THE KATYN
ORDER

Also by Douglas W. Jacobson

Night of Flames

a novel

douglas w jacobson

McBooks Press, Inc.
www.mcbooks.com
ITHACA, NY

Published by McBooks Press, Inc. 2011

Dust jacket, cover illustration and interior design by Panda Musgrove.

Cover collage made of two photos by Jack Delano, courtesy of American Memory and The Library of Congress: 1. Headlines posted in street-corner window of newspaper office Brockton, Mass., 1940. 2. In the roundhouse at a Chicago and Northwestern Railroad yard, Chicago, Ill., 1942.

Library of Congress Cataloging-in-Publication Data

Jacobson, Douglas W., 1945-
The Katyn Order : a novel / Douglas W. Jacobson.
p. cm.
ISBN 978-1-59013-572-3 (hardcover)
1. Warsaw (Poland)--History--Uprising, 1944--Fiction. 2. Katyn Massacre, Katyn', Russia, 1940--Fiction. 3. Poland--History--Occupation, 1939-1945--Fiction. 4. World War, 1939-1945--Fiction. I. Title.
PS3610.A35675K38 2011
813'.6--dc22

2010051537

Visit the McBooks Press website at www.mcbooks.com.

Printed in the United States of America
9 8 7 6 5 4 3 2 1

For Janie

Acknowledgments

I have heard it said that the most difficult book for an author to write is the second one. I have, indeed, found that to be true. The story that finally came to fruition as *The Katyn Order* took many twists and turns along the way, as well as several false starts. As with my first book, this effort could not have succeeded were it not for the help of many people.

At the top of that list is my editor, Jackie Swift, of McBooks Press. Were it not for her seemingly inexhaustible patience, sound advice, and flat-out awesome skill as an editor, this book never would have happened. Jackie knew what story I wanted to tell and was determined not to let me off the hook until I told it.

Many thanks to Swalomir Debski, who again served as a valuable reference, particularly on the background of Katyn and Soviet-Polish relations during this time period.

My friends and fellow authors at Redbird Writers Studio in Milwaukee continued to provide their usual candor and constructive critique, which was extremely helpful in developing the relationship between Adam and Natalia.

My friend Krystyna Rytel, of Elm Grove, lived through the occupation of Poland and the Warsaw Rising as a child. In sharing her experiences, Krystyna helped provide an emotional understanding of those unimaginable times.

I also want to thank the real Tim Meinerz for his generous donation to the Multiple Sclerosis Society Scholarship Fund. It was a privilege to name a character in this story after him.

And, as always, I am eternally grateful for the patience and encouragement of my wife, Janie; Kevin and Mary; Kerri and Filip; and our seven grandchildren who, once again, put up with my absence while I burrowed away for countless hours.

Warsaw City Center & Old Town

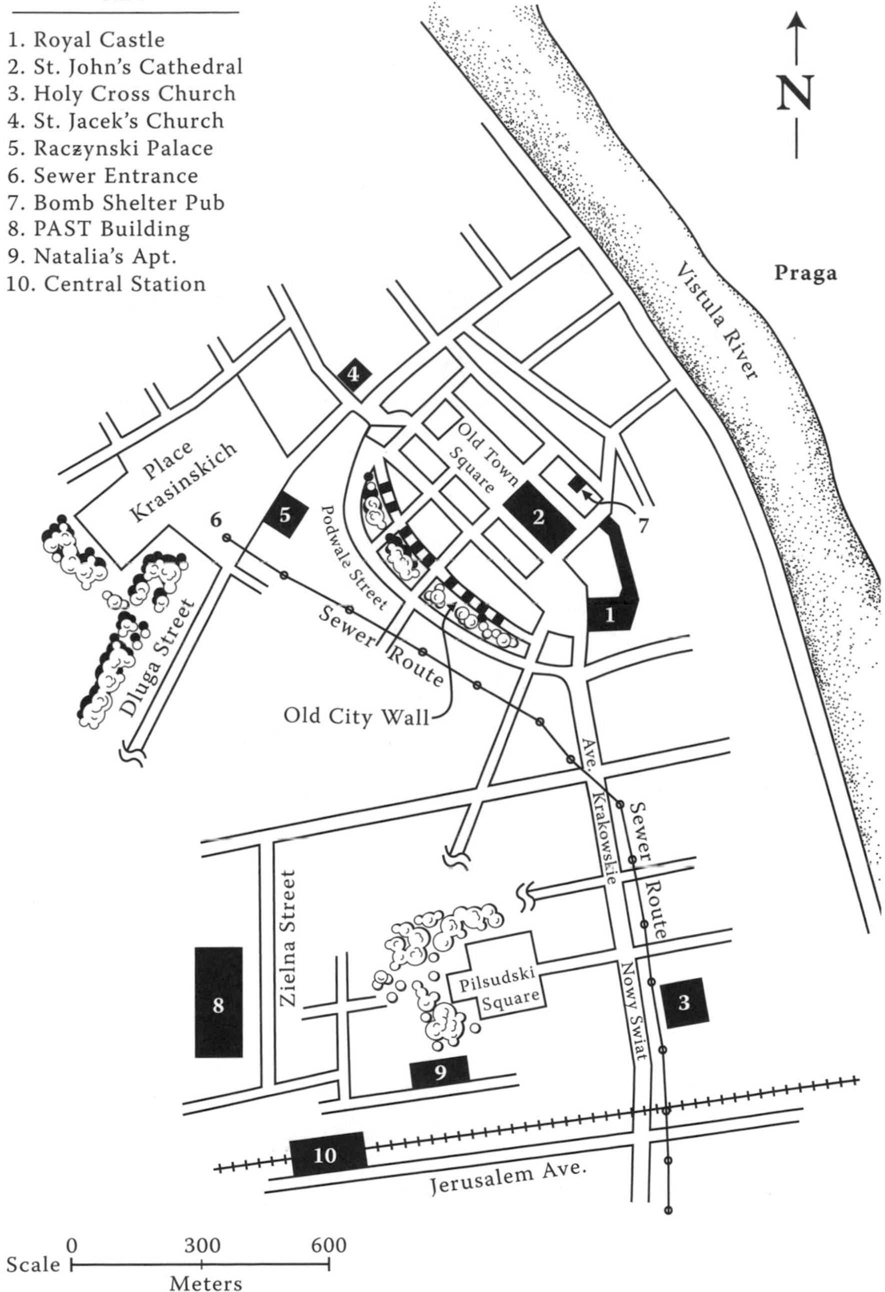

Krakow

City Center, Stare Miasto & Kazimierz

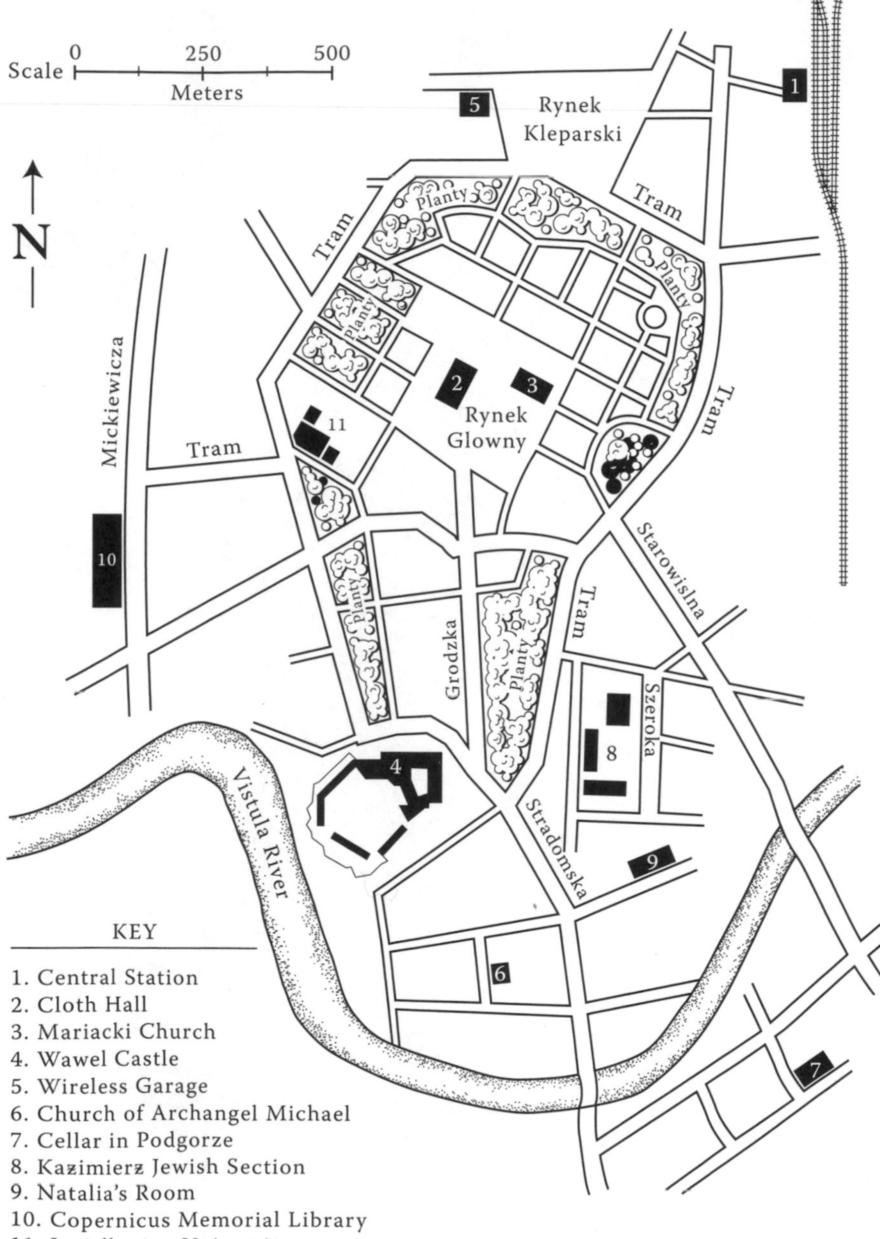

Courage is the first of human qualities . . .
because it is the quality that guarantees all others.

—*Winston Churchill*

THE KATYN
ORDER

Prologue

KATYN FOREST
NEAR SMOLENSK, RUSSIA
APRIL, 1940

THE POLISH OFFICERS knew they were in trouble when the train stopped.

At first they were quiet. After a time some began to pray, some cursed. But most stood in silence in the dark interior of the boxcar, waiting. They were officers, their pride untarnished in defeat. And they waited.

From outside, heavy boots marched on the gravel rail siding, dogs barked and soldiers shouted orders in Russian.

The doors of the boxcar were pulled back, grinding and scraping on rusty tracks. The officers filed across the rail yard as instructions in Polish blared over loudspeakers.

Autobuses arrived, their windows blackened, their rear doors open wide like the jaws of serpents. Inside the buses were cages: one Polish officer per cage, thirty officers per bus. The doors slammed shut.

Darkness.

A rutted road led deeper into the forest, out of earshot, away from prying eyes . . . away from everything.

The officers' hands were bound. Names were recorded in books that would never see the light of day.

A narrow path disappeared into the trees, still deeper in the forest.

It was a crisp, clear April morning. Tree sparrows flitted about, crocuses were budding, the forest awakening. The ferns were wet with morning dew, the air heavy with the dank odor of moss—and the stench of death.

A Russian major stood near an open pit, a gaping hole, an obscene scar on the pristine landscape.

The major barked a command, and Russian soldiers shoved a Polish officer to the edge of the pit. The Pole stared into the carnage, then looked at the major. Their eyes met for an instant. The major turned away.

A Russian soldier put a pistol to the back of the Polish officer's head. It was easier if he didn't have to look them in the eye.

A gunshot echoed through the silent forest.

The sparrows flew away.

The major made a check in his log. There would be more than twenty thousand checks before it was finished.

According to *the Order.*

One

5 AUGUST 1944

THE ASSASSIN STOOD IN THE SHADOWS of an alcove and watched the activity on the other side of the street. The lamps along Stawki Street, just west of Warsaw's City Center, had been shot out during the first days of the Rising, but the night sky was illuminated with brilliant, yellowish-white flashes. German artillery units were pounding the Wola District two kilometers to the west, and an acrid, smoky haze hung in the air. The ground trembled beneath his feet with each jarring concussion.

But he waited.

And watched.

A few minutes earlier, two canvas-covered trucks had pulled up in front of the deserted three-story warehouse, and several prisoners wearing black-and-white concentration camp uniforms had jumped out and begun unloading wooden crates. Two German SS troopers with automatic rifles watched over them, glancing at the western sky whenever a particularly loud burst of artillery echoed through the streets, shattering the last unbroken windows. The SS troopers appeared nervous, though this neighborhood was still under German control.

The assassin checked his watch. It was almost time. He brushed the dust and specks of ash off the front of the uniform he'd taken from the dead Waffen-SS trooper the night before. He had made sure it was a clean shot to the head so as not to soil the jacket with blood. He wanted to look his best for SS-Sturmbannfuhrer Karl Brandt.

At exactly 2200 hours, a flash of headlights swept through the gloom as a long, black auto wheeled around the corner and screeched to a stop behind the trucks. The driver jumped out and opened the rear door of the powerful German-built Horch. The assassin watched as SS-Sturmbannfuhrer Brandt squeezed out of the backseat like an over-ripe melon and tugged on the bottom of his uniform tunic in a futile effort to cover his sagging beltline. The obese officer barked a command to the SS troopers and plodded toward the warehouse.

The assassin stepped out of the alcove and marched across the boulevard, his right hand resting lightly on the holster strapped to his waist. As he approached the automobile, he shouted loudly enough to be heard over the bursts of shelling, *"Guten Abend, Sturmbannfuhrer!"* With his right forefinger, he flipped open the strap of the holster.

SS-Sturmbannfuhrer Brandt stopped and turned toward the street, a bewildered look in his eyes. *"Ja, was ist—"*

The assassin drew the Walther P-38 from the holster and in one smooth motion fired a single shot into Brandt's forehead, then a second into the chest of the driver. He stepped over Brandt's body and fired two quick shots at the SS troopers, who stood staring at him in frozen astonishment. One of them went down instantly. The other required another round.

The striped-uniformed prisoners dropped the crates and stood ramrod stiff, arms in the air, their faces white with fear. An instant later, a group of men wearing red-and-white armbands bolted from the shadows of a building across the street. Brandishing an assortment of weapons, they charged past the stunned prisoners and barged into the warehouse.

From inside, shouts in Polish and German—

Gunshots—

Then it was quiet.

The assassin calmly approached the quivering prisoners and holstered his gun. From his pocket he withdrew a red-and-white armband, emblazoned with the Polish eagle, and slipped it on. "We're AK," he said. "Armia Krajowa, the Home Army. Get inside."

He followed the prisoners into the building and down to the cellar, glancing around in satisfied amazement. It was better than he had thought. Jammed into the damp, earthen-floored room, stacked floor to ceiling, were hundreds of wooden crates, their contents clearly identified with stencils in typical German thoroughness: Gew-43 rifles, MP-38 submachine guns, 7.92mm anti-tank rifles, Mausers, Lugers and thousands of rounds of ammunition. It was a cache of weapons the AK desperately needed. It would keep them going for another week, perhaps longer.

Two of the AK commandos dragged Brandt's body and those of the SS troopers into the building, stripped off the troopers' uniforms and put them on. They took the automatic rifles and went back outside. The assassin dispatched a runner to the City Center AK commander, who would send in reinforcements and move up the barricades. The AK had gained another kilometer of territory.

Then he motioned to one of the other commandos, who tossed him a canvas bag. The assassin untied the drawstring, withdrew a handful of red-and-white armbands and held them out to the prisoners. "You're free men now. You can join us or not. It's your choice."

The prisoners stood immobilized, their dark, sunken eyes wide with astonishment. They were a scrawny lot—dirty and unshaven, lice crawling through their hair—and they were wary, accustomed to expecting the worst at any moment. Finally one of them, a tall emaciated Jew with a yellow star sewn on his uniform, stepped forward and whispered, "Thank you." He took an armband, slipped it on and saluted with a trembling hand. One-by-one the rest followed.

When the unloading activity resumed, the assassin sat down on one of the crates, removed his eyeglasses and carefully cleaned them with a handkerchief. He put them back on and lit a cigarette. His name was Adam Nowak, or it *had* been, back in another life. It was a name he hadn't used in five years, a name almost forgotten, like the life that had at one time existed for a reason other than murder and mayhem. To his comrades in the AK he was known by a code name, as they all were. His was Wolf. An appropriate name he'd always thought, a night stalker, an *assassin.*

Adam glanced at the beamed ceiling as the building shook, sending dust and bits of plaster drifting downward. The shelling was getting closer every night. He brushed the dust off his jacket. The AK had taken the Germans by surprise when they launched the Rising a week ago and had managed to take control of Warsaw's City Center, Old Town and a few other areas. But the victory was short-lived. Now they would pay the price under a barrage of German artillery.

Adam stood up, dropped the cigarette butt on the earthen floor and ground it out under his heel. He walked to the back of the cellar where an enormous, broad-shouldered man with a shaved head stood guard over two other SS troopers captured by the AK commandos when they stormed the cellar. The big man's code name was Hammer. He stood with beefy arms folded, glowering at the SS troopers, who sat on the dirt floor with their hands tied behind them.

Adam was short and slender, though deceptively strong. With his thinning hair and wire-rimmed glasses, many would expect that he was a banker or an accountant—or a student in law school which, in fact, he had been in his previous life. Standing next to Hammer, he seemed to take up hardly any space at all.

"What do we do with these two?" Hammer asked.

Adam looked down at the German soldiers. They looked young, he thought, just boys. Then he drew the Walther P-38 and shot both of them in the head.

Two

6 August

The train slowed around the last bend, rocking from side-to-side, steel wheels scraping against steel rails as it neared Warsaw's West station. Standing in the passageway between the fifth and sixth cars, Natalia Kowalska held onto a handrail with her right hand and glanced at her watch to check the time. They were three hours late. It was just past five o'clock in the afternoon, but it seemed like the middle of night. She'd seen the fires as the train approached the western suburbs, sliding deeper into the cloud of hazy smoke with every kilometer.

Natalia bent down to see out the window as they crept slowly into the station, passing a line of grim-faced German SS troopers, who stood on the platform clutching submachine guns. When the train finally shuddered to a halt with a blast of venting steam, Natalia jumped to the platform, blinking her eyes against the sting of smoke and ashes. As she pulled out the step to assist the departing passengers, she heard a clatter of hobnail boots pounding down the wooden platform. A guttural voice barked in German, "*Raus! Raus!* Everyone out!"

As the SS officer approached her, Natalia adjusted her blue railway conductor's cap and shouted to be heard over the noise, "This train is continuing on to—"

The officer jabbed his nightstick into her ribs. "Everyone off! *Schnell! Mach schnell!*" Then he marched on ahead, banging against every window, waving his hand, "*Raus! Raus!*"

Instantly it was chaos: bewildered people stumbling off the train and scurrying along the platform, dragging luggage and children behind them; SS troopers shouting; dogs barking; the air thick with smoke and haze. Natalia backed up against the brick wall of the station and watched for a moment, keeping her eye on the SS officer, who was trotting farther up the train, banging on windows, jerking people out of the cars and onto the platform. She removed her conductor's cap, stuffed it into the black bag clipped to her belt and stepped into the flow of departing passengers.

Outside, the chaos turned to mass pandemonium. Thousands of panicked and disorientated people clogged the streets, pushing and shoving in all directions. Fires raged while German army trucks plowed through the crowds, running over anyone who couldn't get out of the way. Soldiers leaned over the sides of the trucks, shooting indiscriminately at terrified civilians.

Pulled along with the frenzied crowd like a cork on the ocean, Natalia desperately tried to get her bearings. She was only vaguely familiar with this part of Warsaw, but the rendezvous with her contact was to be at a church in the Wola District, which she knew to be north of this station. The dense smoke and ash made it difficult to see the sun, but Natalia realized the crowd was moving south to escape from the fires. She had to get back across the tracks and head north.

After a few minutes, which seemed like an hour, the stampeding throng crossed a bridge over the railway, and Natalia spotted a breach in the chain-link fence running along the tracks. She shoved and elbowed through the crowd, glancing around to see if any soldiers were nearby, then scrambled down the embankment, dropped to her knees and crawled through the fence.

In the smoke-filled confusion of wailing people, machine-gun bursts and thumping artillery fire, Natalia sprinted across the tracks, then turned and trotted parallel to the fence line until she found another breach—this one caused by the charred remains of a bus that had plowed through the fence—and emerged on the north side.

Keeping to the side streets where there were fewer fires, Natalia made her way north, darting across intersections and ducking between burned-out buildings whenever she heard growling truck engines and clanking tank treads. She rounded a corner and was about to cross over the tram tracks that ran down the center of Avenue Kasprzaka when a crowd of shrieking women and children, running in the opposite direction, knocked her back against a building. As the frantic crowd rushed past, Natalia regained her balance and glanced in the direction they had come from. She froze and stood motionless as her mind tried to comprehend the gruesome scene before her.

Fifty meters away, in the middle of the street, a bulldozer was at work, scooping hundreds of human corpses onto a pile. A gang of SS troopers tossed scraps of wood and paper onto the pile, while another trooper wielding a flamethrower set it ablaze. Beyond the pile, a bus had overturned, and a third gang of SS troopers methodically machine-gunned the passengers crawling out through the windows.

Natalia crept back into the shadows between two buildings and leaned against a brick wall for support, swallowing hard as trucks rumbled past delivering more bodies to the blazing pile. She felt lightheaded and her stomach was churning, so she stayed a few minutes longer until the noxious stench of burning flesh finally forced her to move. Her legs tingled as she crept unsteadily between the buildings, found an alleyway and made a wide circle around the blazing corpses.

An hour later Natalia slipped through the side door of the Church of the Sacred Mother in the center of the Wola District, and was once again assaulted by the scent of death. This time it wasn't an actual smell—though the air was heavy with a pungent sulfurous haze—but more of an aura, an ominous feeling that something dreadful had just happened. She hesitated just inside the door and glanced down the shadowy hallway that led to the sanctuary as the last hazy glimmer of twilight filtered through the transom windows above the door. She took a step into the hallway and—

"Don't!"

She stopped.

"Don't go in there," whispered a voice from behind her.

The hairs on the back of her neck bristled, and she stood still for a moment, waiting until she could take a breath, then turned slowly toward the voice. As her eyes adjusted to the dim light, Natalia saw a figure standing in a narrow doorway at the end of the hall opposite the sanctuary. "Falcon?"

"Yes. Come quickly."

She took a step closer, and the tall, muscular man motioned with his hand. "Follow me. They may come back."

Natalia followed him through the doorway and down an ancient stone staircase. A lighted kerosene lantern hung from the wall, and Falcon grabbed it and continued on through another doorway. They hurried along a damp corridor with rough stone walls and a beamed ceiling for fifty meters, then entered a small windowless room.

Falcon closed the door behind them and set the lantern on a wooden table. In stark contrast to the madness outside, it was eerily quiet, the air musty, as though they had entered a tomb. "I thought you might not make it," Falcon said. He turned and placed a hand on her shoulder. "You've seen what they're doing out there?"

Natalia stared at Falcon in the flickering light of the kerosene lamp, then shrugged off his hand. "It's barbaric, even for the Nazis. There are bodies everywhere: women, children, piled up in the streets like cordwood. They're setting *fire* to them!" She ran a hand through her short-cropped brown hair and rubbed her irritated eyes. "Who on earth chose *this* location for the rendezvous?"

"Stag, of course. But we held this area until twenty-four hours ago."

Natalia cursed under her breath. "We got as far as the West Station," she said. "Then the SS ordered everyone off the train. Everything was on fire, and the area was crawling with storm troopers. I just barely got out of there."

Falcon hand-rolled a cigarette and lit it. He was a whole head taller than Natalia, with thick black hair and steely dark eyes. The bars of an AK captain were prominent on the collar of his makeshift uniform.

"The church?" she asked.

He shook his head. "They're all dead. The SS herded the whole group into the sanctuary—priests, nuns, a dozen or so children. Gunned them all down. Happened just before you got here. Damned good thing you didn't walk into the middle of it."

Natalia took the cigarette from him and inhaled deeply.

"What did you see on the way into Warsaw?" he asked. "We've

heard they're bringing in reinforcements."

"That's why it took so long to get here. We were diverted onto sidings three times for German transport trains—tanks, armored cars, artillery, dozens of troop carriers." She glanced around the small, austere room, suddenly feeling claustrophobic, and took another drag on the cigarette. "The word is that Hitler's furious and he's gone berserk. Imagine a motley bunch of Poles wanting to take back their capital city."

Falcon managed a grim smile that faded quickly. "They'll step up the artillery barrage again right after dark, so we'd better get the hell out of here." He pointed at the black bag hanging from her belt. "Anything from Krakow? From the Provider?"

Natalia removed the folded conductor's cap from her bag, thumbed through the railway schedules, ticket vouchers and a variety of other official odds and ends, then carefully lifted up the false bottom. She removed an envelope and handed it to Falcon.

Suddenly, a thundering blast shook the building, and a beam cracked in the ceiling above their heads. Natalia instinctively dropped to her knees as the beam sagged, and a giant chunk of plaster broke loose and shattered on the floor.

Falcon shoved the envelope into the breast pocket of his jacket and grabbed the lantern. Natalia scrambled to her feet, and they bolted from the room as a second blast brought down the rest of the ceiling.

They raced through the corridor and up the stairs, retracing their steps back to the main hallway, which was miraculously still intact. They burst out the side door, into a narrow cobblestone street and onto Avenue Wolska amidst shrieking artillery shells, shattering glass and a thousand bricks cascading onto the street in heaps of rubble.

Natalia's heart pounded as she followed Falcon past the remains of once-stately buildings that lined the east–west thoroughfare, through a blurred pandemonium of terrified people, faces streaked with dust and ashes, bleeding, crying and cursing. A man staggered from an alley and almost knocked her down, a bloody stump dangling from his shoulder.

Then a monstrous explosion hammered Natalia's eardrums. The ground fell away, and she landed hard on shattered cobblestones.

Ignoring the piercing bolt of pain in her hip, she got to her feet and lurched to the right as a second eruption of bricks and glass obliterated the street. Falcon shouted something, then disappeared into a storefront. She followed him through a maze of toppled shelves and broken crates, out a back door and into another street. Choking on dust and smoke, they continued on, dodging flying debris, climbing over rubble, heading east.

Eventually the shelling was behind them as they made their way, breathless and covered with dirt and soot, from the Wola District into the City Center. Slowing to a walk they rounded a corner where barricades loomed ahead, fashioned from paving blocks, railroad ties and sheets of corrugated metal. Tattered red-and-white flags fluttered from makeshift poles alongside banners emblazoned with Poland's white eagle. Sweat ran down her face, and her legs felt like rubber as Natalia walked in silence beside Falcon, toward a group of men and women wearing the armbands of the AK.

It was close to midnight when the shelling finally ceased, but fires raged on in the Wola District and most of Warsaw's other western suburbs, sending clouds of thick, black smoke and a stench of death billowing into the night sky. But an uneasy quiet hung over the area of the city occupied by the insurgents of the AK. In a small three-room apartment near Pilsudski Square that served as an AK district headquarters, Natalia sat on a faded brown sofa, smoking a cigarette.

She didn't really enjoy smoking but it was something to do, something to keep her hands busy and her mind off the bloody faces and burning corpses she'd seen on the street that day. She blinked away the images and exhaled slowly, glancing around the dingy parlor. A red-and-black banner displaying the letter "P" fashioned from an anchor along with the words *Polska Walczy*—Poland Fights—hung on the wall between the windows.

Across the room, Falcon sat at a table opposite Colonel Stag, an AK officer Natalia had met once before. Falcon handed over the envelope Natalia had carried from Krakow. Colonel Stag slit it open, extracted the documents and looked them over carefully, one-by-one, shaking his head, occasionally grunting.

When he was finished Stag dropped the last page on the table and pushed back his chair. "Jesus Christ, the depravity of these Nazi bastards is beyond belief. *New efficiencies in gas-fired ovens?* You'd think they were talking about baking bread." He stood up, walked over to the window and stared out at the street where a group of AK commandos sang songs around a bonfire. Stag was a short, stocky man, built a bit like a large bulldog. He sighed, his broad shoulders sagged. "My brother and his family were sent to Treblinka, you know."

Still staring out the window, Colonel Stag took another drag on his cigarette, then stepped back to the table and ground it out in an ashtray. He grabbed his chair, carried it across the room and sat down facing Natalia. "You've done excellent work. And so has the Provider, whoever he or she is. I've passed along every document you've given to Falcon."

Natalia thought about the Provider, and the others in Krakow, the risks they'd taken over the years, the lives that had been lost. "Not that it did much good," she said.

"It's evidence," Stag replied, "and it's in the hands of our Allies. Someday these monsters will be made to pay." Then he leaned forward, his ice-blue eyes intense. "But now, you're with us, here in Warsaw where we'll make our stand. This could all be over quickly."

Natalia tensed. "The Russians?"

Stag nodded. "The Red Army has reached the east bank of the Vistula: twelve divisions, a tank corps and heavy artillery just south of Praga, less than ten kilometers away."

"Ha!" Falcon sprang to his feet and paced around the room. "It's true? They're coming in to help us crush these Nazi bastards?"

Colonel Stag was silent, and Natalia watched him closely. He appeared thoughtful, a flicker of doubt in his eyes.

Three

12 August

Natalia raced up the stairs and followed the boy into a vacant room. She knelt at an open window and watched the horrific engagement unfolding before her eyes. From the second floor of the deserted office building she had a clear view of the hospital across the square. A German Panther tank had blown several holes in the outer walls of the building, and a fire raged inside. Patients in hospital gowns spilled out of the doors and ground floor windows, coughing and gagging, some reaching back to help with stretchers.

The boy crouched next to Natalia. He was thin and wiry and not much taller than she. He was young, about twelve or thirteen she guessed, but his face was fixed in determination, as though he'd done this many times.

"Ready?" she asked.

The boy nodded and calmly unbuckled the canvas knapsack he'd been carrying.

Natalia turned back to the window. Twenty or thirty men converged on the hospital wielding clubs and crowbars, a few with handguns. They were Ukrainian conscripts, tough violent brutes recruited by the Nazis. A German Waffen-SS officer flanked by three storm troopers stood near the Panther tank, arms folded across his chest as the gang of Ukrainians broke into a run, charging forward in a mad frenzy, shouting and cursing, bashing heads, kicking and beating the sick and wounded patients.

Then a sudden burst of gunfire erupted from a building on the other side of the square. The Waffen-SS officer and two of the storm troopers went down instantly. A Ukrainian was shot. Then another.

Gunshots erupted from a second building and caught the Ukrainians in the crossfire, picking them off one after another. The third storm trooper dove for cover behind the tank.

It lasted only a few minutes. The few surviving Ukrainians scattered, and the shooting died down. Then it was quiet, except for wounded hospital patients moaning and crying for help.

Natalia dug her fingernails into the rotten wood of the windowsill. After five years of war she was used to Nazi barbarism—at least she thought she was—and when Colonel Stag had sent out the appeal for help in Warsaw, she had quickly volunteered for what everyone in the AK knew would be Poland's last chance for freedom. And now, after seeing the slaughter in the Wola District, and watching the wanton brutality taking place beneath her in the hospital square, she knew they were in a struggle to the death. For years she had followed orders and done her duty, smuggling documents, dodging the SS and Gestapo. But now the stakes had been raised.

Natalia jerked her head to the left at the sudden clamor of clanking steel treads and a growling diesel engine. She slipped her right hand into her jacket pocket, feeling the cold steel of her pistol, then stood up and moved out of sight at the edge of the window.

The Panther tank crept forward along the street directly below. The monstrous machine's turret swiveled, and the gun barrel arced upward, pointing at the building across the square where the first shots had come from. The tank commander stood in the open hatch, shouting directions, his black leather beret cocked to one side.

Natalia withdrew the pistol and glanced at the boy, who held a Molotov cocktail in one hand and a lit match in the other. She counted to three then stepped in front of the window, gripped the pistol with two hands and leaned out. The tank was almost directly below her. She sighted on the center of the black beret, held her breath and pulled the trigger.

The beret disappeared in a splatter of red and black as the tank commander toppled over the side. Natalia quickly backed away from the window and in a blur of motion the boy stepped in front of her.

Without hesitation, he held the match to the Molotov cocktail's cloth wick, leaned out the window and tossed the flaming bottle of petrol into the open tank hatch. Then he whirled around, and the two of them dove to the floor as a fireball erupted with a jarring *whump!*

A blast of heat washed over their heads.

Natalia jumped to her feet and scrambled for the door, the boy right behind her, clutching the knapsack as they fled from the room and hustled down the stairs to the ground floor. She stopped in the hallway near the back door of the building to catch her breath.

"Hah, we *fried* those sons-a-bitches, didn't we?" the boy chirped, slapping his hand on his knee as he leaned against the wall. He smirked as if he'd just scored a goal in a football match. This was their first assignment together, but Natalia had heard about him before. He was a skinny lad with tousled blond hair and a grimy face. She wondered how many others he had *fried* since being recruited into the AK.

She slowly pulled the door open, checking the street to make sure it was clear. They stepped out and sprinted through the alley and down the street to another building.

Natalia glanced back at the boy, who followed close behind her as they inched along the side of the building. "Stay alert," she said, though it was rapidly becoming apparent that he needed few instructions from her in the tactics of guerilla warfare. She turned back and continued on until they had a view of the hospital square.

Thick, greasy smoke from the burning tank drifted across the open area where dozens of hospital patients lay bleeding on the grass among dead Ukrainians. The patients that could walk huddled together in a tight group and stumbled across the lawn toward the street, several of them carrying others on stretchers. Two AK commandos wearing red-and-white armbands ran across the lawn and took up a stretcher. A few local citizens emerged tentatively from the cellars of adjoining buildings and stood watching. A man and woman ran toward the patients. Two others followed, then three more, taking up the stretchers, helping the patients cross the street.

Then another tank appeared.

Natalia's mouth dropped open, stunned at the inconceivable sight.

Three women stumbled along in front of the Panther tank, acting as human shields. A rope was tied around each of their waists and secured to the tank. Waffen-SS troopers trotted alongside, right behind the women who, to Natalia's astonishment, shouted at the AK commandos, imploring them to fire at the tanks.

An instant later the ground beneath Natalia's feet heaved, and she fell to her knees as a thunderous blast erupted from the tank's gun barrel. A cloud of dust billowed into the sky. The side of the building she and the boy had just vacated slid into the street.

As the tank plowed forward into the rubble, one of the women tripped over a pile of fallen bricks and was dragged beneath the clanking treads. The other two, now shrieking and flailing their arms, stumbled over the clutter of shattered bricks and wood, trying desperately to stay on their feet. But the massive growling machine, with scraps of the first woman's blue-and-red skirt caught in its treads, barged into them. Staggering, falling, one after the other, the women finally disappeared beneath the tank.

Natalia went rigid. As the tank rumbled on, she spotted something in the rubble. An arm emerged then a shoulder as the last woman dragged under the tank struggled to lift her head.

Natalia bolted into the street. But she stopped abruptly as one of the Waffen-SS troopers following the tank looked down at the struggling woman, then pointed his rifle at her and shot her in the head.

For an instant everything seemed frozen in time. The SS trooper turned away as though he'd just shot a varmint in a farmyard. Natalia's hand clutched the pistol in her pocket and, before she realized what she was doing, her right arm was extended and the pistol was pointed squarely at the SS trooper's back.

She blinked.

And pulled the trigger.

Then everything seemed to happen at once.

She heard the boy shout. An instant later he was next to her, tugging at her sleeve and dragging her to the ground.

They rolled over on the cobblestones as a gunshot cracked, and the air whistled above their heads.

When Natalia looked up, a second SS trooper stood over the body of the one she'd just shot. He chambered another round and aimed directly at her.

Another gunshot echoed off the buildings, this one from behind her. The SS trooper slumped to the ground, his rifle clattering on the street.

Natalia got to her knees and looked back in the direction of the second shot.

An AK commando sprinted forward, waving his hand for them to stay down. He dropped to one knee, raised his rifle and fired twice over their heads, dropping two other SS troopers with deadly precision. Then he lowered the rifle and ran up to them. He was a thin, serious-looking man with wire-rimmed eyeglasses. "Get back against that wall," he said quietly but firmly.

The boy grabbed Natalia's elbow, and they backed up against the building as three other AK commandos sprinted into the center of the square, carrying a PIAT anti-tank gun. She crouched low with her hands over her ears as the PIAT's barrel flashed. The Panther tank shuddered with a deafening *bang!*

The tank's turret rotated toward the square.

The PIAT flashed again, and the tank rocked with a second *bang!*

The turret stopped.

The hatch popped open, and black smoke billowed out. A tank crewman frantically clawed his way out the open hatch, face blackened with soot, his shirt on fire. He was halfway out when he collapsed and slid back into the burning tank.

Natalia stood ramrod stiff. Her ears rang so badly she couldn't hear, but she caught a sudden flash of movement from the corner of her eye.

On the other side of the square, a German Army truck barreled onto the lawn and skidded to a halt. Waffen-SS troopers leaped from the back of the truck and charged across the lawn toward the PIAT crew. An instant later a horde of screaming AK commandos poured out of the buildings surrounding the square.

Gunfire erupted from every direction—

SS troopers fell—

Commandos fell—

Bodies clashed in a melee of hand-to-hand combat—

Then it was over.

In a haze of gun smoke, a small group of breathless commandos stood motionless in the center of the square, surrounded by dozens of dead bodies.

Natalia leaned back against the building and wrapped her arms around her chest, staring at the carnage in the square. Overwhelmed by the madness and the senseless, brutal slaughter, her mind went blank. She felt . . . numb.

In the street, the woman who had struggled to lift her head was now still.

The boy crouched next to her. Blood trickled from a cut on his cheek, and his blond hair was matted with dust. He was called "Rabbit" by the AK commandos because he could run like the wind, and he knew where the stockpiles of Molotov cocktails were hidden in the cellars, trash bins and sewers throughout Warsaw's City Center.

Natalia slowly slid down and put a hand on the boy's knee. "Thank you," she said quietly.

Rabbit shook his head. "I didn't do anything. We'd both be dead now if it hadn't been for Wolf."

"Wolf?"

"The commando wearing the glasses, the one they call 'the assassin.' Damn, I wish I could shoot like that."

Natalia searched the square for the slender AK commando, but the haze was too thick and dozens of people were milling around. She leaned her head back against the building and wiped the sweat from her forehead.

Rabbit rolled a cigarette. He licked the edge of the paper, stuck the limp cylinder in the corner of his mouth and struck a match. He inhaled deeply then handed it to her.

Natalia took a drag from the flimsy cigarette and held the smoke in her lungs for a moment before exhaling slowly. It helped. She took a second drag and handed it back. "Where is your home?" she asked.

"Anywhere I happen to be," the boy said with a shrug. "Fuckin' Krauts bombed our house in '39. But I'm still here. They aren't gonna haul *me* away like they did my brother."

"Your brother?"

Rabbit picked a bit of tobacco off his lip and spit in the street. "He was two years older than me. We were the only ones who made it to the cellar that night. But six months later a couple of SS bastards stopped him on the street . . ." He took a drag on the cigarette and stared at the ground.

"You've haven't seen him again?"

Rabbit shook his head. "I stayed with my aunt for a while, but she got sick and died. AK's my family, been that way for most of the war."

The boy looked up, staring silently into the street and the square beyond, holding the cigarette between his thumb and forefinger. After a few minutes he flicked an ash and said, "He was bigger than me, but I could beat his ass in football anytime." His eyes widened, and he smiled broadly as though he were seeing the game being played out in front of them. "He'd always line up on the opposite side, and he'd try like hell to give me a shoulder or take a swipe at my ankle, but I was too fast, way too fast. He'd curse at me, call me every name in the book and try to run me down, but I'd just laugh and pound the ball into the goal."

"What was his name?"

The smile slowly slid off his face. Then he carefully stubbed out what was left of the cigarette and put it in his shirt pocket. "We don't have names, remember?"

They sat quietly for awhile, watching the square as the last of the hospital patients were carried off. Another group of AK operatives appeared, riding in a battered truck filled with concrete paving blocks and railroad ties. Barricades went up and flags were raised. Territory was gained, perhaps to be lost again the next day.

Four

15 August

Colonel Stag rapped his knuckles on a table, and the chatter in the room subsided. It was warm, the air heavy with cigarette smoke and body odor as more than fifty AK officers and commandos jammed into the cellar of the Polonia Bank building. Natalia sat next to Falcon on the right side of the room, occasionally glancing up at the ceiling at the sound of German artillery fire, now less than a kilometer to the west.

It had been three days since her encounter with the Panther tanks, and she and Rabbit had been involved in several other firefights since then, but none nearly as bad as the bloodbath at the hospital. She'd been lucky so far: just some scratches and bruises, and her hip still ached from the fall on the first day. But she was tired. She hadn't slept well, seeing images of the women dragged under the tank every time she closed her eyes.

Falcon put his arm around the back of her chair as Colonel Stag started the briefing. His hand brushed against her shoulder. She didn't respond. Sometimes she did but not always. It was a casual thing, their affair. Nice enough at times, but generally . . . tedious.

The building shook again, harder this time, and several of the AK commandos near Natalia glanced around nervously. The Germans were firing massive anti-siege howitzers from railcars that launched projectiles weighing more than two tons, the infamous "screaming cows" that could flatten entire buildings with a single strike.

"We've lost the Wola District," Colonel Stag said gravely, his hands folded tightly on the table in front of him. A murmur of curses swept through the room. The colonel stood up and stepped over to a map of Warsaw hanging on the back wall. With a red marker he drew a line along the western edge of the City Center. "General Bor has ordered all remaining AK units in Wola to pull back behind this line. The barricades are being reinforced tonight. The last of the weapons have been removed from the warehouse on Stawki Street and relocated to Old Town." He took another marker and made five *X's* along the red line. "We'll set up machine guns and mortars at these points. Riflemen will be positioned in the windows of the buildings behind them. We expect they'll hit us hard tomorrow. At all costs, we hold this line."

"What about communications with our units in the Jolibord District?" someone asked from the center of the room.

"We're running telephone lines through the sewer mains," Stag replied. "The work has already started. We've pulled Rabbit and some of the other boys off 'cocktail duty' to help out, especially to crawl through some of the smaller tunnels."

A few good-natured cheers and bursts of laughter broke out as someone shouted, "Rabbit better not carry those cocktails with him. The fumes will set them off!"

Natalia turned to see who made the joke. It was a heavysct, barrel-chested man with a full beard, clenching a cigar between his teeth. Then she noticed someone else, another man, who stood nearby, yet slightly apart from the crowd. He looked like—

Her attention was diverted back to the front of the room as the colonel rapped the table again. "We've received reports from the British that we can expect an RAF airdrop tomorrow night. This time the target area is Place Krasinskich."

Another murmur rippled through the crowd. A man behind Natalia muttered, "Good Christ, flying right through the city with smoke as black as hell and anti-aircraft guns firin' those fuckin' 88s."

"What about the Russians?" another commando asked. "When are they coming in?"

Colonel Stag's face tightened. "We've had no direct contact with them, but our intelligence reports say they will be arriving soon."

Natalia shook her head. She knew it was all lies. Colonel Stag probably did too. She had been raised in a small village in eastern Poland. Her brother had been a cavalry officer, captured by the Russians after their sneak attack in September of '39. Then, two weeks later, when the Red Army entered their village and burned it to the ground, her parents and her uncle and aunt had disappeared along with hundreds of others. None of them had ever been heard from again.

As Colonel Stag was about to adjourn the briefing, an AK officer wearing the uniform of a Polish Army captain stood up and cleared his throat. Natalia recognized him. His code name was Pierre, the commander of AK forces in Wola. He was a friend of Falcon's and about the same age, but tonight he looked much older. His face was drawn, and there were dark pouches under his eyes. His voice cracked as he spoke. "More than thirty thousand civilians in the Wola District were murdered *just last week,* Colonel. Women, children, even priests and nuns, their bodies tossed into heaps and burned like garbage."

The room fell silent.

Pierre took a long breath before continuing. "It's that monster Heisenberg and his SS Twenty-Ninth Brigade. More than half of those vicious bastards are criminals the Germans released from concentration camps. The rest are conscripted Russians and Ukrainians. They're just wanton killers, slaughtering innocent people! We've been ordered to pull out of Wola, but we've got to *do* something about that son of a bitch!"

Colonel Stag was silent for a moment, his expression darkening. "SS-Hauptsturmfuhrer Heisenberg is under surveillance," he said finally.

Pierre persisted. "Do we have a plan—?"

"Wolf will take care of it."

Heads in the group turned to the left. Natalia followed their gaze to the man she had noticed earlier, the one who stood apart from the group. He was slightly built, but in a wiry, rugged sort of way, with thinning hair. He wore glasses—

"Natalia?"

"What?"

Falcon leaned close. "I said we should go."

She nodded.

The man called Wolf looked directly at her; their eyes met for an instant, then he turned away and headed for the door.

The meeting was breaking up, but Natalia remained in her chair, staring at the doorway.

Falcon put a hand on Natalia's shoulder and squeezed. "Wolf?" he whispered. "You know him?"

Natalia shook her head. "No . . . I don't." She managed a thin smile. "It's nothing. Let's go."

Adam sat on the edge of the bed smoking a cigarette in his tiny third-floor room overlooking the square in Warsaw's Old Town. The briefing had ended an hour ago, and he was mulling over some details of tomorrow's mission when his thoughts drifted to the young woman wearing a railway conductor's uniform who'd been sitting across the room next to Falcon. The uniform must be a cover, allowing her to travel safely from Krakow to Warsaw. He'd heard that someone was making that run—an AK operative in Krakow, an undercover courier who'd been smuggling Nazi documents for years.

Adam realized he had seen her once before, a few days earlier, in the midst of the battle at the hospital when she had run into the street to rescue one of the women who'd been dragged under the tank. She was petite and rather plain, not remarkable in any way. Yet, there was something . . .

He shook his head to clear away the distraction. What did it matter? Nothing mattered except the mission. That's the way it had been for years, just the mission, no distractions, no connections, nothing—just the killing. And that was fine with him. The killing was what mattered. It pushed everything else into a dark corner of his mind and kept things simple. Just the way he wanted it, one single emotion to keep him focused: revenge . . . simple, uncomplicated revenge.

Adam stared at the glowing end of the cigarette for several long moments. Then he stubbed it out and reached under the bed. He pulled out a leather briefcase, unlocked it and removed the surveillance report on SS-Hauptsturmfuhrer Heisenberg.

• • •

Natalia was still wide awake. She rolled over and tilted the brass clock on the nightstand so it caught the moonlight streaming in the window. It was two o'clock. On the cot next to her in the tiny second-floor bedroom, her friend Berta slept soundly. Natalia sat up and stretched. Falcon had wanted her to come home with him last night, but he had started drinking right after the briefing ended and it soon turned ugly. Someone shoved him and he shoved back. There was a fist fight, broken bottles and bleeding noses. He apologized, but she put him off. He was drunk, she was tired, and it wouldn't have meant anything, so why bother?

Frustrated, Natalia got out of bed, grabbed her coat from the back of a chair and slipped quietly from the bedroom, pulling the curtain closed behind her. She tip-toed down the creaky stairs, stepped carefully around a dozen women commandos asleep on cots jammed into the parlor of the vacant apartment. Formerly occupied by a tailor and his family, who had fled the city, the apartment was an unusual affair with a parlor, kitchen and bathroom on one floor, and a small bedroom upstairs. It was situated above the ground-floor tailor shop and was one of only a few residential apartments—now all vacant—in the five-story office building on Trebacka Street in the City Center, north of Pilsudski Square.

Natalia made her way to the cramped, white-tiled kitchen and rummaged through her coat pockets until she found a leftover cigarette. She lit it and sat at the round, wooden table, staring out the dirt-streaked window at a rubble pile—all that remained of the building across the street. In the distance she could hear the dull thump of artillery.

It was only a matter of time—another few weeks, maybe less—before the Germans crushed the Rising. The AK insurgents were fighting valiantly, but less than a third of them had real weapons, and most of those were rebuilt relics left over from '39. Ammunition was scarce, the food and water supplies were running out, and the corpses were piling up. It couldn't last much longer.

Then what? The Russians weren't coming in to help. That much Natalia knew for certain. Where she grew up, danger had always come from the monster to the east. She inhaled the stale cigarette smoke deeply and thought about her brother, Michal, and the one letter she'd received, sent from a Russian prison camp somewhere near Smolensk. Most of the words had been crossed out with thick black ink, but he had said he was being well-treated and would be home soon. That had been five years ago. Natalia took a last drag on the cigarette then grimaced and ground it out. If there was a force on earth more evil than Hitler's Germany, it was Stalin's Russia and his secret police, the NKVD.

A drink, she needed a drink to clear her head. She took a bottle of vodka from one of the brightly painted, green-and-yellow cabinets on either side of the sink, poured some in a glass and swallowed it. She poured another, carried it back to the table and sat down, looking out the window again.

Gradually, her thoughts turned to the AK commando standing off by himself during last night's briefing, the same one she and Rabbit had encountered in the hospital square that day—the sharpshooter. The man they called Wolf.

Natalia had heard about him. She'd heard he was an American, trained by the British and dropped into Poland years ago. Perhaps it was just a myth, or a rumor: things like that were rampant among the operatives of the AK. But it could be true. There were some like him, she knew, covert agents trained as assassins and dropped behind the lines with instructions to kill high-level German officers. They were highly skilled and deadly, with no identity, no background—and nothing to lose.

Another burst of artillery jarred her back to the moment, and Natalia flinched at a shadow in the doorway.

Berta stepped into the kitchen and whispered, "Sorry if I startled you. I couldn't sleep. Apparently you couldn't either."

"Oh, I'm fine, just a little restless. But you were snoring up a storm when I left the room."

"The damn artillery fire woke me. Christ, sometimes I have this dream that one of those screaming cows lands right in my bed. Probably be as good a way to go as any, I guess."

Natalia took a deep breath and held up the glass of vodka. "Maybe this will help. Want one?"

"No, if I get started I'm not going to want to stop. I'll save it for your birthday party."

Natalia smiled but felt a sudden twinge in her stomach. Her birthday was a week away, and she would turn twenty-nine. She wondered if she would live to see thirty.

"You didn't go with Falcon last night?" Berta asked with a shiver and grabbed her coat from the hook.

"He was drunk again, and I don't need that."

"Getting a bit tired of him are you?"

"I don't know . . . maybe . . . it's getting annoying. He's way too possessive, like I'm a piece of his property."

"Well, if you decide to dump him, let me know. I could use a good roll in the hay right now." Berta sat down and dropped her elbows on the table with a heavy sigh. She was several years older than Natalia, with gray streaks running through her short brown hair. She had been a dispatcher for the railway during the time when Natalia was making her courier runs from Krakow to Warsaw.

"It looks like I'm losing my 'cocktail chucker,'" Natalia said, changing the subject.

"Rabbit?"

"He's being reassigned to sewer duty. It was announced at the briefing. You weren't there."

"I was exhausted," Berta said. "Besides, sometimes I feel better not knowing too much."

"Hah, you *always* want to know what's going on."

"I used to . . . in the days when there were just a few of us making decisions, running our own show, like we did during those years on the railway."

Natalia nodded. "You ran a good operation then, Berta. I learned a lot from you."

Berta shrugged and sat back in the chair. "You always knew what you were doing. I just covered your tracks once in a while when you took a few too many chances."

"Or when I was just plain stupid, like the time I ordered the Gestapo agent off the train because he didn't have a ticket."

Berta laughed but caught herself, trying not to wake the others.

"Christ, I'd almost forgotten about that. He wanted to have your head on a platter, bitched and carried on like a madman."

"Well, he also didn't have his ID, claimed he'd left his wallet at home, so I didn't know who he was. Just another arrogant ass who spoke German."

"And there were plenty of those characters around."

"Didn't you give him a bottle of cognac or something to calm him down?"

"Not just a bottle—a whole damn *case*. I offered him a bottle, but the greedy son of a bitch followed me into the store room and spotted the case. The station manager almost had *my* head on a platter when he found out. It was his own private stock." Then, still chuckling, Berta leaned over the table and said, "And what about the time the SS cleared the whole train just before you were due to leave Krakow because they were convinced there was a smuggler on board."

"Oh God, that's right. I remember they searched every one of the passengers and tore through every piece of luggage."

"And all the time you were standing right there with stolen documents hidden in your conductor's pouch."

Natalia's neck tingled as she recalled the incident. "To this day I remember being absolutely terrified that I'd wet my pants." She paused and was silent for a long moment. She put her hands up to her face, covering her eyes, remembering that day.

Berta touched her arm. "What is it? Something wrong?"

Natalia sat still, looking at Berta, trying to decide. Finally she said quietly, "There's something else . . . something I never told anyone . . . something that happened later that day."

"When, on the train?"

"Yes, just before we got to Warsaw. A man was walking toward me in the aisle of the first-class compartment, and just as we passed each other he suddenly stopped. He gripped my shoulder and whispered in my ear, 'I know what's in the bag.'"

Berta flinched. "Good God, what did you do?"

"Nothing—I mean, not right then. I turned around, but he walked away very quickly and passed through into the next car. A few minutes later we were in the station. I was petrified because I really didn't know what he looked like. It all happened so fast, I never got a good look at him, and . . . I was afraid to get off the train. I was certain that he'd be there, waiting."

"Did you meet your contact? Did you report it?"

"No. I said, I've never told anyone. Falcon was my contact—I guess I can tell you that now that it's all over. Anyway, we'd just started working together the week before. I was afraid that he . . . this man, whoever he was, I was afraid he'd see us."

"So, what did you do?"

Natalia dropped her eyes. "I destroyed the documents."

Berta was silent.

"I rushed into the toilet inside the station and closed myself in a stall. Then I took out the documents—there were only about a half dozen pages this time—and I tore them up into little pieces and flushed them down the toilet."

"Did you ever see the man?"

"No. Not then, or ever again. It's almost like it never really happened, like I just imagined it." She paused again, remembering the man whispering to her. She could almost feel his hand on her shoulder and his warm breath on her neck. "I didn't meet Falcon that day, just got on the train again for the run back to Krakow."

"And you didn't tell anyone."

"No, I was too . . . I don't know . . . ashamed, I guess. It was the only time I failed to complete an assignment and I just couldn't . . ."

Berta gazed at her for what seemed like an eternity. Then she took Natalia's hand. "You did the right thing."

Natalia pulled her hand away, pushed back her chair and got to her feet. "No, I didn't. You wouldn't have done that, not destroyed the documents. I should have taken evasive action, circled around through the opposite door of the station, seeing if I could spot him again."

"But you didn't know what he looked like. How would you have spotted him again? You did the right thing, and it's exactly what I would've done."

"But those documents could have been important. They *were* important, or else they wouldn't have been passed along." She stopped.

Berta had her arms folded across her chest, an impatient set to her mouth. "OK, so you would have done the same thing. That doesn't make it right."

"Make it *right?* Christ, Natalia, don't beat yourself up for something that happened a couple of years ago. Not after all you've done. Remember what we were taught: Survival is the most important thing. Live to fight another day."

"I guess you're right . . . as usual."

Berta smiled. "Feel better now that you've got that off your chest?"

"Yeah, sure. Thanks."

Berta put a hand on her shoulder. "Well, we lived through all that, so I guess we can get through the mess we're in now. I'm going to try to get some sleep."

Natalia nodded as her friend shuffled out of the room. Then she tossed back the vodka and sat down, staring at the empty glass.

Five

16 August

The following morning Adam woke up an hour before dawn, precisely as he'd planned. He dressed in the Waffen-SS uniform and gave his black boots a quick shine. He checked the clip on the Walther P-38 and slipped the pistol into the holster on his waist, then strapped a second holster to his right leg, just above the ankle. He inserted a knife with a black walnut handle into the ankle holster, slipped on his red-and-white AK armband and left his room.

Adam walked briskly across the cobblestone expanse of Old Town's central square, mostly deserted at this hour save for a few groups of commandos huddled around bonfires near the immense Gothic façade of St. John's Cathedral with its towering spires and ornate wrought-iron gates. He passed under the two-story-high arch of Queen Anne's Corridor that connected the cathedral to the Royal Castle and glanced at the clock high in the castle's onion-dome tower, though he knew exactly what time it was. He continued south, past the soaring granite column topped with a bronze statute of King Zygmunt III overlooking the Medieval streets that wound through the ancient city.

The eastern sky was brightening, but the persistent sooty haze hanging over the city would blot out the sun for most of the morning. Old Town and much of the City Center were still firmly in the hands of the AK, and Adam passed a barricade where a group of commandos stood guard, waiting nervously for the attack that would come at dawn. He shouted a greeting and made sure they saw his armband so he didn't get shot.

Fifteen minutes later he crossed into the German-held area of the City Center and arrived at Pilsudski Square. He removed the armband and checked his watch. He had a few minutes to spare.

At the far end of Pilsudski Square stood Saxon Palace with its colonnade-topped arcade housing Poland's Tomb of the Unknown Soldier connecting the two symmetrical wings. The palace was now the headquarters of the German garrison. Every morning at precisely 0500, a black Horch driven by a single Waffen-SS trooper rendezvoused with a motorcycle at the palace arcade and picked up SS-Hauptsturmfuhrer Heisenberg in front of the equestrian statue.

Fortunately for Adam, the motorcycle driver, also a Waffen-SS trooper, was as predictable in his habits as Heisenberg. He always arrived at Pilsudski Square ten minutes ahead of time to smoke a cigarette before driving on to the palace. There was normally no one else in the square at that hour.

At exactly 0450 Adam heard the rumble of a motorcycle engine and watched the single headlight beam as the vehicle pulled into the square and stopped less than ten meters away. Adam hung back in the shadow of a large oak tree and waited while the driver killed the engine and parked the motorcycle on its kickstand. The driver removed his leather helmet and goggles, then reached into his pocket for a pack of cigarettes.

Adam removed a cigarette from his own pack and held it unlit in his left hand. Then he removed the knife from his ankle holster, held it tight against his right leg and stepped out of the shadow, approaching the motorcycle driver who had just lit his cigarette. "*Guten Morgen, Unterscharfuhrer.* Would you give me a light?"

The startled motorcycle driver turned abruptly. Adam casually held up the cigarette. The driver hesitated, staring at Adam in the gray predawn light. Then he appeared to recognize the uniform and held out the cigarette lighter. "*Ja, ja,* you surprised—"

In one swift movement, Adam extended his right arm and thrust the knife into the driver's throat. He stepped back quickly out of the way as blood spurted from the wide-eyed man's neck. The mortally wounded driver's mouth opened wide as he staggered forward, reaching for Adam. Then his knees buckled and he collapsed.

Adam removed the knife, wiped the blade on the dying man's pant leg and slipped it back into the holster. He put on the helmet and goggles, kick-started the motorcycle and drove off to meet Herr Heisenberg.

As he entered the palace arcade, Adam flicked his right hand in a quick wave to the SS trooper behind the wheel of the Horch, then stopped the motorcycle in front of the black auto. A moment later the image of a tall, solidly built SS officer appeared in the cycle's vibrating rearview mirror. SS-Hauptsturmfuhrer Heisenberg with another SS trooper at his side, walked across the arcade in long confident strides toward the waiting automobile. The SS trooper opened the rear door, and Heisenberg disappeared inside. Then, to Adam's surprise, the SS trooper opened the front passenger door and slid in next to the driver.

When the driver of the Horch tapped the horn, Adam gunned the motorcycle and led the car out of the palace arcade. Following the route described in the surveillance report, Adam drove south on Nowy Swiat, turned onto Jerusalem Avenue and headed west, all the while working out a revision to his plan. With two SS troopers in the car, the knife was useless. Fortunately, he had a few extra minutes to think, since they weren't headed directly to the Wola District. Heisenberg's enthusiasm for murder wasn't the only reason he was an early riser. He had a girlfriend.

She was a Polish woman in her thirties, not especially attractive, but well-endowed, and apparently willing to trade sexual favors—and information—for her life. According to the report Adam had studied, Heisenberg kept her in an apartment beyond the West Station in the Ochota District and visited her every morning.

With the hazy eastern sky behind him and ominous clouds of black smoke from the fires in the Wola District ahead of him, Adam continued west on Jerusalem Avenue. He kept to the side of the wide thoroughfare staying out of the way of the heavily armed German convoy rumbling toward him. The convoy was headed east, toward the City Center, and as he sped past Adam counted at least a dozen Panther tanks and twice that number of trucks towing heavy artillery. Hundreds of conscripted soldiers—Hungarians, Serbs, Ukrainians and a smattering of Russians—were crammed elbow-to-elbow in the back of the trucks, all destined to serve as cannon fodder against the AK while German SS officers hung back and watched the show.

Ten minutes later Adam made a hard left turn off Jerusalem Avenue, then maneuvered carefully through a maze of shattered residential streets pockmarked with craters and littered with debris. He finally stopped in front of a three-story apartment building he had scouted out the day before in a neighborhood Heisenberg had obviously decided to spare for the time being. It was an east–west street, and Adam parked the motorcycle pointing into the haze of the rising sun.

Adam took his time as he killed the motorcycle's engine, climbed off the seat and set the kickstand, keeping an eye on the rearview mirror. Artillery shelling had commenced in the City Center, and thumping detonations echoed through the area, rattling windows and keeping pedestrians off the streets. The SS trooper in the front passenger seat of the Horch jumped out and opened the rear door. Heisenberg emerged and headed straight into the building. A man on a mission, Adam thought.

Still watching the rearview mirror, Adam removed his goggles and pulled off the helmet as the SS trooper got back into the front seat of the car. The driver lit a cigarette and held out the pack to his partner. Adam glanced quickly up and down the street then, turning to his left, he slipped the Walther P-38 out of the holster and held it tight against his right leg. In a brisk but unhurried motion, Adam took three strides toward the car.

The driver squinted into the smoggy sunlight with a hand over his eyes. It was already a warm day, and the window was rolled down.

Adam stepped up to the car and, without a word, fired a single shot into the side of the driver's head. He took a step to his left and shot the other SS trooper between the eyes.

He wasn't sure if the sound of the artillery would drown out the gunshots, but he wasn't about to waste any time. Holding the pistol at his side, he walked up to the apartment building and pulled open the door. The apartment was number 2B, on the second floor, and he took the steps quietly, two at a time, holding the gun out in front. He didn't see Heisenberg. The man must have gone right to work.

Adam stopped at the second floor landing and took a breath. He could still hear the artillery shells. He reached with his left hand for the handle on the door marked 2B and pulled it downward. It was locked.

He took another breath and stepped back, pointed the pistol at the door handle and fired. With the gunshot reverberating off the walls of the confined space like a cannon blast, Adam kicked open what was left of the door.

Across the room, Heisenberg knelt on the floor facing the sofa with his pants down to his ankles. He whirled around clumsily and struggled to stand up, stumbling over his bunched-up trousers. The woman sat on the sofa with her nightgown unbuttoned to her waist, her eyes wide in confused terror.

Adam fired a shot into Heisenberg's groin. The SS officer's eyes bulged. Then he curled into a ball, gasping for breath and clutching at the bloody mass that gushed from between his legs. Adam took a step closer, looked down at him and fired a second shot into the back of his head.

The woman shrieked wildly, the SS officer's blood dripping from her face and bare chest. She stared at Adam in horror. Then she scrambled off the sofa and ran to the bedroom, slamming the door behind her.

Adam turned to leave but stopped at the shattered door leading to the hallway. He stood there for a moment. Then he cursed under his breath, marched over to the bedroom door and kicked it open.

The woman cowered on the floor at the foot of the bed with black, mascara-streaked tears running down her cheeks. "Please, I didn't tell him anything," she sobbed, pulling the blood-spattered nightgown over her ample breasts. "Nothing he didn't already know. He *forced* me to do it. He was a pig! I had no choice!"

Adam raised the Walther and fired a single shot through her forehead before he had a chance to think about it a second time. Then he holstered the gun and walked out of the room.

Six

19 AUGUST

THE MORNING WAS HOT and windless, and the smoky haze that hung in the air made it difficult to see much beyond a hundred meters. But from his perch in one of the copper-clad twin towers of Holy Cross Church, Adam had a good view of Avenue Krakowskie. Farther down the avenue, beyond the AK barricade, a German bunker and machine-gun nest guarded the white stone walls and wrought-iron gates at the entrance to Warsaw University. Beyond the gates several hundred German soldiers patrolled the tree-lined pathways of the university grounds. The bodies of five Waffen-SS troopers and a handful of Ukrainian conscripts lay in the street between the university and the barricade.

The shelling had intensified during the night as German Panzer units attacked with greater fury since the discovery of Heisenberg's body. But the barricades protecting Old Town had held . . . at least for now.

Adam knew it had been a risk. Assassinations led to reprisals. But it wasn't something to be concerned about now. He'd followed his orders and it was done. Heisenberg was a murderous butcher who deserved to die, along with his collaborator girlfriend. But that didn't matter, either. Emotion played no part in it. The man was a target, and he had taken him out. It was that simple, just the way it had been ever since the British dropped him back into Poland. Identify the target and take it out.

It was close to noon when Adam heard someone climbing the

staircase leading up to the tower where he'd been positioned since daybreak. Though the church was behind the barricades, in territory still held by the AK, Adam tensed and moved to a corner where he had a clear view of the top of the staircase.

"Captain Wolf, it's Rabbit," a young voice called from halfway up the stairs. "I have a message."

Adam relaxed. Though he had no official rank in the quasi-military organization of the AK, Rabbit always called him "captain." "Come on up," he called back. "I promise not to shoot you."

The skinny lad's blond head poked up through the opening, a broad smile on his face. He was one of the good ones, Adam thought, tough enough to be trusted and streetwise beyond his years, yet young enough not to worry about the inevitable consequences.

"I have a message from Colonel Stag," Rabbit said. "You're to report to his headquarters immediately."

Adam flicked on the safety of his American-made Springfield A4 sniper rifle and slung it over his shoulder.

"When are you gonna teach me how to shoot that rifle," Rabbit asked a few minutes later as they walked through the barricaded streets of Old Town, shells bursting in the distance and thick, black smoke drifting in from the western districts of the city.

Adam laughed. "How old are you?"

"Thirteen," Rabbit said, straightening up and throwing his shoulders back.

"This thing would knock you right on your ass."

"The hell it would. I'm a lot tougher than I look, you know. Besides, I'd rather be a sniper than crawl through the damn sewers, dragging telephone lines."

Adam laughed again. "Maybe some day, Rabbit. But, in the meantime someone has to know the way through the sewers. That may be our only way out of here."

The boy kicked a stone. "Nah, we're goin' to beat these fuckin' Krauts. Me and the Conductor have fried a bunch of 'em."

"The Conductor?"

"Yeah, the one with the uniform. Remember that day in the hospital square? Me and the Conductor were caught in the middle of the street, and you took out three of those SS pricks, shot 'em right over our heads. Damn, that was something to see. You *gotta* teach me to shoot like that."

Adam shrugged. He remembered the day at the hospital, of course. And he had seen her again a few days later, sitting with Falcon at the briefing. But what did it matter? She'd probably just get herself killed, like they all would.

"We're going to beat these Krauts, don't you think?"

Adam put a hand on the boy's shoulder and nodded, marveling at the optimism of youth. He was about to respond when someone shouted at Rabbit from across the street. The boy said, "It's Bobcat, gotta go. See ya later."

Adam watched with a smile as Rabbit ran up to the taller, dark-haired boy called Bobcat and punched him in the arm, then ducked out of the way as Bobcat took a swipe at his head. A moment later they were both running down the street, laughing and calling each other names.

The AK district command center had been moved from Pilsudski Square to the cellar of the Polonia Bank building in Old Town. Located just a few streets off the central square, the bank was nestled in the middle of a row of three-story, seventeenth-century merchant houses and guild halls that had so far withstood the sporadic shelling with only a layer of soot darkening their multi-colored façades.

As Adam descended the staircase and entered the crowded, smoky room in the cellar of the bank, a brawny commando with a shock of jet-black hair and a scowl on his face brushed past him and stomped up the stairs.

Adam watched the commando for a few seconds, then glanced around the hot, stuffy room, lit with bare bulbs strung across the wood-beamed ceiling. He spotted Colonel Stag at a small table in the far corner, away from the other AK officers, who were poring over maps and scratching out dispatches for the runners.

The colonel waved his hand for Adam to join him. His face was heavily creased and pasty-looking, his eyes showing fatigue. "We've been instructed by General Bor to make contact with the Russians,"

Stag said as soon as Adam sat down, not wasting any time with small talk. "The situation here is getting critical, and it's imperative we know their intentions."

"Has there been any movement on their part?" Adam asked.

Stag shook his head. "No, they're still sitting there on the east bank of the river, south of Praga. They've had firefights with the Germans up and down the river, but our scouts report they've shown no inclination to move into Warsaw." Stag leaned over the table and lowered his voice. "The Russians won't talk with us directly, of course, so as soon as we can set it up, we're going to send you over there."

Adam stiffened. He understood the reality of the situation. As historical enemies, Russian officers would never communicate directly with their Polish counterparts, would never acknowledge them as equals, even though since 1941 they were technically allies. "What makes you think they'll talk to me?"

"You're an American. Our intelligence people have made some probes and have reason to believe they'll receive you."

"Even though I've been fighting with the AK and carrying out orders given by Polish officers?"

"The Russians won't know that. They might know who General Bor is—and maybe who I am and one or two of the other officers, if their spies are any good. But there are thirty thousand insurgents fighting here and, even if they cared, it would be impossible for them to know who you are. Hell, you've been so deep under cover *I* don't even know who you really are."

"So, when I get over there, who or what will they think I am?"

"A story is being planted that you're an American emissary from London, representing the Polish Government-in-Exile."

Adam thought about it for a moment. "Does anyone else know about this?"

Stag shook his head.

"What about Falcon? As I came in he almost knocked me down stomping out of here. He looked pretty pissed off about something."

"That's just the way he is," Stag said with a shrug. "He's been badgering me for a week to let him lead an assault on the German garrison at Saxon Palace. It's out of the question, of course. Without armored protection, they'd get slaughtered, but he doesn't see it that way. Just between you and me, I think he also wanted to be the one to take out Heisenberg."

Adam nodded. He'd met Falcon only once but knew him by reputation as a fearless fighter, though something of a bully and impulsive, prone to taking unnecessary risks. He folded his hands on the table and looked at Colonel Stag. "Will I have a name, identification?"

"Nothing, no name, no ID. That's the way it's being set up."

"So there's no record. No matter what happens, I was never there."

Stag rubbed a hand on his stubbly chin and smiled. "That's the idea. It may take a few days to get everything set up, so just be ready to go."

"Who will I be meeting?"

"A Red Army general named Kovalenko. We don't know much about him except that he's in command of an armored division just south of Praga and he reports directly to Rokossovsky."

Seven

19 August

General Andrei Kovalenko was furious. From his vantage point on the east bank of the Vistula River he watched the smoke rising from Warsaw and knew they were running out of time. The AK insurgency had lasted almost three weeks, longer than anyone had thought possible, but the Germans were bringing in reinforcements. Very soon, he knew, it would be too late.

His attention was diverted by the sound of an approaching automobile, and he abruptly turned away from the riverbank. A black four-door GAZ-11, streaked with dust, pulled up and stopped behind a long line of idle T-34 tanks. A Red Army captain named Andreyev emerged from the backseat and walked briskly across the gravel road to meet the burly, broad-shouldered general. The captain saluted smartly and held out an envelope. He was taller than the general but very thin, almost gaunt. The left side of his face was scarred from shrapnel wounds, and he wore a black patch over his left eye. "Orders from Marshal Rokossovsky's headquarters, sir."

General Kovalenko snatched the envelope from the captain's hand and ripped it open. He removed a sheet of paper, read it quickly, then crumpled it in his thick fist and tossed it on the ground. "Fucking idiots," he muttered and headed back to the river.

Captain Andreyev retrieved the crumpled wad of paper and caught up to the general. "*Shto sluchílas'*, what's wrong?" he asked. "Are we not attacking?"

Kovalenko glared at the young captain, his most trusted subordinate.

He removed his cap and ran a thick hand through close-cropped gray hair. "*Nyet,* we're not attacking. Our orders are to sit here on our dead asses and watch, while the Germans destroy one of Europe's great cities." He waved his hand at the line of tanks and armored cars, his voice rising in frustration. "We've had these Nazi bastards on the run for months! We've got five hundred tanks and twelve divisions of infantry with heavy artillery, ready to finish this! Now is the time, Goddamn it!"

"Then why aren't we attacking?"

Kovalenko was silent. Across the river smoke billowed into the summer sky. He knew there wasn't a chance in hell that the insurgents of the AK could succeed in their Rising against the Germans without help from the Russian Army. But he also knew why they weren't attacking. He knew about the plans that Stalin and his thugs in the NKVD had for Poland. And there wasn't a damn thing he could do about it.

Andreyev stood next to him and looked across the river, seeming to sense his thoughts. "Don't they know when they're defeated, when to give up?"

"Would *you* know, Captain Andreyev?" Kovalenko demanded. "Would any of us? When the German Wehrmacht threatened to overrun us at Stalingrad, were any of us prepared to admit defeat and give up? Weren't we ready to throw every last man, woman and child into the breach to turn back these fascist Nazi pigs?" He paused and took a breath, remembering the horror of Stalingrad where he'd certainly have lost his life if it hadn't been for the heroics of Captain Andreyev, who had been disfigured in the process. When he continued, the general softened his tone. "I'm certain the insurgents of the AK feel exactly the same way, Captain. Our own armies, as well as Germany's, have been trampling over Poland for the last three hundred years. Perhaps they've finally had enough."

"And they've had just twenty years of freedom," Andreyev said.

Kovalenko grunted. "That's enough to know what it tastes like, enough to not want to lose it again, no matter the cost." He turned and faced the younger captain. "So, after five years of Nazi occupation, at the precise moment when the German Army is on the run, and the Poles have one chance to take back their capital before *we* move in, is it any surprise that they choose to fight?"

"The only surprise is that they've lasted this long," Andreyev said.

"Yes, indeed it is, Captain. It shows you how desperate they are to avoid getting out from under German occupation only to live under Soviet occupation."

"But the AK can't possibly succeed. Hitler will never allow it. He's demanded that they be crushed and Warsaw burnt to the ground." Andreyev contemplated the crumpled message in his hand. "And we're not going to help them, are we?"

Kovalenko spat on the ground. "*Nyet,* Captain Andreyev, we're not going to help them."

Eight

20 August

It was close to midnight as the moon slipped silently from behind the clouds, casting a silvery glow and spidery, ghostlike shadows onto the cityscape. Natalia crouched behind the wreckage of a burned-out Panther tank and studied the imposing structure on the other side of Zielna Street. The Warsaw Telephone Exchange—known as PAST—was housed in the concrete-reinforced building that stretched for an entire city block. It consisted of two four-story sections on either side of an eight-story central tower. The building had been the target of intense fighting since the first day of the Rising.

As the German Army's main communications link between Berlin and the eastern front, PAST was vital to their operations and was held by a 150-man garrison protected by tanks and armored cars. But the AK's resolve to take the building had been unrelenting. Day after day for the last three weeks, AK commando units had assaulted the enemy stronghold with Sten guns, homemade Filipinka grenades and crossbow-launched Molotov cocktails. But the German machine gunners situated at the top of the tower had an unencumbered field of fire, and AK casualties had mounted steadily. Steadfastly refusing to quit, however, Colonel Stag had stepped up the attacks until finally today, just before dusk, the AK had surrounded PAST. The moment for striking the final blow had come.

Natalia turned around at the sound of someone shuffling across the cobblestones. She smiled at Berta as her friend knelt down next to her.

"This waiting is driving me crazy," Berta whispered. "Let's just get going and get this over with."

Natalia glanced around at the other AK commandos huddled nearby. They were all women, a specialized unit known as Minerki that Natalia and Berta had volunteered to join. The unit leader was Zeeka, a former engineer and an expert in explosives. Iza, Ula, Alida and Berta, along with Natalia made up the balance of the Minerki team, a unit organized hastily and in secret by Colonel Stag to throw German spies off the track. She looked back at Berta. "A bit impatient, are you?"

Berta shrugged. "Yeah, I guess."

"You just don't like not being in charge," Natalia whispered back.

"No, I'm fine with someone else being in charge of *this* operation. I don't like messing around with explosives."

"Zeeka knows what she's doing."

"Yeah, yeah, I know. We get in, we get out. No problem."

At precisely midnight, Zeeka motioned for the others to gather around and whispered the instructions one last time. She was taller than the rest of the women, with dark, intense eyes and jet-black hair that she always wore in a ponytail under a green felt cap. Natalia had often wondered if she might be a gypsy. "The Kalinski Battalion has succeeded in blowing open a breach in the concrete wall just below the south end of the tower," Zeeka said. "In exactly fifteen minutes the battalion will launch another grenade barrage at the Panzer units at both ends of Zielna Street. At the same time, the Sten gunners will spray the top of the tower. That's when we run across the street and slip through the breach into the basement."

"How many Germans are inside the building?" Ula asked, adjusting the chinstrap of the World War One vintage steel helmet she'd taken off the body of a dead AK commando earlier in the day.

"We don't know for sure, at least a hundred." Zeeka held her wristwatch up to the moonlight. "Twelve minutes to go. Gather up your packs."

Natalia picked up her heavy canvas pack and slung it on her back, pulling the cinch-strap tight across her chest. Like three of the others, her pack contained twenty kilos of a homemade incendiary explosive mixed with paraffin and fashioned into bricks. Iza, a round, solidly built woman and the second-in-command, carried the flamethrower with a petrol canister strapped to her back.

The mission had been planned as well as could be expected on short notice, and the six-woman Minerki team had practiced the assault under tight security twenty-four hours earlier in the cellar of a bombed-out church in Old Town. They would have exactly four minutes after entering the basement under the PAST tower to place incendiary bricks along the outside walls in a specific pattern that Zeeka had designed for maximum impact. Then they would exit where they had come in, and Iza would ignite the charges with the flamethrower.

Natalia squinted at her own watch, but the moon had slipped behind the clouds again and she couldn't make out the time. She swallowed hard and waited. It was true they had practiced the mission, but they hadn't actually *done* it.

Berta stood next to her, impatiently shifting her weight from one foot to the other. Natalia turned and smiled, though she could just barely make out her friend's face in the darkness.

At exactly 0015, the night sky erupted into a blaze of flashing lights and jarring *whumps* as the Kalinski Battalion launched the grenade barrage. A few seconds later the clatter of Sten guns echoed off the buildings, Zeeka shouted the order and the Minerki team sprinted across the wide street. Natalia was fourth in line behind Ula and ahead of Berta.

Suddenly a searchlight from the top of the tower illuminated the street, and a burst of machine-gun fire ripped along the cobblestones. But the Sten gunners took out the searchlight, and the street was dark again.

Zeeka was the first to arrive at the base of the enormous building and disappeared through the breach, lighting the way for the others with a flashlight.

When Natalia crawled through the breach and jumped into the damp, cavernous basement, the two women ahead of her had already opened their packs and were placing incendiary bricks under Zeeka's direction. Berta was right behind her, and the four women set the explosives precisely in a predetermined chain that could be ignited from outside the building with the flamethrower. In three and a half minutes they were back on the sidewalk.

The Sten gunners started in again, spraying the tower with covering fire as Iza moved into position with the flamethrower, and Zeeka yelled for the others to get back across the street.

But the enemy machine gunners at the top of the tower refused to quit, spraying the entire length of the street with random, hammering bursts, shattering the last of the windows and filling the air with flying chunks of concrete and stone.

Natalia lowered her head and dashed into the street right behind Ula and Alida. She'd taken only a few steps when she heard a grunt from behind, and Berta stumbled forward, almost knocking her down.

Natalia reached back to grab Berta's hand, but her friend fell to the ground and rolled over on the cobblestone street, clutching her left leg. Natalia dropped to her knees and crawled back to Berta, who lay curled in a ball, trembling and moaning, her shredded trouser leg already soaked in blood.

Natalia screamed for Ula, then grabbed Berta under the arms and tried to drag her forward. A second later Ula was alongside, cursing loudly as a bullet struck her steel helmet and knocked it off her head.

Holding Berta under the arms, the two of them dragged her across the street and behind the tank as bullets ricocheted off the steel frame. Natalia dug into her pack, pulled out a knife and quickly sliced away what was left of Berta's blood-soaked trouser leg.

"Jesus Christ," Ula muttered when she saw the wound.

"Grab her arm and roll her onto her stomach," Natalia said sharply. "Alida, get over here!"

Berta groaned deeply as the two women commandos rolled her over, and Natalia examined the wound. It was a ragged laceration several centimeters wide running up the back of her leg from the knee to just below the buttocks. Blood seemed to be everywhere. It pooled on the ground, and Berta moaned louder as Natalia felt around with her fingers on either side of the ugly gash.

"I don't think there are any broken bones," Natalia said as she straightened up and ripped off her blue uniform coat followed by her cotton shirt. She quickly folded the shirt into a rectangular pad, then placed it over the back of Berta's leg and pressed down hard. "Take off your belts and cinch them around her leg," she shouted at Ula and Alida. "Right over this pad, quickly, we've got to get the bleeding under control."

From across the street Natalia heard a *whoosh* from the flamethrower, then a momentary pause, followed an instant later by a rising crescendo of concussions that felt like hammer blows in her eardrums. The incendiary charges ignited in rapid succession, thrusting a monstrous fireball upward from the bowels of the PAST building.

Their faces blackened with soot and dripping with sweat, Zeeka and Iza dashed across the street, scrambled behind the tank and dropped to their knees. Zeeka crawled over next to Natalia. "I saw her go down. How bad is it?"

"Nothing's broken as far as I can tell, but the back of her leg is badly lacerated and she's losing a lot of blood." Natalia shot a quick glance at Alida. "Tighten that belt!" Blood was already soaking through the makeshift bandage, and Natalia motioned to Zeeka. "Help me roll her onto her back again, gently, and we'll get that leg elevated. We've got to get her to a medic fast or she'll—"

Her voice was drowned out by a thunderous roar from across the street as the wall of flames engulfed the lower two floors of the eight-story PAST tower, climbing rapidly, blowing out windows in a relentless upward thrust. Dozens of shrieking German soldiers, their clothes ablaze, stumbled out through the main entrance or tumbled out first floor windows. The flames rocketed upward, engulfing floor after floor until they reached the top where dozens of men were trapped in the tower.

Natalia watched, dumbstruck with horror, as German soldiers leaped to their deaths, dark silhouettes flailing against the fire-lit sky.

Nine

21 August

Natalia dipped a cloth in a pan of cool water, wrung it out and laid it gently across Berta's forehead. She placed the back of her hand against her friend's cheek. It was warm, but not hot, and that was good. Though it had been more than twelve hours, she knew Berta was still in danger. The few remaining doctors in Warsaw were all working round-the-clock in makeshift hospitals. But Zeeka had somehow managed to dig up a stretcher and then find a medic, as the others carried Berta from what was left of the PAST building to the women commando's quarters on Trebacka Street. It had taken almost two hours and fifty stitches to close Berta's leg wound, but there were no antibiotics and Natalia knew that the greatest danger over the next few days would be infection.

Fortunately the medic did have morphine. He'd given Berta two shots to get her through the procedure, and she had slept fitfully through the rest of the night and most of the next day. Natalia stayed with her, dozing on and off, and holding Berta's hand whenever her friend woke up. By evening the morphine had worn off, and Berta was awake, groaning whenever she moved her leg. "God . . . damn it," she muttered in a mushy, slurred voice, "of all . . . the . . . rotten luck."

Natalia set the cloth aside, brought over a bowl of weak vegetable soup and fed her a spoonful.

Berta grimaced. "Ach, that's . . . horrible."

Natalia nodded, "Yep, same as always. But it's all we've got, and you've got to keep up your strength." She lifted the sheet and examined

Berta's leg, which was elevated with her left foot resting on a wooden crate. The jagged line of stitches ran up the back of her thigh, ending just under the buttocks. The medic had done an adequate job, but her leg was badly swollen. The skin on either side of the stitches was taut and deep red with a yellowish puss oozing from the wound.

Berta looked at her with bloodshot eyes. "So, former medical student . . . how does it look?"

"You're lucky it didn't get your knee," Natalia said half-heartedly, knowing that wasn't Berta's real problem. More than half the deaths among the AK commandos were the result of infections from the unsanitary conditions and lack of medicines.

Berta gripped Natalia's hand. "Listen to me," she said, her voice dropping to a raspy whisper. "You can't . . . stay here . . . and nursemaid me. Go get some rest. I'll be fine."

Natalia smiled at her, wiped her brow again and picked up the spoon. "Shut up and eat some of this delicious soup."

Ula and Zeeka arrived a little after ten o'clock that evening. Ula was carrying a white cotton shirt that she handed to Natalia.

"My God, where did you get this?" Natalia exclaimed, taking off her coat and slipping on the shirt.

Ula shook her head. "You don't want to know."

Natalia nodded. "OK, I understand." She buttoned it up and tugged at the bottoms of the sleeves. "It even fits . . . sort of." Then she noticed that Zeeka had something in her hand. It was wrapped in brown paper, and she held it gently as though it were a precious gem. "What is that?"

Zeeka glanced at Berta, who had fallen asleep again, then passed the mysterious package under Natalia's nose and, with a conspiratorial wink, began to unwrap it.

The aroma hit Natalia, and she grabbed the package out of Zeeka's hand and peeled back the rest of the paper revealing two golden brown, plump *pierogi*. She picked one of the small, semi-circular dumplings off the paper and closed her eyes, breathing in deeply. "Onions and mushrooms! Wherever did you get it?"

"Rabbit brought them into the pub about a half hour ago," Ula said. "An elderly man handed him the package outside. He said it was for the women who killed all those Germans at the telephone company. His wife used the last of their flour and what was left in the garden to make them."

Natalia held the vegetable-filled dumpling in her hand, almost reluctant to eat it because then it would be gone. But, with her stomach growling and her mouth watering, she finally gave in, eating it slowly with baby bites to make it last. "My God, I'd forgotten what they taste like. It's heaven."

Zeeka re-wrapped the last one in the brown paper and set it on the table. "We'll give it to Berta when she wakes up." Then she pointed at the door. "Now *you* get out of here."

"What are you talking about? I can't just leave her."

"So, you don't think *we* can take care of her? It's your birthday, for God's sake, and you need a break. Go over to the pub and have a drink."

The Bomb Shelter Pub was located in the cellar of an abandoned warehouse on a narrow, twisting street behind St. John's Cathedral in Old Town. It was a makeshift operation, born during the first week of the Rising when euphoric AK commandos hauled in an eclectic mix of tables and chairs from deserted homes in the neighborhood, cleared away the dust and cobwebs, and opened for business. Red-and-white Polish flags hung from the ceiling and, when the electricity was on, a phonograph played the beloved melodies of Chopin, heard in Warsaw for the first time in five years. AK banners were tacked to the posts. A painted caricature of a death's-head wearing a Nazi helmet, along with the words *One Bullet – One German,* adorned the wall directly opposite the stairway.

As the fighting dragged into the third week, Warsaw's western districts were being pounded into oblivion. But Old Town and much of the City Center remained in the hands of the AK, and the pub was bustling with activity twenty-four hours a day. It was alternately a soup kitchen, a medical clinic, a meeting hall, a wedding chapel and, during long tension-filled nights, a tavern where beleaguered AK commandos roused each other on to a victory that seemed less likely with each passing day. As in the rest of the city, food and water were scarce, but vodka plentiful. So they gathered, glasses in hand, sometimes mourning losses, other times celebrating victories, turning up the volume of the phonograph to drown out the shelling.

Despite the desperate struggle, the night of 21 August was an occasion for cheer, and the revelry in the sweaty, smoke-filled cellar was more boisterous than ever, celebrating the destruction of the PAST building the night before. More than a hundred German soldiers had been taken prisoner and dozens more had jumped to their deaths as a vital link in Germany's battle communications had been severed.

The vodka flowed freely. Glasses were raised in toasts to the Minerki team amidst raucous cheers and shouts of "Poland Fights! Poland Fights!"

And the loudest voice in the group belonged to Falcon, who had started drinking early and now stood unsteadily atop a table, waving a bottle in the air.

"It's all over for the fuckin' Nazis!" he bellowed hoarsely. "They'll tuck their tails between their legs and run back to their sniveling, knob-kneed Fuhrer!"

Someone shouted from the center of the room, "Give the bastards hell, Falcon! And the same to the Russians!"

Falcon spun around and threw both hands in the air, responding with a mighty roar. "The *Russians?* Fuck the Russians! Let them sit on their sorry asses. We don't—"

He lost his balance. The vodka bottle flew from his hand, soared across the room and shattered against the phonograph, sending the needle screeching across the record. Falcon staggered once, then fell backward off the table on top of a half dozen men, who all toppled to the floor with loud bursts of profanity and uproarious laughter. Falcon's friend Pierre helped him to his feet and tried in vain to boost him back on the table.

Natalia stood in a corner of the room watching the uncouth display, growing more disgusted by the moment. She'd never considered her affair with Falcon anything more than casual. And she'd been losing interest rapidly over the last few weeks as he'd become increasingly possessive. She could still tolerate him when he was sober. But not when he was like this, which was becoming more frequent all the time.

Some break her friends had given her, Natalia thought. When the table split down the middle and collapsed, she had seen enough. She forced her way through the sweaty mob, climbed the stairs two at a time and pushed open the door.

Outside, she stood on the cobblestone walkway and took a deep breath, inhaling the cool night air. It was her birthday, but she didn't feel like celebrating. Her best friend had been badly wounded and, as much as she loathed the Nazis, the sight of desperate men leaping from a burning tower was another in a long list of horrendous images she knew she would carry forever.

She glanced down the street where a family huddled around a small fire. The father held a stick with a clump of something on the end while two little boys, one wrapped in a blanket on his mother's lap, stared listlessly at the flames. Smoke wafted up, drifting toward Natalia in the breeze, carrying the pungent odor of horsemeat.

She turned away and looked in the other direction, then froze as a figure emerged from the shadows of a building across the street. She took a step backward, instinctively reaching into her jacket pocket and gripping her pistol. From inside the pub she heard Falcon's voice, hoarsely bellowing another curse.

The figure stepped into the street and came toward her. "Sounds like things are getting pretty wild in there."

In the moonlight, Natalia could now make him out: a thin man wearing glasses. "Wolf?" she asked.

The man motioned toward the raucous party inside the pub. "That sounds like Falcon. Is he always like that?"

"Only when he drinks . . . He's . . ." She stopped, conscious of her hand still in her jacket pocket, clutching the pistol. "He's just someone I . . ." She stopped again, realizing she couldn't tell him any more. Falcon had been her contact for the documents she smuggled from Krakow. "You and I met once before," she said, changing the subject, "that day at the hospital square."

The man called Wolf took a step closer. "Yes, I know. Are you always that impulsive?"

"That bastard just shot her . . . like she was . . ." Natalia shuddered as the hideous scene of women being dragged beneath the tank flashed through her mind. "I guess I should thank you. You probably saved my life."

Wolf shook his head. "I think Rabbit did that. Besides, the woman would've died anyway."

"That doesn't mean we can't try!"

"You were doing what you had to do. Except that pistol you carry around in your pocket probably wouldn't have stopped the tank."

Natalia felt her face flush. She let go of the pistol and removed her hand from her pocket. "Well, thank you anyway."

"You were part of the Minerki team?"

"Yes, I was."

"That was good work."

She nodded, but a shiver ran down her spine as the images flashed back: German soldiers leaping from the tower, dark silhouettes against the flames.

"They go away eventually," he said. "The memories . . . they eventually go away if you put them out of your mind."

"Is that what you do?"

"Yes, I do." He seemed to be studying her uniform jacket. "They call you the Conductor?"

Natalia brushed some of the dust from the jacket, though it was a futile gesture after weeks of fighting in the streets. "That's what I was, before all this started. I worked the run from Krakow to Warsaw."

"So, you're from Krakow?"

"Not originally. I'm from a small village in eastern Poland, but I moved to Krakow when I got the job on the railway."

They stood in silence for a moment, the quiet broken only by sporadic laughter from the pub and the constant echo of artillery shelling in the distance. Wolf was thin and wiry, and standing in the shadowy moonlight, Natalia thought he looked far less formidable than he had that day in the hospital square. "They say you're an American," she said, though the instant she said it she knew he probably wouldn't tell her if he was.

"Do I sound like an American?" His Polish was without any trace of accent, but cultured and refined, like he'd been raised in the city.

"No, you don't. Do you live here, in Warsaw?"

He shook his head.

"Then I'll bet you're also from Krakow. You were, let's see . . . a banker, perhaps?"

He laughed but stopped abruptly and cleared his throat. "A banker? Good Lord, I couldn't stand to be around all that money. I'd probably steal it."

He seemed a bit restless. Natalia had the impression that he wanted to talk but was uncomfortable about it, as though he wasn't used to being around people. "So, if you're not a banker, then . . . a doctor?"

"No, not even close."

"A schoolteacher?"

"You ask a lot of questions."

"I know. It's my worst quality. I guess I'm just naturally curious. So, *are* you a schoolteacher?"

"If I were, what would I teach?"

"Well, now we're getting someplace. Let's see . . . maybe, economics?"

"Economics? Banking? What is it with you and money?"

Now they both laughed. "I have no idea," she said, catching her breath, "I've certainly never had—"

The door of the pub banged open, and Falcon lurched out, followed by Pierre and another commando, who stumbled into him when he stopped abruptly. Falcon swayed back and forth, clutching a bottle in his hand and staring at Natalia. "There ya . . . there y'are," he slurred and took a wobbly step closer.

Natalia pointed at the door. "Go back inside," she snapped.

Pierre grabbed Falcon's arm and tried to pull him back into the pub. "You heard the lady. Let's go."

Falcon pushed him away. "Get the fuck off me!" The bottle dropped from Falcon's hand and shattered on the cobblestones. He stood upright, shot a quick glance at Wolf, then glared at Natalia. "What the hell . . . what's . . . going on?"

"Get him out of here," Natalia said sharply to Pierre.

Falcon grabbed her hand and pulled her toward him.

She jerked away. "Goddamn it—"

But Falcon lurched forward again and grabbed both of her shoulders. His eyes were glazed, and his breath stank of alcohol. "Don't get smart with me you—"

She pushed him hard. "Take your hands off me."

Falcon stumbled back, then straightened up and looked beyond her. "Hah, he's gone. Looks like your new friend doesn't . . . want any trouble. Now, come over here."

He reached for her hand again, but she turned away. The street was empty except for the family huddled by the fire.

Wolf was gone.

She stepped into the street, but Falcon was on her in a second. He grabbed her arm and jerked her back. "Goddamn it! You don't walk away from me!"

She whirled around and slapped him across the face.

Falcon seemed stunned for a second, then punched her in the side of the head, a hammer blow that sent a searing bolt of pain like an electric shock all the way down her back. He grabbed her by the throat and shoved her to her knees. "You bitch! Now I'm not good enough?"

"Falcon!" Pierre shouted. "That's enough!"

Without taking his eyes off Natalia, Falcon roared, "Shut up and get out of here or you're next!" He squeezed hard on her throat. "We'll see who's not good enough."

Natalia reached into her pocket, fumbling for the pistol. Her head felt like it was split in half, and she could barely breathe. She tried to break loose, but he was too strong, his fingers digging into her throat. Her vision began to blur when she saw a flash of movement out of the corner of her eye.

Falcon's grip abruptly fell away.

Natalia tumbled backward, coughing and gagging, trying to catch her breath. She saw Wolf, his hands clutching Falcon's shirt, driving the larger man backward toward the building.

Falcon's arms flailed wildly as Wolf shoved him to the ground, then kicked him hard in the groin.

Falcon howled and rolled onto his side.

Wolf grabbed him by the hair, lifted the big man off the ground and drove his fist into his stomach.

Falcon coiled up into a ball.

Wolf turned toward Pierre. "Pick him up and get him out of here," he said with an unmistakable tone of menace.

Pierre motioned toward the other commando, who grabbed Falcon under the arms and dragged him into the building.

"I'm sorry," Pierre said. "I should have stopped him sooner. Once he gets worked up he just—"

"Forget it," Wolf said. "Just keep him away from her."

Pierre nodded, then put a hand on Wolf's shoulder. "I've been meaning to thank you . . . for taking care of that bastard, Heisenberg."

Wolf lifted Pierre's hand off his shoulder and turned him back toward the pub. "I was just doing my job. Now take Falcon back inside and keep him there."

Natalia got to her feet, blinking away the stars that danced in her vision, and gently touched the side of her face. She opened and closed her mouth, relieved that her jaw wasn't broken.

Wolf stepped up and took her elbow. "I think we'd better go."

Ten

21 AUGUST

THEY WALKED QUICKLY away from the pub and across Old Town's central market square. In the last five days the enemy shelling had advanced eastward, and now more than half of the Medieval buildings lay in ruins—three centuries of history reduced to rubble piles of multi-colored stucco, shattered leaded-glass windows and broken roof tiles. Flames flickered up through the wreckage, lighting the night street. The acrid odor of smoke hung heavily in the air as groups of AK commandos huddled around their bonfires and pots of soup with rifles slung over their shoulders. They passed around bottles of vodka and cigarettes, glancing up occasionally when a particularly loud artillery burst echoed through the square.

Adam was three paces ahead of the woman in the railway conductor's uniform. He detoured around a massive heap of smashed bricks and glanced down into a crater where the remains of the mermaid statue, the symbol of Warsaw, protruded from the smoldering debris. Her sword pointed to the sky as if she were sending an appeal to heaven. He stepped over the keystone block of a smashed archway, cursing under his breath for letting his guard down. What the hell had he been thinking? Falcon was a drunken lout; there was no doubt about that. But the woman was an AK commando, and she was carrying a gun. Adam sensed that she was used to Falcon's behavior and could've handled him by herself under normal circumstances. *Except the crazy bastard went nuts when he saw me*. And that, Adam knew, was exactly the kind of situation he couldn't afford to get mixed up in.

The woman caught up to him and grabbed his arm, jerking him to a halt. "I'll be fine," she said with determination. "You don't have to go out of your way. Really, I'm fine." In the light from the bonfires, Adam could see the welt on her left cheekbone was turning black-and-blue.

Suddenly the ground shook, and a fireball belched into the air from a shattering blast somewhere in the City Center. The commando groups began to disperse, carrying their cups of soup into what was left of the narrow alleyways leading away from the square. Adam motioned toward the north end of the square. "We should get off the streets."

Five minutes later they arrived at St. Jacek's Church, a stout, gray fortress that stood alongside a copper-domed bell tower at the head of Dluga Street. Adam stopped, glancing back over his shoulder to make sure Falcon or any of his friends hadn't followed them. What he didn't need right now was any more attention.

He pulled open one of the thick, ornately carved wooden doors, and they stepped into a tiny vestibule with a stone floor and thick stone walls. It was cold and damp, with a musty odor that suggested the candles on the wall sconces hadn't been lit for many weeks. They passed through another set of double doors into a three-story-high sanctuary, illuminated only by the dancing light of nearby fires that flickered through the arched windows like demon's tongues. Moving slowly in the semi-darkness, Adam led the way down the marble steps to an aisle along one side of the sanctuary and motioned for the woman to slide into the last pew. The solid oak back and square posts were worn smooth over the centuries. He sat down beside her with his back to the wall, being careful not to get too close.

They sat in silence. As his eyes adjusted to the dim light, Adam noticed clusters of people scattered around the sanctuary, many of them asleep in the pews, others huddled close together holding children on their laps. A group of AK commandos sat on the steps that led to the altar, passing around a cigarette and talking quietly.

After a few minutes the woman leaned over and whispered, "You didn't have to get involved, but thank you anyway. I'm fine now."

Adam nodded.

"I don't even know you, but it seems like I'm always thanking you for something," she said.

"It isn't necessary. It was nothing."

"Well, like I said, I'll be fine. You probably have to be somewhere."

That's right, Adam thought. That's exactly what he should do: get up and leave. She probably would be fine. These things happened all the time, especially now, in this city under siege with no one knowing if they'd live through another day. A guy got drunk, a little disorderly, and his girlfriend got angry. No need for him to get involved. And he *couldn't* get involved.

But he didn't leave.

Time passed and the church was quiet, except for the creaking of wooden pews and a few anxious whispers that rippled through the sanctuary whenever an artillery blast rattled the windows and the brass chandelier suspended from the arched ceiling. Adam was exhausted. The nights were always the worst. Though the enemy tanks and infantry battalions usually retreated behind their lines after dark, sporadic artillery shelling continued. There was the ever-present threat that the next shell might be the one.

The woman cleared her throat and turned toward him. "So, why do they call you Wolf?" she whispered. "Is it because you're a loner?"

Adam hesitated then slid closer, keeping his voice down. "Wolves aren't normally loners," he said. "They usually live in packs."

"Ah, but sometimes a wolf is driven from the pack. Then he's a loner."

Adam clenched his jaw as a shiver ran down his back. *Driven from the pack*. She didn't know how close she was.

"You know, the rumors are that you're an American."

"I know. You said that earlier."

"So, are you . . . an American?"

"I've already answered that."

"No, you didn't. You merely asked me if you *sounded* like an American, and I said you didn't, which you don't because you have no accent."

He looked away. "This is giving me a headache."

"Hey, *I'm* the one with a headache. So, what's the answer?"

"You're very persistent, you know."

"Yes, that's another of my bad qualities."

"And annoying."

"Yet another."

Adam hesitated again, longer this time. There were other AK operatives who knew he was an American, though none of them knew any more than just that, not his real name, where he came from, nothing. So, it would be no real breach of security to tell her and, at any rate, there was little chance any of them were going to survive long enough for it to make a difference. He tensed at the crack of a mortar blast, followed by the muted sounds of men shouting outside the church. When it calmed down again, he said quietly, "Yes, I'm an American."

"But your Polish is excellent. You have no accent at all. How long have you been here?"

"I was born here, in Krakow, as you guessed. My father and I immigrated to America when I was eleven years old."

"And you came back? What on earth for?"

Adam contemplated her question. Emotions he'd not allowed himself to feel for many years flared up suddenly. *And you came back? What on earth for?* He knew why he had come back, but it made no difference now. A young man whose father had just died, returning to the country of his birth, searching for his roots, for the family he'd always longed for. But it made no difference; it had all been abruptly and brutally torn away.

Adam shook his head, driving the emotions back into the far corners of his mind. Then he leaned close to her and whispered, "If I tell you any more, I'll have to kill you."

The woman laughed then stopped abruptly and clamped a hand over her mouth, looking quickly around the sanctuary. No one seemed to notice. "My goodness, I've forgotten who you are," she whispered. "You probably mean it."

Adam woke abruptly at the sound of an infant crying and people shuffling down the aisle. He was confused for a moment and struggled to get his bearings. Then he realized where he was. He turned his head slowly, working out the kink in his neck, and looked around. The sanctuary was brighter now, and he could make out the large wooden cross and two statues prominently displayed on the white stone wall at the front of the sanctuary. Under the arched windows on either side of the altar were two elaborately framed paintings. He was too far away and the light still too dim to make out the subject of the artwork, though it wasn't hard to guess.

Several other people were stretching and moving around. Adam glanced down at the woman curled up next to him on the pew, then raised his left hand and checked his watch. It was five thirty in the morning. *My God, we've been sitting here all night. When did I fall asleep?*

He blinked and came fully awake at the sound of artillery fire in the distance, voices outside and the rumble of an engine starting up. As he shifted his weight, the pew creaked, and the woman lifted her head, looking at him with a puzzled expression. Then she sat up abruptly and rubbed her eyes. "What time is it?"

"Five thirty," Adam said.

She stretched and ran her hands through her short brown hair. "Were you sleeping as well?"

Adam nodded, suddenly irritated with himself. In four years he had never just fallen asleep unless he knew exactly where he was and that it was safe. What the hell was he thinking? Besides, he had orders to meet with Colonel Stag at 0600. He slid out of the pew, removed his glasses and rubbed the bridge of his nose. Then he put them back on and said, "I have to go."

She raised her eyebrows, but slid out of the pew after him. "Well, alright then, Mr. Wolf. I enjoyed our little chat."

"I didn't mean to be rude . . . it's just that . . ." Adam backed up against the wall as an emaciated, middle-aged man and a hollow-faced, young boy squeezed past them in the narrow aisle. The man hobbled on a homemade crutch. He was missing his right leg. The blood-soaked trouser was pinned at the knee.

The woman waited until the man and boy moved farther up the aisle, then said, "Yes, I understand. You have to be somewhere. I do as well."

"We shouldn't leave together."

"No, of course not, you go first."

Adam started for the door but felt a hand touch his shoulder. He turned back to the woman.

"Natalia," she whispered. "My name is Natalia. Maybe someday you'll tell me yours."

Eleven

22 August

The sun was coming up as Natalia cautiously made her way from St. Jacek's Church to the women commandos' quarters on Trebacka Street. The streets of Old Town and the AK-controlled section of the City Center were feverish with activity as commandos lugging PIATs and mortars trotted through the rubble, heading for the barricades to relieve their weary comrades who had stood guard during the night. Gunfire cracked from rooftops, and artillery shells streaked overhead, exploding an instant later in the random destruction of houses and shops. Civilians burrowed deeper into their cellars as survival in Warsaw became a game of chance, with longer odds every day.

Near Trebacka Street, Natalia felt twinges of bitterness and anger as she passed the shattered remnants of the monument of Adam Mickiewicz, Poland's greatest poet. He was her father's favorite, and she would never forget the winter evenings in front of the fire when her father would read Mickiewicz's poems aloud, especially "Konrad Wallenrod," with its thinly veiled depiction of the hatred between Russians and Poles. The monument had been destroyed by the Germans two years ago in their never-ending quest to stamp out Polish culture. Natalia's stomach tightened. Between the Russians and Germans, it was hard to decide who she hated more.

She quickened her pace as she turned onto Trebacka and glanced up at the second story window on the corner of the block-long building that housed their apartment. A young girl, perhaps five or six years old, sat in front of the window, combing her doll's hair. Natalia had seen her before, sitting in that same spot with her doll. As she'd done on the other occasions, the girl waved. Natalia waved back, wondering what would become of her.

The apartment building was a magnificent structure with meticulously carved stone pillars framing the entryways of the now vacant ground floor merchant shops. The first-floor windows were set deep in elaborate stone alcoves, and above the windows, wrought-iron railings projected gracefully from second-floor balconies. With the city falling down around her, Natalia thought it was a miracle the building was still intact.

She felt a bit guilty for not returning last night. But Ula and Zeeka were watching over Berta, and for the first time in three weeks she had actually slept soundly for several hours without nightmares. Who would've guessed that on a night when everything was falling apart—her best friend wounded, Falcon in a brutal drunken haze—that she'd actually be able to fall asleep . . . in a church?

She touched the side of her face. It was still tender, but her headache was gone, and she managed a smile when she remembered how she'd laughed when Wolf said he'd have to kill her if he told her any more. It was the first time in months she'd laughed at anything—and he was probably *serious*. And yet, he had acted as nervous as a schoolboy, tripping over his words as he was about to leave that morning. He was indeed a special case, she thought, reclusive and clearly dangerous. But there was something else, something under that hard exterior that intrigued her. In those few hours she thought there had been a connection between them . . . perhaps just a bit.

She entered the building through the arched doorway next to the vacant tailor shop and climbed the wooden stairs to the first floor. As soon as she stepped through the door of the apartment Natalia knew something had happened. The cots had been removed from the parlor and the bare, wooden-floored room echoed with emptiness. She reached into her jacket pocket, pulled out her pistol and stepped slowly across the parlor, peeking into the kitchen. Glasses and plates filled the sink, and crumbs littered the table. She backed away and moved over to the stairway leading to the second-floor bedroom. At the base of the staircase she leaned against the wall, and pointed the pistol up the stairs. "Ula? Zeeka?"

Zeeka shouted back, "Up here, come quickly!"

Natalia took the stairs two at a time and rushed into the bedroom. Zeeka and Ula knelt on the floor next to Berta, who lay on a stretcher. "Good God, what's—"

Zeeka stood up and wiped a film of perspiration from her forehead with her shirtsleeve. She was normally calm and unflappable, a long-time AK operative who had conducted sabotage against the enemy all over Poland. But this morning there was a decided edge in her voice: "Berta's fine. But the Germans have breached the barricade on the north side of Pilsudski Square. We've got to get out of here and make our way to Old Town."

Natalia looked around the tiny bedroom. The plaster walls were painted a light yellow, and frilly pink curtains framed the single window, reminding her of curtains she'd had in her own bedroom as a child. She remembered the first time she'd entered this room, almost a month ago. She'd wondered then if the tailor and his wife had shared it with a young daughter.

"The medic was here just a few minutes ago," Zeeka said. "Rabbit and Bobcat brought him over. He'd found some morphine, which should keep her quiet while we move her."

Natalia glanced at Rabbit, who leaned against the wall. Another boy stood next to him. He was about the same age as Rabbit but taller, with unruly black hair and a pockmarked face. She recognized him as Rabbit's friend, the one they called Bobcat.

"Move her where?" Natalia asked.

"The medic said there's a vacant schoolhouse on Podwale that's being used as a hospital," Zeeka said. Then she cocked her head. "What the hell happened to you?"

Natalia touched her face. "Ah . . . just a bump. They were a little wild at the pub last night." She flinched as the building shook from a nearby mortar blast. Podwale wasn't far—a little more than half the distance she'd just walked from St. Jacek's Church—but it was daylight now and the snipers were out.

"Can we get there?" she asked Rabbit.

The boy nodded. "No problem."

• • •

Slowed down by the stretcher, Natalia knew they'd have to stay off the streets or they'd be easy targets for the snipers and dive-bombing Stukas. The civilians still living in the area had taken to their cellars, many of which were interconnected with passageways hacked through the walls. Rabbit, who instinctively seemed to know how to get around the city with stealth, directed the stretcher-bearing group down three flights of stairs to the earthen-floor cellar of their building. Then, guiding the way with a flashlight, he led the way through a twenty-meter-long, two-meter-high passageway of slimy cobblestone that Bobcat said was an abandoned sewer main. The passageway led them into a foul, dimly lit labyrinth of cellars beneath the residential apartment buildings of the City Center.

It was slow going. The cellars were crowded with grim-faced, terrified people. The sick and wounded lay on cots, mattresses or the bare dirt floors. Ragged women hunched against rough, stone walls, clutching dirty, silent children on their laps. Others breast-fed whimpering babies or stirred pots of soup, while elderly men distracted the older children with stories and card games.

The AK commandos took turns carrying the stretcher as dirt and plaster rained down on their heads following each random burst of artillery. Berta moaned and occasionally thrashed, then drifted into unconsciousness again. With the stench of human sweat, excrement and urine mingled with must and kerosene from the lanterns, Natalia found it difficult to breathe. Her headache returned.

A half hour later, they climbed a flight of rickety wooden stairs and emerged from the last cellar. Natalia squinted against the sunlight and took a welcome breath of fresh air as she peeked around the corner at the open expanse of the cobblestone square in front of the Royal Castle.

They huddled for a moment. Rabbit gave each of them precise instructions: "Zeeka, you and Bobcat man the stretcher. Natalia and Ula, one on each side, with a hand on Berta. I'll lead the way."

"We're gonna have to run like hell across the square," Bobcat said.

"Yeah, I know." Rabbit looked around at the others. "I'll be the lookout. You all stay right behind me. Keep your heads down and don't trip."

With that, the group sprinted across the Castle Square, past Zygmunt's Column and turned onto Podwale, with Rabbit watching the sky and glancing at rooftops every step of the way.

The former schoolhouse was a four-story red-brick building located at Number 46 Podwale, the semi-circular street fronting the old city walls. At one time a neighborhood of wealthy merchants and aristocracy, it was now mostly deserted, a grim collection of broken windows and shattered roofs. The windows of the school building were boarded up, and a large red cross was painted on the door. "I hope they also painted one on the roof," Natalia mumbled as they trudged up the steps and pushed open the door.

The scene inside was overwhelming. Natalia's head pounded as she glanced around: Kerosene lanterns cast a gloomy, yellow glow. Cots lined every inch of the floor with barely enough room for the nurses to squeeze through to groaning patients. The stifling air reeked of disinfectant, blood and urine.

A priest looked up from beside one of the cots. He held a blood-soaked bandage against a small boy's head with his right hand. With his left, he pointed toward the back of the room.

Natalia led the way as they carefully navigated the stretcher between the rows of cots to the farthest alcove where a stout, elderly nun wiped blood off her hands with a sliver of cloth obviously torn from her habit. The nun tossed the soiled rag into a bucket of red water and plodded over to the stretcher. She shot a cursory glance at Berta's bandaged leg, placed a pudgy hand on her forehead and shrugged. "Not much of a fever yet, so that's a good sign." She motioned wearily toward a staircase that led to the cellar. "Take her downstairs. There are a few empty cots at the back. I'll keep an eye on her."

"What about antibiotics?" Natalia asked. "There's seepage from the wound. We've got to prevent infection."

The nun glared at her as if she'd asked for gold bars. "Young lady, we barely have clean bandages and water." Her brow furled. "Do you have any medical training? If you do we could use some help here."

Zeeka glanced at her watch and shook her head. "We have to meet Colonel Stag, and we're already late."

"Maybe later," Natalia said to the nun. "Later I could—"

The nun waved her hand dismissively and turned her attention to a sobbing young girl, no more than ten years old, with ragged shrapnel wounds in her neck and chest. "We'll keep an eye on her and check the wound," she snapped. "A doctor should be around a bit later. Take her down and find a spot for her. I'll check on her later."

Zeeka put a hand on Natalia's shoulder. "It's the best we can do for her. Now we've got to go."

Natalia came back early the next morning, grimacing at the stench as soon as she stepped through the door. She hadn't thought it possible to jam any more patients into the tiny, stifling hot schoolhouse, but apparently they had. She scraped her knee trying to wedge between two cots in the narrow aisle, now almost impassable since they'd added another row. Halfway through the room, she stopped and gripped the out-stretched hand of an elderly man. His eyes were bandaged, his withered face pockmarked with shell fragments. When she kissed his grizzled cheek, he wheezed a barely audible "thank you."

At the top of the stairway she encountered the elderly nun carrying an armload of soiled sheets. Without breaking stride, the nun motioned with her head toward the stairs. "There's a young boy down there who came in an hour ago with a head wound. Find a clean bandage and change the dressing. He's over in the corner near your friend. You can check on some of the others while you're down there."

Natalia nodded and descended the stairs to the cellar. She made her way carefully through the jam-packed room, smiling at patients who were awake, touching a few hands, patting a few shoulders. In the middle of the room, another nun, younger and harried-looking, knelt next to a man and cut away his blood-soaked trouser leg. The man gripped the sides of his cot, eyes closed, jaw clenched.

Natalia bent down and took a closer look, then whispered to the young nun, "It's a bad break, but the bone isn't exposed. We can probably splint it to make him more comfortable. I'll be back to help you in a few minutes."

Natalia found the boy with the head wound, curled up in the fetal position, sucking his thumb. He appeared to be about seven or eight years old, stick-thin and pale as a ghost. She knelt next to the boy's cot and put her hand on his forehead. "Are you awake?" she asked quietly.

He nodded, but didn't lift his head.

"I'm here to help you. May I look at your wound?"

He nodded again, then whimpered, "It hurts."

"I'll be very gentle," she said. She slid her right hand under his skinny shoulder and gently rolled him onto his back.

The boy groaned. His eyes were shut tight.

Carefully, Natalia unraveled the bloody bandage and examined the wound. It was a jagged laceration that extended from just above his left eyebrow, across his forehead, ending just above the hairline. It wasn't deep, and the blood had coagulated, but the wound was filled with dust and grit.

After gathering a bowl of water, a few clean rags and tweezers, Natalia painstakingly extracted the bits of dirt and gravel, and cleaned the boy's wound. Tears trickled down his cheeks and he gritted his teeth the whole time, but he didn't cry. She wrapped his forehead with the last clean scrap of cloth she could find, wishing again for antibiotics. She stayed with him for a while, telling a few stories, until he seemed to fall asleep.

She checked on Berta, but her friend was also asleep. Her face was flushed, her brow furled with pain. Natalia decided to let her rest, and spent the next three hours doing what she could to help the priest and two nuns in what was clearly a futile effort.

Dozens of people—many of them no older than Rabbit—lay semiconscious on blood-soaked cots, with mangled hands or feet, chest wounds, burns or shrapnel wounds. They groaned and twitched. Sweat dripped from their ravaged, soiled bodies. Natalia knew most of them wouldn't survive more than a few days without real medical attention.

Finally, Natalia wiped blood from her hands and sweat from her forehead, and went back to see Berta. She edged her way through the line of cots, carrying a tin cup half full of precious, scarce water.

Berta's eyes were open now, and she managed a smile when Natalia knelt down and took her hand. "How do you feel?"

"Awful," Berta croaked. "It's so damn hot . . . I can barely . . . breathe." Her face glistened with perspiration, and Natalia put a hand on her forehead. The cellar was sweltering. Natalia was so hot herself it was impossible to tell if Berta's fever had worsened. And even if it had, there was nothing they could do about it.

Natalia held the cup of water to Berta's lips. She took a sip and laid her head back on the stained, wafer-thin pillow. "When can I get out of here?" she asked. Her voice was little more than a croaky whisper, her eyes glazed and distant.

Natalia smiled at her. "As soon as you can put some weight on that leg, I'll get you out of here. Maybe a day or two."

"Yeah, sure. Nice try." She pointed at Natalia's face. "What happened to you?"

Natalia had to think for a second, then remembered how she must look. "Oh, it's nothing. I bumped into a post."

"Looks like someone . . . took a poke . . ." Berta's eyes closed. "It's . . . so hot in here . . ."

Natalia glanced around. The elderly nun was on the other side of the room changing the dressings of a severely burned young girl, who was mercifully unconscious. Natalia cursed under her breath. She had to get back to her unit. But she didn't want to leave Berta. One patient with an infection wasn't going to get any special treatment in this makeshift hospital with virtually no staff and no medications. Berta couldn't walk, and even if she could, where could she take her? Now that they'd abandoned the apartment on Trebacka Street, Natalia and the rest of the commandos in her unit hunkered down wherever they happened to be, like the rest of the AK now trapped in Old Town. As crappy as this place was, at least Berta was off the streets.

"Do you remember . . . when we first met?" Berta had opened her eyes again.

"Yes, I doubt I could ever forget it," Natalia said, remembering the gruesome incident on the train. "You were the strong one that day. I'm not sure if I could have continued on if you hadn't been there for me."

Berta reached over and took her hand with a surprisingly strong grip. "You'll survive this."

Natalia's eyes clouded up. "So will you, Berta. We'll survive it together. I'll come back tomorrow."

"Don't worry about me. I'll be fine. Like you said . . . in a day or two."

Twelve

26 August

Adam knelt with his elbow resting on the sill of the second-floor window and squinted into the late afternoon sun. His body was heavy with fatigue, and sweat dripped down the back of his neck as he silently cursed the Weaver scope on his Springfield sniper rifle. It was fogged up again. He'd had it specially mounted by an AK gunsmith so he could top-load five cartridges, but the damned thing still fogged up in humid weather.

He had been at it for three straight days, working with AK commando units that dashed from barricade to barricade, desperately trying to keep the enemy Panzers out of Old Town. In the days following the destruction of the PAST building, the Germans had brought in thousands of reinforcements, including battalions of battle-hardened Wehrmacht troops to fight alongside the Ukrainian and Russian conscripts. Stukas bombarded the city with aerial assaults, while Panzer units and infantry battalions hammered one neighborhood after another from dawn to dusk. Artillery fire continued nonstop through the night, bringing the last feeble remnants of civilian life to a grinding halt. The AK still hung on to Old Town, but the noose was tightening.

Adam wiped the moisture off the scope's lens with a handkerchief, then peered through it again, adjusting the focus knob. A Panther tank came into view and, a moment later, the tank commander's head poking up through the open hatch. Adam shifted an inch to the left, bringing the target directly into the center of the crosshairs. He exhaled slowly and squeezed the trigger.

The tank commander's head exploded as Adam moved the rifle a few degrees farther left and located a second target: an SS officer standing next to the Panther tank. The officer reacted to the gunshot and turned his head toward the tank as Adam smoothly chambered a second round, squeezed the trigger and shot him in the neck.

He found two additional targets. One went down cleanly with a shot to the forehead. The other doubled over, howling, his hands clawing at the entry hole in his stomach. Adam got to his feet and bolted from the room, taking the stairs two at a time.

He knew the drill well. They had been repeating it for days. The AK was desperately short of PIAT anti-tank guns, so when the Panzer units approached, the commandos waited behind the barricades while Adam picked off as many of the tank crew as he could. Then the commandos charged forward with rifles and Molotov cocktails, attempting to capture or disable the tank. But if they didn't make it before the tank gunner rotated the turret and sighted in, the building Adam was about to vacate would be reduced to a pile of rubble.

He emerged from the building and sprinted down Podwale Street, away from the barricade. He continued for another fifty meters, then ducked into a partially demolished building at the intersection with Senatorska Street. The front façade had been blown away in an aerial bombardment two days earlier, and a broken water main had flooded the cellar, drowning more than a dozen people who had taken refuge down there. There hadn't been time to recover the bodies, and Adam held his breath against the stench as he carefully negotiated the rickety staircase.

He'd selected the building because what was left of the first floor gave him a clear view down Senatorska where a second group of AK commandos had encountered an older Panzer II tank. Adam got into position, reloaded the Springfield and sighted in on his targets. Thirty seconds later he descended the stairs and exited the building.

The Panzer II was captured by the AK, but the Panther tank was not. As Adam looked back down Podwale Street, he saw the massive machine bash through the barricade. AK commandos scattered to get out of the way, but the tank's machine guns mowed them down. The Panther tank crunched over the debris, then stopped in the middle of the street.

Adam dropped to one knee and raised his rifle, but the tank hatch was closed with no targets in sight. One of the badly wounded commandos, his jacket and trouser legs dripping with blood, managed to light a Molotov cocktail and hurl it before collapsing. The bottle hit the side of the tank, and it burst into flames with no effect.

For a moment the tank just sat there. Then the turret rotated toward a schoolhouse with boarded up windows and a bright red cross painted on the door.

A second later Adam was knocked flat as a thunderous blast roared from the Panther's 75mm cannon. In a deafening concussion, the first and second stories of the school building collapsed, belching a cloud of dust fifty meters in all directions. Frantic commandos raced toward the demolished building as the lethal machine turned away and rumbled back across the smashed barricade, its brief mission of retribution complete.

It was well after dark by the time Adam and a dozen other grim commandos finally gave up digging through the ruins of the collapsed school building. They'd recovered twenty-one bodies, and carried them onto the grassy area between the street and the old city wall, but many more lay buried deep beneath the rubble.

A priest who'd been helping them slumped to the ground, his thick, black hair plastered to his forehead with sweat and dust. "I just stepped out to try and locate some bandages," he croaked, "and when I returned the building was . . ." He looked up at Adam, tears streaming down his dirt-caked face. "There were forty-three patients in there. Nineteen were just children!" Adam extended his hand to help him to his feet, but the priest waved him off, his head drooping to his chest.

Adam stood there for a moment. In the brief flashes of light from artillery bursts he could make out a beaded rosary in the priest's hands. When he was a young boy in Krakow his aunt and uncle had taken him to church regularly while his father was off fighting with the legions. His aunt taught him to pray the rosary, which he did to please her. He remembered questioning, in those long ago days, whether it did any good. Now he was certain that it didn't.

Adam wandered away and plodded along Podwale Street, dead tired, every bone in his body aching. He finally stopped and slumped down on the steps of a three-story building with black shutters and a red tile roof that was still mostly intact except for a ragged hole about a meter in diameter near the chimney. He thought wearily that an unexploded shell was probably lying somewhere inside the house.

The enemy Panzers and infantry units had pulled back for the night, and—except for scattered artillery fire—the area was quiet, at least for the moment. He pulled his last cigarette from the soggy, crumpled pack and lit it, staring at the purple sky, illuminated on and off by exploding shells like flashbulbs from a thousand cameras. A haze hung over the area, heavy with the acrid smell of smoke and ammonia. How much longer? he wondered.

He had killed thirteen German soldiers today, at least eight of them officers as far as he could tell. How many did that make in all since he was dropped into Poland by parachute on a bitterly cold night in the winter of 1940? He'd kept track at first, but lost count somewhere over a hundred. Maybe it was two hundred by now, all of them easily justified in his law student's mind as a *casus belli*—justification for acts of war—a principle upheld for centuries in most civilized societies.

He took a long drag on the cigarette thinking of the insanity of civilized societies clinging to some legal principle as an argument for the slaughter of millions of people. And it was equally insane, he knew, to have devoted years of his life to the study of law, the guiding principles of humanity in an enlightened world—then to become an assassin. The more he thought about it, sitting on the steps of a house with a hole in the roof, in a city about to be destroyed by a ruthless enemy, he decided that justification was irrelevant. Simple revenge might be more to the point.

At least Colonel Whitehall would be pleased, he supposed. He imagined the portly, disheveled officer of the SOE, Britain's covert organization for sabotage behind enemy lines, smiling that complacent smile of his. Adam had been one of Whitehall's first recruits. At the time he had been desperate to exact revenge on those who had taken everything from him: his home, the only family he ever knew, the hard-won freedom of his birth country. And Whitehall had been more than pleased to provide him with the training and means to carry out that revenge.

Adam thought about Natalia—the Conductor, as Rabbit had called her—and the question she'd asked still nagged at the back of his mind. *You came back . . . what on earth for?* It was a simple question from a very straightforward woman. Yet it was a question that resurrected distant memories of another world, in what now seemed like a lifetime ago. Another world when he had reunited with his Polish family: the aunt who'd cared for him and raised him as a child, the uncle who'd been a second father to him, mentored him and taught him the most important values in life. They were memories he'd buried a long time ago, the day when that world was abruptly shattered.

Adam was jerked back to the moment when he heard someone shouting. It was a woman's voice, shrill, panicky—and familiar. He got to his feet, slung the rifle over his shoulder and jogged back down Podwale, following the voice toward the demolished schoolhouse.

Natalia stood on top of the rubble pile shouting at two AK commandos. The commandos slowly backed away, shaking their heads. "Get back here and help me, Goddamn it!" she shrieked. "We've got to find her!"

Adam hesitated for a moment then tossed the cigarette on the ground, climbed over the rubble and touched her shoulder. "Natalia—"

She spun around like she'd received an electrical shock. "Wolf?" She took a step back and looked around, thrusting her hands in the air. "What the hell happened?"

"A tank attack, about three hours ago. We—"

"It was a hospital!"

"I know. I was—"

"A hospital . . . with a big red cross painted on the door!"

"I know, I—"

"They're monsters! Goddamn them to hell! They're nothing but . . ." She ripped off her cap and slapped it hard against the side of her leg, stomping around in a tight circle on top of the debris pile.

"We left her here so she'd be safe! We left her and . . . now this." She stopped and clenched her fists.

Adam put both hands on her shoulders and looked into her contorted face. "Natalia," he whispered. "Natalia, I know. I was here."

A tear trickled down her bruised cheek. "But it was a hospital!"

"Yes, I know," he said, uncertain what more to say. "It was tragic, but we've all seen it before . . . you've seen worse than—"

"Not when it was my *friend!*" she hissed.

"Your friend? I didn't—"

"No, of course not! How could you? Her name was Berta, and . . . Oh Christ, I'm just—"

An artillery shell screeched overhead, and Adam instinctively pulled her close as it exploded with a numbing blast a half block away. He looked around the rubble-strewn area, trying to recall a place where they might escape the line of fire. He took her elbow and led her off the debris pile, across the grassy area and to a breach in the city wall.

She stopped. "No, I've got to go back. I've got to find her."

He tightened his grip on her elbow. "She's gone."

She looked at him for a long silent moment, then turned away and ducked through the breach.

On the other side of the wall they rounded a corner onto Piekarska Street, a narrow, cobbled lane of brick and stucco buildings, once populated by a number of bakeries. They jogged down the street, past the only one that managed to stay open a day or two a week, until they came to an arched doorway that led to a staircase.

Feeling his way in the dark, with one hand on damp, moss-covered bricks, Adam led the way down a long flight of wooden steps. At the bottom he spotted a faint light emanating from a deep cellar few people knew existed. He took Natalia's hand and led her silently through a narrow tunnel, following the light.

Thirteen

27 August

The cellar was a subterranean cavern about ten meters square, constructed of rough stone walls that arched upward, forming a domed ceiling. The room was illuminated by a single kerosene lantern nailed to a thick center post that Adam guessed had been added at some point to help support the ceiling. Stacked against one of the brick walls were a dozen wooden crates of ammunition. Adam had been here once before, shortly after the AK transferred the weapons they'd captured at the warehouse on Stawki Street. At that time, the room had been full.

Two commandos, who had entered the room from a second tunnel, looked at them curiously then picked up one of the wooden crates and carried it out.

Natalia leaned back against one of the stone walls. She sighed, then slid down and sat on the dirt floor.

Adam's exhaustion returned with a rush, and he slumped down next to her. He removed his glasses and rubbed his eyes, irritated from the smoke and dust. "We should be safe here for a while, unless they drop one of those screaming cows on us."

Natalia nodded. She sat for several minutes, barely moving, staring at the dirt floor. Finally, without looking up, she said softly, "Do you have any friends, Wolf?"

The question took him by surprise. He glanced at her then looked away, suddenly wishing he had a cigarette. *Friends?* He could barely remember a time when he had friends. He'd had friends when he was a boy, first in Krakow and then in America. And he had friends—acquaintances, actually—at Jagiellonian University where he'd resumed his study of law after returning to Krakow. But that was before the war started and most of them—and what was left of his family—were arrested by the SS, and he was deported from Poland. It was before Whitehall recruited him in London and arranged for his "training," then sent him off on his solitary mission of murder. "No, I don't have any friends," he said quietly.

Natalia hunched forward, wrapping her arms around her knees. "Berta was the only real friend I've had for years. We met in '42 after an incident on the train that I had nightmares about for months afterward." She paused and Adam could hear her breathing. When she continued, her voice was distant, as though she were far away. "I was punching tickets in one of the compartments and this thin, dark-haired girl—she couldn't have been more than seven or eight years old—handed me her ticket. Two SS officers walked past the compartment. One of them stopped. He looked in and said, '*Jude.*' Then he came into the compartment and grabbed the girl by her hair. He dragged her out, down the aisle to the end of the car. She screamed for her mother." Natalia stopped and took a long, deep breath, trembling as though she were suddenly cold. "I will *never* forget that scream. Then he dragged her to the opening between the cars and . . . dropped her under the wheels."

Natalia was quiet for a long time. When she continued again, her voice was barely a whisper. "The girl's mother was hysterical. The other passengers had to hold her down. Finally the SS officer came back and he . . . he put his pistol to her head and shot her. I'd never seen anyone shot like that before! He ordered me to drag her body to the door and throw it off the train. I was so petrified, I couldn't move, but one of the other passengers helped me. We dragged her body to the end of the car and just . . . threw her out."

She sat back against the wall and wiped her eyes with the sleeve of her jacket. A tear trickled down her cheek, the purple welt now mostly obscured with a layer of dirt. "By the time the train arrived in Warsaw, I could barely function. Berta was the dispatcher. I hardly knew her, but she saw what a state I was in and took me to a café for coffee. She knew more than I did, about the Resistance, about refusing to bow down to the Nazis. We talked for a long time that day, and eventually we became friends. Whenever I needed to talk to someone, Berta was always there." She turned her head toward Adam. "She was also an American."

"Berta, an American . . . ?"

"Well, she'd never actually been there, but her father was an American. Her mother was Polish. I'm not sure how they met, but they lived in Warsaw when Berta was born. Her last name was Andersen. It's funny, she was one of the few people whose last name I actually know." Natalia crossed her arms over her chest and shuffled her feet back and forth in the dust. "Do you know what that's like, Wolf, to have someone you can talk to when you're desperate and alone?"

Adam shook his head.

"Don't you miss having a friend, someone you can talk to, someone you can share things with?"

"I don't think about it."

"Hah, that's a lie!" she retorted. "*Everyone* wants a friend they can talk to. Even us, doing what we do in this lousy war, or we're not human. I could talk to Berta, cry with her sometimes, laugh at other times, but she was always there." She closed her eyes. "But not any more."

The sounds of sporadic gunshots and artillery shells, muted by the thick stone walls, drifted into the cellar. Adam looked down at his dirt-caked boots. There was nothing he could say that would help. He'd seen so much death and destruction—much of it by his own hand—that he knew he was far too jaded to be of any comfort.

But there was something about this woman. Something he hadn't seen before. She was tough, of that he was certain, and she'd certainly seen her share of the same death and destruction that he had. But there was a difference. She still cared enough to mourn the loss of her friend. Maybe she still had a soul.

Natalia hunched forward and wrapped her arms around her knees again. She cocked her head. "Tell me about America."

"America?"

"Yes, you're an American, so tell me about it."

His mind was suddenly blank, caught off guard by the incongruous question. "I don't understand. What do you want to know?"

Natalia threw her hands in the air. "God, this is like pulling teeth. I'm not asking for state secrets, Wolf. I'm making conversation. Where did you live? What did you enjoy doing? What kind of food do Americans eat? It's better than talking about dying, isn't it?"

Adam squirmed, more than a little uncomfortable under the glare of Natalia's penetrating eyes. What was it about her that could so easily throw him off stride? "It's just a question I haven't been asked for a long time."

"Well, I'm asking you. We're going to be here for awhile, and anything is better than just sitting here listening to the damn artillery shells."

"I lived in Chicago."

"Chicago? OK, good, that's a start. That's somewhere in the middle, isn't it?"

He smiled in spite of himself. "It's what we call the Midwest. It's a big city, bigger than Warsaw. There's more than a half-million Poles living there."

"A half-million Poles? In Chicago?"

"There're also Germans, Czechs, Irish—immigrants from all over."

"Do they get along with each other: the Germans, the Czechs and the Poles?"

Adam nodded. "Sure, I mean they kind of live in separate neighborhoods, but it's not like it is here. Many of them work at the same factories or offices, and there's just so many people in Chicago that . . . well, I guess everyone just sort of blends in."

"Are there any Jews?"

"Chicago has the largest Jewish population in the Midwest. A lot of them live in a suburb on the northwest side called Skokie."

"How are they treated?"

Adam shrugged. "It's kind of hard to describe. They pretty much keep to themselves, some people make jokes about them, there's some discrimination—not like with the Negroes—but they all work or keep shops and live pretty much like everyone else."

"You said, 'Negroes' . . . like Jesse Owens?"

Adam laughed. "Well, he's not from Chicago, but yes, they're black, like he is. They mostly live on the south side, and a lot of people in Chicago don't like Negroes. It's hard for them to get jobs; they have separate schools and churches. I lived in a neighborhood called the 'Polish Downtown' on the northwest side of the city. There weren't any Negroes there."

"I've heard that Negroes aren't allowed in your army."

"That's not true, but . . . they have separate units. It's better that way."

"Why?"

He thought about it. *Why indeed?*

"And they were once slaves, isn't that right?"

"That was a long time ago—"

"Then America really isn't so much different from here, is it?" Natalia tensed as an artillery shell burst nearby, and the lantern flickered. Bits of plaster drifted down from the ceiling, and she brushed them from her hair. "I'm sorry. I ask too many questions."

He smiled at her. "Your worst quality?"

She smiled back. "I think we've had this conversation before. OK, no more questions."

"No, it's fine. Really, I don't mind."

"Then tell me about your neighborhood, this 'Polish Downtown' in Chicago."

Adam paused as the memories slowly drifted back. It had been a long time since he'd thought about those days: when his father was alive, when he had some friends, when life seemed very simple. "My neighborhood reminded me a bit of where we lived in Krakow, except that it was bigger and noisier, more motorcars and trucks, more people. And the trams run on tracks high above the streets."

She looked perplexed, as though trying to imagine trams running above the streets, but Adam continued as it all came back, the wonderful, vivid memories of a young immigrant boy growing up in Chicago, becoming American. "But there were Polish food stores and cafés in our neighborhood. We had *pierogi* and *galumpki* and *kielbasa*. We had festivals in the summer where they played polkas in the afternoon and Chopin in the evening. But the best part was the Coca-Cola."

Her eyes widened. "Coca-Cola. I've heard about it. What does it taste like?"

Suddenly there was nothing in the world Adam would rather have. "It's sweet and bubbly. And cold, it has to be cold. And we'd eat corn-on-the-cob."

She grimaced and wrinkled her nose. "You ate corn . . . right off the—?"

"Yes, I mean, no; it's different, a different kind of corn than you feed to the pigs. This is a special corn, very sweet, and you boil it in water, then pick it up and eat it." As he was gesturing with his hands, Adam could almost taste the sweet kernels and feel the melted butter running down his chin. He slumped back and closed his eyes. His stomach ached with hunger.

"Do you have churches?"

Adam indulged himself for a few more seconds, thinking about Coca-Cola and corn-on-the-cob, then took a breath and sat forward. "Churches? Hundreds of them. The church we attended, St. John Cantius, looks very much like the Mariacki Church in Krakow, with a big copper-topped tower. It even has an inscription, 'God save Poland' right below a huge triangular pediment dedicated to the January Rising."

"The January Rising? That was over eighty years ago. They know about it in Chicago?"

Adam nodded. "The Polish people do. You can bet on that!"

Natalia picked a stone off the dirt floor and tossed it away. "My grandfather told me about it," she said bitterly. "He said a squadron of Russian hussars rode into his village one night and set all the houses on fire. He and his younger sister tried to run away, but one of the horsemen chased them and trampled her to death. She was ten years old." She shook her head, as though purging the thought. "So, living in Chicago was like living in Poland?"

"Oh no, in America there's more of everything. Big stores filled with clothing, toys, radios, fabrics, pots and pans, books and games."

"So, everyone is rich."

"There are rich people—there were a lot more before the Depression—but we weren't rich. Neither was anyone else in our neighborhood. My father was an engineer. But when he returned from the Great War he couldn't find work in Poland. That's why we immigrated to America. He'd been promised a job, and when we got to America he worked hard. He was one of the fortunate ones. He was able to keep working through the hard times, but we certainly weren't rich."

The lantern flickered again as a vibration rumbled through the earthen floor. Natalia leaned back on her hands and glanced up at the ceiling. "What do you miss most?"

"Baseball."

"What? Out of all that, you miss . . . baseball?"

"Of course! Everyone in America loves baseball. I learned to play during my first summer. I even had my own glove. You know about baseball?"

She shrugged. "Like Babe Ruth?"

Adam got to his knees and brushed the dirt off his hands. "Sure, Babe Ruth, the best ever. He played in New York. But all the big cities in America have a baseball team. It's called the Major Leagues. They're professionals, just like you have the Polish Football Union here. We have two teams in Chicago, but my favorite is the Cubs."

"Did you watch them play?"

Adam nodded. "When I was younger my father would take me sometimes, on the weekends, when he didn't have to work. Later on, when I had my own money I'd go with my friends." He saw it all again: the stands packed with happy, cheering people, the peanuts and popcorn, the perfection of the baseball diamond. "I'll never forget the first time I went to a game. The grass in the outfield was so green it looked like a carpet. And the dirt in the infield was raked so smoothly you couldn't see even a ripple, and the bases, the shiny white bases—"

Natalia shook her head. "Wait, wait . . . outfield, infield, bases, I don't understand."

"Here, let me show you." Adam spotted a stick. He picked it up, then got to his knees and brushed off a spot between them on the dirt floor. "Now, the playing field is shaped like a diamond . . ."

• • •

Natalia woke with a start at the sound of voices. She sat up, rubbing her eyes. In the far end of the cellar, two AK operatives hoisted an ammunition crate onto their shoulders and started up the staircase. She glanced at her watch, barely visible in the weak glow of the kerosene lantern. It was five o'clock.

Where's Wolf?

Natalia got to her feet and raced up the same staircase she had descended the night before. Outside it was still dark, but just down Piekarska Street a fire was glowing under a large kettle, and a group of people huddled around, sipping soup from tin cups.

Wolf turned and waved at her, then walked up, holding two mugs of steaming soup. He handed one to her and took a sip from his own.

Natalia took the mug and sipped the watery concoction as the fog of sleep slowly lifted. It tasted vaguely like turnips and potatoes, with a few bits of onion floating around. She remembered Berta's grimace as she fed her a similar concoction the night after she'd been wounded. She sighed. "When did you get up?" she asked Wolf.

"About an hour ago," he said. "You were sleeping very soundly."

She brushed her hand through her hair and took another sip from the cup. "I think I dreamt about baseball."

"Christ, I must have bored you to death."

"Not at all, it helped a lot. Besides, I enjoyed watching you smile about something. You even laughed once or twice."

He looked at her for a moment as though he were trying to think of something to say, then downed the rest of the soup and glanced at his watch. "I've got to go."

Natalia nodded. Then, after a moment, she said, "I'll try to come back here again tonight. Will you?"

"I don't know . . . I've got to—"

Natalia held up her hand, stopping him. "It's alright, I understand." She stepped up to him, cocked her head slightly and kissed him on the cheek. "Thank you for being my friend."

Fourteen

28 AUGUST

AT NINE FORTY-FIVE that night Adam stood just outside the breach in the old city wall and slowly rolled a cigarette. He took his time because it was the last of his tobacco, and he had no idea where or when he'd be able to get more. But that wasn't the only reason. He was stalling. And he hated it. He hated indecision.

For the last four years, if there was one thing he was, it was decisive. He had to be; his life depended on it. He got an assignment, carried it out, moved on and never looked back. That's just the way it was—until now.

Adam licked the edge of the paper, stuck the cigarette in his mouth and lit it, inhaling deeply. It had been a brutal day. He'd been in the tower of Holy Cross Church covering a squad of AK commandos who were engaged in a furious firefight with a band of SS and Ukrainians at the barricade on Avenue Krakowskie. When two Panther tanks arrived and bashed through the concrete and sheet steel fortifications, the commandos beat a hasty retreat into the church building.

Adam had held his ground in the tower, firing round after round and dropping more than a dozen Ukrainians. Then one of the tanks stopped, its turret and 88mm cannon slowly arcing upward toward the tower. Adam made it down the stairs just before a deafening blast sheared off the top of the tower, sending down an avalanche of bricks, wooden beams and copper cladding.

Another troop of AK commandos arrived with two PIAT anti-tank guns, and the battle continued around the church until nightfall when the Panther tanks retreated behind the lines. The AK lost sixteen commandos. But the barricade was rebuilt, reinforcements arrived and Adam staggered away wondering how, and why, he'd survived another day in this seemingly endless war.

That was more than two hours ago, and he was still wondering what the hell he should do about Natalia. Just through the breach in the wall and around the corner, he knew, she was waiting for him in the ammunition cellar. Perhaps he should go to her. After all, what was the harm? She just wanted a friend. Certainly he could do that, be a friend, couldn't he?

No, what am I thinking? Of course he couldn't be her friend. It wasn't possible; he wasn't anyone's friend. He was an assassin. He'd murdered more men—and women—than he could count. And it didn't bother him, not for a moment. He'd shut the door on emotions long ago. If she needed a friend, she'd have to look elsewhere.

So, he should just leave. Go back to his room, if it was still there, and get some sleep. She was a bright girl; she'd figure it out, and that would be the end of it. That's what he wanted . . . wasn't it?

He tossed the cigarette to the ground and crushed it with his boot. Then he stepped through the breach and headed for the ammunition cellar.

He was almost there when someone called out, "Captain Wolf!"

It was Rabbit.

The boy ran up to him, dripping with sweat, breathing hard. "I've been looking all over for you." He bent over, taking deep breaths. "Colonel Stag sent me to find you."

Adam knew what that meant. The meeting with the Russians was on. "When do we have to leave?"

"Right now," Rabbit said, glancing at his watch. "It took me a while to find you."

Adam turned toward Piekarska Street and the archway leading to the ammunition cellar. It would only take a minute to go and tell her. He hesitated, then turned back to Rabbit. "Let's go; you lead the way."

"We'll take my special route."

Adam nodded grimly. He also knew what *that* meant.

• • •

They entered the sewer through a manhole on Avenue Krakowskie just beyond Holy Cross Church. Adam held his breath as he descended the climbing irons and stepped gingerly into the greasy muck. When he finally let out the breath and inhaled, he gagged at the sulfurous stench and his eyes began to water.

Rabbit met his eyes in the yellow glow of the kerosene lamp and laughed. "You'll get used to it after a while, Captain. But it's slippery, so be careful or you'll fall on your ass."

Adam reached out and touched the wet brick walls for support. "How far is it?"

Rabbit glanced back over his shoulder. "Only about two kilometers, but it may take awhile. Depends on how many detours we have to make. The fuckin' Krauts keep tossin' grenades down the manholes."

Storm clouds had been moving in, and Adam wondered if they would be crossing the river yet tonight. But he knew there was no point in asking Rabbit. It was the usual drill, and he'd been through it a hundred times during the war. Rabbit would only know about his part in the mission—getting Adam to a pick-up point and handing him off to someone else, whoever that may be, and eventually, if they weren't captured along the way, Adam would wind up confronting some Russians.

It was almost three o'clock in the morning when Rabbit slid back a manhole cover, and a wave of fresh air blew into the sewer along with a torrent of rain. The boy motioned for Adam to stay back as he slowly poked his head through the opening. Then he quickly slid the cover all the way back, scrambled up the last three climbing irons and waved for Adam to follow.

Sprinting hard to keep up with Rabbit as he bent over against the driving rain and sloshed through ankle-deep puddles, it took Adam a moment to get his bearings. By the gloomy light of a street lamp that had somehow escaped being shot out, he saw what looked like some warehouse buildings and judged that they were in an area south of Jerusalem Avenue and east of Nowy Swiat. It was a district that had been AK territory since the beginning of the Rising, but judging by how fast Rabbit was running, Adam guessed that might now be in jeopardy.

Rabbit ducked into a narrow walkway alongside a building with boarded up windows and a massive hole in the roof, then glanced back at Adam before disappearing around the back corner.

Adam rounded the corner just as the boy dropped to his hands and knees and slid backward through a cellar window, beckoning for Adam to follow.

Adam slid through the window and dropped to a soft earthen floor. The cellar room was lit with a kerosene lantern hanging from a wood-beamed ceiling. A half-dozen chairs, and an upholstered sofa that had seen better days, were arranged in a semicircle in front of a table piled high with maps, books, files, and an array of coffee cups and vodka glasses.

A man sat at the table, barely visible in the dim light and a haze of cigarette smoke. After a moment, he stood up and plodded across the room. He was thick and beefy, about a head taller than Adam with a scruffy growth of beard and an enormous stomach that protruded from beneath his undershirt. With a cigarette hanging precariously from the corner of his mouth, the man looked Adam up and down, then turned to Rabbit and grunted, "You're late. I expected you last night."

Rabbit stood tall and looked the man in the eye. "You were misinformed."

"We expected a woman."

"What woman would come here?"

Dripping wet, Adam listened silently to the exchange, which was obviously a series of codes. Finally the pot-bellied man took a last drag on the cigarette, dropped it to the floor and extended his hand to Adam. "Welcome, I am Bravo. You look like you could use a drink."

"Yes . . . I'd love a drink," Adam said, wincing from Bravo's vise-like grip, "and a towel."

The burly man laughed heartily, plucked a grimy towel off the back of a chair and tossed it to Adam. Then he produced a bottle of vodka and filled three glasses. He handed one to each of them, held his glass up and grunted, "Long live the AK!"

Adam and Rabbit repeated the toast, and they all knocked back the potent drink, Rabbit downing his like it was water.

A few minutes later Rabbit crawled back through the window and headed for the sewer in the pouring rain. Bravo led Adam to a corner of the cellar where there was a wash basin, soap and clean towels. A neatly folded pair of trousers and a clean shirt rested on a stool next to the wash basin. "You can wash up and change here," Bravo said. "Then I suggest you get some sleep. I'll be back later with some food."

Eager to get out of his foul-smelling clothing, Adam stripped off his shirt. "When do we leave?"

"After dark, the rendezvous is set for 2100."

Fifteen

29 August

Bravo returned shortly after sunset and prepared a meal of boiled potatoes, cabbage and black bread. Adam had slept until early afternoon and had been pacing anxiously around the damp cellar room ever since, wondering where his pot-bellied host had gone and when, or if, he was returning. But when Adam smelled the warm food, his anxiety abruptly disappeared, and he ate heartily without asking how the man had managed it. Black market dealing was always better left unsaid, and besides, it was the most he'd had to eat in a week.

Shortly after eight o'clock they climbed the stairs to the ground floor and left the building through the rear door. In the darkness, Adam followed the heavyset man across a gravel drive to a dilapidated wooden shed. Bravo pulled open a sheet-metal door, which creaked loudly on rusty hinges, kicked a rock in front of it to keep it open and struck a match.

Adam was taken aback at the sight of a long, sleek Mercedes Benz. "Jesus Christ!" he blurted. "Where the hell did you get that?"

Bravo shook out the match. "It was the staff car of some SS officer prick that got a little careless one night. We spotted it parked down by the river. The officer was in the backseat fuckin' some woman while his driver, dumb shit that he was, sat in the front reading a magazine with a flashlight. A few quick shots, and we had ourselves a nice vehicle, complete with the appropriate uniforms. We didn't even get a lot of blood on the seats."

Adam clapped Bravo on the shoulder, slipped on the SS officer's coat and hat, and climbed in the backseat.

Bravo pulled on the driver's coat, which was a tight fit, squeezed behind the wheel and brought the auto's powerful engine roaring to life. "You'd better keep down," he said, as he eased the Mercedes out of the shed. "The first kilometer is the most dangerous, while we're still in AK territory. Most of the regular commandos in this sector know about the car. But in all the chaos, new ones are coming and going every day, and this thing's a hell of a target."

"Christ, that's just great," Adam grumbled as he slumped low in the backseat, contemplating the irony of getting killed by his fellow commandos after managing to survive four years of warfare.

"Ah, we'll probably be fine," Bravo said and stomped on the accelerator, sending a shower of gravel and rocks in all directions as the long, black motorcar bolted forward. "Let's go find some fuckin' Russians!"

Though darkness was on their side, Bravo drove dangerously fast, screeching around corners and dodging piles of debris. The big car sped down the broad thoroughfares of Nowy Swiat and Wazdowskie Avenue, then made a hard left turn and shot past an AK barricade near Lazienki Park. Bravo shouted out the window at the surprised commandos, "Poland fights! Poland fights!"

A few minutes later they emerged "safely" into a German-held section of the Mokotow District. Bravo slowed down as they continued on, waving occasionally at groups of Wehrmacht soldiers, SS troopers and the ever-present conscripted Ukrainians, who huddled near their own bonfires, drinking schnapps and eating tinned sausage, waiting for dawn and another day of stomping out the Polish insurgency.

Adam sat up straight, adjusted his cap and looked out the rear window at the enemy soldiers, wondering what they thought. Did they think it was worth it, wasting all this time, ammunition and their own lives to obliterate a city that was already lost? They had to know that every day they stayed here, they came closer to being surrounded and obliterated themselves by the hundreds of thousands of Russian troops camped just a few kilometers away on the other side of the river. Adam knew the Germans were famous for following orders, but this was a death wish, imposed on them by the lunacy of their Fuhrer.

He sighed and slumped back in the soft leather seat and rubbed his temples. It all depended on the Russians, and whether or not they would finally decide to enter Warsaw and help the AK end this madness. And that, Adam guessed, he would find out soon enough.

They drove south along the broad, tree-lined avenues of the Mokotow District. The vast expanse of parks and open areas, stately mansions and modern, upper-class apartments—only a few of which showed any evidence of the conflict raging in other parts of the city—passed like a mirage outside the Mercedes' windows. It seemed another world from the brutal chaos of the City Center or Old Town, though no one was on the streets save for German soldiers. Most of the windows were dark and there were no lights anywhere. Adam guessed that the civilians in the area, if they hadn't yet taken to their cellars, were lying low.

As they continued south from Mokotow through the Wilanow District—the summer residence of Poland's kings—Adam remembered coming there for the first time as a boy with his uncle. They had toured the section of Wilanow Palace that had been turned into a museum. Though it was too dark to see any of it now, he recalled the Asian artwork hanging in parquet rooms the size of most houses, the vast gardens and marble fountains. He had especially loved the ornately sculpted sundial relief on the palace's south wall and Uncle Ludwik's patient explanation of how it worked.

Eventually the broad streets turned into gravel lanes winding through orchards and farm fields, past wooden barns and thatched-roof cottages. When they drove through the last German checkpoint well south of Wilanow, Bravo waved to the weary-looking Wehrmacht soldiers without even slowing down.

"Do you have enough petrol?" Adam asked. There was precious little available in Warsaw to anyone except the Germans.

"The tank was full when we got the car," Bravo said with a shrug. "We've got enough for this trip. After that, who knows? Hell, we'll probably all be dead in a few weeks anyway."

Twenty minutes later they arrived at a dusty crossroads with a thatched-roof farmhouse on one corner and a tidy brick church on the other. Bravo turned left onto a rutted, dirt road, overgrown with grass, and headed east toward the Vistula River. After another few minutes, he rounded a curve, and the auto's headlight beams illuminated the rendezvous point.

Bravo brought the auto to a stop, and Adam leaned forward, looking through the windshield. It was an abandoned barge dock, nothing more than a cracked and buckled concrete pier extending perhaps ten meters into the river. Ancient truck tires hung from chains attached to rotted wood posts, and the rusted-out hulk of what was most likely the last barge sat mired in the muck. The night air was heavy with the odor of dead fish and rotting algae.

Bravo turned around. "Well, this is as far as I go," he said quietly. The big man's good-natured bluster was now replaced with a note of concern. He reached over and clasped Adam's hand. "I'll be right here tomorrow night at this same time. I hope you are too."

Adam nodded silently and stepped out of the car.

As the tail lights of the Mercedes disappeared around the bend, Adam started down the rutted road toward the barge dock, his right hand resting on the butt of the Walther P-38 strapped to his waist. Colonel Stag had assured him that the Russians knew he was an American and were prepared to receive him, but when Adam spotted the three figures emerging from the shadows, he tightened his grip on the pistol.

He stopped and watched carefully as the figures approached, trying to identify their uniforms in the moonlight. A moment later he realized they were Red Army regulars and not NKVD. He breathed a bit easier, but since two of them carried submachine guns leveled directly at his chest, he kept his hand on his pistol.

The trio stopped three meters away and stood silently for a moment. The one in the middle between two Red Army troopers was an officer. He was tall and very thin with a patch over his left eye. After another moment of silence he finally asked, "*Amyerikanyets?*"

Adam nodded. "Yes."

"*Gavařit pa rúski?*"

"No. Do you speak English?"

The officer took a step forward and asked in perfect English, "Are you looking for the bridge?"

It was the question he'd been told to expect, and Adam answered, "I'm told the bridge is unsafe. But I require passage to Praga."

The officer eyed him carefully, then said something in Russian to one of the submachine-gun-toting troopers, who stepped up, relieved Adam of the Walther and searched him thoroughly. The Russian trooper slipped the pistol into his own pocket, then motioned for Adam to proceed toward the water's edge where a rowboat was beached.

Adam climbed into the boat and sat in the prow while the officer took a seat aft with one of the Red Army troopers, who continued to point the submachine gun at him. The other trooper sat in the middle and took up the oars.

Without another word they rowed across the Vistula River under a dark sky, illuminated only by a half moon and the glow of fires from Warsaw.

Toward evening of the following day, General Kovalenko sat at a metal table in his sparsely furnished field command tent. His tank corps commander, Colonel Roskov, was on his left and Captain Andreyev on his right. Across the table sat his visitor, the American emissary from Warsaw. They had kept him isolated and under guard since his arrival the previous night. He was a scrawny man with thin hair and the wire-rimmed spectacles of a schoolteacher. Yet, as Kovalenko studied him, there was a hard look in the man's eyes and a bearing about him that suggested he was not what he seemed.

The four of them sat in silence for a few moments, the visitor with his hands folded on the table in front of him, his eyes on Kovalenko. Finally, the general nodded, and Captain Andreyev, who'd brought the visitor across the river, spoke first. "You are an American and an emissary of the Polish Government-in-Exile in London?" he asked, in English.

"Yes, that is correct," the visitor replied.

"You've been in Warsaw?"

"Since the beginning of the Rising."

"And what is the situation there?"

The visitor glanced first at Kovalenko, then looked back at Captain

Andreyev. "The AK have thirty thousand armed men and women in the streets of Warsaw. They have seized the City Center and Old Town, and areas of the Jolibord District in the north, as well as several sections of Mokotow in the south."

The tank corps commander, Colonel Roskov, leaned forward and spoke tersely in Russian. Kovalenko nudged Andreyev, who then translated into English for the visitor. "Colonel Roskov asks what these men and women are armed with?"

The visitor replied, "Rifles, pistols, grenades—"

Andreyev began translating back into Russian, but Roskov broke in.

Andreyev stopped, smiled at the visitor and said, "The colonel asks if the weapons are all left over from the '39 campaign?"

Kovalenko watched silently as the visitor spread his hands on the table and locked eyes with the tank corps commander. "Not all," the man said firmly. "There have been airdrops from Britain, and during the first week the AK captured a substantial German weapons cache in a warehouse building—MP-38 submachine guns, anti-tank rifles—"

Roskov interrupted the translation again. Andreyev listened then said, with a hint of annoyance in his voice, "The colonel heard that the AK has assassinated several high-ranking SS officers. The Germans will make them pay for that."

Kovalenko watched the visitor closely. Something flickered in the thin man's eyes, but his expression remained inscrutable as he leaned forward, glaring at Roskov. "The Poles are at *war,* sir. We all are! Against Nazi Germany, our common enemy. Isn't that correct?"

Captain Andreyev spoke up, obviously trying to lower the tension. "Does the AK have any artillery?"

The visitor continued to stare at the Russian tank corps commander for a moment, then turned to Andreyev. "They have mortars, some American bazookas that were air-dropped—"

"Nothing larger?" Roskov asked, this time in English.

Kovalenko knew it was an old trick of Roskov's to throw an unsuspecting American off guard, but the visitor seemed unperturbed, as though he knew all along Roskov could speak English.

"A squad of your T-34 tanks would be very useful right now," the visitor replied.

The group lapsed back into silence. Kovalenko waited a few moments then pulled a pack of Lucky Strike cigarettes from his shirt pocket and offered one to the visitor. "One of our politicians visited with some of your American generals last week," he said, in his own fluent English. "He brought these back for me."

The visitor took a cigarette, and the general lit it for him. He inhaled deeply, apparently enjoying the taste of prime tobacco. Then he folded his hands on the table and addressed Kovalenko. "When can the AK expect the Red Army to cross the Vistula and enter Warsaw, General?"

Roskov leaned across the table and snapped, "The AK has no military standing in this—"

Kovalenko cut him off with a wave of his hand. He slowly lit his own cigarette and looked at the visitor who had never even blinked during Roskov's final attempt at intimidation. "I am waiting for final orders," he said. "You may report to General Bor that we will be there soon."

"How soon?" the visitor asked. "The AK are fighting like hell, but casualties are mounting. They can't hold out forever."

Kovalenko studied his cigarette, then abruptly shoved his chair back and stood up. Everyone around the table stood as well. "Tell them to keep on fighting," he said to the visitor. "We will be there soon."

Sixteen

31 AUGUST

ON THE LAST DAY OF AUGUST, Colonel Stag transmitted a secret message to the British Special Operations Executive.

> *31 August 1944*
>
> *From: AK Headquarters, Warsaw*
> *To: SOE, London*
>
> *Situation in Warsaw desperate. Forty percent City Center destroyed. Air bombardments and artillery shelling constant.*
>
> *Hundreds of civilians killed daily. Hospitals destroyed. Thousands homeless. Burns, shrapnel wounds and disease.*
>
> *Food and water critical. If no relief, all supplies gone in ten days.*
>
> *Our forces reduced by half. Continuing to fight. Weapons and ammunition critical. Airdrops unsuccessful. Old Town in severe jeopardy. Evacuation imminent.*
>
> *Russian forces remain idle on east side of Vistula.*

When the transmission was finished, Stag wearily climbed the stairs from the cellar of the Polonia Bank building and stood on the cobblestone street to wait for Falcon. He expected the commando to bring him a report from the AK command post at the south end of the City Center. That, of course, depended on whether Falcon could make it through the rubble-filled streets in one of the few AK vehicles still operating.

Stag was beyond fatigue. He was so tired that he twitched all over as though a million ants were crawling under his skin. He lit a cigarette and leaned back against the building as the ground shook beneath his feet. The battle had surged into Old Town and degenerated into a savage street-by-street, building-by-building bloodbath that Stag knew was hopeless. German artillery bombardments and Stuka attacks continued around the clock, and the civilians still in the area huddled in their cellars like frightened rodents. Artillery shells exploded just a few streets to the west, and Stag realized that he was risking his life just standing out in the open. But he'd been suffocating in the cellar command post, and a moment in the outside air, though polluted with smoke and dust, was a relief.

Suddenly Stag heard the all-too-familiar, high-pitched scream of a Stuka dive-bomber. It was coming from his left and closing in fast. He dropped the cigarette and started for the doorway when he saw an automobile careening toward him, bouncing along the cobblestones. He waved desperately at it, warning it off, but then a shattering blast knocked him face down onto the marble foyer just inside the doors.

Stag struggled to his feet. His ears rang and his head pounded. Blood dripped from his nose. He leaned against the wall to catch his breath as the whine of the enemy aircraft receded into the distance. He waited for a moment, then stepped slowly through the doorway and peered down the block.

A three-story building had collapsed into the street. Just beyond the rubble-pile, a black, four-door auto lay on its side, the roof caved in, the left front wheel still spinning. Stag put his hand over his mouth to keep from choking on the dust, and stepped closer. Then he stopped and leaned against a broken lamp-post for support. The body of a large man hung out the driver's door of the wrecked auto. Half of his skull had been ripped away.

Stag didn't have to go any closer to know that it was Falcon.

• • •

The ammunition cellar was empty now. The final crates of weapons had been hauled out since Natalia had last been there the previous night. Strangely, the kerosene lantern was still lit. With her boot, Natalia nudged the five-liter metal can next to the post. It was empty, like the rest of the cellar. Barely able to keep her eyes open, she wandered to the far wall, slumped down on the earthen floor and took a bite from a half rotten potato. It was the only thing she'd had to eat all day.

The jarring explosions outside were coming closer. The cellar walls shook, cracks widened and chunks of mortar dropped from the ceiling. The Germans had pounded Old Town with unrelenting ferocity for three straight days, and in the streets above the cellar St. John's Cathedral and the Royal Castle lay mostly in ruins.

In the escalating chaos Natalia's commando unit had been decimated, and those that survived were hunkering down wherever they could. Even so, she'd managed to find a way through the rubble to come to the cellar every night, hoping he would be here. But she knew from the battle raging in the streets that time had run out. She was filthy, hungry and exhausted. And all she could think about was Wolf.

It was crazy. What did they have? A few hours of conversation, a few brief hours when they each let down their guard? She hadn't been surprised when he didn't show up that first night, but she'd come back every night since, hoping he would return. She was disappointed, perhaps even saddened, but not surprised. Anything could have happened. He could have been sent on another mission, he could be injured, he could be . . .

She shook her head. It could also be that he just decided not to come. She knew what he was.

No, that wasn't right.

She knew what he'd *become*. What the war and the killing had turned him into. She didn't have any idea what this man called Wolf had been like before, except an enthusiastic American boy who loved baseball.

The potato slipped from Natalia's hand as her eyes closed, and her head drooped to her chest. She had almost drifted off when she felt someone shake her knee. She looked up, her eyes bleary. She couldn't focus in the dim light.

He knelt in front of her, leaned close and whispered, "Natalia."

Wolf? "My God!" She grasped his hand. "I'm so glad to see you. I've been—"

"We're evacuating Old Town."

She stood up abruptly. "Evacuating? When?"

"Tonight. I just got the word from Colonel Stag. General Bor has ordered the AK to evacuate Old Town. It's the only way to save the civilian population."

"What? That's crazy! These Nazi bastards have been murdering civilians for five weeks. Why would they stop now?"

"Bor has made an arrangement with the German Commanders. If the AK evacuates Old Town, they'll let the civilian population leave peacefully. We can't hang on any longer; it's the only way. The entire district will be pulverized to dust in the next few days."

Natalia wiped the grime from her forehead. "So, what happens to us, the AK? They're just going to let us walk out?"

Wolf shook his head. "The deal is, we lay down our guns and surrender. Then the Germans will treat us as prisoners of war instead of insurgents."

"Like hell they will!" Natalia hissed.

"Colonel Stag is giving every AK operative in Old Town a choice. Assemble in the square at noon tomorrow and lay down our arms—"

"Or?"

"Or escape, at midnight tonight, and regroup in the south end of the City Center."

She glanced at her watch. It was a little after ten. "Escape how?"

Wolf was silent. But she already knew the answer.

They sat on the dirt floor, a few meters apart, facing each other but not talking. The shelling was almost constant, the damp ground trembling beneath them, the air musty and thick with plaster dust. Adam scratched at the dirt with a stick, twisting it into the ground, still seething at the blatant lie he'd been told by the Russian general, Kovalenko. He'd known it the instant the general said, "We'll be there soon." He could see it in the man's dark eyes. It was nothing but a fucking, bald-faced lie.

"The Russians aren't coming, are they?"

Adam flinched. "What did you say?"

"The Russians aren't coming."

Adam cleared his throat. *What the hell?*

"I could have saved you the trip," she said sarcastically. "They're devious, murdering barbarians, and they will never—not in a million years—lift a finger to help Poland."

"What are you talking about?"

"That's where you went. They sent you across the river to talk to the Russians."

"Jesus Christ, Natalia, how did you—?"

She smiled at him. "I guessed. But it makes sense. Sooner or later Bor and Stag had to find out for sure. The Russians would never talk directly with the Poles, so they sent *you*. You're an American. You've been gone for three days, and now we're evacuating."

Adam stared at her, unable to respond.

"I'm right, aren't I?"

He kept silent.

"And I'm willing to bet that whatever lying, son of a bitch Russian you talked to assured you they were coming in to help. That we should keep on fighting and they'd be here soon. I'm right about that too, aren't I?"

Adam glared at her, slowly shaking his head. "I said once before, you ask too many questions."

"And you're an expert at silence. But it doesn't make any difference now, does it? We'll all probably die before we get out of here."

"I can't talk about it."

"Can't . . . or won't?"

He didn't respond. *What is it about her?* No one had ever been able to get under his skin like this.

They were silent for several moments. Finally she looked directly into his eyes. "What are you doing here?"

"I came to get you, to tell you about the evac—"

"No, I don't mean *right now,*" she interrupted. "I already know that. I've been coming here every night hoping to see you, hoping we might . . . and when you finally show up . . . it's to deliver a news bulletin."

"I'm sorry, but I just got the word and I thought—"

"What are you doing in Poland, Wolf? In this war, what are you doing here?"

He felt his face flush, but there was nothing he could tell her.

She persisted. "Seriously, I'd like to know. You're an American. Why would you come back here and get involved in all this?"

Adam abruptly stood up. *Goddamn it, get out. Get out while you can.* He took a step toward the tunnel, then stopped and stood facing the opposite wall. Fighting back the anger that could so quickly rise to the surface, he silently recited the mantra: *Focus on the mission. The past is over. You have no past.*

"My, there's an awful lot going on in that head of yours," Natalia said.

He turned and looked down at her. "I've got to go."

"No, you don't have to go, Wolf. You have to *run*. Run away from whatever it is you're trying to escape from."

"What the hell do you know about it?" Adam snapped. "You don't know a thing about me!"

"Oh yes I do, an awful lot more than you think. I can see it in your eyes. You're hurting. You lost something that was very important."

"So, now you're a psychologist? I met a psychologist once, a long time ago, and broke the little prick's nose."

"Ah, now we're getting somewhere," she said.

"No we're not. I said I've got to go."

Natalia shrugged and motioned toward the tunnel. "OK, go on, run off. But let me tell you something, Mr. Wolf, or whatever the hell your real name is, you're not the only one who's lost someone. We *all* have—some more than others. I lost my parents when the Russians invaded. And I lost my brother, Michal. He was a cavalry officer, captured by the Russians and probably murdered in that forest in 1940—the Katyn Forest—where those Bolshevik bastards slaughtered thousands of our officers, then blamed it on the Germans." She pulled her knees to her chest and wrapped her arms around them, turning her head away. "So go ahead and run off."

Adam stared at her for a long moment knowing that he should leave right now. There was no point in doing anything else. He stood there for what seemed like a lifetime, then finally sat down next to her. The ground shuddered and the support post in the center of the room creaked. He thought about what she'd just said about her brother, and wondered if there was anything that any of them could do now that could possibly make a difference.

"It's Adam," he said quietly. "My name is Adam Nowak. And I know about the Katyn Forest and . . . I'm sorry."

Seventeen

31 August

The memories drifted back. Adam could feel them pushing their way out of the darkness where he'd left them. He had managed to get through years of brutal warfare and to reconcile the killing, the assassinations, because he'd so successfully buried his past. Adam Nowak had ceased to exist, as much in his own consciousness as in the clandestine world of the dark and silent.

But now, as he sat on the cold, dirt floor of an empty ammunition cellar next to this annoying woman, who had somehow managed to bore into his soul, the memories returned . . . and he was powerless to stop them. There was something about Natalia that he couldn't explain, something that he wasn't sure he'd ever be *able* to explain.

He said quietly, "You asked me why I came back to Poland."

She nodded.

He pressed his fingers to his temples, a part of him still wondering what he was doing here. They hardly knew each other, and yet . . .

When he spoke again he barely recognized his own voice. It was as if someone else were telling the story. "My father died while I was in the American Army. I never really knew him when I was a boy living in Krakow. He was away, fighting with the Polish Legions in the Great War. My mother died when I was a baby, and I was raised by my uncle and aunt."

Adam paused, listening to the pulsating throbs of artillery shells. "My father worked hard during our years in America and managed to send me to college. I knew he wasn't happy when I dropped out of law school and joined the army, but he never said anything, and when he died . . . I don't know . . . everything changed for me. I loved America. I loved being an American soldier, but that was 1936 and there was no future in the army. I served out my three-year enlistment, but something was missing."

Natalia touched his knee. "You came back to the uncle and aunt who'd raised you when you were a little boy?"

Adam nodded and swallowed hard, thinking of his uncle—the larger-than-life presence who had always seemed to be there when he needed him, the steadfast Polish patriot who helped shape the country's hard-won freedom yet took time to tutor his young nephew in philosophy, history and literature. "His name was Ludwik Banach," Adam said. "He was a law professor at Jagiellonian University, and when I returned to Krakow he arranged for me to resume my studies in law school. I lived with them for three years. It was the closest thing I ever had to a family."

Adam stood up and paced slowly around the cellar room. Shadows danced off the rough stone walls. The constant thump of artillery and cracks of rifle fire echoed through the subterranean chamber.

"What happened to them?" Natalia asked.

"My uncle was arrested by the Nazis in November of '39 and sent to a prison camp in Germany—a place called Sachsenhausen. They sent hundreds of professors and teachers there. My aunt was arrested the next day. I'm sure they're both dead by now."

Adam closed his eyes and thumped his fist against the post, rattling the lantern. He recalled every detail of the moment when the German SS officer told him about his uncle's arrest: the moment he became consumed with rage, consumed with his quest for revenge. He hadn't talked about this with anyone—not since Whitehall sent him to see that psychologist before recruiting him, a sniveling little weasel who declared that he was too *angry* to be of any value. It was apparently just what Whitehall needed to hear.

"I wanted to kill someone," Adam said, "or have them kill me; it didn't matter."

He looked at Natalia. There was an expression on her face that said she understood.

"It's ironic," he said. "My uncle was like you. He always feared the Russians more than the Germans. He was an internationally known legal scholar who traveled all over Europe, especially to Germany. And right up until the day the Wehrmacht marched into Krakow, he was convinced that Hitler was bluffing. 'It's the Russians we have to fear,' he always said."

"I think he got it right," Natalia said sharply, "despite what happened to him." She got to her feet and stepped up to him. "The Russians could stop this, Adam. They could have stopped it a month ago. But they're not going to. They're going to sit on the other side of the river like vultures and let the Nazis destroy us. Then *they'll* destroy the Nazis. The Russians will sweep through Poland, seal off the borders and hunt down every last one of us in the AK. Then they'll turn everyone that's left into good little communists."

Natalia kicked a stone across the room. Adam watched her, fascinated by her passion. She cocked her head and looked at him. "So, how was it that you got away from the Germans when your uncle and aunt were arrested? You were related to them, after all."

Adam shrugged. "The SS kept me in jail for a few days, threatened me, beat me up a bit . . . but even though I was born in Poland, I was an American, a civilian with a valid U.S. passport, and we weren't at war yet. So, I was deported."

"Back to America?"

"That was their intention. I was put on a train with a dozen other Americans who were all being deported back to the states, some of the last ones left in Krakow at the time. But the Germans turned us over to the Belgians when we got to the border. We got off the train in Antwerp, and the rest of them boarded a bus for the port to catch a ship back to America."

"But you stayed behind."

"The day before my uncle was arrested he gave me a name and a telephone number—in case anything happened. The name was Stanley Whitehall and the telephone number was the SOE in London."

"Your uncle was connected with SOE? Sounds like he was more than just a college professor."

Adam nodded. "I suspected it back in '39 when the war broke out. But after he was arrested . . . I don't know. I didn't think about it . . . I just wanted . . . revenge."

The shelling was closer now. The walls shook, and pieces of brick fell from the crumbling ceiling. At least the dampness was gone, driven away by the heat of fires that were raging in the streets above them. As they huddled together in a corner of the cellar, Natalia wondered if they'd ever get out of there. *And if we do, then what?* It had been so long since she'd had any kind of normal life she couldn't even imagine it.

Suddenly a very loud, very close artillery blast shook the walls of the cave-like cellar. Natalia flinched as the vibration through the earthen floor ran up her spine. The lantern swung back and forth precariously on the post, and Adam slid his arm around her, pulling her closer. "Tell me about your village," he said.

"My village?"

"Yes, where you grew up. Tell me about it."

She pulled away. "Why?"

"Because I'd like to know. Besides, like you said the last time we were here, it's better than just listening to the shelling." There was a softer expression on his face, something she hadn't seen before. He seemed . . . more relaxed.

She leaned back against the wall and sighed. It was so long ago. "I grew up ten kilometers east of Lwow, a rural area, mostly peasant farmers who'd been there for generations. My father was a doctor, and there was a small hospital. I worked there when I wasn't at university in Lwow."

"What did you study?"

"Medicine, of course. When your father's a doctor, what else would you study? The medical school reserved ten chairs for women, the same number they reserved for Jews and Ukrainians. Very civilized, don't you think?"

He nodded. And when he smiled at her she felt something pass between them, a magnetism that seemed to draw them closer. For the first time since they'd met, she felt that he really *cared* about what she was saying.

"I was in Lwow when the first German soldiers arrived. The fall term hadn't started yet, but all the students were there anyway. We'd seen the airplanes almost every day since the beginning of September and we knew what was about to happen. There was only a small Polish Army garrison to defend the city at the time, so we all signed up and did what we could—set up barricades, dug anti-tank ditches, raced back and forth with messages, food and water." She paused and shook her head. "Sounds familiar, doesn't it?"

He reached over and took her hand. "Yes, too familiar."

"Then the Luftwaffe flew in, dropping incendiary bombs. It was hell . . . fires everywhere. Just like hell. Our soldiers hung on, and we did everything we could to help. But then . . ."

"The Russians?"

Natalia clenched her jaw. "Yes, the Russians. Everyone was stunned. We had no idea what was happening. At first they sent in an envoy. He said they were here to *help us*. Of course, it was a lie; the only criminal worse than Hitler is that treacherous son of a bitch Stalin."

She dropped his hand, and propped her elbows on her knees, rubbing her forehead. Lwow had been so beautiful: the opera and ballet, the churches and palaces, the magnificent Baroque and Renaissance architecture . . . "The next day the Germans pulled out, the Russians moved in and the NKVD started arresting people."

Adam placed a hand on her shoulder. When she continued her voice was just above a whisper. "I managed to get out of the city and walked back to our village, taking all the back roads and paths through the forests to avoid the Russian soldiers. But when I got there . . ."

She swallowed hard and brushed away a tear. *Don't cry, damn it!* "When I got there the village was . . . there was nothing left. The fires were still smoldering, our house was destroyed and they were . . . my parents, my relatives, everyone . . . they were just . . . gone."

Tears ran down her cheeks, and she wiped them away, cursing

under her breath. "I left . . . got lost, actually . . . in the forests. Then, several days later, I met some people. They were partisans, forming a resistance movement. We eventually became part of the AK."

"When did you go to Krakow?" Adam asked.

"About a year later, in the autumn of '40. The commander of our AK unit arranged for me to get a job on the railway."

Adam smiled again. "Hence the name, 'Conductor.'"

Natalia shrugged. "Not very original as code names go."

"So, I assume you did more than just punch tickets on the train."

"Eventually, but not right away. I worked strictly as a conductor for almost two years. I hardly heard from the AK. I'd actually started to think they'd forgotten about me."

"And then . . . ?"

"In the spring of '42 I heard from a priest, of all things. He gave me a new assignment. Then someone I never met, called 'the Provider'—"

A thundering explosion rocked the building, and the center support post sagged. An instant later a section of the ceiling collapsed, and the lantern shattered on the floor in a blaze of sparks, buried instantly under the rubble and plunging the cellar into blackness.

Natalia groped in the darkness and found Adam's hand. They scrambled to their feet, choking on dust and stumbling over piles of plaster and wood, until they found the tunnel exit.

They ran through the tunnel and up the staircase, following the reddish-yellow glow from outside.

The scene beyond the doorway was every bit as hellish as Lwow had been—blazing fires and thick, black smoke, blinding flashes in the sky, and the constant thud of bursting shells. Every building in sight had been reduced to a shattered ruin.

Adam squeezed her hand. "We've got to run for it."

She nodded.

But he didn't move.

He stared at her for another moment, his eyes reflecting the softness, the growing feeling of togetherness she'd felt in the cellar.

Then he leaned over and kissed her.

She slipped her hand around the back of his neck and pulled him close as they kissed again. Longer this time, his hand sliding around her waist.

Then he abruptly broke it off.

He took a step back. “We have to go.”

She reached over and brushed his cheek. “Yes, I know.”

He smiled at her, but the look in his eyes that had been there a moment ago was gone.

Eighteen

1 SEPTEMBER

ADAM GLANCED BACK at Natalia. She motioned for him to keep going as they made their way through the rubble on Piekarska Street, then climbed over a half-demolished stone wall. Twelve other AK commandos were waiting for them on the other side, including Rabbit, who stood at the front of the line, his face flushed and his trousers soaked with muck.

"Let's get the hell out of here before they blow our fuckin' heads off!" the boy yelled as soon as he spotted Adam and Natalia. Even from two meters away, Adam could smell the stink of sewage on him.

Through a swirling vortex of shrieking artillery shells, deafening concussions and raging fires, Rabbit led the group into the ancient maze of winding streets bordering Old Town's main square. Only a few skeletal brick façades remained standing, their dark, blown-out windows looming eerily like the eyes of a death's-head. The commandos kept their heads down, circling around the ruins of St. John's Cathedral, its magnificent spires, archways and statuary now pulverized into dust. A few minutes later they rendezvoused with a second group, hunkered down in front of St. Jacek's Church—incredibly still intact—at the head of Dluga Street.

Rabbit glanced at his watch, then turned to the combined group of commandos, shouting to be heard over the thundering detonations. "Bobcat is at the sewer at the south end of the street, at Place Krasinskich. That's where the manhole is. In exactly ten minutes he'll signal with a flashlight, twice. I'll return the signal by flashing three times. Then you all run like hell! Single file. Just follow me!"

Adam put a hand on Natalia's shoulder. "You stay right behind Rabbit."

She grabbed his coat and pulled him toward her. "What about you?"

"I'll be along later. I have another assignment."

"I'm coming with you."

He shook his head. "You can't. We have orders. You have to go now and I'll—"

She jerked harder on his coat. "I'm not leaving without you!"

He bent down and kissed her. Then he gripped her shoulders and looked into her eyes. "You're going *now*. I'll find you."

Defiance flashed through her eyes, and she turned away.

Rabbit shouted again at the group. "No matter what happens, keep running, and don't stop until you're in the sewer! When we're down there, follow me; I know the way. Bobcat will bring up the rear."

The fires and bursting artillery shells lit up the midnight sky, giving Adam amazingly clear glimpses of Dluga Street—from the stout façade of St. Jacek's at the north end to Place Krasinskich at the south end. From his vantage point on the top floor of Raczynski Palace, he spotted Natalia in her blue coat kneeling next to Rabbit in front of the church.

Adam did not want it to end this way. But he knew it would. There was a part of him that wanted to run back into the street and take her in his arms. But that part was just barely alive, buried under years of murder, rage and the quest for revenge that had driven him since Whitehall sent him back into Poland.

He leaned against the edge of the window, watching her in the flashes of light. He had to make her go. He knew that. The AK were out of options. They were trapped in Old Town, and the route through the sewers held the only way out. Surrendering to the Germans would be a death sentence. And when the Russians finally decided to enter Warsaw, Adam knew the terror squads of the NKVD would be right behind the Red Army. Any AK commandos still alive would spend the rest of their days in a Siberian gulag.

But Adam wasn't headed back to the sewers. Raczynski Palace served as a field hospital for hundreds of wounded AK commandos who couldn't escape. If the building survived the bombardment, he knew that SS storm troopers would move in and finish off the wounded men. Colonel Stag knew it too. But there was nothing he could do about it. And Adam knew there was nothing *he* could do about it either. He couldn't stop it. But, when the time came, he could take out some of the storm troopers with him. Perhaps, at long last, all of the killing might actually mean something.

A light flashed twice from the south. Then three flashes from the north, and a moment later Rabbit's group was on the move, running single file down the street, dodging around the rubble.

A burst of artillery shook the palace building and lit up the street like a searchlight. Adam stood ramrod stiff and clenched his fists, watching the slender figure in a blue uniform running right behind Rabbit. Silently, he urged her along. *Run! Run!*

Then a massive concussion knocked him to the ground. Adam groped around to retrieve his glasses and scrambled to his feet. He fumbled to slip them back on, then looked in horror through a cracked lens at the street below where a massive cloud of dust billowed up from a crater three meters across. The runners in the second half of the single-file line had disappeared.

Frozen with fear, Adam watched helplessly as the runners in the front half of the line stopped and looked back. There was instant commotion. Natalia waved her arms, frantically pointing back up the street at the smoking crater. Rabbit tugged at her arm. Some of the others pushed her forward.

Natalia hesitated and continued to point at the crater.

Adam pounded on the window frame and shouted out loud, "Run! Goddamn it, Run!" Only the hospital patients in the next room heard him.

But that's exactly what she did.

And then she was gone.

Nineteen

1 September

The smell was overpowering. Sharp sulfurous gas and the stagnant stench of mold and human excrement swept over Natalia. She fought off a wave of nausea as she stepped off the climbing iron into the foul, knee-deep wastewater with muck up to her ankles. Torrents of water swirled around her, and she stumbled forward, almost falling. Hammer, the husky commando in front of her, grabbed her around the waist as she struggled to lift her right foot from the muck.

"The rope! Grab the damn rope!" Rabbit shouted from the head of the line, the faint glow from his lantern swinging back and forth, briefly illuminating the slime-covered walls.

Natalia put one hand on Hammer's shoulder and felt around in the filthy, rapidly flowing water until she found the rope. It was slippery, and she had to hold tight with both hands to keep from falling. She heard Rabbit shout something, and the rope suddenly went taut, jerking her forward as the group set off into the dark, forbidding labyrinth. Natalia hung on, swallowing hard to keep from vomiting. She concentrated on lifting one foot at a time, praying she wouldn't lose a boot.

They plodded forward, the rope jerking back and forth as people slipped and stumbled, splashing in the squalid wastewater. Suddenly, the rope went slack and someone in front of Hammer cried out, "Jesus Christ, it's a body!"

"Keep moving!" Rabbit yelled back.

The rope went taut again and a moment later Natalia stumbled over a squishy hump underfoot. She clung fast with both hands and kept her eyes forward, focusing on Hammer's broad silhouette to force the grisly image out of her mind as she stepped over the submerged corpse.

They continued on, torrents of putrid water rushing past, carrying not just human waste, but rotting plants, sticks, gravel and broken boards that slammed into the back of Natalia's legs. Her trousers were shredded by the jagged splinters. Wastewater oozed through the brick roof, dripping on her head until her hair was sticky and matted, and her eyes burned.

"Step up!" Rabbit yelled as the group made a left turn into a smaller tunnel with the main flow of water rushing off in a different direction. It was drier and the footing better, though the tunnel's low ceiling forced them into a crouched position. Natalia banged her head a few times and, in front of her, Hammer crawled on all fours.

Overhead she heard crunching noises and the unmistakable clatter of steel tank treads as Rabbit called out, "Passing under Holy Cross Church!"

Then a thunderous *bang* echoed off the brick walls.

The rope went slack. Voices shouted and shrieked.

"Grenade!" shouted Bobcat from his position at the rear of the line.

Another *bang,* and the tunnel filled with smoke.

"Get moving!" Rabbit shouted. "The fuckin' Krauts are throwin' grenades down here! Get moving!"

The line jerked forward, and Natalia stumbled, scraping her knee on the concrete floor. Hammer reached back and grabbed her elbow until she regained her footing. Choking on the acrid smoke, she clung desperately to the rope as the line surged forward.

The group staggered on through the narrow, tube-like tunnel for what seemed like an eternity. Hunched over, her back aching, her knees bruised and bleeding, Natalia thought about Adam, about Berta, about her job on the railway—anything to push away the paralyzing dread that the roof would collapse, that this is where it would end, here in the sealed tomb of a sewer tunnel.

Finally, they turned right and climbed down into a larger tunnel, the shadows from Rabbit's lantern flickering on greasy, oval-shaped walls. Up and down the rope line, the commandos fell quiet now as fatigue settled in. This tunnel had higher ceilings—even Hammer could straighten up—but they were back to flowing wastewater and dozens of corpses lying in the sticky, ankle-deep muck. Natalia had lost any concept of time but was certain that hours had passed. Rabbit's voice became hoarse and weary as he called out their locations.

Progress slowed as they passed under Warsaw University. The area above their heads crawled with SS troopers and Panzer brigades. Overhead, the crunching sounds of tank treads, clattering machine guns and exploding artillery shells hammered Natalia's eardrums until she thought her head would split open.

The fearsome screeching of dive-bombing Stukas signaled that dawn had come, and the rope went slack whenever the group neared a manhole. Rabbit doused the lantern and crept forward searching for any crack of daylight and the ambush that might be waiting.

They slogged southward under Nowy Swiat, and had just passed the intersection with Jerusalem Avenue when Natalia heard the metallic clank of a manhole cover being pried off behind her.

A sudden burst of daylight illuminated the tunnel.

"Run!" Bobcat shouted from the rear. "Run! Run! Get mov—!"

A blinding flash! An instant later a searing wave of heat from a flamethrower knocked Natalia face down into the muck. She scrambled to her knees, struggling to grab the rope, but her feet slipped sideways on the greasy floor.

The rope jerked wildly. The tunnel echoed with agonized wails from those at the back of the line.

Rabbit stood frozen at the head, staring back into the tunnel, the eerie glow of the lantern reflecting the horror in the boy's eyes. Then he turned away.

The rope surged forward. The man behind Natalia clawed frantically at her back, screaming for her to get moving. Hammer reached back and found her arm; his massive hand gripped her wrist like a vise and pulled her along.

The group stumbled forward into the darkness, slipping and sliding in the muck. The rope continued to jerk back and forth as the injured commandos at the rear lost their balance, and others tried desperately to hold them up.

Gradually the wails receded into painful moans, and there was less resistance on the rope as those not able to continue fell away. Natalia plodded on, placing one foot after the other, tears streaming down her grimy face, her heart wrenching in agony for Bobcat and the others who'd been lost. Then her mind went numb.

Time passed. The sounds from overhead became muted and less frequent. Apparently too tired to call out locations, Rabbit had fallen silent. Natalia had no idea where they were. Her legs tingled, her ankles had swollen and every bone in her body ached. Her temples throbbed, her throat was raw from the caustic fumes and her hands were so blistered from clutching the rope that she feared she wouldn't be able to hold on for another second.

And just as she was certain she would pass out, a draft of fresh air suddenly washed over her. It became a breeze, a miraculous cooling breeze from up ahead.

"Thank God!" someone behind her shouted.

The line surged forward for a moment, then went slack, and Natalia slammed into Hammer, as she slipped on the greasy floor.

"Quiet down!" Rabbit hissed. The group fell silent.

Hammer turned back toward Natalia and whispered, "It could be a trap. We don't know who's up there."

Rabbit doused the lantern. Natalia could hear him moving forward, slowly and cautiously, sloshing through the fetid water.

There was a loud clank and a heavy scraping sound as the manhole cover was dragged away. Then shouts from above—in Polish—and the commandos in the tunnel surged forward again, yelling loudly, pumping fists and clapping each other's back. Natalia grabbed hold of Hammer's belt and hung on to avoid getting knocked down in the rush.

Rabbit shouted for order. "One at a time! Slow down, Goddamn it! One at a time!"

Hammer took hold of Natalia's shoulders, and an instant later she was on the climbing irons, staring up through the open manhole at the outstretched hand of an AK commando.

A half hour later, the commandos who crawled out of the sewer stood shivering around a bonfire in the middle of a wide street that ran alongside an abandoned canning plant. The building's windows were broken out, and its roof caved in on one end. A sign hung from a rusting chain-link fence indicating that the property was for sale. Across the street stood an enormous, three-story paint factory. Natalia feared it was likely to erupt into a blazing inferno if the shelling came any closer to this area at the south end of the City Center.

But the area seemed secure for the moment. There were barricades at every intersection, and two PIAT anti-tank guns were positioned near the paint factory along with a German Panther tank that the AK commandos had somehow managed to commandeer. To the north, the sky was ablaze where the fires in Old Town raged out of control.

Fortified from a cup of bitter coffee and a thick slice of black bread that had miraculously appeared on a table near the bonfire, Natalia spotted Rabbit, sitting alone on the steps of the canning plant. She sat down next to him.

"Did you get something to eat?" she asked.

The boy shook his head.

She held out a chunk of the bread. "Here, take some. You certainly earned it."

He glanced at her, then looked away. His eyes were red, his grimy face streaked from tears.

She laid a hand on his thin shoulder. "I'm sorry about Bobcat."

Rabbit didn't respond.

"I know that he was your—"

"I don't want to talk about it," Rabbit snapped. He spit on the ground and turned away from her. A moment later he hunched forward, gripping his knees, his back arching up and down as the sobs wracked his skinny frame.

Natalia moved closer and wrapped her arm around him. "I'm so sorry," she whispered.

Rabbit leaned against her, then slowly laid his head in her lap, covering his face with his hands.

A few minutes later, he straightened up and wiped his face with his shirtsleeve. "Do you believe in God?" he asked.

Natalia was startled by the unexpected question, and it took her a moment to respond. "Yes. I do. Do you?"

The boy shrugged. "I don't know. If there was a God, why would he let the fuckin' Krauts kill Bobcat? Why would he want any of this to happen?"

"I don't think God wants this to happen, Rabbit. And I'm sure he didn't want your friend to get killed."

"Then why the hell doesn't he stop it?" the boy croaked. He turned to look at her, his dirty face streaked where tears had slid down his cheek.

"God doesn't work that way," she said. "He doesn't interfere." *He just lets us slaughter each other.* She paused for a moment and bit her lower lip, then put a hand on Rabbit's shoulder. "I think God wants us to learn how to live together."

"Hah! I'll bet God didn't have to live with the fuckin' Nazis."

Natalia smiled in spite of the irreverence of the boy's remark. "Do you go to church, Rabbit?"

The boy shook his head. "Nah, not any more. My Ma made me and my brother go. But ever since they . . . you know, since then I never went again." He was quiet for a moment, then turned to look at her. "Do you go to church?"

"I used to, when I lived in Krakow."

"My Ma went to Krakow once. She said it was beautiful, with lots of big churches."

Natalia nodded. "It *is* beautiful. And there are many, many churches."

"Which one did you go to?"

"My favorite is the Mariacki Church. It's on the Rynek Glowny, right in the heart of the city. It's a basilica. And it has this magnificent vaulted nave. The walls are painted in blue and gold and decorated with elaborate friezes."

"Friezes," the boy repeated. "What are those?"

"Decorations on a wall, usually sculptures or paintings. Sometimes they tell a story."

Rabbit spat on the ground again. "I'll bet none of those stories are about fuckin' Nazis burnin' kids in a sewer."

It took a moment for Natalia to reply. Then all she could manage was, "No . . . they aren't."

"Did you go there often?"

"Well, not on a regular basis, not every Sunday. But I would go sometimes during the week, especially if I was troubled by something, or just wanted to think." She squeezed his shoulder. "Maybe someday you could go there with me."

"Yeah, maybe. I'd go with you . . . but I wouldn't talk to God."

They sat for a long time, Natalia with her arm around the tough young warrior who'd just lost the only thing that mattered.

A tear trickled down her cheek, and she wiped it away.

She knew exactly how he felt.

Twenty

1 October

By the first of October, few buildings remained standing in the section of the City Center west of the canning plant. Natalia hobbled along a narrow cobblestone walkway and finally slumped down, exhausted, in the shadows between two of those buildings. She gingerly touched her swollen ankle, wincing in pain. She'd twisted it badly several hours earlier, running along Okrag Street looking for Rabbit and Hammer. They had vowed to stick together, but the constant artillery barrage over the last three days had created such chaos that she'd lost sight of her friends in the panicked crowds.

And now she was alone.

They'd been on the run for a month since evacuating Old Town through the sewers, and Natalia wasn't sure she could last another day. She doubted any of them could. They were out of ammunition, there was no food or water, the streets were littered with corpses and communications had completely broken down. They were surrounded by the enemy, and the last flickers of life in the insurgency were about to be snuffed out. Natalia knew it was only a matter of time. For some units of the AK still entrenched in isolated areas, perhaps a few days. In her case, perhaps just a few minutes.

Natalia leaned back against the brick building and closed her eyes, thinking about Adam. She knew where he'd gone that night on Dluga Street, just before she followed Rabbit into the sewer. A commando in one of the last groups to escape had seen him entering Raczynski Palace, the makeshift hospital where hundreds of wounded

AK commandos were trapped. Trying to protect them from the SS was a suicide mission. But considering the torment in Adam's heart, the hatred and revenge that had driven him for years, she knew why he went there.

A week later she heard the news. When the Germans moved into Old Town, the SS stormed Raczynski Palace and murdered everyone—doctors, nurses, patients in their beds. She had cried that night, cried for what might have been.

She heard a noise.

It was the all-too-familiar clanking of tank treads, and she slid backward on her rump, deeper into the corner between the two buildings where the late afternoon shadows provided some cover.

The same chaotic streets that had separated her from her friends a couple of hours ago were now suddenly deserted as the grinding noise of the enemy tanks drew closer. The moment the artillery barrage ceased, those who were still standing knew what was coming next. They abruptly vanished, scurrying into cellars and alleyways like rodents before a flood.

The rumbling diesel engines and creaking treads escalated into a deafening crescendo. A shiver ran down Natalia's back as she scrunched against the building. The noise echoed off the buildings, and the ground shook violently as the monstrous machines approached.

A loud *bang* jolted every bone in her body.

Another *bang!*

Then guttural shouts in German: "*Raus! Raus!* Fucking Polish Dogs! *Raus jezst!*"

Natalia crouched, frozen with fear as a blur of black-uniformed SS troopers flashed past the walkway, tossing grenades through cellar windows.

Screams and belching smoke filled the air. Doors flew open, and terrified civilians raced up the cellar stairs and into the walkway, faces blackened with soot. A man with his clothes on fire rolled on the ground, screaming. A woman clutching a baby drenched in blood wailed in agony, then sank to her knees.

Natalia struggled to her feet, ignoring the pain in her ankle, as a squad of SS storm troopers charged into the walkway, sealing it off from the street. The people who had fled the cellar suddenly fell silent, huddling together, moving backward, shoving Natalia against the building.

The SS troopers advanced.

A thunderous burst of machine-gun fire reverberated off the brick walls.

The people screamed in panic and clawed at each other.

A hot, piercing pain shot through Natalia's forehead and dropped her to her knees. The man in front of her grunted and collapsed backward, knocking her flat. Someone fell on top of her and jammed her face into the ground.

Then it was quiet.

Natalia lay still, her head throbbing, the dead weight of the bodies on top of her threatening to crush her ribs. She struggled to turn her head to the side and get some air. Boots scraped on the cobblestones as the troopers kicked at the bodies. They grunted German phrases and laughed. Then the boots walked away.

Through the tangle of bodies, Natalia caught a glimpse of blood-stained cobblestones in the fading sunlight. A puddle of blood had pooled in a depression; red slowly faded into brown as the liquid soaked into the earth between the stones. The puddle blurred and then smeared into darkness.

Twenty-One

2 October

Movement awakened her. Natalia opened one eye. Her other eye, pinned against the cobblestones, was crusted shut. She heard voices—heavy, crude voices—laughing and cursing.

Ukrainians.

She caught a glimpse of their boots in the dim light. It was daylight, but probably early, she thought, just after dawn. They were shabby boots, dusty and worn, holes in the soles. *How many are there?*

The pile of corpses on top of her shifted, and the weight on her ribs lightened a bit as the Ukrainians pulled off one of the bodies. She could understand only a few words, but enough to realize they were looters. It sounded like there were two of them. As another body was dragged onto the cobblestones, Natalia wished now she'd been killed by the Nazi machine gunners.

The body lying directly on top of her moved, and Natalia closed her eye, playing dead, praying they wouldn't touch her.

But she knew what would happen.

A large, calloused hand grabbed her collar and jerked her up. She yelped as her swollen ankle was dragged across the stones.

The Ukrainian bent down and grabbed her hair, forcing her head back. He had a round, almost boyish face, blue eyes and a shock of unruly brown hair. He laughed and said something to his partner, his breath stinking of onions and tobacco. Natalia couldn't understand him, but it didn't matter.

The Ukrainian grabbed her by the lapels of her uniform jacket and hoisted her to her feet. The pain in her ankle almost caused her to pass out. His partner now appeared in her field of vision. This one also looked young, though taller, with broad shoulders and a dark, stubbly beard. Both of them were grinning like children with a new toy. The round-faced one reached under her jacket and fondled her breast, then rolled his eyes and spat on the ground. The bearded one jostled him out of the way and reached for her belt.

Natalia twisted her body, trying to back away, but Round Face slapped her, sending a searing bolt of pain through her forehead where the bullet had grazed her. He grabbed her by the hair again and jerked her head back.

Someone shouted from the other end of the walkway. At first Natalia couldn't make out the words. Then she heard them again. *"Halt! Stoppen Sie!"*

Round Face's grip loosened, and his hand fell away.

Two soldiers marched toward them from the street.

Natalia's stomach tightened as she realized they were Germans.

The one on the right, an officer, glared at the two Ukrainians. *"Raus!"* he commanded and jerked his thumb toward the street. *"Raus! Schnell! Mach schnell!"* He reached for the pistol strapped to his waist and shouted again, louder. *"Raus! Schweinhunds!"*

The Ukrainians made a wide circle around the two Germans, then bolted for the street.

Natalia slumped to the ground.

The officer put a hand on her shoulder. "Can you stand?" he asked in German-accented Polish.

Natalia flinched.

"Yes, I know," the officer said. "I get that all the time, a German officer who speaks Polish." He looked to be in his fifties with a narrow face, and a pencil-thin, gray mustache. His uniform was Wehrmacht. Though Natalia could barely breathe, she was thankful that at least he wasn't SS.

"I was a military attaché to Poland in the thirties," the officer said casually. "I lived here in Warsaw for six years. So, can you stand, or do you need help?"

Natalia swallowed and shook her head. "I can't . . . it's my ankle."

The officer barked a few terse commands to his subordinate, who turned and jogged back toward the street. Then he knelt down and touched her ankle gently. When Natalia flinched again, he took his hand away.

The younger soldier reappeared carrying a canvas pack and a crutch. "Unteroffizier Brunkhorst is our company medic," the officer said. "He'll take care of that ankle." Then he brushed back her hair, examining the bullet graze on her forehead.

Natalia's skin crawled, and she had to fight the urge to slap away his hand.

But he withdrew it, as though sensing her anxiety. "I'd say you were pretty lucky, young lady. Brunkhorst will clean that up as well."

The medic gently removed Natalia's boot and began to tape her ankle. He appeared to be in his late teens or early twenties, with a fair complexion and short, stubby fingers. His uniform was soiled with dirt and blood, but his young face was clean and so smooth it appeared he hadn't yet started to shave. He glanced up at her once, then blushed and looked back down at his work.

The officer lit a cigarette and studied the bodies of the civilians lying in the walkway, shaking his head. "My SS colleagues get a bit carried away at times, but this insurgency is a bad business." He exhaled a perfect smoke ring, holding the cigarette delicately with his little finger extended. "It's a shame. I loved my time here; it was a magnificent city. Are you from Warsaw?"

She shook her head. "Lwow."

The officer raised his eyebrows. "Lwow? That's too bad. The Russians are such brutes."

Natalia stared at him, feeling like a prop in some bizarre stage play. *Who is this character, and what the hell is going on?* Suddenly she was aware of something very strange. There was no shelling, no grinding tank treads, no gunfire.

The officer smiled again. "You're wondering why it's so quiet?"

Natalia nodded.

"They've called a ceasefire."

It took a moment for her to process the thought. "A ceasefire . . . I don't understand . . . when?"

"Your General Bor and our high command agreed to a ceasefire beginning at 0700." He glanced at his watch and nodded. "Ah, right on time."

Natalia was stunned. *Just like that . . . it's over?* Then she remembered the Ukrainians and shuddered: she might have had her throat slit by those filthy brutes on the very day the nightmare finally ended. "What happens now?"

The officer shrugged. "As soon as Unteroffizier Brunkhorst has you fixed up, you can use that crutch and walk out of here. But, of course, Brunkhorst and I will leave first." He pointed to the soiled red-and-white armband on her right sleeve. "After all, it wouldn't do for me to be seen assisting an enemy combatant, would it?"

Natalia sat quietly as Brunkhorst finished wrapping her ankle. Then he carefully cleaned the graze and bandaged her forehead. His touch was so gentle that she had to smile, which made the boy blush again. She thought about Rabbit. Perhaps in some other world, he and this young German boy might have become friends. When the medic was finished, he held out the crutch and, with a firm grip on her elbow, helped her to her feet. Natalia sighed with relief and hobbled around a bit to get her balance. "It feels much better. Thank you."

The boy smiled briefly, then knelt down to close up his pack.

"Well, we shall be on our way now," the officer said. He looked at her for a moment, then saluted smartly. He turned on his heel, and the two Germans marched away.

Cautiously negotiating the uneven cobblestones on her crutch, it took Natalia several minutes to make it to the end of the walkway. When she reached the street, she stopped, dumbfounded.

AK commandos milled about openly, laughing and joking, passing around bottles of vodka and hand-rolled cigarettes under the watchful eyes of German soldiers, who stood near their tanks yet kept their distance. Natalia scanned the faces of the Wehrmacht soldiers but didn't see either the officer or the young medic. She looked down at her wrapped ankle and felt the bandage on her head, reassuring herself that she hadn't just imagined the whole thing.

She hobbled around for a while, smiling at some of the commandos she recognized, accepting a swig of vodka from an outstretched hand.

An exuberant teenager slapped her so hard on the back she almost fell. A young woman hugged her. Finally she stopped near a couple of commandos she recognized from the escape through the sewers.

"The AK's been disbanded, and we're all civilians now," one of them said. He was a stocky, bearded man whose name she couldn't recall. His tattered army uniform was streaked with dirt and blood, his right arm in a sling.

"Yeah, and I'm Jesus Christ!" his friend retorted. "You just watch. The fuckin' SS will show up any minute, and we're all dead meat."

"Bullshit! I heard from—"

He was interrupted by a weary-looking AK officer banging a steel bar against the side of a dented oil drum. The drum held a blazing bonfire.

"I have an announcement from General Bor," the AK officer croaked, his voice breaking with emotion. "This announcement is being read by officers in every sector of Warsaw still held by the AK." The crowd fell silent as he unfolded a single sheet of paper and began to read. "All military operations of the AK in Warsaw shall cease immediately. All AK personnel will be afforded combatant status and will be under the control of the German Wehrmacht as prisoners of war under the terms of the Geneva Convention."

The crowd instantly erupted into a cacophony of voices, some cheering and waving red-and-white AK flags, others shouting loudly that they'd been sold out.

The officer banged the iron rod against the drum again. When the crowd quieted down to a ripple of murmurs, he continued. "As military combatants—and not insurgents—you are ordered to march out of the city beginning at 0700 tomorrow, weapons shouldered, wearing AK armbands and carrying banners. At the city limits you will surrender your weapons to the German Wehrmacht and will be interned as prisoners of war according to the convention."

The crowd broke into dozens of animated conversations, though less boisterous this time. Questions and opinions flew back and forth from group to group. Natalia recalled that the mysterious German officer had referred to her as a combatant and not an insurgent. She wondered if that helped explain his actions. Or, was he just someone doing a good deed?

"Natalia!" a familiar voice shouted.

She turned around and saw Zeeka pushing through the crowd with Hammer and Rabbit right behind her. Natalia hobbled toward her comrade-in-arms, whom she hadn't seen in over a month. "My God, you're still alive!"

"I've been in the Mokotow District," Zeeka said breathlessly. "Colonel Stag sent me down there with Ula and Iza on a demolition mission. We were almost finished when we got surrounded . . ." Zeeka's voice tailed off, but the look in her eyes told Natalia what had happened to the others. "I heard about Berta," Zeeka added quickly.

Natalia nodded. The remorse was still there, though it now seemed as if it had happened a long time ago.

"These two have been looking all over for you," Zeeka said. "By some miracle, I ran into them just a few minutes ago."

Natalia dropped her crutch and reached out to Rabbit. The boy wrapped his arms around her while Hammer hung back, nodding and running a thick hand over his bald head. But she noticed that the big man's eyes were moist.

Hammer picked the crutch off the ground and looked it over before handing it back to Natalia. "Nice crutch," he grunted. "Did you steal it from the Germans?"

Natalia felt her face flush and absently touched the bandage on her forehead, thinking that someday she might tell the story . . . but not now. "I didn't steal it, but the medic who taped my ankle probably did."

Zeeka drew the four of them together, maneuvering away from the crowd. "I have something important to tell you," she said lowering her voice. "Colonel Stag took me aside a few hours ago. He told me about the ceasefire and the terms of surrender."

Natalia listened silently to her former Minerki unit leader, sensing that something important was coming next.

"I was desperately hoping that I could find all of you," Zeeka said. "Colonel Stag has ordered me to gather a small group who are willing to try to escape."

Natalia glanced at Hammer and Rabbit. Neither of them said a word, but they edged in closer.

Zeeka continued. "We're not the only ones. Stag said there will be other groups, but we're not to know who, and we are not to act together. Our instructions are to dispose of our weapons, armbands, badges—anything that would connect us with the AK—then blend in with the civilians as they're evacuated from the city."

Natalia instantly understood. "The AK is being disbanded," she said.

Zeeka nodded. "*Officially*, that's true. General Bor has saved our lives by negotiating combatant status for the AK. As insurgents we would be immediately executed. But the AK as an official fighting force is being disbanded. Those who surrender to the Wehrmacht can expect to be detained in POW camps until the war is over."

"And then wind up in the hands of the Russians," Hammer growled. "So, fuck 'em, why surrender? We may as well continue to fight and die right here."

Zeeka shook her head. "It's the only way to save the civilian population. If the AK refuses to disband and surrender, the Germans will burn the city to the ground and everyone in it—women, children, old people, everyone. There is no other choice. The AK has to surrender and march out of the city."

"But not all of us," Natalia said.

Zeeka looked each one of them in the eye. "No, not all of us. My orders from Colonel Stag are to select a small group I can trust and who are willing to take the risk. If we're successful in escaping, our orders are to lay low for several months, blend in with the local population and then make contact with designated AK cells and carry on the fight." She paused. "You have to understand that if we're caught by either the Germans or the Russians, we'll be executed on the spot."

Natalia glanced again at Rabbit and Hammer. They all looked at Zeeka and nodded.

Twenty-Two

17 January 1945

General Andrei Kovalenko ordered his driver to halt at the midway point of the pontoon bridge over the frozen Vistula River. In the freezing cold he stepped out of the GAZ-11, braced against the wind and stared at the snowbound ruins of Warsaw. By now he was beyond the frustration that had gripped him for more than four months while his army was ordered to sit by idly. He was beyond trying to rationalize any tactical reason for the Red Army's inaction when his vastly superior forces could have swept in at any time and crushed the Nazi bastards.

From his command post on the east bank of the Vistula last August, he had watched the destruction of the City Center and Old Town. He knew about the escape through the sewers of several thousand AK commandos. The poor bastards had continued their futile struggle through September, before the inevitable capitulation. And then the forced expulsion of the remaining citizens of Warsaw: more than four hundred thousand souls, who plodded out of their city under gunpoint to transit camps many kilometers away.

Then, for another three months, Kovalenko had watched the Nazis systematically destroy every remaining structure in Warsaw. While other Red Army units to the north and south overwhelmed the German Wehrmacht, pushing them westward across the plains of Poland, he continued to follow his orders, standing by while German tanks and flamethrowers laid waste to the city.

Kovalenko shivered in the cold, but he stood on the windswept bridge for another moment, gazing at the frozen rubble beyond the river. Then he got back in the car and ordered the driver to proceed into what was left of Warsaw.

By noon, a temporary command post was set up in the barely recognizable central square in Old Town. Nothing remained standing. The Royal Castle, home of Poland's royalty for three hundred years had been leveled, together with St. John's Cathedral, which had stood on the same site since the fourteenth century. The merchant houses and guild halls, the shops, cafés, art galleries and museums were reduced to piles of rubbish. The windblown, snow-covered streets were deserted and, save for a few stray dogs struggling through the snowdrifts, not a single sign of life remained.

Russian tanks, fitted with plows, had pushed back enough of the rubble to erect a headquarters tent. Diesel-powered generators and heaters were set up and a communications center established to serve notice that the Red Army was now in control of what little was left of Warsaw.

When General Kovalenko's car pulled up in front of the headquarters tent, two Red Army soldiers scrambled to attention and one opened the rear door. Kovalenko stepped out, glanced around quickly, then entered the tent. He handed his greatcoat to a soldier at the door and surveyed the cadre of officers scurrying around with messages and instructions for the regiments that were about to enter the wasteland of Warsaw.

Captain Andreyev sat at a table in the center of the tent studying a report. He stood up and saluted smartly. "*Dóbraye útra*, General," Andreyev said loudly enough to stop all activity inside the tent. "Welcome to Warsaw."

Kovalenko grunted and waved his hand, signaling everyone to carry on, then stepped over and tossed his hat on the table. He pulled a pack of cigarettes from his shirt pocket.

Andreyev produced a lighter and lit the general's cigarette. "You have a visitor," he said.

Kovalenko blew out a cloud of smoke and sat down at the head of the table. "A visitor? Here?"

Andreyev nodded. "An NKVD officer. Major Tarnov."

"Tarnov? What the hell is *he* doing here?"

"He arrived first thing this morning in his own automobile, as soon as we crossed the river. Do you know him?"

Kovalenko thought back to a dreary, rainy night in Siberia in 1940. But Andreyev didn't need to know about that. At least, not yet. "I know the name, that's all. What does he want to do, hunt down rats in the sewers? There's nothing left."

Andreyev shrugged. "He wouldn't say. Just insisted on talking with you as soon as you arrived."

Kovalenko stood up. "Go get him. Let's find out what service we can provide for the secret police."

Andreyev left the tent and returned a few minutes later accompanied by a short, stocky NKVD officer. Andreyev stood back as the officer stepped up to the table, saluted the general and said, "Major Dmitri Tarnov, NKVD 105th Frontier Guards Division."

Kovalenko nodded without speaking.

Tarnov continued. "I have orders to detain and interview any terrorist insurgents of the AK held in your custody."

Kovalenko studied the thick-necked NKVD officer, who obviously didn't recognize him from the incident in Siberia. Then he smiled, sat down and took a long drag on his cigarette. He didn't offer Tarnov a seat. "Well, Major Tarnov, did you look around when you arrived in Warsaw this morning? If you did, then you must have noticed that there is nothing left—no buildings, no churches, no houses. There's no fucking *people* left, Major, let alone *terrorist insurgents.*"

Tarnov appeared unfazed. "We understand that several thousand AK terrorists escaped from the German Wehrmacht at the time the city was evacuated. I have orders to—"

Kovalenko cut him off with a wave of his hand and addressed Captain Andreyev. "Captain, please explain to our guest what we know about the fate of the AK in Warsaw."

Andreyev stepped up to the table. "Of course, you realize, Major Tarnov, that the Red Army was not present in Warsaw at the time of the evacuation. However, we understand that more than ten thousand members of the AK surrendered to the Wehrmacht and were subsequently sent to POW camps in Germany."

Tarnov nodded impatiently. "*Da,* we have the same intelligence, Captain. But we also know that there were several thousand more AK insurgents who slipped through, blended in with the civilians and escaped. What can you tell me about—?"

Kovalenko cut him off again. "We don't know anything about them, Major Tarnov. They could be anywhere. Now, unless there's anything else, we are quite busy this morning."

Tarnov withdrew an envelope from a leather folder and laid it on the table. "As a matter of fact, General Kovalenko, there *is* something else. I have further orders. And these orders come directly from Commissar Beria."

Kovalenko leaned back in his chair. "That's very interesting, Major. What orders do you have from the Commissar of the NKVD that brings you here to Warsaw—other than hunting for the remnants of a defeated nation's Home Army?"

"These orders do not concern Warsaw or the AK, General Kovalenko. These orders require that you provide me with safe passage to Krakow immediately."

Kovalenko ignored the envelope. "You want safe passage to Krakow? What the hell for?"

"I am not at liberty to answer that, General. I am on official NKVD business, and it is imperative that I get to Krakow and the former German headquarters at Wawel Castle immediately."

Kovalenko took another drag on his cigarette. *What's so important at Wawel Castle?*

Tarnov persisted. "You *are* moving on to Krakow, are you not, General? Our information is that—"

Kovalenko abruptly ground out the cigarette in an ashtray. Then he shoved his chair back and stood up, towering over the NKVD officer. "*Da,* Major Tarnov. We are heading on to Krakow. The Germans are retreating, and we will be moving into Krakow within the next few days."

"My orders require me to get to Krakow immediately, General. I must request that—"

"Goddamn it, Major, are you deaf? I don't give a shit what orders you have. The Germans are retreating from Krakow now, as we speak. Red Army units will be moving in within the next few days. *That's* when you'll get to Krakow."

Tarnov nodded. "Very well, General, I will pass that along to Commissar Beria." He gestured toward the envelope. "If you'd care to inspect the orders?"

"I don't have time to inspect your orders, Major. Show them to Captain Andreyev on your way out."

Three days later, the Red Army entered Krakow. For the second time in the war, the city had escaped major damage. The Germans had fled, and Krakow had been taken without a shot being fired.

General Andrei Kovalenko sat in the backseat of the GAZ-11 with Captain Andreyev as they drove along the narrow, cobblestone streets of the ancient city, the Mecca of Poland for a thousand years. They drove through the Rynek Glowny, Krakow's central market square dominated by the Baroque, fifteenth-century Mariacki Church and the colossal Renaissance façade of the Cloth Hall. They passed the City Hall Tower, proceeded south along Avenue Grodzka and up the hill to Wawel Castle.

In the auto right behind them was Major Dmitri Tarnov of the NKVD.

Twenty-Three

8 May

Startled by the sound of an approaching truck, Adam scrambled off the dirt road and crawled into the high grass. He lay flat, holding his breath. It was well past midnight, a dark night, and the Red Army soldiers in the truck were probably drunk. But that only made them more unpredictable and dangerous.

As the vehicle passed by, a bottle tossed casually from the back landed less than a meter away and broke, splashing the left side of his face and his left eye with vodka. Adam exhaled slowly but didn't move for several minutes, cursing himself for his lack of vigilance. Here on the Baltic coast, with the sea less than fifty meters away, the noise of the wind and surf made it difficult to hear anything. And he was tired, dog tired, but that was no excuse. The area was crawling with Red Army troops and NKVD agents, hunting down the AK. There was little margin for error.

He waited another minute then stood up slowly and glanced around in the darkness. He pulled out a handkerchief and wiped the liquid from the left side of his face. He could barely feel the cloth against his skin due to the numbness, a result of the bullet wound that had mangled his left ear and come within a centimeter of ending his life at Raczynski Palace the previous September. He'd also lost most of the hearing in that ear, which was probably why he hadn't heard the truck until it was almost too late. Another reason to remain vigilant, he thought, cursing again.

He stepped back on the road and continued on, looking back over his shoulder every few paces. He knew from the map he'd studied that the road ran along the crest of a high bluff, which descended down sandy cliffs to the sea. There was no moon, and he found his way along the road by staying near the edge where the high grass rubbed against his leg. He kept his eye on the white foam of breaking waves on the beach below, which formed a half moon shape as it curved around a bay.

Adam trudged on, alternately glancing over his shoulder and down to the beach, until he was at the midpoint of the bay. He paused and listened to the crashing surf for a moment, then stepped off the road and walked carefully through the high grass to the edge of the bluff.

Am I early? He glanced at his watch but couldn't make out the numbers in the darkness. It had been close to midnight when he'd snuck around the outskirts of the seaside town of Ustka, staying clear of the marauding Red Army soldiers. He had followed the back routes and footpaths until he reached the coast road, and he guessed at least an hour had passed before he was surprised by the truck. That had been at least a quarter of an hour ago. The rendezvous was set for 0200. Not much longer.

Time passed. Adam knelt in the grass, staring into the blackness of the sea. Several times he thought he'd spotted a light and stood up, then nothing. The wind was stronger here, and the noise of the pounding surf enveloped him completely. With his spine tingling, he looked back toward the road every few minutes, making sure no one was sneaking up behind him.

He'd been on the move for seven days ever since receiving the message from London at an AK safe house in the Tuchola Forest. Seven days of plodding along muddy, rural roads on foot; in the back of ox carts; in ancient trucks owned by sympathetic peasants, who shared what little food they had. Seven days of avoiding the Red Army and, above all, the NKVD. But Adam was used to that part, he'd been a hunted man for years—first the Germans, now the Russians.

A flash, out at sea, slightly to his right.

He peered into the blackness. Nothing.

He waited.

Another flash, then a second. He was certain of it.

He glanced back toward the road, then slid down the sandy cliff on his butt, tumbling over at the bottom. He got to his knees and shook the sand from his woolen cap. He removed his glasses and wiped off the sand with his handkerchief, being careful with the cracked left lens. He put them back on and scanned the shoreline until he spotted several wooden pilings silhouetted against the foaming surf. That was the spot. He took one last glance at the top of the bluff then sprinted across the beach to the pilings.

Adam braced himself against one of the rough, wooden posts—the remains of a pier long since vanished—and stared in the direction where he'd last seen the flash. The spray soaked him instantly, the chill of the piercing wind driving straight through to his bones. Within minutes he was freezing and felt dizzy. The occasional dizzy spells were another result of the bullet wound last September. He'd had his thirty-fourth birthday two weeks ago, but on nights like this he felt twice his age. He clung tight to the post, shivering and waiting for the dizziness to pass.

He saw it again. Another flash.

What did the message say? Three quick flashes? Answer with two flashes?

Adam reached into his pocket for the flashlight he'd taken from the AK safe house. His hand trembled from the cold as he held it and fumbled for the switch. He flicked it on and off twice, wondering if it were strong enough.

Then he glanced back at the bluff again. *Goddamn it!*

Headlights bounced along the coast road.

He turned back toward the sea and was startled when he saw the light almost on top of him. Then, out of the gloom, the shape of a boat appeared, its rounded bow rising and falling in the surf. He flicked the flashlight again, twice, as the boat swept ashore.

Two figures emerged, one holding a line, the other racing toward him. He was a large, husky man, wearing a black rubber suit, his pistol drawn. He shouted in English, "We are looking for Oskar!" The voice was deep and strong, the accent British, the words expected.

Adam shouted back, "Oskar has taken the train."

A gunshot from the bluff—

The British marine fired back—

Then he grabbed Adam's arm. "Let's get out of here, chum. You're off to London."

Twenty-Four

10 May

The hotel room in London was small but clean, with fresh sheets and a private bath. There were clean clothes in the bureau, a new suit in the closet and room service. Adam thought he'd died and gone to heaven.

The first day after his arrival, he had stumbled about in a fog. The entire journey seemed surreal, like something he might expect to see in the cinema—tough men in a rubber raft, a submarine, a small twin-engine plane. He'd been whisked to the hotel in a limousine with instructions to get some sleep and, in no uncertain terms, to stay put.

By the afternoon of the second day, Adam was restless. He wore clean clothes for the first time in many months. The food was good, the best he'd had in years, and more than he could possibly eat. Apparently his hosts had special connections. He couldn't imagine that even Londoners ate this good in wartime.

The bed was firm—a real bed with real sheets and pillows—though he still woke abruptly in the middle of the night, as he'd done almost every night since Warsaw. He would stare into the darkness, hands trembling, his back clammy with sweat. The dream varied little from one restless night to the next, though the faces would change—dead faces, their eyes wide open, staring back at him.

The proprietor of the hotel, a proper sort in a tweed jacket, pipe clenched in his teeth, had delivered the *London Times* to his room. The paper was still overflowing with news and pictures of V-E Day celebrations. Adam read it all, from front to back, scarcely able to believe the war had officially ended. It certainly hadn't for the Russians, hunting down the AK in Poland.

Finally, at four o'clock in the afternoon, there was a knock on the door. It was the chauffer, the same one who'd driven him to the hotel without speaking. This afternoon he said, "You have an appointment." That was all.

As the sleek, black Bentley dodged between black taxis and double-decker buses in the congested streets of London, Adam observed the condition of the city. He had left London in 1940, before the worst of the Blitz, but he had heard the reports about nonstop bombing raids. He noticed that part of the British Museum had been destroyed, several tube stations reduced to craters and the Commons Chamber of Parliament badly damaged. A number of windows were boarded up at Buckingham Palace, but Big Ben and Westminster Abbey still stood. Compared to Warsaw, London seemed virtually untouched.

The Bentley pulled into a garage underneath a familiar office building on Baker Street. The chauffer opened the rear door and handed Adam off to a pretty young woman, who introduced herself as Margie, Colonel Whitehall's assistant.

They took the elevator to the fifth floor and walked down the same drab hallway he remembered from his previous visits. At the end of the hall, he was ushered into the same cluttered office he recalled, with two large windows overlooking an interior courtyard. A heavyset man with a pink, fleshy face and a shock of unruly white hair hoisted himself from his chair and stepped around the desk, hand outstretched.

"Adam, jolly good to see you again. What's it been, three years, four? Have a seat."

"Almost five," Adam said as he shook Whitehall's thick hand and sat down on the straight-backed chair in front of the large wooden desk covered with an array of file folders. Whitehall shuffled back around the desk and plopped heavily into the chair. He seemed much older.

"Had a nice rest?" Whitehall asked, rummaging through the folders.

"It was fine." Adam watched the colonel curiously, wondering what the old man had in store for him this time. As one of the founders of SOE—the Special Operations Executive—Whitehall was a shrewd old war horse appointed by Churchill himself with orders to "set Europe ablaze."

They'd certainly accomplished *that,* Adam thought grimly. He'd left behind more than enough corpses to attest to it.

Whitehall found the file he was looking for, flipped through a few papers, then leaned forward, peering over the top of his reading glasses. "Can you guess why you're here?"

It was the type of mind game Whitehall loved, but Adam had little patience for it. Not now. Not after Warsaw. SOE had financed and directed hundreds of sabotage and covert resistance operations throughout the war but, like everyone else, they had looked the other way when Warsaw was leveled. Now the Germans were gone, and the Russians had moved into Poland—different enemy, equally dangerous. "No, Colonel, I really have no idea," he said.

Whitehall grunted, removed a sheet of paper from the file and passed it across the desk. Adam picked it up and read the single paragraph.

> *Sachsenhausen prison camp at Oranienburg, Germany, liberated 22 April, 1945, by Soviet Red Army. Less than 3,000 survivors including, 1,400 women. Most starving and too weak for transport to medical facilities.*

"If I remember correctly, that's where Ludwik Banach was sent after he was arrested by the Gestapo in 1939," Whitehall said.

Ludwik Banach. Hearing his uncle's name so abruptly after all these years took Adam's breath away. After a moment he looked at Whitehall, nodding slowly.

Whitehall opened another folder. "A war crimes investigation team is being sent to Berlin to negotiate with the Russians. They want to get into Sachsenhausen as soon as possible. The Americans are taking the lead, along with some of our boys, but the Polish Government-in-Exile here in London wants a representative on the team. I've recommended you."

Adam had been struggling to follow what Whitehall was saying, suddenly consumed with thoughts of his uncle. "I'm sorry . . . I don't understand. You want me to join a war crimes investigation team . . . representing the Polish Government?"

Whitehall lifted his bulky body out of the chair, lumbered across the room and closed the door. When he sat down again, he took back the sheet of paper and closed the file. "Your uncle, Ludwik Banach, was one of the original founders of the AK. He was known under a code name—the Provider—and he set up an information channel several months before the war broke out to smuggle secret German documents to Warsaw, which were, in turn, passed on to us here in London."

Adam shifted in his chair. He wondered about the code name "Provider," trying to recall if he'd heard it before. He thought that he had, but where, when? A dozen images flitted through his mind like random puzzle pieces, but nothing clicked.

"I didn't discuss any of this with you when you arrived here in '39," Whitehall said, "because your uncle's involvement in the AK was known to only a select few within the Polish Government. At the time, you didn't need to know. Now you do."

"But what's all this got to do with a war crimes investigation—?"

Whitehall held up a hand, stopping him. "Here's something else we know." He paused for a moment, glancing briefly at another piece of paper. "Last month the government of the Soviet Union invited sixteen of the surviving commanders of the AK to a peace conference in Moscow—then arrested them."

Adam sat silently. He had heard about the arrests.

"Do you know what became of them?" Whitehall asked.

"I heard they're locked up in Lubyanka Prison. The whole thing was a sham, a trick to destroy the remaining leadership of the AK."

Whitehall looked at Adam for a long silent moment, then leaned across the desk. "You're quite right. The leaders of the AK are now in Russian hands, all of them, the last roadblock in the takeover of Poland by the Russians. All of them, that is, except Ludwik Banach."

"Banach? My uncle was sent to Sachsenhausen six years ago, Colonel. He's probably . . ." Adam's voice trailed off as he remembered the last time he'd seen his uncle. He was dressed in his best suit and heading off to a "seminar" at the university. He never returned. But that night, before he left, he'd given Whitehall's name and telephone number to Adam.

"I know how much he meant to you, Adam. And it's quite possible he didn't survive. But, then again, perhaps he did. You saw the report, there *were* survivors."

Whitehall pushed back from his desk and stood up, a clear signal the meeting was over, the issue decided. "The Polish Government-in-Exile wants a representative on that investigation team," he said matter-of-factly. "Ludwik Banach is important to them. He's an icon, symbol of Polish independence and all that, especially now, since the arrest of the other AK leaders. They want to know what happened to him."

Whitehall stepped around the desk and laid a big hand on Adam's shoulder. "Sleep on it. We'll meet tomorrow with one of my staffers, chap named Donavan. He'll give you the run-down on Sachsenhausen." Then he cocked his head and looked closely at the thin scar on the side of Adam's face and his mangled ear. "Nasty wound. That happen in Warsaw?"

Adam nodded.

"Well, could've been worse. But we should get those glasses of yours fixed while you're here."

Twenty-Five

11 May

Adam didn't get much sleep. He had dinner in his room, drank half a bottle of wine and smoked cigarettes—real ones from a package, instead of the limp and soggy, hand-rolled ones he'd put up with for years, filled with as much sawdust as tobacco. He lay on the bed and stared at the ceiling for most of the night, thinking about Ludwik Banach, the man who had been like a father to him during the first eleven years of his life, the man who had taken him in a second time, years later, and become his teacher and mentor. The man who had given him a family.

And then, in September of 1939, it was all abruptly and brutally torn away. His uncle's arrest had been part of a *sonderaktion,* the beginning of the Nazi plan to strip Poland of its professors and teachers, its lawyers and political leaders. At least that's what Adam had always thought.

But the conversation with Whitehall brought back forgotten details, memories of his uncle that didn't quite fit the picture Adam had constructed of him. They were just fragments, a few bits and pieces, things that Banach seemed to know when no one else did.

He recalled a conversation in August of '39 when Banach speculated about the secret treaty between Germany and Russia—a week before it happened. Then, just two days into the war, Banach knew before anyone else that Krakow would not be defended. And, two weeks later, he wasn't surprised when the Russians attacked.

An "information channel," Whitehall had called it. And Ludwik

Banach, one of the original leaders of the AK, had set it up. *That's* why he was arrested. Adam thought again about his uncle's code name, "the Provider," almost certain he'd heard it before . . . but then again . . .

He lit another cigarette, watching the smoke curl its way toward the ceiling, remembering the moment when he learned of his uncle's arrest and the cold, ice-blue eyes of the SS officer who delivered the news. Though seething with rage, Adam hadn't had the opportunity to kill that particular officer at that moment. But in all the years since then he'd sought his vengeance through sabotage and assassinations, forcing every emotion from his heart except pure hatred for his uncle's murderers. It drove him, it kept him going, and he'd shut out his past.

Until Warsaw.

Until Natalia . . . a ray of light in a dark world.

But at the one moment when it might have mattered, he had been incapable of doing anything. It was as though his feet were buried in the same cement that had hardened his heart. At the moment when he stood watching from the window of the hospital in Raczynski Palace, he had desperately wanted to run to her and embrace her. But he was immobilized by his fear, his smoldering anger . . . his guilt.

And then she was gone.

Adam woke at dawn, after finally drifting off for a few restless hours. His back ached and his mind was a murky haze. Coffee helped. The English breakfast—with real eggs and real bacon—helped even more. By nine o'clock, when the taciturn chauffer arrived, he was ready to face the day, though he was still uncertain what good would come from a tour of a German concentration camp.

Whitehall's staffer, Tom Donavan, was a tall, lanky man in shirtsleeves, sporting a colorful bow tie. He slid into a chair in Whitehall's office with a file folder on his lap and sat quietly, waiting for instructions.

"Very well, then," Whitehall said, "shall we get started?" He glanced at Adam. "I realize that some of this may be a bit difficult for you, old chap, but God knows, you've undoubtedly seen worse."

Whitehall motioned to Donavan, who opened the folder and removed a sheet of paper. He studied it for a moment before he began. "The Sachsenhausen camp was constructed in 1938 at Oranienburg, just north of Berlin. Before the war most of the inmates were German communists and other political dissidents. After the invasion of Poland the camp was expanded, and the number of inmates grew significantly—Jews, trade union leaders, political prisoners from Germany, Czechoslovakia and, of course, Poland." He looked up from the paper. "We estimate the total number of prisoners sent to Sachsenhausen at more than a quarter million."

"The survivors?" Adam asked.

Donavan laid the sheet of paper on the edge of Whitehall's desk. "We understand there were approximately three thousand survivors when the Russians liberated the camp. We don't have any names, of course, but the Russians will have the records."

"What happened to them?"

Donavan shook his head. "I'm afraid we don't know. The SS guards apparently ran off before the Russians got there, and some of the survivors simply walked away. Those that were left were mostly the ones too sick or weak to leave."

Adam turned to Whitehall. "What happens next?"

Donavan gathered his papers and left the room.

When they were alone, Whitehall said, "You'll be going to Berlin, to join the investigation team and to find out what you can about Ludwik Banach. Of course, we'll provide you with an entire list of names the Poles are supposedly interested in—to make it seem more logical, you understand."

"The *Russians* control Berlin. How are you going to get me in?"

Whitehall leaned back in his chair, which creaked in protest. "A conference is being arranged between Stalin, Churchill and the new American president to implement the Yalta agreements. It will take place at Potsdam, a suburb of Berlin that is still mostly intact. British and American officers are being allowed in to make arrangements." Whitehall swung around and hoisted himself off the chair, once again indicating the meeting was over. "It's a frightfully tedious process, but we should be able to get you in. It'll take a few days to work up the papers. I'll give you a ring."

Three days later Adam met Whitehall for dinner in a small, private dining room at the Lion's Head Pub just down the street from SOE headquarters. It was a smoke-filled, dimly lit place with cracked leather booths and creaky floors. "Is everything set up?" Adam asked when they sat down.

Whitehall was silent as a waiter appeared, delivered two pints of ale and departed. The portly colonel took a sip of ale. "Everything's in order. I've managed to get your U.S. passport renewed and cleared the mission with your State Department. God, they're a bloody tiresome lot, wanting to know what you've been up to the last five years and all that rubbish." He slid the blue passport across the table.

Adam slipped the passport into his pocket and picked up his glass, though he hated the warm, flat British beer. He'd give anything to plunge his hand into a bucket of icy cold water and pull out a frosty bottle of Budweiser. "So, what did you tell them, Colonel? What's my cover story?"

"Yes, yes, I'm getting to that. It's all been worked out. Quite simple actually. Almost everything is exactly the way it really happened. You're a naturalized American citizen and a former American soldier who was born in Poland. You returned to Poland in '36, lived with your aunt and uncle in Krakow, and went to law school. When the Germans invaded in '39, you were deported and came to London—and this is the new part—where you've been ever since, working as a liaison between the British Government and the Polish Government-in-Exile."

Adam took a swallow of beer, grimaced and set the glass down. "So, I've been a diplomat for the last five years instead of an assassin."

Whitehall shrugged. "Bit of a stretch, perhaps, but your State Department bought the story. We threw a lot of paper at them, and they filed it all away."

"I doubt the Russians will be as easy to fool, Colonel."

"No, I'm sure they won't be. And of course that's the sticky part.

The Russians are very suspicious about the Americans and the British, and vice versa. Tensions are high. Everyone is treading lightly to make sure this conference comes off."

"Yes, I understand."

"The Russians, as you know, will not communicate directly with the Poles. That's why I chose you. But they'll investigate. Even though you're an American, and a civilian, the Russians will try to find out everything they can about you. And I don't have to tell you what their attitude is toward the AK."

Adam snorted. "Their *attitude* is to wipe out the AK. But it's a little late to worry about that now, isn't it?"

"It's never too late to change plans. What I want to know is, are you sure the Russians don't know who you are? Are you sure they don't know the name *Adam Nowak?*"

Adam set his glass down. "I haven't used that name in six years." The mention of his name to Natalia in the ammunition cellar flitted through Adam's mind, but he ignored it. "I haven't used it since the day I arrived in Antwerp in November of '39 and telephoned you. I was nobody then, a former student who'd been doing research for his uncle, and I was being deported from the country. And Poland has been in chaos ever since." He paused, glancing around the small dining room, making sure they were alone. "If the Russians knew who I was, Colonel, I wouldn't be here. I'm exactly what your people trained me to be: *dark and silent.*"

Whitehall beamed. "Well then, *Adam Nowak* is back."

The food arrived: baked fish and cold vegetables. They both picked at it with little enthusiasm. After a while, Whitehall wiped his mouth and dropped the napkin on top of his plate, obviously eager to get on with the business at hand. "The Russians will go through the motions at the Potsdam conference, but we doubt they have any intention of allowing free elections in Poland," he said. "According to our intelligence, they're organizing a group of Polish communists in Lublin as the new government."

"I know about those bastards," Adam said. "They're puppets, dancing on strings for Stalin." He folded his hands on the table, clenching his fingers so tightly his knuckles turned white, thinking about the

Russian general, Kovalenko, who lied to him, then watched Warsaw burn. He thought about Natalia and her family in the small village near Lwow, and her brother, the cavalry officer captured and murdered by the Russians.

"I know what the Russians are capable of," Adam hissed. "They're worse than the Germans. They proved that back in 1940 when they murdered thousands of Polish officers in cold blood in the Katyn Forest."

Whitehall grunted and flicked his hand in the air as if dismissing an old myth.

Adam swallowed a gulp of the warm, flat ale and set the glass hard on the table, glaring at Whitehall. "I know the Russians claim the Germans committed the massacre at Katyn, Colonel. And the British and Americans are buying the story. After all, the Russians are our *allies*. I understand the risk. Now, when do I leave?"

Twenty-Six

16 May

The U.S. Army transport plane banked to the left as it began its final approach into Berlin's Templehof aerodrome. Adam looked out the window to catch a glimpse of the city, but the view was obscured by a thin veil of fog.

The American Air Corps officer sitting next to him leaned over and tapped the window. "That's dust," he said.

"Dust?"

The officer nodded. "I'll bet you thought it was fog. I thought so, too, when I flew in here last week. It's dust from all the collapsed buildings. The heat from the fires carries the dust into the air. The whole city's covered with it—what's left of it, anyway."

As they dropped in altitude, snatches of the ground became visible, and Adam turned back to the window. Images emerged through the dust, spreading out in all directions in a brownish-gray monochrome, images that reminded him of pictures he'd seen of the ruins of ancient Rome . . . images that reminded him of Warsaw.

Adam leaned back in the seat and closed his eyes, a jumble of emotions racing through him. For the first time in many years he was back in the company of American soldiers. But these soldiers were different from those he served with in the thirties, during the ambivalence of a peacetime army. In those days he'd worked at his sharpshooting and sniper training with relish because he enjoyed it, but there was always the undercurrent that it really didn't matter because America was at peace and unconcerned about political tensions half a world away.

But the soldiers sitting around him now were different. They had a strong, confident edge, and the battle-hardened swagger of soldiers who had just won a war. He'd fought the same war, though he fought it differently and perhaps for different reasons. All the same, he was pleased to be in their company.

For the first time in what seemed like an eternity, Adam thought back to his arrival in America when he was eleven years old. That first year had been difficult. He hated to leave Krakow, had cried off and on for days, missing his uncle and aunt terribly. When they finally arrived in Chicago, he had felt lost and alone. He had to learn a new language, new customs. Though there were many Poles in their new neighborhood, it was still very strange, very different from Krakow—bigger and noisier, tall buildings, motorcars and elevated street cars.

But gradually, as the months went by, he'd come to feel at home. He had made friends, learned to play baseball and did well in school. Then, seven years later, he had graduated from high school and become an American citizen all in the same day. It was the proudest day of his life. He remembered every detail with complete clarity: writing the test answers, signing the documents, then standing with his father and facing the red-and-white striped flag with the glittering blue field of stars, his right hand over his heart, reciting the pledge of allegiance to his new home. That was the day he decided he would become an American soldier.

Adam looked out the window again, thinking of that simple, carefree time when it seemed as though everything were possible, as though every dream would come true and he could be whatever he wanted to be.

He glanced around at the American soldiers in the transport plane. He felt a kinship with them, but at the same time he was an outsider. They were the first of his countrymen he'd actually been around since the war began.

In all the years Adam had been fighting his own covert war of sabotage and murder behind enemy lines, he'd encountered numerous German soldiers. Most of them had been officers he'd eventually assassinated. And then there were the hundreds of Polish soldiers he'd fought with. They had set aside the sting of defeat and joined the covert warfare of the AK. They had sabotaged German trains and destroyed fuel depots, smuggled information and forged documents. The Americans had fought, and they had suffered hardships and lost friends. But they could never know what it meant to face the enemy on their own home soil, to witness the destruction of their homes and the deaths of their family members—and then to lose that fight. Adam was an American, and he would always be an American. But he was also a Pole, and he knew a part of his heart would forever belong to the country of his birth and the courageous people who faced tragedy again and again without surrendering.

The big four-engine plane bumped hard onto the uneven runway, roaring past wrecked tanks and burned-out trucks. The plane swung to the right, and the terminal building came into view. Adam turned to the air corps officer. "I'm surprised the terminal is intact."

"We didn't want to bomb it because we thought we'd need it," the officer said. "And when the Russians moved in they were in such a rush to get to the Reichstag, they just bypassed it. Hell, Lufthansa was still operating commercial flights out of here until the end of April."

Adam pointed to the Soviet hammer-and-sickle flag flying from the top of the building, just below the enormous stone sculpture of the Nazi eagle.

The officer shrugged. "Yeah, I know. Supposedly, the aerodrome is in our sector, but the Russians are finding every way possible to delay the handover. So far, between us and the Brits, we've only been able to get a little over two hundred men into Berlin. More are trickling in every day, but the Russians have twenty divisions here, so they're calling the shots."

The plane came to a halt, and a detachment of Russian soldiers marched out of the terminal, forming a corridor between the plane and the building. Their khaki uniforms were accented with grayish-green hats adorned with red bands and a solitary gold star.

The air corps officer nudged Adam's shoulder. "NKVD," he said. "A little intimidation as our welcome to Berlin. They're the Russian equivalent of the German SS."

No, they're actually quite a bit worse than the SS. But Adam nodded and peered out the tiny window at the familiar soldiers, the very bastards he'd been evading for months. And now he was going to walk right up to them in broad daylight?

He stood up, put on his new, gray overcoat and fedora, and straightened his tie. His credentials and documents were supposedly solid, identifying him as a Civilian Liaison Officer attached to the U.S. Judge Advocate General—War Crimes Investigation Team. Adam exhaled slowly. He was having a difficult time just remembering the title.

He retrieved his suitcase from the luggage cart and followed the air corps officer into the terminal. They queued up behind a table where two NKVD soldiers, wearing the distinctive blue hats of officers, checked documents. The officers were flanked by a half-dozen NKVD riflemen. Beyond the checkpoint, milling about in a cloud of cigarette smoke punctuated with bursts of laughter and profanity, a group of American and British soldiers awaited the new arrivals.

When Adam reached the table, he handed his credentials to one of the officers who gave him a long hard look, then muttered something in Russian. The second officer laughed at the apparent joke and looked up at Adam, shaking his head.

Adam remained silent and kept his eyes on the officer holding his credentials, wishing he had a pistol under his coat. It was the first time in many years he'd been without a weapon, and he felt naked. The officer was a major with the NKVD 105th Frontier Guards Division. He looked to Adam exactly like every cartoon he'd ever seen of Russian officers—a squat, thick-necked *Ivan*.

The major studied Adam's credentials for a long time, then looked up and snarled a question in Russian.

Adam responded in English, "I don't understand."

The major scowled and called over his shoulder to one of the riflemen.

The rifleman stepped forward, bent down and listened to whispered instructions. Then he straightened up and stepped toward Adam.

"Hold on!" someone shouted from behind the table.

The din of chatter and laughter in the terminal abruptly ceased as an American army officer pushed through the crowd, followed by two American Eighty-Second Airborne troopers toting submachine guns.

The American officer, who was about average in height, but solidly built with curly black hair, looked down at the NKVD major and pointed at Adam. “This man is with us. May I have his papers?”

The Russian glared at the American, and Adam knew that this *Ivan* wanted nothing more than to be able to stand up toe-to-toe, but the American officer had moved in too close. A momentary stare-down ensued. Finally, the Russian major turned back to Adam and held out the papers, gesturing with a jerk of his head for him to move on.

Adam snatched his papers and squeezed past the Russian rifleman, who had not backed off. The two Eighty-Second Airborne troopers fell in behind Adam and the American officer as the crowd of American and British soldiers opened a pathway for them to the terminal exit. Adam heard a British voice shout, “Way to go, Yank. Give the bloody bastard hell!”

Outside, the American officer led the way to the first of two Jeeps flying U.S. flags and motioned for Adam to climb in the backseat. A very young-looking American corporal sat behind the wheel. A moment later, a Russian Army truck rumbled alongside with two NKVD officers in the cab and four scruffy, unshaven Red Army soldiers sitting on benches in the open rear compartment. The driver nodded at the Americans, gunned the engine and swerved in front, spraying the Jeep with dust and bits of gravel. The young American corporal spit the dust from his mouth and mumbled an obscenity as he shoved the Jeep into gear.

As they followed the Russian truck out of the aerodrome, the American officer leaned over to Adam and extended his hand. “Colonel Tim Meinerz, with the Judge Advocate General’s office. I’m head of the investigation team.”

Adam shook his hand. “Adam Nowak. I’m your ‘Civilian Liaison Officer,’ whatever that means.” He jerked his thumb back toward the terminal. “Thanks for your help.”

Colonel Meinerz nodded. “I’m sure they piled it on a little extra for a civilian diplomat. So far they’ve been assholes about everything.”

“Well, you did the right thing. The only way to deal with them is to stick your nose in their face." *Or a knife in their ribs.*

Meinerz laughed. "Of course, a couple of Eighty-Second Airborne troopers carrying submachine guns always helps."

They exited the grounds of the aerodrome, and Adam looked around, squinting, his eyes watering from the dust. He cleaned his glasses and took another look. As far as he could see, not one building was intact. All had been reduced to nothing more than heaps of rubble with an occasional chimney, or the jagged edge of a wall poking through the debris. A smell hung in the air, a musty, masonry smell, like wet concrete mixed with smoke. It did, indeed, look very much like his last memory of Warsaw—and it gave him a morbid sense of satisfaction.

"Technically this area is in our sector," Colonel Meinerz said loudly over the roar of the Jeep. "But both sides are still arm wrestling about the timing of the handover. For now, the Russians are our 'escorts,' and we're under instructions to follow them. They'll take a roundabout route to make sure you see the sights. They seem proud of their handiwork."

Had Adam not been in Warsaw during the last days of the Rising, he wouldn't have believed it possible to lay waste to a city to this extent. Amidst a never-ending expanse of destruction, the only human activity Adam noticed were small isolated groups of women, ragged shawls over their heads, listlessly clearing away piles of bricks from the fronts of shattered buildings. The closer they got to the center of the city, the more appalling the destruction. The piles of debris became mountains, many still smoldering, the rising heat carrying a nauseating odor of rotting flesh. Burned-out tanks and wrecked trucks stood half-submerged in the muck of bomb craters filled with water from broken mains.

By the time they reached the Landwehrkanal, even the rubblewomen had disappeared. Sewer pipes dangled from beneath sections of smashed bridges, disgorging thick, brown liquid into the scum-covered waterway. Adam put his hand over his face to fend off the stench and turned away, glancing up ahead at the Russian truck. The Red Army soldiers lounged in the back, smoking cigarettes.

They followed the roadway along the stinking canal for several minutes, then headed south, away from the city center. Gradually the destruction became less complete, and they passed through neighborhoods where perhaps a third of the buildings were still intact. Little glass remained in any of the windows, and the streets were littered with debris, but the rubble-women had reappeared, shoveling bricks into carts. Now and then a few ragged children scampered over the piles, and two old men, struggling with a cart filled with boards and corrugated metal, stared at them with blank, sullen eyes as the Jeep rumbled past.

Later, they were sitting on the terrace of an immense three-story mansion in Schoenberg, part of the American district of Berlin. The elaborate brick-and-stone structure, complete with marble columns, tiled gables and wrought-iron railings, had somehow survived the Russian bombardments with only a few broken windows.

"The house used to be owned by some big-shot German industrialist," Meinerz said, handing Adam a bottle of dark and refreshingly cold German beer. "He owned some chemical plants in the Ruhr valley, a loyal Nazi, so I heard. Apparently he and the family fled just before Berlin fell, took only what clothes they could carry and the contents of a wall safe in the drawing room. We commandeered it for American officers, and guests."

"How fast the mighty can fall," Adam said, glancing out at the neatly trimmed hedges that surrounded a rose garden just beginning to bloom.

Meinerz took a long swallow of beer, then ran a hand through his thick, curly hair. "I looked over the dossier we received from the Brits. You're a former American soldier with medals in marksmanship and sniper training?"

"That's right."

"But you spent the war as a diplomat in London?"

Adam had prepared himself for how strange that would seem. "I served back in the thirties, peacetime army, Fort Benning, Georgia." He tapped his eyeglasses. "Since then my eyesight's gone bad. Probably from all the damn books we had to read in law school."

Meinerz smiled, taking another swig of beer. "Amen to that." He pointed at Adam's left ear. "You get that at Fort Benning?"

Adam shook his head. "London, buzz-bomb explosion, lost part of my hearing as well."

Meinerz nodded, though Adam guessed he wasn't completely convinced. "The dossier also said you're fluent in German as well as English and Polish. And you studied law at Jagiellonian University in Krakow."

"I returned to Poland in '36, following my discharge from the army."

"So, are you up to speed on what we're doing here and the doctrine of 'crimes against humanity'?"

"That was part of my course work at Jagiellonian."

"Though I guess the operative term now is *genocide,* isn't it?" Meinerz paused for a moment then added, "By the way, wasn't it some Polish fellow who coined that term?"

Adam set his beer on a glass-topped table and looked Meinerz in the eye. "Are you testing me, Colonel?"

Meinerz was about to respond, but Adam held up his hand, stopping him. "The man's name was Lemkin, Raphael Lemkin, a Polish legal scholar who is now an adviser to the U.S. Army. You may have read his book, *Axis Rule in Occupied Europe*. And, you're correct; he did coin the term, 'genocide,' based on his studies of the slaughter of Armenians by the Ottoman Turks. It seems he agreed with Churchill: 'the world has come face-to-face with a crime that has no name.'"

Meinerz finished his beer. "No offense, Mr. Nowak—"

"You can call me Adam."

"No, offense, Adam, but this mission is likely to get pretty dicey. I don't like surprises."

"I don't either. And you may as well know: while I'm here to help you if I can, I represent the Polish Government-in-Exile, and their main concern is to determine the fate of a number of specific individuals."

"I see. You have a list?"

"I do. Would you like to see it?"

Meinerz shook his head. "Let's wait and see how cooperative our Russian allies are first. It may take some doing to get into Sachsenhausen. Another beer?"

Twenty-Seven

17 May

Adam was up early the next morning, woken first by the usual dream, then by sounds of an idling engine and voices from outside. He pulled back the curtain and looked out the window. A U.S. Army truck stood on the cobblestone drive, and two soldiers were unloading crates from the back. A gray-haired civilian wearing a tweed suit coat waited nearby.

After he'd washed up and shaved, Adam put on the new navy-blue suit provided by SOE. He left his second-floor bedroom and made his way along the hallway to the main staircase. Amidst the ruins of Berlin it was hard to comprehend the elegance that now surrounded him. He descended the broad oak staircase, glancing at oil paintings of German landscapes lit with wall sconces, powered by a generator Meinerz said was located on the premises. At the bottom he made his way through a richly decorated parlor with a cavernous stone fireplace flanked by floor-to-ceiling bookshelves.

He paused at one of the bookshelves and scanned the titles. They were mostly German, but included a smattering of English and French, even some Polish. He noticed an entire shelf of German legal volumes: maritime law, taxes, labor law. He skimmed through the volume on labor law, shaking his head at the sections dealing with fair pay and penalties for discrimination. He shoved it back on the shelf, guessing it was written before the Nazis took over, and headed for the kitchen.

Adam stepped through the swinging door, just as the gray-haired man in the tweed coat dragged a crate filled with vegetables and fresh bread through the kitchen. He stopped abruptly and straightened up, to stand stiffly, staring at Adam.

"Guten Morgen," Adam said.

The man nodded. *"Guten Morgen."* He appeared to be in his sixties, thin and tired-looking. The tweed coat was well-worn but clean. The man fidgeted, his eyes darting around as though he were trying to decide what to say next. Before he could respond, a woman stepped into the kitchen from the same back door.

She bowed her head to Adam and said in fractured English, "Good morning. I Frau Hetzler. This is husband." She wore a crisp white apron over a flower print dress, her gray hair knotted in a tight bun. She shot a sharp glance at her husband, who bent down and dragged the crate into a large pantry. Then she bowed again and stepped through a second set of swinging doors, beckoning Adam to follow.

They entered a room Adam had not seen the night before. It was apparently a breakfast room with floor-to ceiling leaded glass windows, half of them boarded up, overlooking the terrace. A massive oak table dominated the center. On a sideboard stood a coffee urn, cups and saucers; a cream and sugar service; and a platter of dark bread and cheese. Frau Hetzler served coffee, then gestured toward the cream and sugar, and the platter of bread and cheese.

Still having trouble adjusting to this sudden abundance of food, Adam settled for coffee, holding the cup under his nose for a moment, savoring the sweet aroma. He was stirring in the cream when a man's voice from behind said, "The coffee is real and so is the cream."

Adam turned and saw Colonel Meinerz standing in the doorway. Frau Hetzler had disappeared. "Good morning," Adam said, and took a sip of the first real coffee he'd had in years. "How is it possible?"

Meinerz stepped over to the sideboard and poured a cup for himself. "The owner had a pile of ten-kilo sacks of coffee beans squirreled away in the cellar along with a dozen blocks of cheese, some bags of sugar and a case of French cognac. As for the cream, the Hetzler's keep a cow locked in a garage in back of the house."

"The Hetzler's are the caretakers?"

Meinerz nodded as he carved a slice of cheese. "Yes. We're all amazed the cow is still here."

"That's because *Ivan* cares more about drinking than eating," said a new voice from the doorway. A stocky crew-cut American officer entered the room and stepped up to Adam. "Major Mark Thompson."

Adam shook the officer's hand and introduced himself.

"According to Herr Hetzler," Thompson said with a laugh, "there was a lot more than one case of cognac in that cellar before the Russians got here. They probably got so plastered they couldn't even see the cow, let alone try to shoot it."

"Mark was the first one here," Meinerz said, "so he got all the inside dope from Herr Hetzler."

Thompson had poured himself a cup of coffee and was stirring in a third spoonful of sugar. "Yeah, it was just the old man and me for the first two days. Frau Hetzler was so terrified of being raped by the Russians that she locked herself in the garage."

Frau Hetzler returned with boiled eggs and sausages, then backed out of the room again as Colonel Meinerz pulled out a chair. "Well, gentlemen, shall we have breakfast?"

When they were seated, Thompson immediately began to spread strawberry jam on a slice of bread. "So, you're the chap representing the Polish Government?" he said to Adam. "And you're American?"

"An American with special ties to Poland," Adam replied.

"You've spent time in Poland, then?"

"I was born there."

Meinerz cut in. "I'll explain it all later." Then he turned to Adam. "I'm not sure I mentioned it last night, but we're the only ones staying here at the moment. Since we don't have clearance from the Russians to visit Sachsenhausen yet, the rest of the team has gone down to Dachau. At least that's in the American sector, and we don't need their fuckin' permission. Mark will be joining them later today. You'll go with me to visit the Russians here in Berlin and see what we can get done."

It was mid-afternoon before Colonel Meinerz was able to set up a meeting. The same young corporal arrived with the Jeep, and Adam and Meinerz climbed in the back.

"No 'escort'?" Adam asked.

"The boundaries of our access zone change almost daily," Meinerz said. "As of 0100 this morning the entire suburb of Schoenberg is part of the American sector. But you can bet your ass they'll be waiting for us at the Kommandatura."

"The Kommandatura?"

"The Allied Control Council, where the occupying powers are supposed to work out the administration of the country."

The Kommandatura was housed in a former Supreme Court building in Schoenberg, a four-story, fortress-like structure with marble stairways arching up from either side, leading to stout, three-meter-high, oaken doors. As Meinerz predicted, a Russian Army truck was waiting for them in front of the building. This time, however, the scruffy Red Army soldiers in the back had been replaced by snappily uniformed NKVD riflemen.

"Looks like we've moved up in the world," Adam said. "Who are we going to see?"

"A Red Army general by the name of Kovalenko."

Adam inhaled sharply then coughed, trying to hide his surprise.

Meinerz glanced at him. "Something wrong?"

"It's nothing," Adam said. "Just some of this damn dust in my throat."

There was a suspicious look in Meinerz's eyes, and Adam turned away, thinking about Kovalenko, wondering if the general would remember him. Most likely he would, but all Kovalenko would have known on that night eight months ago was that Adam was an American diplomat, an obscure envoy sent by the Polish Government-in-Exile. It was the same story now. There was no connection to the AK, no connection to "Wolf."

The driver retraced the same route back to the Landwehrkanal, then crossed the foul-smelling waterway on one of the only intact bridges and headed toward what was left of the Berlin city center.

Adam found some vengeful comfort in the destruction on the other side of the canal. Detouring around craters and mountains of rubble, they followed the Russian truck through a maze of barely passable streets lined with demolished buildings and eventually entered a vast open area of fetid swamps on either side of a pockmarked road. The remains of armored vehicles lay mired in muck, scattered among thousands of charred tree stumps. It took Adam several minutes, mentally recalling maps of Berlin, to figure out where they were. He nudged Meinerz's shoulder. "The Tiergarten?" he asked, remembering pictures he had seen of Berlin's magnificent central park.

"What's left of it," Meinerz said. Then he pointed to a shadowy silhouette off in the distance. They turned right and followed an intersecting road through the murky swamp, drawing closer to the silhouette, now recognizable through the haze as the shattered remains of a colossal building with four towers and a domed top. "The Reichstag," Meinerz explained. "The SS Nordland Battalion was holed up there in the final days of the assault. The Russians circled it with heavy artillery and spent a whole day shelling it before the battalion surrendered. It's a wonder there's as much of it left as there is."

Farther on, they passed the Brandenburg Gate. Atop the heavily damaged monument, where a goddess in her chariot had overlooked the city since the beginning of the nineteenth century, a Soviet flag fluttered in the breeze. Smoky, dust-filled air burned Adam's throat as they turned onto Wilhelmstrasse, the main artery of central Berlin and its administrative center since the days when it was the Kingdom of Prussia. A shiver ran down the back of Adam's neck as they drove past the bombed-out Reich Chancellery, where a cadre of NKVD riflemen stoically guarded Hitler's vacated Fuhrerbunker.

Meinerz leaned over. "I was attached to the Sixty-Ninth Infantry Division, First Army Group. We made contact with the Russians on the Elbe, west of Berlin. The higher-ups had decided that the Russians were going to take Berlin, so we stopped and sat there while the Red Army pounded the hell out of the city for over a week with heavy artillery and Katyusha rockets. They had a million troops closing in on Berlin from three directions, probably killed as many of their own men as they did Germans."

Adam knew about Katyusha rockets, incongruously named after a Russian wartime song about a girl longing for her lost lover. The rocket launchers weren't very accurate but, when they were massed in large numbers for saturation bombardments, they created a hell of a paralyzing shock on enemy troops and civilian populations.

Adam imagined the scene: So Meinerz had just sat there with the rest of the Americans, watching as the Russians laid waste to Berlin, watching those rockets blast the life out of the city. Wasn't it the same thing the Russians had done in Warsaw, standing by while the Germans blew it to hell? Did it matter whether it was Germans or Poles, Russians or Americans? Did it make a difference depending on which countries were allies at the moment? He didn't know. Nobody did.

A moment later they drove past a group of Red Army soldiers smoking cigarettes and jeering at a couple of elderly women hoisting rubble into a horse-drawn cart. Adam instinctively jerked his thumb toward the Russians. "These are the same fucking cowards who sat in their tanks and *watched* while a quarter of a million Polish civilians were slaughtered in Warsaw and the rest driven out of their homes!" He stopped abruptly, realizing he couldn't say any more without creating doubts about his cover story. Meinerz was a savvy, no-nonsense officer, and that suspicious look in his eye had returned. But with that spontaneous outburst Adam realized he had just answered his own question. What happened in Warsaw and Berlin *were* different. They were different because he was in Warsaw when it happened, and Poland was his birth country. It wasn't a matter of who was right and who was wrong. But it *did* make a difference. It made a difference to *him*—because it was personal.

Meinerz raised his eyebrows. "Christ, if you hadn't told me differently, I'd swear you were right there watching it happen."

"We got the reports in London," Adam replied quickly, then changed the subject. "I understand the only German troops left to defend Berlin by the time the Russians got here were old men and the Hitler youth."

Meinerz looked at him for a moment before responding. "Yeah, and most of them ran away when the Red Army moved in. The Russians charged through the streets tossing grenades into the cellar windows of wrecked buildings. They didn't care who they killed—women, children, it didn't matter. Then they'd kick in the doors, drag out any women still alive and rape them."

Adam took a last glance at the Red Army soldiers, wishing once again for a weapon.

Farther along Wilhelmstrasse, the Russian truck slowed as they approached a massive seven-story structure surprisingly intact in this area of almost complete devastation. "Here we are," Meinerz said. "It's the Air Ministry building that Hermann Goering built in honor of his Luftwaffe. I'm told the ceilings of the upper floors were constructed with sixty centimeters of steel-reinforced concrete. That's why it's still standing."

The truck came to an abrupt halt, forcing the corporal to slam on the Jeep's brakes. He mumbled a curse as the NKVD riflemen jumped off the truck and came to rigid attention. Adam and Meinerz climbed out of the Jeep. Adam stiffened as the thick-necked major from the aerodrome emerged from the cab of the Russian truck. He glared at Adam and Meinerz, then spun on his heel and marched briskly toward the steps of the imposing structure. One of the riflemen motioned for them to follow.

Soviet flags stood on each side of the entrance next to hand-lettered signs in Russian and English, indicating this was the headquarters of the Soviet Military Administration. Inside the building, broad corridors extended in two directions as far as Adam could see. Russian officers scurried past them carrying briefcases and armfuls of documents, the sound of their boots echoing off the hard marble surfaces. Three NKVD officers and a young woman in a Red Army uniform sat behind an enormous reception desk flanked by hard wooden benches.

The thick-necked major stepped up to the desk, spoke briefly to the woman, then marched off without a word. Adam and Meinerz looked at each other and turned to follow, but one of the riflemen blocked their way. He motioned toward the benches instead.

Half an hour passed, then forty-five minutes. Finally, the woman emerged from behind the desk, stepped over and said in English, "Gentlemen, if you please to follow me."

She led them down the corridor to the left, up two flights of steps and down another corridor. She stopped at a set of double doors. Adam tensed when he saw the brass plate fixed to the wall. He couldn't read the Cyrillic letters but he knew the name was *General Andrei Kovalenko.*

"Please to wait here," the woman said and stepped inside the office. A moment later she reappeared and motioned for them to enter.

The office was about the same size as the parlor of the mansion Adam and Meinerz were staying in and just as lavishly furnished, complete with oriental rugs and soft leather chairs. Enormous, oak-framed windows, two of them still boarded up, covered the wall opposite the door, offering a gut-wrenching view of the ruins of Berlin. On the wall to the left was a fireplace flanked by oak shelves filled with books, photographs and various trophies.

Adam studied the books while the woman laid a file on the general's desk, spoke a few words to him and left the office. The books were all German—military texts by Clausewitz, Guderian, Rommel, von Kluck, and works of philosophy and science by Goethe, Engels and Einstein. Adam wondered whose office this might have been before the Russians took over. Goering's perhaps?

The tall, broad-shouldered Red Army general that Adam remembered from that night on the other side of the Vistula River stood behind the desk with his hands clasped behind him. Now, however, instead of the dusty field jacket he'd been wearing the last time, General Kovalenko wore a crisp dress uniform with gold epaulettes and rows of campaign medals. Adam thought he looked older, his close-cropped hair grayer, his face more heavily creased.

Sitting on one of the two settees in front of the general's desk was the aerodrome major. He did not stand up.

"I am General Andrei Kovalenko," the general said. His voice was deep and coarse, but his English was as fluent as Adam remembered. He gestured toward the major, who had not looked up or acknowledged their presence. "This is Major Dmitri Tarnov, of the NKVD. I believe you met."

Meinerz stepped forward and held out his hand to the general. "Colonel Tim Meinerz, American First Army, now assigned to the Judge Advocate General."

Kovalenko nodded but did not offer his hand. He turned to Adam, his dark, sunken eyes moving up and down, taking in his civilian clothing. There was not the slightest hint of recognition.

Adam stood where he was and kept his hands at his side. "Adam

Nowak, Civilian Liaison Officer, also assigned to the Judge Advocate General."

Kovalenko stared at him for a long moment then said, "You're an American, Mr. Nowak?"

"Yes, that's correct."

"And what is your connection to the Polish Government, which is in exile in London?"

Adam thought that either Kovalenko did not remember him or that he was very accomplished at deception. Based on his previous experience, he decided on the latter. "I was asked by the British to serve as the representative of the Polish Government for the purpose of investigating war crimes."

Silence hung in the room for a moment as the three men stood on either side of the mammoth desk. Finally General Kovalenko gestured to the settee opposite the one where Major Tarnov sat and then lowered his husky frame into his desk chair. He shook a cigarette from a pack of Lucky Strikes and lit it with a gold-plated lighter. He took a long drag, exhaled a cloud of smoke and asked, "So, what service may we provide, Colonel Meinerz?"

Meinerz leaned forward. "As we indicated in our correspondence through General Parks' office, the Allied War Crimes Investigation Team requests assistance from our Russian allies to visit the Sachsenhausen concentration camp at Oranienburg."

Kovalenko's dark eyes were blank. "Correspondence? We received no correspondence." He took another drag on the cigarette.

Meinerz pressed on. "The correspondence was sent by courier from General Parks' command center to your attention here at the Soviet Military Administration last week."

Kovalenko shrugged. "You have seen the size of this building, Colonel Meinerz. Many hundreds of Russian officers work here. Perhaps it will turn up."

"Yes, perhaps it will," Meinerz replied. "However, since we are here now, shall we discuss arrangements for a visit?"

Kovalenko blew out another cloud of smoke, then he turned to Adam. "So, an American diplomat is representing the interests of Poland and investigating war crimes?"

"Several million Polish citizens were sent to concentration camps," Adam replied.

"*German* concentration camps," Kovalenko said. "You are investigating *German* war crimes."

Adam thought about the hundreds of thousands of Poles sent to Russian gulags, and the murder of thousands of Polish officers at the hands of the NKVD in the Katyn Forest. But he wouldn't talk about that . . . not now. "Yes, General, *German* war crimes."

Kovalenko stared at him in silence and took another long drag on the cigarette before crushing it out in a silver ashtray. Then he abruptly stood up. Major Tarnov stood as well.

Adam and Meinerz both got to their feet. Meinerz said, "General, about the visit—"

Kovalenko cut him off. "I am very busy right now. There are many demands on my time. When I receive your correspondence I will look into the matter."

Behind them the door opened, and a Red Army officer stepped into the office carrying a thick folder. He said something in Russian that included the name "Marshal Zhukov," the Supreme Commander of Russian forces in Berlin.

General Kovalenko glanced at Meinerz and signified with a quick nod of his head that the meeting was over.

Twenty-Eight

21 May

Natalia pedaled her bicycle up the long hill that ran alongside the Rawka River, pushing hard to keep up with Rabbit. Following the winding pathways through dense stands of birch and aspen trees, they often raced the three kilometers from the thatched-roof cottage buried deep in the Bolimowski Forest to the village. It was a race she routinely lost to the skinny, but deceptively strong, lad. He seemed to have grown a head taller in the last eight months, and much hungrier.

And today was no different. As they embarked on their weekly ride to the village to replenish their supplies, Rabbit had challenged her to another race, the winner getting the first pick of whatever vegetables might still be available at the village's market. Natalia knew he would win, of course, and she certainly didn't care. It was fun, and eight months after the nightmare of Warsaw she was thankful for just being alive, let alone having a bit of fun now and then. Especially since they'd been cooped up in the tiny cottage all winter.

Finding the abandoned cottage had been a godsend after their narrow escape from the collection point outside Warsaw, Natalia thought as she watched Rabbit disappear around the bend. The escape had been a stroke of pure genius, planned by the streetwise youth, who had a knack for getting out of tight spots. Natalia, Zeeka and Hammer, along with Rabbit, had blended in with the civilian exodus and slipped out of Warsaw following the defeat of the Rising. When they met up at the first collection point, Rabbit snooped around—just a curious boy asking questions—and learned that every train included a baggage car at the end, used by the Germans to haul supplies beyond Prushkov. Natalia still wore her Polish railway conductor's jacket, Rabbit had pointed out, and though it was filthy and tattered, she didn't look any worse than anyone else. Besides, the train would be packed with fatigued, hot and ornery people, who wouldn't give a damn about anything except getting to the next stop. If Natalia could exert some authority and lead a small group to the baggage car at the back of the train, it might work.

It had succeeded as planned. The four of them had concealed themselves among crates and large canvas sacks filled with everything from works of art to sterling silver, jewelry and clothing that the Germans had plundered during their systematic destruction of Warsaw.

The following day, wearing new clothing and toting two suitcases filled with winter coats, sweaters and hats they'd pilfered from the baggage car, along with a few thousand zlotys that Rabbit had found in the lining of a black leather briefcase, they departed the train at Zyrardow, forty kilometers west of Prushkov on the edge of the Bolimowski Forest. Two days later, as they trudged through the dense forest, Rabbit had spotted the abandoned cottage.

As Natalia pedaled past a meadow, now alive with red poppies and blossoming apple trees, the bright mid-afternoon sun warming her back, she thought about the long, cold winter they had endured in the tiny cottage. The forest had provided ample firewood, and they had been able to find odd jobs with the farmers in the area in return for a stockpile of potatoes, turnips and a bit of salted pork before the weather turned and the snow set in. Hammer had even bartered a log-splitting job for a Russian Mosin-Nagant rifle and some ammunition. Armed with the rifle, he had managed to provide an occasional treat of fresh venison. He had also obtained a Browning 9mm pistol, which Natalia carried in the pocket of the gray woolen coat she'd stolen from the baggage car. She had never asked Hammer exactly how he'd gotten the Browning.

They had escaped the clutches of the Germans and, so far at least, they had managed to avoid Red Army troops and NKVD agents. But Natalia knew the enemy was out there. Zeeka had made contact with an AK cell in Zyrardow that had a wireless radio. She had brought back reports of the NKVD tracking down AK operatives all over Poland and arresting them—or shooting them on the spot.

Natalia took one last glance at the shimmering meadow and inhaled the sweet scent of the apple blossoms before she pedaled back under the green canopy of budding birches and aspens. They'd survived one war, but they were entering another.

When she finally cleared the forest, Rabbit was waiting for her at the edge of the village. It was a dusty, ramshackle collection of thatched-roofed wooden cottages, a cinder-block grain elevator, and a two-story wood-frame building with peeling paint that housed a post office and a blacksmith shop. The most substantial building in the village was a tiny church of white-washed brick with a faded red-tile roof. In a grassy area next to the church stood the weekly market—a dozen wooden stalls with faded canvas awnings covering plank tables set on sawhorses.

"I already checked it out," the boy chirped triumphantly, leading the way to the market. "They have potatoes and beets. I choose potatoes."

Natalia laughed. "You *always* choose potatoes. Why not beets?"

"Because I won the race, that's why."

Natalia and Rabbit filled their backpacks with the potatoes *and* a few beets, along with a half-dozen strips of salted pork, a bag of ersatz coffee and two bars of lye soap. They paid the merchants a few zlotys. Mounting their bicycles, they headed down the pathway toward the forest. As they neared the gravel road that headed west out of the village, Natalia noticed two men standing next to a black, four-door auto parked alongside the road.

"This doesn't look good," Rabbit said. "Maybe we should—"

Natalia cut him off with a sharp look, shook her head and continued on, instinctively sliding her hand in and out of her jacket pocket, feeling for the Browning 9mm pistol. One of the men wore the khaki uniform and gray-green hat of an NKVD trooper, and turning back now would look entirely too suspicious.

They were about to pass the auto when the uniformed trooper abruptly stepped out into the path. Natalia almost fell off her bicycle as she swerved to avoid him.

"Izvinítye," the trooper said and grabbed the handlebars to steady the bike. He was short and plump with a grisly growth of red beard and thick hands.

He had said "excuse me," one of the few Russian phrases Natalia understood. The hair on the back of her neck stood up at the sound of Russian. The trooper said something else, which Natalia didn't understand. She glanced at Rabbit, who shrugged. Then she turned back to the trooper. "It's fine," she replied in Polish. "No problem."

The trooper continued to grip the handlebars.

Rabbit stopped his bicycle next to Natalia, and the trooper launched into a long string of Russian. The boy shrugged again. "I'm sorry, I don't understand?"

"He said to get off your bicycle," the second man said in Polish.

Rabbit dismounted but kept a firm grip on his handlebars.

This man was taller than the trooper and clean-shaven. He wore a dark blue suit, with a black tie and a red hammer-and-sickle pin in his lapel. He was clearly an NKVD agent and the one in charge. He approached Natalia and said, "May I see your papers, please?"

Natalia reached into her pocket and produced the identification card that Zeeka had obtained from the forger at the AK cell in Zyrardow. Obtaining new identification cards and ration coupons had been one of their first orders of business after arriving in the area last fall, but up until this moment, Natalia had never had to use hers. Trying to control her breathing, Natalia handed the intentionally weathered-looking card with her picture on it to the agent.

The Russian studied it for a long time, glancing back and forth from the card to Natalia. Finally he asked, "Where did you get this?"

Natalia feigned surprise. "Where did I get it? At the city clerk's office in Warsaw, as you can see."

The agent frowned. "Yes, I can plainly see that is what is printed on this card. But where did *you* get it?"

Natalia felt her face flush and cursed silently. *Stay calm. Just stay calm.* "I got it at the city clerk's office in Warsaw, in 1938, when I applied for a job in the civil service."

The agent took a step closer. He had a ruddy complexion and narrow, dark eyes. He glanced at the card again, then back at her. "And your name is Katolina Archowski? You were born in Warsaw in 1915?"

"Yes, that's correct."

"And what are you doing in this filthy little backwater, Katolina Archowski? Working for the 'civil service'?"

"No, I'm not. As you know, everyone was forced out of Warsaw by the Germans last September. My brother and I"—she motioned toward Rabbit—"are temporarily staying in the area, doing odd jobs, just trying to survive."

"Staying where, exactly?" he asked.

"In a cottage owned by my family, about three kilometers down this pathway." Natalia pointed toward the spot where the pathway disappeared into the forest. She watched the agent's expression as he studied the pathway, obviously not eager to hike several kilometers into the forest to check out her story.

"Your family owns this cottage?"

Natalia nodded. The four of them had rehearsed the cover story many times. "Our father used it occasionally with some of his friends—for hunting and fishing."

"And your family is there now, in the cottage?"

"No, just my brother and I, and two cousins. Our parents were both killed during the Rising."

"How convenient. And the documents proving your family's ownership of this cottage?"

"I assume they're on file at my parent's bank in Warsaw."

"A bank which is now destroyed, of course." The agent exchanged a few words with his comrade, who still gripped the handlebars of Natalia's bicycle. "You will both have to come with us until we get this cleared up," he said.

"Come with you?" Natalia asked. Her heart pounded so loudly she was surprised the agent couldn't hear it. "Where?"

"That is not your concern. Trespassing is a serious offense."

Suddenly Rabbit lunged toward the agent and rammed his bicycle hard into the man's groin.

The stunned agent doubled over and dropped to his knees, gasping for breath. Rabbit jumped on the bicycle and pedaled hard toward the forest.

The trooper let go of Natalia's handlebars, pulled a pistol from the holster on his belt and spun around, taking aim at the escaping boy.

It all happened in an instant, but it was just the diversion Natalia needed. She pulled the Browning from her jacket pocket and fired into the back of the trooper's head before he could get off a shot.

The NKVD agent stared wide-eyed at the trooper, who collapsed to the ground with a gaping hole in his forehead. But he recovered in an instant. He struggled to stand up, reaching inside his suit coat for his gun.

He wasn't fast enough.

Natalia pointed the Browning at him and shot him in the stomach.

The agent stumbled backward then fell to his knees, gazing down at the widening circle of blood on his white shirt. He mumbled something as blood dripped from the corner of his mouth, and tried to raise the pistol in his right hand.

Natalia took three quick steps and kicked the gun out of his hand.

He looked up at her with glassy eyes, his mouth opening and closing, producing only a raspy wheeze.

The blood from his wound was pooling on the ground, and Natalia was amazed he was still on his knees. She grabbed him by the hair, jerked his head back and thrust the barrel of the Browning into his mouth. She leaned close and whispered. "This is for my brother, you son of a bitch." Then she pulled the trigger.

Natalia stood for a moment staring down at the two dead men, wondering if either of them had actually been among the murderers at the Katyn Forest five years ago. She decided it didn't matter. They were NKVD. That was close enough. She retrieved her identification card and took both of their pistols before jumping back on her bicycle and pedaling quickly into the forest after Rabbit.

"We can't stay here," Zeeka said, pacing back and forth in the cottage's living area a few hours later. "We should get out now, while we have the chance."

Hammer glanced at his watch. It was a little after seven o'clock. "The sun will set in about a half hour," he said. "If they haven't come by now, they certainly won't attempt to find this place in the dark."

"Don't be too sure," Zeeka said. "With two of their agents shot to death, the NKVD will be swarming over this entire area like flies on a manure pile." She looked at Natalia and held up her hand. "I know, I know, you had no choice. Getting in their automobile would've been a death sentence."

"You're damn right," Hammer growled. "We should take out these Bolshevik bastards every chance we get. Besides, I'm certain the villagers had both bodies buried in the forest and the auto hidden away before Rabbit and Natalia got back here."

Zeeka glared at the big man with her hands on her hips. "And when those two agents don't report in at the end of the day? Then what? Do you suppose their superiors are just going to go home and have their dinner?"

Hammer grabbed his rifle from the corner near the wood-box. "You two decide what to do. I'll go help Rabbit keep a lookout."

After Hammer left, Natalia propped her elbows on the table. A wave of guilt washed over her. "Goddamn it, I feel terrible for those villagers. Hammer is right; I'm sure they got rid of the bodies and the auto. But we know what the NKVD is like. Sooner or later they'll show up in that village, and they'll find out what happened one way or the other."

Zeeka pulled up a chair and sat down facing her. "And when those poor folks have a gun pointed at their heads and their daughters are about to be raped, they're going to lead them right here."

Natalia slumped back in the chair. "Christ, what a mess."

"Look, what's done is done. If I'd been in your shoes I'd have shot those sons-of-bitches too. But right now we have to decide where to go. I don't think we should even wait until morning. We should move out now. The AK cell in Zyrardow has a safe house. We could hide out with them for a day or two until we sort things out."

"If we leave right after dark we should get there before dawn," Natalia agreed. "And they have a wireless. They can send out an alert."

Twenty-Nine

22 May

Almost a week had passed since the brief, unproductive meeting with General Kovalenko, and Adam was restless. Colonel Meinerz had given up after three days of waiting for Kovalenko's office to return his calls and had joined the rest of the team in Dachau, leaving Adam alone. Before he left he had instructed Adam to stay in Berlin and work through General Parks' staff to gain access to Sachsenhausen, but after several days of bureaucratic inaction Adam was going stir-crazy.

New American officers had arrived and taken up lodging in the former Nazi's mansion. They were friendly enough, but spent little time there except for meals. Unlike himself, Adam assumed they had real jobs to do. The meals were another thing—heavy, gravy-laden schnitzels with dumplings and spaetzel, all prepared by Frau Hetzler from the incredible supply of food that kept arriving on U.S. Army trucks. It had been years since Adam had eaten this well, and his stomach was rebelling.

So this evening he passed up dinner, took an apple from the pantry and went out for a walk. The weather had warmed during this third week of May, and it was still light when he returned a little after eight to find a group of American officers playing bridge on the terrace. He was chatting with them when Frau Hetzler announced that he had a telephone call. Adam followed her into the house and made his way to the foyer near the front door where a silver-plated telephone stood on an ornate, inlaid-wood table. He picked up the receiver. "This is Adam Nowak."

There was a pause, then a gruff voice said, "Kovalenko."

Adam flinched. He had given up on hearing from the general's office and certainly from Kovalenko himself. He took a deep breath before responding, "Good evening, General. It's good to hear from you."

"Have you had dinner?"

Adam consulted his watch. It was eight thirty and he wasn't hungry. "No, I have not."

"Come to the Adlon Hotel." There was a click, and the line went dead.

Adam slowly placed the receiver back in the cradle. *Dinner with Kovalenko?* The Adlon Hotel was in the Russian sector. Should he go alone? Meinerz and the rest of the team were in Dachau. He wondered if Kovalenko knew that.

After pondering the bizarre situation a few minutes longer, Adam borrowed a Jeep from the group of Americans and drove to the Kommandatura where a Red Army officer stood next to a Russian GAZ-11 with a Soviet flag mounted on the right front fender. It was the same officer from the meeting outside Warsaw eight months earlier, the one with the scarred face and black eye patch. Adam climbed into the GAZ-11, and the officer settled behind the wheel.

Neither spoke during the short drive to the world-renowned hotel on the corner of Wilhelmstrasse and Unter den Linden, long a favorite haunt of journalists, diplomats and celebrities like Herbert Hoover, Charlie Chaplin and Marlene Dietrich. In the silence Adam examined the interior of the GAZ, running his hand across the hard leather seats. As an official staff car, it wasn't nearly as luxurious as the Mercedes-Benz Bravo had stolen from the Germans in Warsaw. It seemed equally powerful though, but it was noisy, and the ride much stiffer, obviously designed for Russian roads.

Adam peered out the window as the automobile slowed and came to a stop in front of the massive hotel building next to the bombed-out wreckage of the British Embassy. Though still primarily intact, the majestic six-story brick façade of the hotel was blackened from a recent fire, and most of the windows were boarded up. Enormous glass lanterns—remarkably undamaged—stood atop stone pillars on either side of the main entrance, which was also boarded up.

The Red Army captain opened the auto's rear door, and Adam stepped out. He followed the Russian through an improvised doorway a few meters from the main entrance, then down an eerily dark corridor and up a flight of stairs, the odor of charred wood hanging heavily in the stale air. They proceeded down another corridor, then entered a brightly lit dining room filled with people.

Adam gazed in astonishment as white-gloved waiters, wearing black waistcoats and red bow ties, squeezed between closely spaced tables, carrying tureens of soup and platters of sausages, potatoes, roast beef and chicken. The captain tapped his shoulder and pointed to a table at the far end of the noisy, smoky room where General Kovalenko sat at a table set for two.

The general looked up as Adam approached the table. "Welcome to the Adlon Hotel, Mr. Nowak." Kovalenko motioned for him to sit, then picked up a carafe of red wine and filled each of their glasses. He took a long drink, draining half of the glass. "The food isn't very good, but I've ordered onion soup and sauerbraten. It may take them a while." He polished off the wine and refilled his glass.

"That will be fine," Adam said, as he took a sip of the sweet wine. "I'm sorry Colonel Meinerz is not here to join us," he added. "He was called to Dachau."

The general lit another cigarette and regarded him through the smoke. "I know. Dachau doesn't interest you?"

"It does, but my instructions are to remain here and arrange the visit to Sachsenhausen."

They sipped the wine. Adam lit a cigarette of his own and glanced around the teeming dining room, marveling at the rich mahogany walls, patterned carpet and plumed pillars that rose to the ceiling. Each table was set with white linens, sterling silver flatware and a single rose in a cut-glass vase. The elegant room was populated mostly by Red Army officers accompanied by young German women with painted faces, incongruously dressed in evening gowns in the midst of this shattered city. "I'm surprised the hotel is still able to maintain such a dining room," he said.

"Marshal Zhukov ordered us to leave it standing. He thought the officers might need a place to dine. Fortunately this section of the hotel was spared the worst of the fire." Kovalenko snapped his fingers, and a waiter appeared with another carafe of wine. "I'm told the SS was dining in this very room, celebrating their Fuhrer's birthday as we were advancing on the city. Do you like the wine? The cellar was well-stocked when we arrived. Apparently the SS left in a hurry."

"It's nice," Adam replied. "What is it?"

"The Germans call it Trollinger. Too sweet for me," the general said. "But we can't have everything."

The trivial conversation continued until the food arrived. Adam tried the soup first. It was thick with onion but lacked cheese or seasoning. The sauerbraten was tough and the potatoes overcooked, but the heavy brown gravy was all he could taste anyway. He would be glad to get away from German cooking. Across the table, Kovalenko appeared to feel the same.

When they finished, the waiter cleared the table and reappeared a moment later with two snifters of cognac. Kovalenko lifted the glass to his nose and inhaled, gently swirling the amber liquor. "Rémy Martin, one of the few things the French ever got right," he said. "The SS were kind enough to leave several hundred cases in the cellar as well." He fixed Adam with a sharp look over the rim of the glass. "Did you serve in the Polish Army, Mr. Nowak?"

The curious question caught him off guard. Was it possible that Kovalenko did *not* remember him from their meeting that night across the river from Warsaw? Adam doubted that and took a sip of cognac before answering. "I'm an American, General Kovalenko. I served in the American Army from 1933 to 1936."

"But you were living in Krakow when the war broke out."

As Whitehall had predicted, the Russians had investigated his background. "I was living there as a civilian, following my discharge from the army. I studied law at Jagiellonian University. I had family in Krakow. But you probably know that."

"The Germans deported you in '39?"

"Yes."

"So, you returned to America?"

"No, I went to London," Adam replied. The well-rehearsed story rolled out more easily than he'd expected. "I worked as liaison between the British and the Polish Government-in-Exile. I was born in Poland, you see, so my fluency in the language is—"

Kovalenko abruptly lit a cigarette and blew out a mighty cloud of smoke. He leaned forward, glancing around the dining room. "A word of caution, Mr. Nowak. Major Tarnov has taken an interest in you."

Adam's spine tingled. "And why would Major Tarnov be interested in me?"

Kovalenko waved a hand dismissively. "Ah, he's NKVD. They're all paranoid. You weren't associated with those AK anarchists in Poland, were you?"

Adam maintained eye contact with Kovalenko. *This is a very clever—and very dangerous—adversary.* "No, General, I wasn't."

The general's expression was inscrutable as he flicked cigarette ashes into the sterling silver ashtray. Then his eyes moved toward the front of the dining room. "Ah, our drivers have arrived."

Two Red Army officers stood at the entrance. General Kovalenko led the way across the room. He motioned toward the officer with the eye patch who had driven Adam to the hotel. "Captain Andreyev will drop you back at the Kommandatura. He will meet you there again at 0700 tomorrow and drive you to Sachsenhausen. Perhaps you will find what you're looking for."

Thirty

23 May

The roadway leading into the Sachsenhausen concentration camp passed through the center of a stately three-story brick building. Captain Andreyev stopped the GAZ-11 in front of the gate and exchanged a few words with the Red Army soldiers standing guard. Adam grimaced as he read the sign in the center of the gate: *Arbeit Macht Frei.* Yes, "work will set you free" . . . *until they send you to the gas chamber.*

The gate opened, and Captain Andreyev gunned the engine. They drove through and stopped on the other side in a vast semicircular courtyard surrounded by concrete and stucco barracks that radiated outward like the spokes of a giant wheel. Standing prominently at the far end of the bloodstained cobblestone yard was a wooden gallows that Adam guessed was large enough for a half-dozen people.

A moment later the car door opened, and a burly Red Army officer with a thick, black mustache climbed into the backseat next to Adam. Captain Andreyev turned around and said in English, "This is Major Vygotsky. He is in charge of the camp detail. I will interpret for him."

Major Vygotsky chattered in Russian, and Andreyev repeated in English, as they drove through the immense facility. Adam forced himself to concentrate on what was being said and tried to keep his mind off his precarious situation—an American, formerly a saboteur and an assassin for the Polish AK, touring a German concentration camp with two Russian officers. He felt relieved every time Vygotsky wanted them to have a closer look at something and he could leave the confinement of the auto.

The Russian seemed eager to display his knowledge of the gruesome camp. As they stood inside one of the empty barracks, lined on each side with three-tier wooden racks still reeking of mold and human excrement, Vygotsky stated matter-of-factly, "There were more than sixty-five thousand prisoners in Sachsenhausen as late as January 1945, including ten thousand women. About half of them were marched out by the SS before we liberated the camp. Most of those left behind were too weak to march, and the SS finished them off in the 'pit' with machine guns."

It sickened Adam to think that his uncle had been here. "I heard you found several thousand survivors," he managed to say.

Andreyev translated, and Vygotsky nodded. "Most of them died within a week. All the rest were taken to hospitals in nearby towns." While Andreyev's facial expression remained inscrutable, his shoulders twitched occasionally. Adam noticed a tightness in his voice as he related Vygotsky's remarks, as though he were disturbed by what he was hearing.

"Do you have their names?" Adam asked.

Upon hearing the translation, Vygotsky roared with laughter. "Names? Yes, we have names—tens of thousands of names, addresses, identification numbers—books full of names. You will see." They got back in the auto and sped off.

They drove on through the deserted facility with Vygotsky explaining the details and Andreyev continuing to translate. They passed factory buildings where slave laborers had worked to death producing bricks, army boots and munitions, past the medical facility where SS doctors conducted medical experiments on prisoners too weak for work, finally arriving at the "pit." Andreyev pulled over and stopped the car next to a concrete trench as long as a football field and about half as wide. The flat bottom and slanted sides were covered in blackish-red stains. "The survivors told us the SS only used this for quick and dirty executions," Vygotsky said, "like right at the end. Most of their work was done at Station Z."

Adam looked at the grisly killing field. *Quick and dirty, like right at the end.* Had his uncle been among them?

After a moment they set off again, and Andreyev drove to a large, windowless, concrete-block structure. He circled around to the back and stopped. A neat row of pressure cylinders were chained to the side of the building, each one bearing a prominent red-and-white placard emblazoned with a skull and crossbones.

"This is Station Z," Vygotsky said. "The SS gassed more than a hundred thousand prisoners here." He jerked his thumb toward the cylinders. "*Zyklon-B,* it's a pesticide, the same thing they used at Auschwitz—very effective. Care to have a closer look?"

Adam stared at the austere concrete building and the lethal gas cylinders, grateful now for every SS officer he'd assassinated. He turned to Andreyev.

The Russian looked him in the eye. With a barely discernible motion, Andreyev shook his head.

"I've seen enough," Adam said.

The final stop was a wood-frame structure that looked like a small house, at the far end of the triangular-shaped camp. They got out of the car and walked up to the door. Vygotsky took out a ring of keys, fumbled around for the right one and unlocked the door. He clicked on the lights and motioned for them to enter.

Adam stood in the doorway and looked around in amazement. Covering all four walls were floor-to-ceiling shelves filled with hundreds of identical leather-bound volumes. A wooden table and four chairs filled the center of the room. Major Vygotsky tossed his hat on the table. He lit a cigarette and turned to Adam. "The records are very well organized, typical SS devotion to paperwork and detail. Now, what can we do for you?"

Adam produced the list of names he'd received from Whitehall. The last one was his uncle's: Ludwik Banach.

It was a tedious process. Vygotsky pulled down volume after volume, while Adam flipped through the pages, read the various entries and wrote down the information. He had to admit, Whitehall's staff had done their homework to make the exercise seem legitimate while obscuring the real reason for the search. Some of the persons on the list had been incarcerated at Sachsenhausen and some had not, as one might expect after the uncertainty of six years of war.

After what seemed an eternity, Adam found what he was looking for. On page 164 of volume 87, an entry read:

> *Reference Number: 23864*
> *Date of Admission: 10 November 1939*
> *Surname: Banach*
> *First name: Ludwik*
> *Domicile: Krakow, Poland*
> *Religion: Roman Catholic*
> *Occupation: University Professor*
> *V293*

Adam stared at his uncle's name, finding it extremely difficult to maintain the detached demeanor of a diplomat investigating a list of names. The cold realization that his uncle had actually been imprisoned in this hellhole crushed him like a vise. He took his time writing down the information, being careful to prevent his hand from shaking. When he finished, he took a deep breath before he trusted himself to look at the Russian officers, who were chatting at the other end of the table. He motioned to Vygotsky and pointed to the last item of the entry. "*V293* . . . what does that mean?" he whispered.

Vygotsky stepped around the table and leaned over the volume. Then, suddenly seeming agitated and talking rapidly, he scanned the shelves on the back wall of the room. He pulled down volume 293 and flipped through the pages.

"He says that this volume contains information on prisoners that were subject to special circumstances," Andreyev said to Adam. "That's very unusual. He says he's only seen it one other time."

Vygotsky continued to rifle through the pages of volume 293, then stopped and ran his finger down a page halfway through the thick leather-bound book. He bent down and studied one of the entries, then turned to Adam, his expression darkening into a scowl.

Adam read the neatly printed words.

> *Reference Number: 23864*
> *Surname: Banach*
> *First Name: Ludwik*
> *Date of Release: 10 July 1940*
> *Destination: Krakow, Poland*

> *Special Orders: Transferred to the personal custody of Hans Frank, Governor, Government General – Poland.*

He read them a second time, just to be sure.

"What does it say?" Andreyev asked.

Adam swallowed hard before he answered. "It says he was transferred to the personal custody of Hans Frank, Governor of Poland."

The next evening, on the terrace of the German industrialist's mansion in Berlin, Colonel Meinerz leaned forward in the wicker chair across from Adam. "Hans Frank?" It was the first time he had spoken during Adam's detailed report of the events of the last twenty-four hours. "Let me make sure I've got this straight. You're telling me that one of the persons on that list of yours was released from Sachsenhausen into the personal custody of Hans Frank, the Nazi Governor of Poland, the son of a bitch they call 'the Jew Butcher of Poland'?"

Adam nodded, still unable to comprehend what it could possibly mean.

Meinerz had come directly back to Berlin upon hearing from Adam. It was late in the evening, and they were alone. "So, after not returning phone calls for a week, Kovalenko suddenly invites you to dinner, then arranges a private tour of Sachsenhausen. Any idea why?"

"No."

Meinerz stood up and paced around the terrace. "Do you know that Hans Frank is in the custody of the American Army? That he is being held in Nuremberg, charged with war crimes?"

Adam felt as though he were drifting through some macabre dream. "Yes, I know."

"Jesus Christ, Adam, the Russians will jump all over this. Most of the big Nazi fish got away from them and surrendered to us—Goering, Speer, Jodl, Frank. They're really pissed off about it and grabbing anyone still out there. You're damned fortunate those prison guards and your driver were Red Army officers. When the NKVD finds out about this, you can bet your ass we'll be hearing from them." Meinerz pulled out a pack of Camels, lit one and blew out a long column of smoke. "Who was this person anyway—the one released into Frank's custody?"

"His name is Ludwik Banach."

"Yeah, that's fine, but who the hell is he? And why was he on that list?"

Adam studied Meinerz. He seemed like a straight-up sort, an honest army officer and JAG lawyer. Adam felt he could trust him, and he owed him something after the deception. But he couldn't tell him everything. "He's my uncle."

"He's *what* . . . your *uncle?*" Meinerz stood with his hands on his hips, glaring down at Adam. "What the fuck is going on here, Adam . . . Mr. Nowak . . . or whoever the hell you really are? Why didn't you tell me right up front what you were looking for?"

"I couldn't. I'm under orders from the British SOE."

"Well that's just great! You've got some secret orders from the British spooks that I don't know anything about. What else haven't you told me? Do the Russians know that Banach is your uncle?"

"Yes, it's possible they do. I know that they've investigated my background. I lived with my uncle when I was going to law school in Krakow. It wasn't a secret."

"But I'll bet they didn't know that your uncle was sent to Sachsenhausen and then released into the custody of Hans Frank."

Adam shook his head. "I'm sure they didn't. *I* didn't know that until yesterday."

Meinerz stubbed out his cigarette in an ashtray. "Why would Hans Frank have had any interest in your uncle, a university professor?"

Adam tried to focus, to come up with an answer, but it was hard to concentrate. His emotions were drained from anxiety over what this could mean. Finally, he just said, "I don't know." It was true. He had no idea, though he had been thinking about nothing else since reading the extraordinary entry in "volume 293." He stood up, so that he was face-to-face with Meinerz. "Look, I'm sorry about the deception. I had no idea about this business with Hans Frank. But I need your help. I've got to report this to SOE, and I've got to do it quietly. It can't go through channels."

Meinerz was silent for a long moment, looking Adam in the eye. Finally he nodded. "Yeah, sure, whatever you need."

Thirty-One

26 May

Adam sat on the front porch of the former Nazi's mansion, reading *Stars and Stripes,* trying unsuccessfully to relax. The front page article was an optimistic report on the upcoming Potsdam conference, filled with flowery references to "freedom across Europe." Adam snorted and tossed the paper to the ground. Obviously the reporter had never dealt with the Russians.

Adam's message had been delivered by special courier to Colonel Whitehall the day before, and he'd received a return message earlier this morning to expect Whitehall's assistant, Tom Donavan. He'd spent most of the last twenty-four hours trying to sort out the stunning revelation about Banach and Hans Frank, but nothing made sense. Especially troubling was the date of his uncle's release—July, 1940. Adam had been sent back to Poland by the SOE in the winter of 1940 and spent the next four years on his covert mission of murder, never knowing his uncle had survived Sachsenhausen and was back in Krakow. How many German officers had he assassinated avenging his death? Did it matter? They were all monsters who deserved to die, weren't they?

Adam sighed, pulled back to the moment as a British army staff car pulled up in front of the house. Donavan exited from the backseat, wearing the same bow tie he'd worn in London and lugging a thick briefcase. They exchanged a brief greeting, and Adam led him to the library.

It was a dark, heavy room of walnut shelving laden with leather-bound books. A large, bronze plaque, emblazoned with the coat-of-arms of the Teutonic Knights, hung above a granite fireplace. They sat facing each other across a mahogany table.

"Your message was a bit of a shock, to say the least," Donavan said without preamble. "Ludwik Banach released from Sachsenhausen by order of Hans Frank—quite extraordinary. If it gets out, it'll cause quite a stir within SOE—and with the Polish Government in London, I should think. Whitehall's keeping a lid on it for now, but it won't last."

Adam kept silent, though it was difficult. Cause a stir within SOE? What the hell did these people think it did to *him?*

"We've been doing some homework on Herr Frank since your call," Donavan said. He opened the briefcase and pulled out a stack of papers. "Obviously, you have no idea why Frank would have ordered Banach's release."

"I can't imagine," Adam said. "Frank didn't arrive in Krakow as governor until a month or two after my uncle's arrest and my deportation from Poland."

Donavan nodded. "Well, let's review a bit about this chap, shall we? Our people have prepared a summary." He pulled a pair of reading glasses from his shirt pocket and scanned the top page of the stack of documents. "Frank is a lawyer, one of Germany's most noted jurists, a degree in economics, as well." He ran his finger down the page. ". . . associated with fascists during his university years . . . joined the German Workers Party in 1919 . . . became connected with National Socialist Party around 1928."

Donavan continued flipping through the pages. "Hmmm . . . elected to the Reichstag in 1930 . . . became president of the Reichstag after the Nazis came to power in 1933, appointed to the post by the Fuhrer himself."

Donavan turned over the last page. "He served as the Reich Commissar for Administration of Justice, the Bavarian State Minister of Justice, and he was President of the Academy of German Law from 1933 until 1942. That's quite—"

Adam held up his hand. "Excuse me, what did you just say?"

Donavan looked back at his notes. "He was the Bavarian—"

"No, the next thing."

"Ah, he was the President of the Academy of German Law."

Adam turned the words over in his mind, trying to remember.

"Does that mean something to you?" Donavan asked, peering over the top of his glasses.

"What were the dates?"

Donavan looked back at the notes. "1933 until 1942."

Adam absently rubbed the thin scar on the left side of his face, though it was numb and he barely felt it. "Banach was very involved in the development of Poland's judicial system," he said, thinking back, reconstructing details from past conversations with his uncle. "He'd studied the system in Germany for many years. In one of his classes on constitutional law he talked about a conference he'd attended a few years earlier, in 1935, I believe. The conference was organized by this group, the Academy of German Law." Adam paused. "Yes, I think that's right, a conference of the Academy of German Law."

Donavan frowned. "Are you sure? That was quite some time ago."

"I was working as his legal assistant when he mentioned it in the class. I helped prepare his lecture notes. I'm sure it was this same organization. You say that Hans Frank was president of the academy?"

"He founded it."

They were both silent for a long time as other things flitted through Adam's memory, more bits and pieces, nothing that had ever seemed out of the ordinary—until now. "This academy, what was it all about?"

Donavan flipped through the file and pulled out another sheet. "The Academy of German Law . . . Frank organized it in the early thirties, I believe. Yes, here it is. That's right, shortly after the National Socialists came to power. It included some of the most prominent legal scholars in Germany." He scanned the document, speaking faster, as if he were warming up to the subject. "Their objective was to structure a legal framework that would preserve Germany's independent judiciary within a totalitarian regime. The academy members consulted with other European legal scholars to safeguard these concepts within the National Socialist Government."

Consulted with other legal scholars?

Donavan looked up from the paper. "What is it? . . . Mr. Nowak?"

"I think my uncle and Hans Frank knew each other," Adam said.

He could barely get the words out.

"Well, it's possible they might have met, at this conference perhaps, but—"

"No, it's *more* than that. This whole thing you just said, the part about an 'independent judiciary within a totalitarian government.' That was one of Banach's major fields of expertise—the same kind of thing this academy was attempting to do. My uncle exchanged correspondence for years with some institution in Germany. I was his assistant, working in his office. I never paid much attention at the time, but I remember packets arriving with German postmarks." He stared up at the ceiling. After a moment he looked back at the lanky Englishman. "My God, I think they really *did* know each other."

Donavan got to his feet and shoved the files back in his briefcase. "We'd better arrange a secure telephone line to London."

They telephoned Whitehall. Then, later in the day, Adam called him a second time, after spending several more hours with Donavan, digging through the stack of research files on Hans Frank. "We found something else," Adam said.

"What is it?" Whitehall asked brusquely.

"A copy of a paper Hans Frank wrote in 1936 describing the circumvention of trial procedures in the Russian Bolshevik government, how the Russian courts were nothing more than *pathetic pawns on the perilous chessboard of the NKVD.*"

"Well, that's damned poetic. But I don't understand. What does it mean?"

"My uncle wrote a paper on the same subject a year earlier," Adam replied. "The year he attended the conference in Germany."

Whitehall grunted. "I still don't—"

"He showed it to me," Adam said quickly, recalling now with complete clarity a meeting one afternoon in his uncle's office. "He kept the paper alongside a thick leather-bound book in his personal library—*The Proceedings of the Academy of German Law*. He wanted me to read the paper and give him my opinion. He didn't do that very often."

"Well, perhaps Frank was interested in the same subject, but—"

Adam interrupted. "It's the phrase—*pathetic pawns on the perilous chessboard*—it all came back to me when I read Frank's paper. Banach used the exact same phrase in *his* paper . . . a paper that was never published."

Whitehall was silent for a long moment. "Well, that might explain something," he said finally.

"What do you mean?"

"The Russians are causing some trouble. Our delegation in Berlin was contacted by Major Tarnov of the NKVD, damned nasty chap, I must say. They've slammed the door on any further visits to Sachsenhausen. And now Tarnov is demanding that all records relating to Hans Frank be off-limits until they complete their investigation."

"Investigation of what?"

"The connection between Ludwik Banach and Hans Frank—and Banach's activities after he returned to Krakow."

Adam almost dropped the phone. "Oh Christ! They think Banach collaborated with the Nazis." He slumped back in the leather desk chair and stared at the ornately carved wooden beams in the ceiling of the former Nazi's study. "This whole thing is insane," he snapped. "My uncle has been back in Krakow since 1940, and I never knew. I was gone, doing what *you* trained me to do. Doing things that—"

"He'll start looking for him," Whitehall said.

"What?"

"This NKVD agent, Tarnov. He'll start looking for Banach."

Adam suddenly felt dizzy. "We've got to find him first."

"Do you have a contact?" Whitehall asked. "Someone in the AK who was in Krakow, someone who might know where to start?"

"I don't know . . . they're all gone . . . they're . . ." Adam closed his eyes to let the dizziness subside. Slowly an image formed in his mind, an image of Natalia sprinting toward a sewer in Warsaw, wearing her blue railway conductor's uniform. That was her code name, *Conductor*. She had mentioned it that last night in Warsaw, in the ammunition cellar. "Not very original as code names go," she had said. Snatches of the conversation gradually came back to him. Just before the artillery shell hit and they bolted out of the cellar, Natalia had said, "I heard from a priest . . ."

And then . . . what else? There was something else, something he had been trying to remember for weeks. Adam forced himself to concentrate, trying to recall her exact words. "I heard from a priest, of all things . . . then someone I never met . . ."

It struck him like a thunderbolt.

". . . someone I never met, called the *Provider*."

Adam abruptly stood up, squeezing the telephone receiver, his knuckles turning white. *Of course! How could I have missed it?* Natalia had never finished the thought, but now it was suddenly clear.

The Conductor . . . The Provider.

She was part of the channel!

"There may be someone," he said into the telephone. "Someone I knew . . ."

"What's his name?" Whitehall asked.

"*Her* name," Adam said. "Her name is Natalia."

Thirty-Two

6 June

Krakow's Medieval Stare Miasto District stretched for almost two kilometers along the Royal Way, from the Gothic tower of St. Florian's Gate in the north to Wawel Castle, high above the banks of the Vistula River, in the south. And in the center of the district, encircled by the wide pathways and greenery of the Planty park, was the Rynek Glowny, the largest market square in Europe, and since the thirteenth century, the heart and soul of the City of Kings.

Natalia walked briskly across the Rynek Glowny and continued south, along the narrow, cobblestone streets of the Stare Miasto, struggling to suppress her anxiety about being back in the city after months of hiding out in forests and AK safe houses. She knew she should keep moving, blending in with the pedestrian flow so as not to attract attention.

But she paused for a moment at the base of Wawel Castle and glanced up at the towering edifice of the royal palace and the adjoining cathedral where every Polish monarch for a thousand years had been coronated. Flags fluttered from the towers high above the stone fortifications that surrounded the castle. They were Soviet flags now, the hammer-and-sickle having replaced the swastika since she'd last been here. The Russians had driven out the Germans, the flags had changed, and the black uniforms of the SS were replaced with the khaki uniforms of the NKVD.

Natalia sighed and turned away from the castle, following the route she had taken dozens of times over the years, through the tree-lined paths of the Planty park then along a labyrinth of narrow, Medieval streets where the rich ensemble of Gothic, Renaissance and Baroque architecture remained unscathed by the war that had ravaged the rest of the country.

The Stare Miasto was crowded at this hour, but subdued. There were few vehicles, and pedestrians avoided conversation with strangers, averting their glances as they'd been conditioned to do through the long, dark period of occupation. The shops had little to sell, the cafés offered only a few meager selections and the hundreds of churches were mostly empty under the atheist influence of the communist occupier.

Natalia continued on, moving briskly, avoiding eye contact. She made her way along the boulevards bordering the Vistula River to the Kazimierz District, once a separate city and for three hundred years the home of Krakow's Jewish quarter. It was a familiar route, a familiar city, remarkably undamaged yet inexorably altered, its royal soul deadened.

Twenty minutes later, in the heart of Kazimierz, Natalia walked down a long narrow street, lined with stone walls on either side, and entered the courtyard of the Church of Archangel Michael and Saint Stanislaus. A rose garden was in full bloom, and an elderly man hunched over, clipping grass at the base of a towering oak tree. The tree shaded a rectangular pond with a granite statute of the saint at its center.

Natalia wore stout shoes and dark trousers, a white long-sleeved shirt and a gray vest. Along with her felt hat and short brown hair, she could be taken for a man by a casual observer, which was safer than a woman alone. But caution was a habit, and she turned away from the elderly man.

She glanced at her watch. It was one o'clock in the afternoon. And it was the sixth of June, a Wednesday. She paused for a moment, studying the red-brick church building with its twin towers and high-peaked tile roof, then slowly climbed the curved, limestone staircase. With her cap folded under her arm she entered the gloomy sanctuary.

There was a faint odor of incense in the air, and she waited a moment for her eyes to adjust. Then she knelt, made the sign of the cross and slipped into the last pew on the right, the one closest to the confessional in the rear of the sanctuary. There were several people ahead of her, and she withdrew a rosary from her pocket. She closed her eyes, absently fingering the beads, thinking about the extraordinary message that had brought her back here.

It had arrived on her last day at the AK safe house in Zyrardow. The NKVD had been closing in, investigating the shooting of the two agents, and it was time to move on. Zeeka had made contact with another AK cell in Lodz and had sent Hammer and Rabbit on ahead. But as Natalia and Zeeka were gathering their things, the AK wireless operator came down from the attic with a message.

"From Lodz?" Zeeka asked.

The wireless operator shook his head. "It's from SOE in London. It was sent several days ago, but it was routed through three different cells before I got it." He handed Natalia the message. "It's for you."

"From the SOE in London? Are you sure it's for me?"

"It's addressed to 'The Conductor' and that's you," he said with a shrug.

Natalia hesitated then unfolded the paper and read the decoded message:

MUST LOCATE PROVIDER

REPEAT: LOCATE PROVIDER

Avoiding trains and keeping to the back roads and small villages, it had taken Natalia a week to get to Krakow. She had traveled first with Zeeka as far as Lodz, where she parted with her friends and comrades-in-arms. Rabbit had wanted to go with her, but whatever awaited her in Krakow, Natalia knew that she had to do this alone.

She had no idea why SOE wanted to locate the Provider. She had never even known there was a connection between the two. During her years acting as a courier, she'd never met the Provider. It was just a name, someone in the channel who passed documents to the priest, or to someone in between. She really didn't know; she didn't need to know. All she had ever needed to know was to kneel at the confessional in this church between one and two o'clock in the afternoon on a Wednesday.

But why would SOE contact *her?* She hadn't been an active part of the channel since she left for Warsaw at the start of the Rising, almost a year ago. *Why now? Why me?* She had no idea. But it was an assignment, and it was not her place to question it. She had been instructed to locate the Provider. And this was the only place to start.

A woman sitting on Natalia's left nudged her elbow, indicating that it was her turn. Natalia took a deep breath, then stood up, and stepped around a marble pillar and over to the confessional. It was an enclosure of rich mahogany wood, a bit larger than a telephone booth, with a peaked roof and adorned with intricately carved scrollwork. A slatted wooden screen allowed the penitent to communicate with the priest waiting inside. Natalia knelt on the velvet-padded kneeler and whispered into the screen, "In the name of our Lord, I come seeking."

There was a moment of silence. Then a voice from the other side whispered back, "Whom do you seek, my child?"

Natalia paused before responding, her tension momentarily relieved at the familiar voice and the customary words. "I seek the one who has provided us with so much."

"It has been a long time," the voice said.

"A difficult time," Natalia answered.

When the voice spoke again there was a slight tremor. "The Provider is no longer among us."

Natalia's stomach tightened as she stared at the wooden screen. She swallowed hard, carefully choosing her next words. "Did he leave anything for me?"

Another moment of silence. Then the voice said, "This afternoon, five o'clock, Dietla and Stradomska. Get on the tram for Stare Miasto."

The tram was crowded, and Natalia had to stand. The priest sat on the right side of the car, a newspaper folded under his arm. When they reached the first stop in the Stare Miasto District, the priest got up and pushed his way through the crowd. Natalia followed him out of the car.

As they walked toward the Rynek Glowny, Natalia waited for the priest to say something, but he was silent. He was a thin, severe-looking man in his sixties with sharp, chiseled features and an imperious manner that Natalia had at first found intimidating. In later years she had little patience for the man's haughty nature and had rarely spoken with him outside of the confessional.

"What happened to the Provider?" she finally asked.

The priest remained silent, walking briskly, staring straight ahead.

"Is he alive?"

The priest slowed his pace and glanced at her. His face, partially hidden under his black, wide-brimmed hat, was pale, his eyes blank and distant. "He's gone."

"Gone where? When?"

"I don't know. The day before the Russians arrived, he was just . . . gone."

They entered the Rynek Glowny, an enormous cobblestone square surrounded by church spires, Medieval merchant halls and former residences of Krakow's elite. They found a table at an outdoor café where they tried to order tea but had to settle for bitter, ersatz coffee. While they exchanged small talk about the weather, Natalia glanced at the folded newspaper which the priest had laid on the table. Inside would be an address handwritten in the margin.

The priest finished his coffee, his dull eyes darting around the busy market square. He whispered, "God be with you, my child." Then he stood and walked away.

An hour later, Natalia found the address in the eastern section of the Kazimierz District. For centuries it had been a crowded, bustling district of apartment buildings, banks and synagogues, tailor shops and jewelers, butchers, clothing stores, and outdoor markets. The Jews who built it were gone now, murdered in the concentration camps of Auschwitz and Treblinka, and little remained in the area except decaying buildings, emaciated stray dogs foraging for scraps in the gutters, and crippled beggars, dressed in rags, holding empty cups in their bony hands.

Repeating the same procedure she had used during the war, Natalia let herself into the run-down apartment building and retrieved a key from the mailbox in the vestibule. She climbed the creaking stairs to the third floor, wondering if anyone still lived there, unlocked the door to a room at the end of the hall and locked it behind her. She opened the window a crack to let in a bit of fresh air, and stood in the center of the room listening to the silence. Then she got down on her knees and reached under the bed.

The package was wrapped in the usual brown paper, but it was smaller than the others she had retrieved in the same manner from other rooms in other shabby buildings. This package felt more like a book than the files of documents she had received during the years she had spent as part of the channel.

Natalia sat on the bed and held the package, turning it over in her hands, thinking about the hundreds of documents that had been passed along this same channel during the years of Nazi occupation, documents that she could never resist reading despite putting herself in even greater jeopardy by possessing the information. There had been meticulously prepared reports, including daily logs and charts filled with numbers, revealing inconceivable atrocities taking place behind the walls of Auschwitz, Treblinka and the other death camps of Poland.

Extreme risks had been taken by everyone along the channel, from the Provider to another unknown contact, then to the priest and finally to Natalia, who carried them on the train to Warsaw. The identities of those involved in the channel were a carefully guarded secret. Natalia knew only those with whom she had direct contact: the priest, Berta and Falcon. The documents had been passed along, and perhaps some had made it to London, New York or Washington. Natalia had no way of knowing. It hadn't done any good. That much she knew. The carnage had escalated. Hundreds of thousands were murdered, perhaps millions.

And now, when the war had ended, the Nazis were defeated . . . *the Provider is gone?*

Natalia stared at the package, her nerves taut as piano strings. Then, very slowly, she removed the wrapping paper. Inside was the customary envelope containing currency, a thin stack of fifty-zloty banknotes to help her with expenses. There was also a book.

It was a leather-bound notebook, similar to a diary. The cover was worn, the edges of the pages frayed, as if having been thumbed through hundreds of times. She opened the cover and stared for a long time, confused by the handwritten words on the first page.

The Journal of Ludwik Banach

Thirty-Three

7 June

Natalia woke suddenly. A noise in the hallway . . . footsteps . . . creaking stairs.

Then it was quiet.

She waited a moment, then stepped quietly across the room, parted the curtain and peeked out the window, squinting in the early morning sunlight. A scrawny, three-legged dog hobbled across the cobblestone alley, sniffing in the gutter. She dropped the curtain and glanced at her watch. Seven o'clock. What time had she fallen asleep? She had no idea.

The journal!

She spun around, her eyes darting to the bed, then to the floor. It was there, the tattered leather-bound notebook that she had spent the night reading. She picked it up and sat down on the bed, leafing through the pages, as though to make certain the words hadn't changed.

She spent an hour going over it again, rereading carefully the last installments of Ludwik Banach's implausible journey that had ended with his disappearance just before the Russians arrived in January. When she finished, Natalia stared at the book, trying to decide what to do, then slipped it in the inside pocket of her vest. She put on her hat, opened the door slowly and peeked down the dim hallway.

Nothing.

She hurried down the steps, then made her way through the eerily quiet, litter-strewn streets, past vacant buildings marred with graffiti and broken windows, until she arrived at Szeroka Street, once the central market area of the Jewish community, now largely deserted. She slipped into a grimy café and took a seat in a booth at the rear.

The foul-smelling proprietor brought over a cup of lukewarm coffee and asked if she wanted anything else. Over at the bar a shriveled ghost of a man sat on a stool, slurping something out of a bowl. She shook her head, and the proprietor shuffled away. Natalia took a sip of the bitter concoction, grimaced and slumped back in the cracked leather seat, overwhelmed by the story of Ludwik Banach.

Ludwik Banach . . . Adam Nowak's uncle . . . was the Provider.

It was almost impossible to believe, but it had to be true. Banach said it himself in the journal, in an entry he wrote in 1940:

> *I waited for this day for nine months, thinking every hour in the hellhole of Sachsenhausen about my Beata, and my nephew, Adam.*

Adam had mentioned his uncle's name—Ludwik Banach—that last night they spent together in the ammunition cellar. Natalia had forgotten about it in all the chaos of the Rising, and it hadn't registered again until she read that entry in Banach's journal.

It was just as Adam had said. Banach was arrested in 1939 and sent to Sachsenhausen. But then, after being released into the custody of Hans Frank, Banach was back in Krakow and working at the new Copernicus Memorial Library, Frank's pet project and the reason Frank arranged for Banach's release from Sachsenhausen. But Banach had used that opportunity to re-start the channel, the channel *she'd* been part of. Natalia recalled the words Banach wrote in the journal in 1942:

> *I realized what had to be done with documents I'd smuggled out of the library. The channel has been resumed. Many are taking risks to preserve what little is left of our humanity. May God grant that our efforts are not in vain.*

Natalia rubbed her forehead, still scarcely able to comprehend it. Ludwik Banach was the Provider. He smuggled documents out of the library—documents describing the unspeakable atrocities taking place within Poland's death camps—and resumed his Resistance work. Banach wrote that entry in the journal in 1942, about the same time she'd been contacted by the priest and given a new assignment. She'd been working as a conductor on the railway since being sent to Krakow by the AK. The priest was her contact, and by 1942 she had a well-established routine, working the daily round-trip from Krakow to Warsaw. With only a slight change in her routine to include "confession" at the Church of Archangel Michael and Saint Stanislaus on Wednesdays, and a modification to her black conductor's bag, she had become part of the channel.

Natalia glanced around the sleazy café that stank of cooking grease and body odor. The bartender was reading a newspaper, and the ghostly man was asleep with his head on the bar. She was hungry but couldn't bear the thought of what might have been in the bowl. She took another sip of the bitter coffee, then propped her elbows on the table and tried to sort things out.

Was it just pure chance that she and Adam had met in Warsaw, in the midst of the Rising, neither one knowing of their mutual connection through Ludwik Banach? As improbable and remarkable a coincidence as it seemed, there was no other explanation.

Natalia thought about their conversation that last night in Warsaw when she and Adam had huddled in the ammunition cellar. Adam had told her about his uncle, Ludwik Banach, who was arrested in 1939 and sent to Sachsenhausen, then his aunt's arrest the next day. "I'm sure they're both dead by now," he'd said. So, on that night, just ten months ago, he hadn't known that his uncle had been released from Sachsenhausen four years earlier.

But someone knew. The British, someone at SOE, must have learned just recently about Banach's release from Sachsenhausen. And they knew he'd been sent back to Krakow in the custody of Hans Frank. Why else would they send her a message instructing her to locate the Provider?

Natalia left the café and walked quickly through the mostly deserted streets of the eastern Kazimierz District, avoiding eye contact with the occasional cripples and beggars and hunched figures lurking in the shadows—the desperate, starving people who could slit her throat for a single zloty.

She made her way back toward the busy Stare Miasto District, where she could disappear into the flow of pedestrian traffic on a work-day morning. Her stomach ached from hunger, and she eventually spotted a small bakery with a half-dozen poppy seed rolls in the otherwise empty display case. She purchased one, found a bench on the Rynek Glowny and sat down, thinking carefully about what to do next.

Why was the message sent to her? If SOE needed to contact the Provider why wouldn't they have sent the message to the priest? Natalia took a bite of the poppy seed roll, then another, and it was all gone. She was still hungry. She considered walking back to the bakery to buy another when the answer suddenly struck her.

SOE didn't send the message to the priest because they don't know about him. They sent it to her because she was their only contact. She was the only one they knew of with knowledge about the Provider.

Natalia's stomach growled, but she ignored it, trying to sort out the mystery. There were only three people besides the priest who knew that the documents she smuggled out of Krakow originated with someone called the Provider: Falcon, Colonel Stag and Adam. She felt a lump in her throat when she thought about Adam and what they might have had together, in some other place, at some other time.

But Adam had died that night at Raczynski Palace.

That left Colonel Stag or Falcon. The hair on the back of her neck bristled, remembering her last encounter with the drunken, abusive Falcon. But he wasn't high enough in the AK chain of command to have contact with SOE.

Was it Stag? She remembered what the colonel had said the day she arrived in Warsaw with the smuggled documents: "You've done excellent work. And so has the Provider, whoever he or she is." Stag's uncertainty about the Provider's gender indicated he also hadn't known Banach's identity.

Natalia stood up and walked around the square to clear her mind. In the end it was insignificant how the British had learned Banach's secret identity. What really mattered was what they *didn't* know. *They know Banach is the Provider, but they don't know about the journal.*

And they didn't know about Banach's stunning discovery in January of 1945, one of the last entries in the journal. As Natalia recalled the revelation she had read in that entry, icy fingers raced up her spine. *What if I'm the only other person who knows this? Banach is gone. Is it all up to me?*

Natalia reached into her vest pocket and touched the journal.

She felt very alone.

Thirty-Four

8 June

At his office in Berlin, General Andrei Kovalenko hung up the telephone and banged his fist on the massive oak desk. *"Výdi von!"* he shouted at the orderly who had just entered the office carrying a tray of coffee and biscuits. As the orderly scurried away, the general glared at Captain Andreyev, who sat across from him. "What the hell is that son of a bitch, Tarnov, trying to pull?" he demanded.

"He's NKVD," Andreyev replied. "You never know with them."

The general gestured toward the phone. "That was the American, Colonel Meinerz, the head of their War Crimes Investigation Team. He wants to know why the NKVD is demanding that Hans Frank's records be sealed. It was the first I'd heard of it. Apparently, Tarnov called him and didn't bother to inform me." Kovalenko leaned over the desk. "And how did Tarnov find out about the American diplomat's visit to Sachsenhausen?"

"I think Major Vygotsky, the commander of the camp detail, was the leak, sir. He's disappeared."

The general pulled a cigarette from a crumpled pack and snapped his gold-plated lighter three times. It didn't light. "Goddamned piece of shit," he grumbled and tossed it into the wastebasket.

Captain Andreyev pulled out his own lighter and lit the general's cigarette.

Kovalenko stared at the younger officer, thinking, considering. Andreyev had been with him a long time. The young officer had put his own life at risk, and lost his eye, rescuing Kovalenko from a Luftwaffe attack in Stalingrad. He could be trusted. And now, perhaps, he could be useful. "What I'm about to tell you, Captain Andreyev, stays between the two of us."

Andreyev nodded.

Kovalenko continued. "I first encountered Dmitri Tarnov in 1940, while I was serving out my sentence in Siberia, thanks to the treachery and deceit of the NKVD. It was in late April, a miserable, rainy night, and I was swabbing the floor in the kitchen of the guard's mess hall . . ." He paused as Andreyev raised his eyebrow. "Yes, swabbing the floor. As hard as it may be for you to believe, Captain, that's what those of us who were caught up in Stalin's great purge were reduced to . . . until they needed us again in '41." He took a long drag on the cigarette. "As I said, I was swabbing the floor, and I overheard a conversation between three NKVD officers sitting around a table in the mess hall with a bottle of vodka. One of them was quite drunk and was bragging about an assignment he'd just carried out in the Katyn Forest."

Andreyev pulled his chair closer. "Tarnov?"

"*Da,* Tarnov. He'd just returned. And he was *bragging* about it, bragging how he'd carried out the execution of four thousand Polish officers—'Polish dogs,' he called them—and bulldozed their bodies into a ditch."

Andreyev whistled softly and adjusted his eye patch. "So it's true . . . about Katyn? It was the NKVD?"

"Of course it was. And that son of a bitch Tarnov was directly involved. More than twenty thousand Polish officers and members of the intelligentsia were all intentionally murdered, at three different locations. One of those locations was in the Katyn Forest. I heard him boast about it with my own ears."

"Does Tarnov know that you overheard?" Andreyev asked.

Kovalenko shook his head and pulled out another cigarette, which Andreyev lit for him. "No, he never knew I was there." The general stood and walked over to the window, looking out over the ruins of Berlin. "I've been loyal to Russia, Captain Andreyev. Even after being fingered by the NKVD in the purge of '37, even when we invaded

Poland in '39. As you know, I'm half Polish, yet I remained loyal and did my duty. But what happened at Katyn . . ." Kovalenko was silent for a long time, smoking his cigarette, staring out at what little remained of Berlin.

Andreyev cleared his throat. "Is there anything you can do about it . . . about Tarnov and Katyn?"

Kovalenko turned around and smiled at his young protégé. "Perhaps. For years, especially after '43 when the Katyn massacre became public and Stalin blamed the Germans, I tried to find out as much as I could about Tarnov. He's related to Beria, you know."

"Beria, the Commissar of the NKVD?"

"A second cousin, I believe. And Tarnov obviously believed that if he carried out the massacre at Katyn, Commissar Beria would be grateful, and Tarnov would move right up the ranks of the NKVD. But it never happened. Beria ignored him, and Tarnov languished in low-level assignments."

"Well, that would explain Tarnov's reputation."

"For being a brutal, vindictive son of a bitch? Indeed it would. All of my contacts informed me that Tarnov was bitter, very bitter, and wanted revenge."

"Revenge against Beria? That would be a dangerous game. What did he do?"

"Nothing. At least nothing I knew about . . . until now." Kovalenko sat down at the desk again and crushed out the cigarette. "You will recall, Captain Andreyev, that when Tarnov showed up in Warsaw last January, he insisted on safe passage to Krakow."

"He'd been given the authority, directly from Beria," Andreyev said, "to take control of Frank's headquarters in Wawel Castle."

Kovalenko waved his hand dismissively. "*Nichivó,* never mind about his authority. That's typical NKVD bullshit. The important thing is that Tarnov spent an entire week personally searching every room in the castle."

Andreyev leaned forward, furling his brow. "What was he looking for?"

"Damned if I know. But it must have been extremely important to him. He also interrogated and beat the hell out of the few grunts

Frank left behind. It seemed a little extreme at the time, even for an NKVD fanatic like Tarnov."

"Some obsession with Hans Frank, it seems."

Kovalenko continued. "Tarnov served in Poland from 1939 until the Germans drove us out in '41."

"Did he ever meet Frank?" Andreyev asked.

Kovalenko managed a wry smile. "A good question, Captain. A question I've been thinking about for some time. And now *you're* going to dig into it and find out."

Andreyev cocked his head, a concerned look in his eye.

Kovalenko sighed. "*Da*, I know what you're thinking. *Nichivó*. Just be cautious. Go about it quietly, ask some questions. See what falls out."

The captain nodded and got to his feet.

"One other thing," Kovalenko said.

"Da?"

"Contact this American diplomat, Adam Nowak, and ask him to meet me tonight for a drink at the Adlon."

"Do you think he'll come . . . after what's happened?"

Kovalenko nodded. "He'll come."

Thirty-Five

8 June

Captain Andreyev parked the GAZ-11 in front of the Adlon Hotel and turned to Adam. "My instructions are to wait for you here. I believe you know the way."

Adam stepped through the opening in the blackened front façade of the hotel, climbed the stairway and walked down the dim hallway, wondering what he was getting into. It had been almost two weeks since he'd heard from Whitehall about Major Tarnov launching an investigation into his uncle's dealings with Hans Frank, and now he'd been abruptly summoned to a late-night meeting with General Kovalenko.

He stepped into the lavish dining room and glanced around. It was eerily quiet. The tables were set with the same white linens and sterling silver as before. But the lights were lower now, there were no vases with roses, and the room was empty except for a table at the far end where General Kovalenko sat smoking a cigarette. As Adam approached the table, Kovalenko snapped his fingers, and a waiter suddenly appeared carrying a silver tray with a bottle of vodka and two glasses. The waiter set the tray on the table and departed.

The general crushed out his cigarette in the cut-glass ashtray and glanced up. "Welcome back, Mr. Nowak. Have a seat." When Adam sat down, Kovalenko filled both glasses and held his up. "*Nazdaróvye!*" he said, draining it in one gulp.

"Cheers," Adam replied and did the same. It was Russian vodka, distilled from wheat with a sharp bite and a hint of charcoal. But it was ice cold and slid down Adam's throat easily.

Kovalenko refilled the glasses, and they drank again.

The general thumped his empty glass on the table, his dark eyes meeting Adam's. "So, your trip to Sachsenhausen was a success?"

Adam was sure that Kovalenko had been completely briefed on everything that had taken place. There would be no point in withholding anything. The only thing he was uncertain of was why Kovalenko had summoned him. "I found the information I was looking for."

"So, it was a success. And this information pertained to a relative of yours—your uncle, to be more precise."

Adam took a moment to light a cigarette. "Seems like you already know everything, General."

"I know your uncle is the university professor who was released into the custody of Hans Frank, the German war criminal."

"Then you know more than I do."

"I doubt that," Kovalenko said. "But do you know that Major Tarnov has issued an arrest warrant for him?"

Adam took a long drag on his cigarette. Meinerz had warned him that a warrant was likely to be issued, but hearing about it from a general of the Red Army was another matter. "My uncle is not a criminal," Adam said in as even a tone as he could manage.

"How do you know? It has been many years since you have seen him. Is that not correct?"

"I *know* my uncle."

Kovalenko persisted. "You have no idea what he has been doing, or what his relationship was with this mad dog, Frank, or why he was brought back to Krakow. Is that not correct?" The general glared at him. "But we all know what took place in Poland and Russia. We all know what happened at the hands of Nazi bastards like Hans Frank."

Adam clenched his teeth. "Why did you ask to meet me, General?"

At that moment the waiter returned and set a platter of *zakuska* in the center of the table. He was a small man with a pasty complexion and black hair, slicked back and greasy. He avoided eye contact as he carefully placed a small plate and fork in front of each man, then backed away.

General Kovalenko reached over, speared an anchovy, placed it on a cracker and popped it in his mouth. "They're from the Black Sea," he said, "very good. Please, help yourself. It's taken some effort to bring Russian food to this place."

Adam detested anchovies and looked over the platter, filled with an assortment of cheese, caviar, marinated mushrooms, pickled herring and smoked salmon. He scooped some caviar onto a thin, rye cracker and took a bite.

Kovalenko refilled the vodka glasses, and they drank again.

Kovalenko casually looked over the *zakuska* platter, apparently not yet ready to explain the reason for the meeting.

"Why did you arrange for me to visit Sachsenhausen?" Adam asked.

"Perhaps I was in a generous mood," the general replied as he speared a pickled herring. "But it seems your discovery has created a fuss with the NKVD—with Major Tarnov, in particular."

"Because he thinks Ludwik Banach is a war criminal?"

Kovalenko nodded. "Of course. But that's just NKVD bullshit. There are hundreds of collaborators and saboteurs out there: Poles, Czechs, Romanians, as well as Germans. This is something else."

Adam leaned back and rubbed his palms on his trousers. "What do you mean?"

Kovalenko's dark eyes narrowed, almost disappearing in the creases of his face. "What *was* your uncle's relationship with Hans Frank?"

Adam hesitated. "I don't know."

Kovalenko picked up the vodka bottle and filled both glasses. He lifted his and tilted it toward Adam. "Be cautious, Mr. Nowak."

Adam sat silently in the rear seat of the GAZ-11 as Captain Andreyev drove back to the Kommandatura. A dozen questions rattled around in his mind, but he doubted Andreyev would be likely to answer any of them. He seemed a decent sort and, unlike Kovalenko, there had been a flicker of recognition in his one good eye when he saw Adam for the first time in Berlin. Adam was certain Andreyev remembered him from the meeting outside Warsaw but, like his boss, he hadn't acknowledged it. He wondered how Andreyev felt about the lie Kovalenko told him that night, how he felt about watching the Nazis destroy Warsaw and the valiant fighters of the AK.

It was almost midnight when they arrived at the Kommandatura. The area appeared deserted except for Adam's borrowed Jeep. He bid Andreyev good night and walked across the gravel parking area.

As Adam approached the Jeep, the headlights suddenly flashed on, freezing him in place. He shielded his eyes as three figures moved toward him, silhouetted against the glaring light.

Major Tarnov came into view, followed closely by two NKVD riflemen. "You out late, Mr. Nowak," Tarnov said, in fractured English.

"The Kommandatura is in the American sector, Major Tarnov, in case you hadn't noticed. There is no curfew here."

From the corner of his eye Adam noticed Captain Andreyev getting out of the GAZ. "Mr. Nowak was at a meeting with General Kovalenko," Andreyev called out.

Tarnov kept his eyes on Adam but shouted at Andreyev in Russian and motioned for him to get back in his car.

Andreyev walked toward them slowly and responded in English. "I am under instructions from General Kovalenko to see to it that Mr. Nowak returns safely to his billet."

"I don't give fuck what order have, Captain!" Tarnov shouted. "This man harbors fugitive, Ludwik Banach, enemy of Soviet Union."

Adam took a step closer to Tarnov, ignoring the riflemen, who abruptly raised their weapons. "Harboring a fugitive? What the hell are you talking about, Major? I haven't seen Ludwik Banach in six years!"

"Turn around, Mr. Nowak, hands behind," Tarnov hissed. He motioned with a flick of his head, and the two riflemen stepped forward.

Andreyev shouted at Tarnov in Russian.

Tarnov shouted back but stopped abruptly as two Jeeps roared into view and skidded to a stop. Four American Eighty-Second Airborne troopers armed with submachine guns jumped from the Jeeps and sprinted forward, instantly surrounding Tarnov's group. The Russian riflemen spun around, shielding Tarnov between them, pointing their weapons at the Airborne troopers.

"Tell your men to stand down, Major Tarnov." Colonel Meinerz marched into the circle of light, pointing a finger at the Russian. His bearing was firm and authoritative.

Tarnov glared at Meinerz but didn't respond.

"Tell your men to stand down," Meinerz repeated sharply.

"This man harbors fugitive. He is under arrest."

"On whose authority?" Meinerz demanded.

"*My* authority! Commanding officer, NKVD in Berlin!" Tarnov barked an order in Russian, and one of the rifleman reached for Adam's arm.

Instantly the American Airborne troopers closed in.

"Don't anyone move!" Meinerz shouted. He stepped closer to Tarnov. "The Kommandatura is within the American sector, Major. If your men lay a hand on Mr. Nowak, I will order these troopers to shoot them."

Meinerz and Tarnov glared at each other.

The NKVD riflemen stood their ground, but their eyes darted around nervously.

Adam's heart beat faster. He clenched his fists and shifted his feet slightly, ready to take out the rifleman who'd reached for his arm.

Finally Tarnov shouted another command, and the riflemen lowered their weapons. His face contorted in rage, Tarnov pushed past Meinerz and stalked across the parking area to another auto that had been concealed in the shadows.

As Tarnov's car sped away, Adam finally relaxed and unclenched his fists. Meinerz slapped him on the back. "Fucking NKVD."

"How did you—?"

"Captain Andreyev called me . . . just before you left the Adlon."

Adam turned to Andreyev, who said, "General's orders."

Kovalenko's final words of caution echoed in Adam's mind. *What the hell is going on?*

"This isn't the end of it," Andreyev said.

Thirty-Six

10 June

Captain Andreyev hesitated at the top of the stairs, peering into the gloom of the shattered building, one of the few still standing in Berlin's Mitte District. While the Mitte had always been the political and commercial center of Berlin, Andreyev found it hard to imagine this shattered section of the city would ever reach those heights again. The entryway of the building was littered with chunks of plaster and bits of broken glass, the window at the far end boarded up. An array of odors assaulted his nostrils—charred wood and masonry dust, human sweat, tobacco and stale beer.

An abrupt burst of light penetrated the murkiness as a door swung open at the bottom of the stairs and two figures emerged, laughing and stumbling. The larger of the two was a Red Army officer, who finally managed to grip the handrail on his third try and pulled an inebriated woman up the steps. The couple staggered past Andreyev and lurched through the outer door into the night.

Andreyev descended the staircase, following the din of laughter and drunken shouts, and peered through the smoky haze of the *Rats Keller.* A long, copper-topped bar was packed three-deep with sweat-soaked Red Army soldiers, all of whom looked as though they'd been there most of the day. Behind the bar, two beleaguered Germans hustled back-and-forth, shoving mugs of beer and glasses of schnapps into dozens of out-stretched hands.

In the center of the stifling room, a few couples swayed listlessly to the barely audible crooning of Frank Sinatra. Small, round tables covered with heavily stained red-and-white checkered tablecloths lined the perimeter of the room. While Andreyev enjoyed some American music, particularly jazz, Sinatra wasn't his style and neither was this disgusting German beer hall. The less time he had to spend here, the better.

It didn't take long for Andreyev to spot her, sitting alone at a table in the far corner. She had silky, black hair tied to one side with a pink ribbon and cascading over her bare left shoulder. The dress was yellow, slinky and low-cut, designed for business in the shadowy world of after-hours Berlin. She nodded when their eyes met, her fingers resting gently on the rim of an empty glass.

Andreyev snapped his fingers at a waiter—a boy of no more than sixteen—ordered two glasses of schnapps and slid into the chair across the table from her. "Fraulein Schmidt?" he asked quietly, though if he'd shouted no one would have heard him over the raucous clamor in the ancient drinking hall.

She eyed him curiously, then fished a package of Chesterfields from a black beaded purse, withdrew a cigarette and held it up, waiting for a light. "That depends on who wants to know."

Andreyev took his time. She appeared to be in her late thirties, her voice was husky, her German refined and cultured, a native Berliner, he thought, upper-class, aristocratic . . . at least she used to be. Finally, he pulled a lighter from his shirt pocket and flicked it open. When she leaned forward to catch the flame, he took hold of her wrist, squeezing it just enough, communicating with his eyes *don't fuck around with me*.

When he let go, the woman sat back and took a short, nervous puff, exhaling quickly.

The drinks appeared. Andreyev tossed the schnapps back in one gulp and pulled out his own pack of cigarettes. "Now, shall we talk?"

She took a tentative sip and set the glass on the table, her eyes darting around. "Here?"

"*Ja*, here. Or, if you'd prefer, we could take a ride."

She twisted a large, ruby ring on her left middle finger. "What is it you want to know?"

"Dmitri Tarnov."

"*Schwein!* A disgusting turd of a man."

Andreyev smiled. "I need some information."

She took another sip of the schnapps, then set the glass down. She stared at it, tapping long, painted fingernails on the table. "*Ja, natürlich,* but what's in it for me?"

Andreyev reached over and put his hand over hers, to stop the tapping. "You could stay alive."

From the window of the train, Dmitri Tarnov watched the peasants who trudged along the muddy roads and queued up at rail stations. Germans slogged westward while Poles, Ukrainians and Czechs headed eastward in the postwar confusion. He soon tired of the dreary scene and sat back in the seat of his first-class compartment. Perhaps most of them would starve along the way, he thought. It would save everyone a lot of trouble.

But Tarnov had more important matters on his mind. He wasn't pleased about returning to Krakow. God knows he'd had enough of Poland over the last few years. But, thanks to Kovalenko, he had no choice. What the hell did that arrogant bastard think he was doing, sneaking an American diplomat into Sachsenhausen? It was a damn good thing Vygotsky had been there, or he might never have known. Tarnov felt a slight twinge of guilt as he thought about Vygotsky, but it passed quickly—just another casualty of war. As it turned out, the whole incident might actually have been a stroke of luck.

Tarnov had been frustrated for months after tearing apart Wawel Castle, searching for the one thing he knew would ruin him. But it wasn't there. And it wasn't among all the documents and diaries the lunatic Frank kept, because they'd been handed over to the Americans, and Tarnov knew that if *they* had found it, the entire world would know the secret . . . and *he'd* be rotting away in a Siberian gulag.

As the months passed, Tarnov had actually dared to believe it had gotten lost. Then, out of the blue, a Goddamn American diplomat representing the Polish Government had waltzed into Sachsenhausen and discovered that his uncle—a university professor from Krakow named Ludwik Banach—had been released into Hans Frank's personal custody. *Five years ago.*

That *had* to mean something. Why would Hans Frank arrange for a Polish university professor to be released from a concentration camp into his personal custody? And what had Banach been doing all those years in Krakow? Did he have access to Frank's personal papers? Had he seen the document? Did he *have* it?

The notion was crazy and so far-fetched it hardly seemed worth pursuing. On the other hand, it was the only lead he had.

Tarnov's anger swelled the more he thought about it. Who the hell was Ludwik Banach? More important, *where* was Ludwik Banach—and what did he know? He stood up and headed for the officer's dining car. He needed a drink.

Thirty-Seven

11 JUNE

A LONG, BLACK MERCEDES pulled up in front of the King William Tower in the center of Berlin's Grunewald District. As Adam approached, a British corporal jumped out of the vehicle. He muttered a quick, "Good evening, sir," and opened the rear door.

"Looks like the British military is traveling in style these days," Adam quipped as he got into the auto.

The corporal merely nodded.

Adam settled into the plush leather seat, wondering what was going on. He had received a message from Colonel Whitehall the previous day, inviting him to dinner. He hadn't known the SOE leader was in Berlin. And the note was vintage Whitehall: terse and to the point, revealing nothing about the real agenda.

Adam recognized the Black Bull insignia of the British Eleventh Armored Division on the corporal's sleeve. "You boys did a hell of a job at Normandy," he said, trying to make conversation.

The British soldier glanced at him in the rearview mirror. "You're a Yank? Were you there?"

Adam shook his head. "No, I was desk-bound in London. Working with SOE."

"Lousy job, that is. I'd take on the bloody Krauts on those beaches again instead of this gig if I had my way. Hate these damn spooks, I do. And hobnobbing with the fuckin' Russians? No good will come of that, mind you."

Adam smiled. "So, how'd you wind up here, working for Whitehall?"

"Whitehall?" The driver snorted. "That ol' fart don't ever talk to the likes of me. I don't work for him; no way I'd want that. I just drive his car and listen to the load of crap he dishes out to whoever's ridin' with him. That's all they think I'm good for after taking a load of shrapnel in the knee at Antwerp."

Adam thought he'd noticed a limp when the corporal walked around the car. "That's the top brass for you," he said, "playing their own little chess game. They don't care who gets caught in the crossfire."

The corporal nodded again, and they drove in companionable silence the rest of the way through Grunewald, the "mansion colony" developed by Otto von Bismarck in the late nineteenth century for Berlin's elite. The winding roads led them through a largely undamaged, heavily wooded area populated with vast estates and hunting lodges situated along streams and small lakes. The peaceful serenity, less than an hour's drive from the shattered ruins of central Berlin, was almost impossible for Adam to comprehend, though he found some satisfaction in the overgrown lawns and shuttered windows of the mostly vacant estates. If it were up to him, he'd burn down the whole damn country.

They turned off the road, and the corporal parked the Mercedes in the center of a broad circular drive. Adam stepped out and stared in awe at the massive, three-story stone structure towering above him. A pair of granite lions flanked broad marble steps that led up to a slate terrace at least ten meters wide. At the top of the steps and across the terrace was the main entrance—double oak doors, five meters high, framed by granite pillars encircled with serpents.

One of the doors creaked open as Adam approached, and a butler appeared, a tall, regal-looking man wearing a pince-nez and a black tuxedo. The butler bowed slightly with a curt, "*Guten tag, Herr Nowak,*" and motioned for him to enter.

Adam was shown into a richly paneled and elegantly furnished drawing room lined on one side by floor-to-ceiling leaded glass windows overlooking the terrace. Stanley Whitehall hoisted his rotund body off a leather chair and lumbered across the room, holding a whiskey glass in one hand.

"Good to see you again, old chap," Whitehall said. "Care for a drink?" He held up the glass. "Glenlivet, from Scotland."

Adam barely heard him as his attention was drawn to the presence of another person in the room. A large, broad-shouldered man in a Russian Army uniform stood with his back to him, pouring a drink at a sideboard.

General Andrei Kovalenko turned around and said, "Good evening, Mr. Nowak."

Adam stiffened, then glanced back and forth from Kovalenko to Whitehall, dumbfounded.

The Russian general stepped up to him and held out a glass. "Have a drink, Mr. Nowak. Stanley will explain it to you. Captain Andreyev will be arriving any moment, and he and I must have a little chat. Then I'll find out what the cook is preparing for dinner. I understand the former owner of this mausoleum used to throw parties for Hermann Goering."

Kovalenko closed the door behind him, and Whitehall gestured to the leather chairs on either side of the fireplace.

Adam eyed him suspiciously and then sat down.

"Andrei uses this house for certain meetings that are better held outside of the Russian sector," Whitehall said. "He and I go way back. I met him in school in London in 1910. His mother brought him there after his father was killed in the Russo–Japanese War. She was Polish."

Adam almost spilled his drink. "Kovalenko's mother was Polish?"

Whitehall nodded. "Born in Warsaw, daughter of some nobleman. His father was a Russian Army officer, who was stationed there. In '04 his father left for Manchuria and never returned. His mother moved the family to London a few years later. Apparently she had traveled there when she was growing up and had connections."

Adam took a long swallow of the whiskey, allowing the mellow liquor to slide down his throat. He set the glass on a side table. "So, you knew that I met Kovalenko during the Warsaw Rising?"

"Of course."

"But I was under cover!" Adam exclaimed, his voice rising. "Even Colonel Stag didn't know who I was. Christ Almighty, did Kovalenko know—?"

Whitehall held up his hand, interrupting him. "Kovalenko remembered meeting a certain American, an envoy representing the Polish Government, who came across the river for a secret meeting. He didn't know who you were at the time, of course. I filled in the blanks for him after the fact. Apparently he was impressed with how you held your ground with one of his officers."

"Then my meeting Kovalenko again here in Berlin was not just a coincidence."

"A minor deception. But necessary."

"*Necessary?* Jesus Christ!" Adam got to his feet and paced around the elegant room. He stopped and turned back to the pudgy, sly man with whom nothing was ever as it seemed. "Are you going to tell me what the hell's going on?"

Whitehall nodded. "Of course, that's why you're here. Care to sit back down?"

Adam glared at him, then sat down.

"When Kovalenko's mother died, he went back to Russia and joined the army, though he's always been somewhat conflicted, given his Polish heritage. At any rate, he advanced through the Red Army officer corps until Stalin's purge in '37, when he was fingered by the NKVD for having connections with foreign intelligence."

"Because of his mother being Polish and her associations in London?"

"Probably. That's how things work in Russia."

"Let me guess: he was exiled."

"To Siberia, along with several hundred other officers . . . those they didn't execute. For good measure, they also arrested his wife and threw her into Lubyanka prison. Then, when the Germans invaded Russia in '41, the Red Army needed officers and he was reinstated. But, to keep him in line, his wife remained in prison—where she died a year later. He's never gotten over it. His hatred of Stalin, Beria and the NKVD is very deeply rooted." Whitehall stood up and plodded over to the sideboard. He refilled his glass and returned with the bottle, setting it on the table next to Adam. "Do you remember the night you and I had dinner in London?"

Adam refilled his own glass. "Yes."

"You made a comment that night . . . about the Russians murdering thousands of Polish officers in 1940."

"The Katyn Forest massacre; you didn't believe it."

Whitehall sat back in the soft leather chair, balancing his drink on the arm. "Another deception, I'm afraid. I most certainly *do* believe it. What's more important, Kovalenko believes it. He's convinced it was all conceived and carried out by the NKVD, and he's been working behind the scenes to help us find proof."

"What makes you think Kovalenko can be trusted? The son of a bitch lied to me about coming to the aid of the AK. Then he and his men sat there on the other side of the river while Warsaw was burned to the ground."

"Yes, he can be trusted. Can you imagine how an atrocity like Katyn must have affected him? He's part Polish, and to have his countrymen commit a crime of that magnitude?"

"Goddamn it, Stanley! If he's part Polish, how could he watch Warsaw burn? How could he let hundreds of thousands of innocent civilians—"

"He was following orders, Adam. You know how things work. Kovalenko didn't make that decision." Whitehall abruptly leaned forward and set his glass on the floor. "Look, there are larger issues at stake here. We all know what's going to happen to Poland." Before Adam could respond, Whitehall pressed on. "Stalin's going to swallow up Poland and everything else east of Germany. It's a disaster, and no one's going to stop him. Churchill saw it coming two years ago. He laid it all out for a select few of us at SOE. 'Get proof,' he said. 'Get proof about Katyn—one of the most despicable war crimes in history—something even the Americans can't ignore.'"

Whitehall glared at Adam, jabbing a pudgy finger in the air. "If there is actual proof that the NKVD carried out those murders in the Katyn Forest, and it's made public before the start of the Potsdam conference, it might be just enough to slow down the tidal wave of communist domination that's about to wash over Europe."

"And you think a *Russian*—a general in the Red Army—is going to help you with this?" Adam couldn't keep the scorn out of his voice.

"Kovalenko contacted me a couple of months ago," Whitehall

replied. “He said he had a lead. It had to do with this NKVD officer, Tarnov.”

“Tarnov? The same bastard who’s—”

“Yes,” Kovalenko said, “the same bastard who’s issued an arrest warrant for Ludwik Banach. Kovalenko was on to something, but he had to proceed cautiously. You can imagine how dangerous this is for someone in his position.”

Whitehall’s shoulders sagged. It was a warm night, and the drawing room windows were open, a gentle breeze floating through now and then. His starched white shirt was wet with perspiration. “We needed a go-between,” he continued. “Someone who could travel back and forth from Britain to Germany without raising a lot of flags, preferably an American . . . but also someone fluent in Polish, someone who knew the country and could go there if necessary. He asked me to get someone I trusted.”

“Me.”

“Yes, you. Kovalenko agreed with the arrangement. The plan was to bring you here to Germany as part of the war crimes team. That was your cover so you could operate freely between Kovalenko and me.”

“But the visit to Sachsenhausen?”

Whitehall sighed. “Just a little something extra—an enticement, so you’d be sure to accept the mission. We knew how you felt about your uncle. Kovalenko agreed to set it up. I couldn’t tell you up front because Kovalenko insisted on meeting you face-to-face before we went any further. He’s very cautious.”

Adam looked out beyond the terrace at the neatly manicured lawn, one of the few in the area being maintained. Then he turned toward Whitehall. “So, all of this about the Polish Government-in-Exile wanting to know what happened to Banach: Another of your *deceptions?*”

“It seemed harmless at the time.”

Adam shook his head. “Yes, harmless—until I found out about Banach and Hans Frank.”

Dinner was an elaborate affair, served in a cavernous dining room of heavy beams, walnut panels and brass wall sconces. The four-meter long, highly polished oak table was set for four with heavy white china and gold-plated flatware. At one end of the room was a two-meter-high fieldstone fireplace with an enormous elk head over the mantel, and at the other end, a magnificent, gleaming black, Steinway grand piano.

Kovalenko presided over the group with a flourish, popping the cork of a twelve-year-old Mercier Brut to get things started, followed by an elegant white Bordeaux with the first course of salmon and white asparagus. "Tonight, gentlemen, we'll have none of that German cough syrup they serve at the Adlon," the general proclaimed. Then, glancing at Adam he added, "I apologize for not being a better host when we first met, Mr. Nowak. The sauerbraten was little more than shoe leather."

Even now, Adam thought, in the private company of Andreyev and Whitehall, the great general would not acknowledge their meeting in Warsaw. The meeting that ended in lies. "Well, I've never thought much of German food, General," he said. "They seem more adept at starting wars than cooking."

Kovalenko laughed heartily and slapped his hand on the table. "Well said, Mr. Nowak. Stanley, I'm sure you would agree with our American friend, wouldn't you? Even what passes for food in London is better than dumplings the size of hand grenades swimming in brown gravy."

Whitehall set his fork down and touched the linen napkin to his lips. "My dear friend, I must say I'm surprised to hear you disparage the food in Britain. You always seemed to devour the fish and chips—and the Boddington ale."

This time it was Andreyev who laughed, then quickly looked down at his plate and finished off the last of his salmon.

Kovalenko, who'd already finished, set his knife and fork on the plate. "You seem in a jovial mood this evening, Captain. Perhaps you could entertain us with a tune on the piano?"

"You play the piano?" Adam remarked.

Andreyev shrugged. "Yes, a bit."

Whitehall chimed in. "The captain is being far too modest, Adam. I've heard him before. He's quite accomplished."

Kovalenko pushed his chair back and lit a cigarette as Andreyev stepped over to the grand piano. "Yes, he is quite good . . . except for that disgraceful American jazz he seems to like. Bad habits he picked up when he lived there."

"So, you spent time in the states?" Adam asked Andreyev, having suspected it given Andreyev's excellent English. "Where did you live?"

"Washington, DC. My father was a military envoy to the U.S. He was stationed there in the early thirties. I attended Georgetown University," Andreyev added with another little shrug.

"The captain's family descends from aristocracy," Kovalenko remarked with a hint of sarcasm. "But they became loyal Bolsheviks when it was the prudent thing to do."

Andreyev took a seat at the piano with a sardonic smile, then, with a groan from the general, launched into a spirited rendition of Duke Ellington's "Don't Get Around Much Anymore." When Andreyev finished, Kovalenko thrust his hands in the air as though surrendering while Whitehall and Adam applauded with enthusiasm.

Andreyev adjusted his eye patch and looked at Adam. "Perhaps a little something in honor of your birth country, Mr. Nowak?"

Adam sat back in astonishment as the Russian captain performed a brilliant interpretation of Chopin's Nocturne no. 2. Andreyev captured with incredible grace and style the essence of the nocturne's reflective mood, gradually becoming more passionate until, near the end, he executed a stunning trill-like passage that tapered off into a calm finish.

The group was silent as Andreyev stepped back to the table and took his seat. Adam watched Kovalenko as the burly, gray-haired general cleared his throat. Then with a softness in his eyes Adam had not seen before, he nodded at Andreyev and refilled the captain's wine glass. *This is the same man who lied to me and watched Warsaw burn? We played Chopin in Warsaw, you son of a bitch, and you sat on your ass while the Nazis destroyed us.* Adam shook his head, unable to comprehend the nature of men that allowed them to appreciate fine music one moment and act as deceitful manipulators the next.

But Kovalenko recovered quickly, standing up and striding over to the sideboard where a dozen bottles of wine were lined up. "How about our second course?" he announced loudly, and the butler appeared an instant later. Kovalenko uncorked a refreshing Sancerre, and the sumptuous meal proceeded with lemon sherbet, followed by thinly sliced veal, acorn squash and two bottles of Chateauneuf du Pape '38.

After dinner they adjourned to the terrace with cigars and cognac. Despite the good-humored spirit of the evening, Adam was still edgy in the presence of the Russians. He remembered what Natalia had told him about the Russians burning her village; about the disappearance of her parents, relatives and friends; about her brother, most likely among the thousands of Polish officers murdered at Katyn and dumped into a ditch. He took a sip of cognac and watched Kovalenko and Andreyev, who were bantering easily with Whitehall. Despite his prejudice against Russians, Adam found himself rather liking Andreyev, feeling some connection with him. He decided he'd better be cautious about that.

Halfway through his second cognac, Kovalenko finally came to the point of the evening. "Gentlemen, I suggest we address the issue that brings us here tonight. I asked Captain Andreyev to see if he could find out what our NKVD friend, Dmitri Tarnov, was up to the last few years. It seems he found a rather—shall we say—*intimate* source."

Andreyev set down his glass and leaned forward. "She's a German woman who followed Tarnov around for a few years until he tired of her. Hans Frank introduced them."

"Frank?" Whitehall exclaimed. "Tarnov had dealings with that monster?"

"A *lot* of dealings," Andreyev said. "From '39 to '41—while Germany and Russia were allies—Tarnov traveled to Krakow on a regular basis, collaborating with Frank on the plunder of Poland. What the woman told me the other night, however, was new information."

Adam and Whitehall exchanged glances. Kovalenko reclined in his chair, puffing on his cigar.

Andreyev continued. "As you can imagine, contact between Tarnov and Frank stopped after Germany invaded Russia in June of '41. Tarnov returned to Moscow and took the woman with him.

However, a year and a half later, in the fall of 1942, when it looked as if Germany might win, Tarnov made a secret trip to Krakow."

Adam stared at the Russian captain in disbelief. "How the hell did he manage that?"

Andreyev smiled. "The woman said it was pretty complicated, a lot of stops at out-of-the way places and—"

"Bloody hell! He took her along?" Whitehall blurted.

Kovalenko roared with laughter. "That's my favorite part. The son of a bitch apparently couldn't get along without her. And then he was stupid enough not to shoot her when he finally dumped her."

"What happened in Krakow?" Adam asked.

"According to the woman, Tarnov carried a briefcase that he never let out of his sight the entire trip," Andreyev said. "She told me that one evening they were invited to Frank's private quarters at Wawel Castle. Only the three of them were present, and late in the evening, after dinner and quite a few drinks, she recalled Tarnov removing a file folder from the briefcase and handing it to Frank. She asked him about it later when they were alone, and Tarnov said it was a secret document about Poland that very few people knew existed. She claimed Tarnov was always boasting about his connections and his access to high-level orders."

"He cut a deal to save his own skin," Whitehall muttered.

"Exactly right! The fucking traitor!" Kovalenko snapped, glaring at the other three. "And what do you suppose that document was? What do you think he gave to Frank in exchange for his personal safety if Germany defeated us?"

The group was silent as the question hung in the air.

Whitehall finally spoke up. "General, now might be a good time to tell Adam what you know about Tarnov."

Kovalenko turned to Adam. "You don't know whether to trust me or not, do you, Mr. Nowak."

Adam looked him in the eye. "No, General, I don't."

"Fair enough, at least you're honest. Well, you can trust me on this. Dmitri Tarnov carried out the murders at Katyn. He did it to curry favor with Commissar Beria, who happens to be his second cousin. But it didn't work out the way Tarnov had hoped. After it was all over,

Beria cut him loose, and Tarnov's dream of a high-ranking position in the NKVD never materialized."

Regardless of what Adam thought of Kovalenko's trustworthiness, there was a look in the general's eyes that left no doubt what he had just said was true. "Is there any proof?" Adam asked.

"Tarnov wasn't acting alone, of course. This atrocity was orchestrated at the highest levels of the NKVD. Something of this magnitude required an order—probably signed by Stalin himself and the other members of the Politburo."

Adam turned to Captain Andreyev. "You think that's what was in the briefcase? Wouldn't an order like that be top secret and securely locked away in the Kremlin?"

"Perhaps someone made a copy." Whitehall chimed in. He addressed Kovalenko: "Tarnov's woman-friend said he was always boasting about his connections. As a relative of Beria's he'd know certain people, he'd have access to things normally above his station, wouldn't you say, General?"

Kovalenko nodded. "It's possible."

Adam absently rubbed the numb, razor-thin scar on the side of his face. "Are you suggesting that Tarnov gave a copy of the Katyn Order to Hans Frank? Why would he do that? He's NKVD. That would be committing suicide."

"Not if he thought the Germans would win," Andreyev said.

"Of course!" Whitehall exclaimed. "It makes perfect sense. When the graves at Katyn were discovered, Germany and Russia blamed each other for the murders. Think of the leverage Hans Frank would have had with Hitler if he possessed actual proof that the NKVD conducted the massacre. They were prisoners of war—*officers,* mind you—murdered in cold blood. Tarnov gave a copy of the Katyn Order to Frank in return for his protection if Germany won the war."

"But Frank never used the information," Adam said.

"No, he didn't," Andreyev responded. "Frank's window of opportunity closed a few months later, when the tide turned and we had the Wehrmacht on the run."

Whitehall nodded. "Quite right, by then Frank would have been preoccupied with saving his own neck—and avoiding capture by the

Russians. He couldn't have risked any connection with that order."

"So, what did he do with it?" Andreyev asked.

"Obviously, no one knows," Whitehall said, "not even Tarnov, who must be desperate to get it back."

"Wait a minute," Adam cut in. "We're all just speculating here. The woman just said that Tarnov gave Frank a document. We don't know for sure what it actually was."

Kovalenko, who had been silent for the last few minutes, took two long strides to the round wicker table and grabbed the bottle of cognac to pour another drink. Waving the bottle in the air he glared at the group. "Six months ago Tarnov tore apart Hans Frank's headquarters at Wawel Castle looking for something. And now, since this revelation about Ludwik Banach and Hans Frank, he's ordered that all of Frank's records be sealed, as though he's terrified there's something he missed. He's obsessed with trying to find something, and I think we all know what it is." Kovalenko filled his glass and stepped over to Adam, holding out the bottle. "You'd better have another drink, Mr. Nowak, because Dmitri Tarnov hasn't yet found what he's searching for . . . and now he's going after your uncle."

Thirty-Eight

12 June

The next day, Adam was summoned back to the estate in Grunewald. It was chilly and overcast, with occasional drizzling rain, a dreary day that matched Adam's mood. He hadn't slept well, and not just because of recurring dreams of wide-eyed corpses. Listening to Andreyev play Chopin had re-opened all the wounds of the Warsaw Rising: the hundreds of AK commandos who lost their lives, the tens of thousands of innocent civilians killed and maimed, the churches and monuments, the history, the culture of a great city . . . all destroyed.

And the conversation after last night's dinner had also gnawed at him all night. Could there actually be a document, a written order, authorizing the secret murder of thousands of Polish officers? And could Tarnov have managed to obtain a copy of that order and given it to Hans Frank? If that were all true, then Dmitri Tarnov was far more desperate—and far more dangerous—than Adam had imagined.

Whitehall was waiting for him in the drawing room, dressed casually in gray flannel slacks and a black cardigan sweater. But the butler still wore a tuxedo as he efficiently served coffee and produced a tray of biscuits and jam. When he left the room, Whitehall said, "We've received a message from your contact in Krakow."

The cup and saucer rattled in Adam's hand, and he quickly set it on a table before spilling the coffee. Whitehall was still speaking. "I'm sorry," Adam said. "What did you say?"

"The message was quite short," Whitehall repeated. "Rather cryptic. It said, 'Find Adam Nowak. We are not pathetic pawns on the perilous chessboard.'"

Adam stood for a long moment, staring blankly at Whitehall as the message slowly sank in.

Natalia was alive.

He hadn't dared to believe it, even after he'd given her name to Whitehall. It had been ten months since—

"Adam? Did you hear what I said?" Whitehall asked sharply. "Do you know what it means?"

"I'm sorry . . . do I know what . . . ?"

"The message, do you know what it means?"

Adam silently repeated the message to himself, *Find Adam Nowak. We are not pathetic pawns on the perilous chessboard.* "My God, where did she get . . . ? I don't understand."

"Nor do I," Whitehall said. "Of course, I remembered the phrase from the research files on Hans Frank. I was hoping you would know why *she* would use it?"

"What else was in the message?"

"A code that she needs help."

"Help? What's wrong? What kind of help?"

"The code she used suggests that she's found something important and needs someone to rendezvous with her."

"When do I leave?"

"It'll take a bit of doing," Whitehall said. "We'll prepare some papers identifying you as an American industrialist doing business with the Russian Army. We'll get you a letter of authorization from General Kovalenko—"

Adam wasn't listening. He was consumed by the memory of Natalia sprinting along Dluga Street that last night in Warsaw while he watched from the window.

"Must be some big deal goin' on," Whitehall's driver said as they pulled away from the mansion. "A couple of Russians here last night, now you come back this morning."

Adam met the driver's eyes in the rearview mirror. "What Russians?"

The driver laughed. “That’s a good one. You keep associating with the likes of Whitehall, and you won’t remember your own name.”

Adam actually enjoyed the man’s impertinence. With everything on his mind, a few moments of light banter felt good. “You know the old saying, if I told you—”

“Yeah, yeah, you’d have to kill me.” The driver glanced at him in the mirror again. “But you don’t look like the type.”

The driver brought Adam all the way back to his lodgings in Schoenberg. Meinerz was sitting in a wrought-iron chair on the front porch when Adam stepped out of the backseat of the Mercedes. The American colonel looked up from the file he was studying as Adam walked up the steps. “Well, well, riding around in a chauffeured Mercedes. Pretty classy,” he said with a smirk.

Adam slumped down in the chair next to him. “It’s not going to last. I’ll be leaving for Krakow soon.”

Meinerz set the file on a round, wood-topped table between the chairs and pulled out a pack of cigarettes. He offered one to Adam and lit both of them. “Has SOE located your uncle?”

“I don’t know. They received a message that our contact in Krakow discovered something important.”

Meinerz cocked his head. “Do you have any idea what you’re getting into here, Adam? A few days ago you almost got arrested by the NKVD and now you’re going off to *Poland?* We can’t help you if anything happens over there, you know.”

Adam nodded. “I understand.”

“Do you?” Meinerz leaned forward, looking him in the eye. “There are a lot of desperate people out there trying like hell to cover up all the atrocities they committed. One more life isn’t going to matter to any of them. That NKVD prick accused you of harboring a fugitive. That’s all the excuse he needs.”

Adam smiled to hide his irritation. Meinerz had no idea what he’d seen and done the last four years, and that was the way it had to stay. “I appreciate your concern, and I’ll be careful. But I’ve got to get to the bottom of this. I sure as hell don’t want my uncle’s name associated with mass murderers like Hans Frank, regardless of what the damn Russians think. Besides, I may dig up some evidence that will be useful in the war crimes trials."

Meinerz shook his head. "Listen to me, Adam. We're making up these damn laws as we go because we won the war—along with our Russian *allies*. We can't trust those bastards further than we can throw one of their tanks. None of this 'war crimes' crap is ever going to stick. The American people don't care. We'll eventually just get tired of the whole tedious process. Then, very quietly, we'll let them all go."

"So, you think we're all just wasting our time here? We're discovering evidence of mass genocide, for Christ's sake! You think everyone will just forget about it?"

"What I'm saying is, we can do all the investigating we want because we're the victors. But there is no legal precedent to conduct war crimes trials against individuals."

"What about the Moscow Declaration? The London Charter?"

Meinerz shook his head again. "Written by Churchill with support from Roosevelt and Stalin during war time. It won't stand up under the scrutiny of international law."

"Then what about the Hague Convention, which protects the rights of civilians in occupied countries?"

"The Hague Convention holds governments responsible for war crimes, not individuals. Look, Adam, I agree with you. All of these Nazi bastards should hang for their crimes—"

"And a lot of Russians."

"My point, exactly. It's certainly not fair treatment under the law, is it? No one knows better than you the extent of the crimes committed by the Russians against the Poles. But since they're our allies—"

Adam held his hands in the air. "I know, I know!" Meinerz's words cut right through to his heart. Was this all just an exercise, a grandstand show by the victors? Could the Americans and British really put Germans on trial for war crimes and ignore what the Russians did in all those hundreds of Polish villages? Could they ignore what the Russians did at Katyn?

Meinerz stubbed out his cigarette and held out his hand. "Look, I'm cynical by nature. Don't pay any attention to it. We'll do our best to hang these bastards. You just watch your back . . . and stay safe."

Adam gripped his friend's hand and nodded.

• • •

Adam left the next day and spent most of the trip from Berlin to Krakow sitting alone in the train's first-class dining car, smoking cigarettes and staring out the window. Morning became afternoon, rain turned to sunshine, but he didn't notice. All he could think about was Natalia.

When he'd given her name to Whitehall, it was with only the slightest hope that SOE would find her. He wasn't even sure she'd made it out of Warsaw, much less avoided capture by the NKVD for the last ten months.

Adam had just barely made it out of Warsaw himself after being wounded when the SS assaulted the AK hospital in Raczynski Palace. The bullet that mangled his ear had knocked him unconscious, which turned out to be a stroke of luck since he'd been left for dead by the SS troopers. When he finally came to, he had managed to crawl out of the palace, and into the street where he'd passed out again. An elderly couple found him and took him to their hiding place, a cellar in an adjacent building. They had tried their best to nurse him, but with the lack of medical supplies, infection had set in. He had been so dizzy most of the time he couldn't stand, much less walk. It had taken a month to recover, and by the time he managed to slip out of the city, Natalia, like everyone else, had disappeared in the chaos.

And now he was on his way to meet her.

The only time in five years he had let his guard down had been with Natalia. They'd only spent a few hours together, sitting in a church, then huddling in the ammunition shelter. But there was something about her, something that had penetrated the protective shell he'd so meticulously created, the shell that sealed off his emotions and kept him going. And it frightened him. It had frightened him that last night in Warsaw, when he had run off on the futile mission to Raczynski Palace . . . then watched her from a window like a schoolboy.

Adam forced himself to think about something other than what he would say when he met her. Had she found Banach? Could his uncle still be alive after all this time? Was it possible he might be re-united with the man who meant more to him than life itself?

And the phrase—*pathetic pawns on the perilous chessboard*—the phrase Banach used in his paper, the same phrase Hans Frank used. Where would she have learned it, if not from Banach?

He looked out the window, rubbing the numb left side of his face, and watched the Polish countryside slip past: gray buildings in war-weary, gray towns, dusty roads winding through the wheat fields, wagons pulled by horses and oxen. He imagined it looked the same as it always had, century after century . . . war after war.

Adam reflected on his conversation with Whitehall the other day when they were alone in the drawing room of the mansion before dinner with Kovalenko. One of Whitehall's comments had struck a chord: *Get proof about Katyn, something even the Americans can't ignore.* He thought about the comment, remembering the Poles he knew in Chicago—most of them, like himself, first or second generation immigrants, and all of them patriotic Americans. While they kept alive their Polish heritage, they were as fiercely proud to be an American as he was.

But Whitehall's comment had made him think. If there *were* solid proof of Russia's treachery at Katyn, would the Americans stand up to Stalin and help Poland? Would his adopted country stand beside the country of his birth at the hour of her greatest need?

Adam knew what the answer would be if he asked any of the hundreds of AK commandos he'd fought with over the years, the proud, stubborn Poles who were fighting to the death to win their freedom. The British and the French may have let them down, but Adam knew that every one of them believed America would be there when it counted. He hoped it was true.

He suddenly felt very tired. He let his head fall back on the seat and closed his eyes, wondering what he would say when he met Natalia.

Thirty-Nine

13 June

The late afternoon sun was quite warm when Adam exited Krakow's Central Station with his suit coat draped over his arm. For the first time since he'd been deported by the Germans in 1939, he walked the familiar streets leading to the Stare Miasto District, grateful the city that had once been his home had survived the war with little damage.

Sweat trickled down the back of his collar as he crossed the Planty park and stopped outside of St. Florian's Gate to get his bearings. He looked around, observing his surroundings and noticing faces. Then he passed through the gate and the remnants of the ancient fortifications, and entered the old city.

Adam walked a short distance down Florianska Street, weaving through crowds of people. He turned into a narrow cobblestone lane, barely wide enough for a horse and carriage, then circled around and came back to where he'd started to make sure he wasn't being followed. Repeating the process another time, he continued down Florianska to the Rynek Glowny.

Adam paused for a moment at the northern end of the vast market square, taking in the view of the Mariacki Church, the Cloth Hall, the vendors' horses and carriages. He'd spent many Sunday afternoons on this square as a boy, sitting at a café with his aunt and uncle, eating ice cream and feeding the pigeons. And he'd spent many hours here after he returned from America, sitting at those same cafés, sipping coffee or beer while studying law books.

The square was much the same, largely undamaged by the war, but it felt different. It was quieter, more subdued. A few of the vendors were at their stations, but there was little in their carriages for sale. And many of the cafés were closed, their awnings rolled up, chairs stacked upon the tables. Adam took a last look around, then walked across the square, proceeding south along Grodzka to Wawel Castle, heading for the rendezvous point in the Kazimierz District.

An hour later, he entered the courtyard of the Church of Archangel Michael and Saint Stanislaus. There was no one around. Adam checked his watch—five o'clock—he was right on time. He lit a cigarette and wandered over to the pond, pretending to study the statue of Saint Stanislaus in the center. The saint had a stern expression on his stone face, as if he were disappointed by human frailty. A few minutes passed. Then a few more and still no one appeared except an elderly man who looked like a caretaker, carrying a basket filled with grass clippings.

The elderly man walked toward him and seemed to be heading for the gate when he suddenly dropped the basket at Adam's feet. The grass spilled out, covering Adam's shoes.

"Ach, what a fool. I'm sorry, sir." The man bent over and scooped the clippings off the ground as Adam shook his shoes clear.

Adam instinctively bent down to help, and the man whispered, "Dietla and Starowislna, at six o'clock. Get on the tram for Podgorze." Then the man picked up the last of the clippings and headed out of the gate.

Despite all of her efforts to keep her emotions under control, Natalia gasped when Adam boarded the tram. She quickly covered it up with a cough when the woman across the aisle glanced at her, but it had been enough, and he turned in her direction. Their eyes met for an instant before the crowd pushed him toward the front of the car.

She could feel the flush in her face and turned to look out the window, not trusting herself if their eyes should happen to meet again. *Is it really him?* Several minutes passed. Finally she couldn't stand it any longer and shifted in her seat, stealing a glance at the front of the car, certain she had made a mistake.

Adam was halfway up the aisle, wedged between two taller men.

He wore a dark blue suit and carried a briefcase. He looked older. There were creases at the corners of his eyes that she didn't remember, and his shoulders sagged a bit, as though he was tired. She swallowed hard when she noticed the thin scar on the left side of his face and his ragged left ear. Half of it had been torn away. Tears clouded her vision, and she turned back to the window.

The tram rumbled over the Vistula River, and Natalia gazed at the slow-moving gray water, fighting the urge to look at him, to get up and push through the crowd. Vivid memories of the last time she had seen him suddenly returned with a rush—Dluga Street in Warsaw, fires raging out of control and artillery shells shrieking overhead as he headed off to the hospital in Raczynski Palace in his suicidal effort to protect the trapped and wounded AK commandos. Natalia had been certain that night she'd never see him again. Then she had heard the reports a week later, confirming that the SS had murdered everyone in the hospital.

And now, as if he'd risen from the dead, Adam was here.

The tram slowed to a stop in the Podgorze District, where the Jewish ghetto had been. Natalia stood up, made her way to the door and stepped from the tram. She could feel him following her. The streets were busy with people on their way home from work or the market, clutching bags half-full with the few meager groceries they could find. She walked with a steady pace, blending in with the crowd but making sure he could keep her in sight.

She continued around a few corners, along the route she'd planned, until she came to Lwowska Street, lined on one side by the high brick walls of the former ghetto. Replacing the German propaganda placards that had been ripped down, the invented word, *grunVald*, with a large capital "V," had been painted along the wall. It was a popular form of anti-German graffiti in remembrance of the Medieval Battle of Grunwald when the Kingdom of Poland defeated the Teutonic Knights. Natalia followed the ghetto wall for a hundred meters, then crossed the street at the intersection with Dabrowskiego, passing through a doorway and down a flight of creaking wooden steps. Scarcely able to breathe, she stood in the center of the dimly lit cellar and waited.

A few minutes passed before Natalia heard him descending the staircase. She fidgeted, suddenly feeling very conspicuous. When he stepped into the room, tears flooded her eyes. She had fantasized about this moment ever since Warsaw, wishing in her heart that it were possible, but knowing in her mind that it wasn't. But it *had* happened. He was alive. The impossible dream had come true. And now, as he stood in front of her, no words would come.

"I watched you," Adam said, "in Warsaw . . . that night on Dluga Street, from a window in Raczynski Palace."

Natalia felt a chill and wrapped her arms around her chest. "I thought I'd never see you . . ." Her voice trailed off and she turned away, a sudden rush of anger, shame and frustration, washing over her all at once. She had believed he was dead. *You gave up hope. You don't deserve this.* The shame was almost more than she could bear.

"Natalia?" His voice was quiet, soft.

She closed her eyes and rocked slowly back and forth. Tears trickled down her cheek.

After a moment he asked, "Have you found Ludwik Banach?"

Natalia spun around and glared at him, scarcely able to believe what she'd just heard. "Have I *what?* You come back . . . you just show up after all this time . . . and then you ask me . . ." She dropped to her knees and buried her face in her hands.

Adam knelt down next to her and put a hand on her shoulder. "I'm sorry. I thought it was a safe place to begin."

She looked up at him. "I thought you were dead."

"I know, and I'm sorry. I can explain." He stood and offered his hand to help her up.

Natalia ignored his hand and stood up on her own, shaking her head. "Not now, not here." She took a breath to calm herself. "I haven't found your uncle. He was alive, and here in Krakow as recently as January of this year. But I don't know where he went."

"Was he captured by the Russians?"

"He left before they got here." She watched Adam run a hand over the scar on his face, his brow furled, as he absorbed the news. "He kept a journal," she added.

"A journal? You have it?"

"Yes, it's all there: how he came to Krakow and started my smuggling channel, Hans Frank, all of it." She cocked her head. "*You* told SOE about me. You're the one who asked them to contact me so I could find your uncle."

Adam nodded. "Colonel Whitehall, the head of SOE, brought me back to London. Then he sent me to Berlin with a War Crimes Investigation Team. Whitehall told me that Banach was 'the Provider' and I eventually realized that you were part of the channel. It's a long story. Perhaps, sometime . . ."

"Perhaps."

"I need to see that journal," he said.

"I've hidden it. We'll have to be careful."

"Yes, of course. But he must have written something—left some clue about where he would go."

"No, there wasn't anything like that. But there *was* something else." Natalia glanced up at the ceiling as a truck rumbled past on the street outside. She waited until the sound disappeared, then took a few steps deeper into the cellar, away from the stairs.

Adam followed her.

"The last entry your uncle made in the journal was this past January," Natalia whispered. "He mentioned a document he had discovered in the Copernicus Memorial Library, where he was working." She moved closer. "It was a copy of an order, signed by Joseph Stalin in 1940, authorizing the murders in the Katyn Forest."

Adam stiffened. "Good God! You have it?"

"No, I don't. Banach mentioned the order in his journal . . . but I don't know where it is."

Adam rubbed the left side of his face again, and paced around the cellar. He stopped and turned back to her. "In your message you said, *we are not pathetic pawns on the perilous chessboard.* Where did you learn that phrase?"

"Those were the last words your uncle wrote in the journal: *to whoever reads this journal: find Adam Nowak and tell him that we shall never be pathetic pawns on the perilous chessboard of the NKVD.*" There were voices in the street, and Natalia held up her hand, listening. It sounded like children, young boys. There was a tinny clanking sound as if a can were being hit with a stick, then footsteps running away, laughter, a few shouts. Then it was quiet again. "We should leave now."

Adam stopped her with a gentle touch on her shoulder. "That phrase—*pathetic pawns on the perilous chessboard*—it's from an unpublished paper my uncle wrote in 1935. Hans Frank copied it and used it in a paper of his own a year later. I discovered it when I was in London."

Natalia shrugged. "I don't understand."

"My uncle and Hans Frank knew each other."

Natalia nodded. "I know; he wrote about that in the journal. But I still don't understand. Why would that be the message he wanted to send to you?"

Adam looked up at the ceiling, as though he was trying to recall something. "I don't understand either," he said, "but there's something else you need to know. When I discovered that my uncle had been released from Sachsenhausen, it caught the attention of the NKVD."

Natalia suddenly felt cold again, icy fingers on the back of her neck.

Adam continued. "An officer by the name of Tarnov has issued an arrest warrant for him."

"Is he here? This Tarnov, is he here in Krakow?"

"Yes, I think so."

Natalia started for the stairs. "We have to leave. I'll go first—"

Adam reached out and took her hand. "That copy of Stalin's order. We have to find it. We don't have much time."

"What do you mean, 'much time'?"

"In a few weeks there's going to be a conference in Germany," Adam said. His face flushed and he talked quickly. "It'll be in a place near Berlin called Potsdam. They're going to decide what happens to Poland."

"Hah! We both know what's going to happen to Poland. The Russians will gobble us up, and the world won't give a damn."

"Not if we can find that copy of the order. If we can pass it along to the right people, it could make—"

"Stop it!" Natalia snapped, suddenly overwhelmed again. "Goddamn it, Adam, I thought you were *dead!* Can you understand that? Do you have any idea how I felt that last night in Warsaw when you decided to kill yourself rather than escape?" She caught herself before he could respond and backed away, waving her hands. "No, don't say anything. I'm sorry, just give me a moment."

She forced herself to calm down, trying to sort things out one more time. A moment passed, and gradually she realized what she had to do. "There's someone I have to see. Go back the way we came and get on the tram. I'm going a different way."

Adam balked. "But how will I find you?"

"I'll find *you*."

Forty

13 June

A long, black Citroën drove from Krakow's Central Station, through the Stare Miasto District and up the winding road of Wawel Hill. It circled around the castle, through the Dragon's Den Gate and stopped next to the cathedral.

Dmitri Tarnov got out of the auto and stomped across the courtyard. He was oblivious to the three-story arcade of spiral columns, balconies and stone archways fronting the palace rooms that had served as knights' quarters, armories and the royal treasury during Poland's golden age. His mind was focused on only one thing as he flashed his identification to the NKVD officer standing guard, then pushed through a discreetly hidden doorway leading to the lower level. He made his way down a hallway, removed a key from his pocket and let himself into a small, windowless room.

Tarnov flicked on the light switch, closed the door behind him and re-locked it. Then he sat at the solitary table and stared at a row of filing cabinets containing the records of his interrogations and search of Hans Frank's headquarters last January.

He realized that his sudden fixation on Ludwik Banach might be nothing more than a wild goose chase. But there was something about this law professor's connection to Frank that compelled him to dig deeper. He was determined to hunt down Ludwik Banach and find out what he knew. And the search had to start here, in these files. It had to be here somewhere, the one thing Tarnov knew he must have overlooked . . .

After more than an hour of digging, Tarnov discovered a file he had set aside as irrelevant last January. It was labeled *Staatsbibliothek Krakau*. He rubbed his eyes, shifted in the hard wooden chair and opened the file. As he leafed through it, he discovered page after page of copious notes written by Hans Frank about *Germanizing* the Copernicus Memorial Library. Tarnov shook his head. No wonder he had tossed it to the side six months ago. Who the hell cared about a library?

As Tarnov kept reading, however, it became obvious that this was a special project for Frank, and he had visited the library often, discussing with the staff the transfer of thousands of books and documents into the new facility. It was indeed a mission, bordering on obsession—the establishment of a new Center of German Culture right here in Krakow, with Frank at the center of it all.

Eventually, digging deeper into the file, a smile came across Tarnov's face as he discovered the name of a person who worked at the library, a person with whom Frank met frequently. Ludwik Banach.

Tarnov read further. There were more notes, written by Frank, about discussions he had with Banach on all manner of subjects—books, periodicals, works of art, the events of the war, the construction of Jewish ghettos—hinting at an importance Frank placed on Banach's opinions. Tarnov propped his elbows on the table. *What does it all mean? What else did Frank share with him?*

Tarnov continued flipping through the file, searching for anything that might provide a clue to Banach's whereabouts. There was nothing.

Then, at the very end, he discovered a list of people who worked at the library. With typical German thoroughness the list was complete with job descriptions, departments in which each individual worked and the dates of their employment. Tarnov studied the list, making notes, cross-referencing the information, until another name caught his attention, someone who worked closely with Ludwik Banach.

Tarnov sat back and took a deep, satisfied breath. He circled the name, folded the list and slipped it in his pocket. He was annoyed and frustrated that he had overlooked the file earlier, but he put it out of his mind. There was still time. Banach was out there somewhere. And now he had a place to start.

Forty-One

14 June

Natalia knelt in a pew at the Church of Archangel Michael and Saint Stanislaus, waiting her turn for confession. She held a rosary in her hand, but she wasn't praying. She'd stopped praying long ago, feeling betrayed by God as everything she'd known and everyone she'd loved had been crushed under the heels of fascists and communists. She wasn't praying, but in her heart there was a feeling that hadn't been there for a long time. There was a glimmer of light in the darkness.

Adam was alive.

Could there still be a chance? she wondered. After all the brutality, the killing and destruction . . . Could there still be a chance?

She hadn't known what to say when she saw him yesterday, standing at the bottom of the cellar stairs. As she thought about it now, she realized at that moment she had been consumed with fear. After all she'd been through, the idea that another person could mean as much to her as Adam did had terrified her.

And she didn't know what to say.

Finally it was her turn, and Natalia made the sign of the cross and stepped over to the confessional. Today was Thursday, and it had been well established for years that contact was only to be made on Wednesdays. But surely the priest would recognize her voice. She cleared her throat and said, "In the name of our Lord I come seeking."

There was silence. Finally the voice from behind the screen whispered, "What have you done with the gift you received from our Lord and Provider?"

Natalia's eyes darted around the semi-darkness of the sanctuary. "It is safe, Father."

"Do you seek consultation?"

"Yes."

Another moment of silence, then the priest said, "Tonight, eight o'clock, on the Rynek Glowny, the southwest corner of the Cloth Hall."

The colossal Renaissance edifice of the Cloth Hall, adorned with Italian gargoyles glaring down from an ornately sculpted roof, dominated the center of the Rynek Glowny. Dozens of arcades and merchant stalls lined both sides of the ground floor where traditionally all manner of goods could be purchased, from dishware to clothing, candy, cigars, amber jewelry and artwork. Though few of the stalls had anything of value to sell in the aftermath of the war, and few of the people milling about had money to spend, it was still one of the busiest locations in Krakow on this warm Thursday evening.

Natalia took up a spot on the southwest corner providing a good vantage point from which to observe the comings and goings of the teeming square. She was still nervous about being out in public in a big city surrounded by thousands of unfamiliar faces. Ever since her escape from Warsaw, and especially since she'd been forced to shoot the two NKVD agents near the Bolimowski Forest, Natalia expected at any moment to feel a heavy hand grip her shoulder.

The priest arrived a few minutes past eight. Tonight he was dressed in a gray suit and fedora, indistinguishable from the hundreds of other men milling about the area.

"We should take a walk," he said in his usual clipped manner.

Natalia nodded, and they walked slowly around the perimeter of the vast building.

"I know that Ludwik Banach is the Provider," she said after a moment.

The priest stopped as abruptly as if he'd walked into a wall. His face was sheet-white. "Where did you . . . ?"

"It was in the journal—the 'gift' you left for me. Didn't you read it?"

"Of course not. I've never read any of the information received from the Provider. I just pass it along."

Natalia doubted that was true.

"And, as I told you," the priest continued, "the Provider is no longer among us."

"I'm aware of that," Natalia replied, "but I must find him. It's extremely urgent. The gift—his journal—has also revealed the existence of a document that could help save Poland. He's the only one who can tell us where it is."

"I suspect it's a bit late for that, my child."

"No, it's not too late. But time is short."

The priest didn't respond.

"I'm not the only one searching for him."

The priest's eyes darted around. Groups of people passed by in all directions, carrying on their own conversations, the sound of a trumpet from a nearby café drowning out most of the chatter. He turned back to Natalia and whispered, "This is very dangerous."

"I know. That's why we have no time to lose."

"What do you want from me?"

"Your contact. The other person in the channel."

"Impossible! You know I can't tell you that."

Natalia took his arm. "Please, it's absolutely crucial. This is our only chance."

The priest shook his arm free. "You know the rules. I cannot divulge the name of a contact. None of us can." He began walking again.

Natalia hurried to catch up to him. "Stop!" she hissed. "Stop and listen to me, Goddamn it!"

He stopped and turned to her. His bony face was crimson. "How dare you—"

"Just listen for one moment . . . please."

His mouth tightened. "As you wish, one minute."

"The NKVD is hunting for Banach. We both know what they're like. They'll eventually find out about all of us. It's only a matter of time. Our only chance is to locate the document, and the only way to do that is to find Banach before they do."

The priest glared at her, looking down the length of his pencil-thin nose as though she were a gnat he wanted to swat away. But he was sweating and there was a flicker in his eyes that gave him away. He was afraid.

"It's the only way," Natalia whispered.

A group of people staggered past, singing and laughing. One of the men waved a half-empty bottle of vodka. The priest waited until they were out of earshot. "We can never meet again. You can never come back to the church. Is that clear?"

Natalia nodded.

"Never," he repeated.

"I understand."

The priest hesitated then said, "His name is Jerzy Jastremski."

"Does he know where Banach went?"

"Yes. He's the *only* one who does."

Forty-Two

15 June

When the telephone rang in Adam's room at the Hotel Polonia he had been awake for a long time, worrying about his uncle. He snatched the receiver off the hook on the second ring.

It was Natalia. "The service is at nine o'clock," she said. "Bring some flowers."

"Christ, it's been—" The line went dead.

Adam placed the receiver back on the hook and stared out the window at the street below, watching the city slowly come to life. He wondered if they could survive this.

At five minutes to nine Adam left the hotel. He paused on the sidewalk. The sun was bright, and there was a warm breeze. It would be hot again today. He spotted the flower stand just a few meters down the street. Natalia leaned against the wall of the adjacent building, reading a newspaper. Ignoring her, Adam walked up to the stand and picked out a bouquet of daisies. As he paid for the flowers, Natalia walked away.

Adam followed her at a safe distance, across the Planty and the Rynek Glowny, into the Mariacki Church. Inside, the sanctuary was quiet. Friday morning was an off time and only a handful of people knelt here and there, praying the rosary to themselves. Adam slid into the pew next to Natalia and laid the daisies on the seat beside him.

He waited while Natalia sat with her hands folded in her lap, looking straight ahead. Finally she turned to him and said softly, "I thought I'd never see you again. I know where you went that last night in Warsaw, and I know why, but . . ." She turned away, shaking her head.

Adam rested his arms on the back of the pew in front of them. How could he explain his actions on that chaotic night? He didn't understand what he'd done any more now than he did then. In the few brief hours they had spent together in Warsaw, Natalia had stirred emotions inside him that he had thought were long dead, emotions that had driven him to try to defend the AK hospital.

He glanced at Natalia. She was as tough and battle-hardened as he was, not hesitating to kill the enemy before they killed her. But there was a difference, something he saw in her eyes every time he looked at her, a tenderness that he doubted he could ever return.

She touched his arm and motioned for him to sit back. Then, as if she had read his mind, she leaned close and whispered, "Don't."

He slid back in the pew. "Natalia, I—"

"Don't," she repeated. "You're here now. That's all that matters."

"Natalia, I . . . Natalia, I don't think . . ." Christ, he had to get this out! He tried again, keeping his eyes on the floor as he spoke. "When I went to Raczynski Palace, I knew I'd die there. I couldn't go with you. I couldn't escape. I wanted to. But I couldn't." He paused and took a deep breath, grateful that she didn't try to stop him before he could get it out. "I wasn't trying to be a hero. But I had to do *something* that would have some meaning. I just needed . . . I needed . . ."

"Redemption?" she asked quietly.

Adam blinked, taken aback by how easily she could see into his soul. *Was that it?* After all the murders, the hatred, the years of cold-blooded killing . . . Was he seeking *redemption?* Was that even possible after everything he'd done? He gripped the edge of the wooden pew, willing himself to go on. "I wasn't the only commando in the palace that night," he said. "There were six of us. The SS opened fire on the building with machine guns and mortars. They kicked in the doors and tossed grenades through the windows. Then they charged in. They shot the patients, doctors, nurses. They went from room to room. We took out a lot of them, but they picked us off one-by-one. I was the only one left at the end. I was driven back to a corner on the ground floor. And then my head . . ." He brushed his fingers over the scar on the left side of his face and slumped back in the pew as the events of that last night rushed back: the anguish on the faces of the doctors, the terror in the nurses' eyes, the crushing frustration and the feeling of absolute futility.

"Then something happened," he went on, still avoiding her eyes. "I remembered that last moment in the ammunition cellar, when the lights went out and you took my hand. And I wanted to live. Suddenly, at that moment, more than anything I've ever wanted in my life, I wanted to live."

Natalia placed her hand on his knee and rubbed it gently. "We've been given a second chance, Adam. We can make this mean something."

He finally looked at her and nodded, not trusting himself to speak.

They decided it would be safer if they kept moving, and a few minutes later they were walking along Avenue Grodzka heading south, away from the Rynek Glowny. They circled around Wawel Castle and followed a path down to the bank of the Vistula River. There was no one else around, and they sat on the grass beneath a giant willow tree. Ducks swam lazily on the river, and a rowboat glided past. Natalia held the bouquet of daisies in both hands, looking down at them.

After a few minutes she laid the daisies on the ground and reached into the vest pocket of her jacket and withdrew a thin, leather-bound book. "We can't take much time now, but there are some sections of this you must read before we do anything else."

Adam watched in silence as she opened the journal written by his uncle, Ludwik Banach. She thumbed through the pages, then handed him the journal, pointing to an entry near the end.

Adam held the journal in his hands for a moment, then began reading. His uncle told of working in the Copernicus Memorial Library six days a week, of sleeping most of the rest of the time, of feeling tired, with a hacking cough. He wrote about a friend, Jerzy Jastremski, who urged him to see a doctor, but he declined, remembering the "hospital" at Sachsenhausen from which no one ever returned.

Then Adam read the account of a meeting his uncle had with Hans Frank, once his colleague, now his jailor, a meeting in which Frank told him about the discovery of a mass grave in the Katyn Forest where thousands of Polish officers had been murdered in 1940.

> *14 April 1943*
>
> *He said that he had known about the murders for some time. He asked if I recalled his visitor last November. Thanks to this visitor and the gift he brought, Frank said, he has proof that it was the Russians who committed this despicable act. He said that proof—solid evidence—was always useful.*

Adam set the journal down, staring out at the river. *Frank's visitor was Tarnov.* It had to be. It all fit with what Captain Andreyev had reported that night on the terrace. Tarnov's lady-friend said they went to Krakow in the fall of 1942 and Tarnov gave Frank a document. The document Frank referred to as a "gift."

Natalia touched his arm. "You should read the last two entries."

> *15 January 1945*
>
> *Today I discovered the "solid evidence" Hans Frank boasted about back in April of 1943. It is a carbon copy of a single document authorizing the massacre in the Katyn Forest! I found it neatly folded in a non-descript envelope intermixed with dozens of other envelopes and file folders in the final box of documents left on the table in room L-3.*

Adam's eyes leaped to the next entry, dated 16 January:

> *I have translated the document. It took more than two hours . . . this is the essence of its contents:*
>
> *On 5 March 1940, at the request of NKVD Commissar Lavrenty Beria, an order was signed by Joseph Stalin and every other member of the Soviet Politburo, authorizing the execution of twenty-seven thousand Polish "nationalists and counterrevolutionaries." The various groups of Poles and their places of execution were itemized—including the four thousand officers of the Polish army whose graves were discovered by the Germans in the Katyn Forest.*

A little later, came the last words his uncle had written:

> *Now, I have but one last thing for which to live. This will be my final entry of the journal. I have been up all night, and I know what I must do. The copy of Stalin's order authorizing the massacre in the Katyn Forest must not fall into Russian hands.*
>
> *To whoever reads this journal: find Adam Nowak and tell him that we shall never be pathetic pawns on the perilous chessboard of the NKVD.*

Adam dropped the journal and closed his eyes, barely able to comprehend what he'd just read: his uncle, obviously quite ill after years in captivity. It was almost more than he could bear. He now realized with absolute certainty that it was all true. Tarnov had given a copy of Stalin's Katyn Order to Hans Frank in 1942. And now he had to get it back. A chill crept down his spine as he thought about the last thing General Kovalenko had said that night on the terrace: "Dmitri Tarnov hasn't yet found what he's looking for . . . and now he's going after your uncle."

Natalia's hand touched his leg. As he opened his eyes and looked at her, his emotions left him reeling. He wanted to take her in his arms, but at the same time an almost irresistible urge to run away threatened to overwhelm him. But Natalia was the one person, perhaps the only person, he knew he could trust. He told her what he knew so far about Tarnov's search for the order.

"Then we have to find it first," she said emphatically, "and to do that we have to find your uncle."

"Where do we start?"

"With your uncle's friend. His name was in the first journal entry you read."

"Jerzy Jastremski?"

"You're about to meet him."

"What? Are you serious?"

"He works in the Reading Room of the Copernicus Memorial Library. You're to go there this morning." She ran her eyes over his new suit. "What's your cover story for being here?"

"Whitehall arranged it," Adam said. He felt self-conscious under her scrutiny. "I'm an American industrialist doing business with the Russian military."

"That's perfect. You're a businessman doing research at the library."

"It's open again?"

"They're getting ready for the university to resume classes this fall, but the library is open now. Jastremski knows where your uncle went when he left Krakow."

"He *knows?* I don't understand. How did you—?"

"I have a contact who told me. Before the war Jastremski was a librarian at the law school."

Adam thought for a moment. *A librarian at the law school.* He seemed to recall Jastremski from the days when he was doing legal research for his uncle—a slender, middle-aged man sitting behind a desk at the law school library. "I think I remember him."

"I thought you might," Natalia said. "Jastremski will have been told to expect a visitor, but he will be extremely wary. Even if he recognizes you, he might not acknowledge it. He's AK, but very covert, very much under cover. Banach was smuggling documents from Frank's personal files at the library—hundreds of documents. Details about the Jewish ghettos, concentration camps, all of it passed through the channel to me. Jastremski was part of the channel, though I never knew his name until yesterday."

"Do you think Jastremski knows about Stalin's order?"

Natalia shook her head. "According to the journal, your uncle never shared that with anyone."

"When I meet Jastremski, what's the code?"

"Ask for some help finding a book. Then tell him you're new in town. Ask him if he knows what time the mass is on Sunday at the Church of Archangel Michael and Saint Stanislaus." She reached into a cloth bag she had been carrying, extracted a folded newspaper and handed it to him. "In the lower left-hand corner of page six I've written an address in the eastern section of the Kazimierz District. I'll meet you there at three o'clock this afternoon. The room is on the third floor, number 34. The key will be behind the radiator at the end of the hall."

Adam suddenly felt uneasy, as though an invisible force was pulling him into a place he wasn't sure he could go.

Natalia smiled as if, once again, she had read his mind. She reached over and took his hand, then brought it to her lips and kissed it. "Three o'clock," she said softly. "You can read the rest of the journal."

Forty-Three

15 JUNE

ADAM STOOD IN FRONT of the imposing multistory structure on Avenue Mickiewicza with his suit coat slung over his shoulder. He glanced up at the words *Biblioteka Copernicus* embossed in the stone façade above the three-meter-high, copper-clad doors of the main entrance. At least the Germans never had the chance to officially change the name. He put his coat back on and passed through the doors into a three-story circular atrium. He walked through a marble archway that led to the main floor section of the new library.

He smiled at the young woman sitting behind a semicircular, mahogany desk under a sign that read *Information* and asked for directions to the Reading Room.

"Take the stairs to the first floor and it will be on your right."

Adam crossed the library's ground floor gallery, heading for the stairs. His uncle had been instrumental in creating this place but, ironically, it had not been completed until after the German invasion. The gallery was a vast, circular room at least fifty meters in diameter with a marble floor and a high, domed ceiling depicting the heliocentric model of the universe conceived by the sixteenth-century Polish astronomer, Nicolaus Copernicus. In the center of the room stood a life-sized, bronze bust of Copernicus perched on a marble pillar. Around the perimeter of the gallery ranged shelves of periodicals and newspapers, mahogany tables and leather-backed chairs. To his left and right, marble archways led to other areas of the ground floor. And on the far side of the gallery, directly across from the main entrance, a wide marble stairway arched gracefully upward to the first floor.

Adam climbed the stairway, turned right and entered the Reading Room—a large, brightly lit area with windows along one side. About a dozen people were scattered about, sitting quietly at sturdy oak tables, studying books and documents. At the far end of the room a woman in a somber gray dress and a middle-aged man wearing a neatly pressed white shirt and tie sat a few meters apart behind a counter, sorting books and making notations on small cards. Adam set his briefcase on an empty table, took his time opening it and rummaged around until the woman picked up a pile of books and disappeared into the stacks behind the counter.

As Adam approached, the slender man glanced up and peered over the top of his glasses. The man's face was familiar: thin, white hair, his skin soft and pale, the look of someone who spent most of his time indoors. His name tag read *J. Jastremski.*

"I'm looking for some records of iron ore production in Silesia," Adam said.

Jerzy Jastremski was silent for a moment, appearing thoughtful, rotating a pencil between his thumb and forefinger as though he was envisioning the exact book and its precise location. Then he nodded and said, "Yes, I think I know where that might be. What period are you interested in?"

"The 1930s," Adam replied.

Jastremski got to his feet and wandered off into the stacks. He returned several minutes later carrying a thick leather volume under his arm. He set the book on the counter and turned to the table of contents.

Adam glanced around. The woman librarian hadn't returned, and everyone else in the room seemed engrossed in their reading.

After a moment Jastremski flipped through the book and said with a note of triumph, "Ah, here it is. I think you'll find what you're looking for on pages 1142 through 1156."

Adam turned the book toward himself and glanced at the pages of dense data. "That looks like what I need."

"Is there anything else I can help you with?" Jastremski asked.

"There is one other thing," Adam said, casually. "I'm new in town and I'm thinking of attending mass this Sunday at the Church of Archangel Michael and Saint Stanislaus. Do you know the time?"

Jastremski stared at him for a moment, a flicker of recognition suddenly appearing in his eyes. His face flushed, and there was a slight tremor in his hands as he withdrew a thin notebook and fountain pen from his suit coat pocket. "There is more than one mass," he said. "I'll write down the times for you." He scribbled a note and handed it to Adam with a barely perceptible motion of his head toward a door at the far end of the counter.

Adam glanced at the note.

Lower Level, Room L-3, thirty minutes.

Adam spent the next half hour staring at charts and tables of iron ore production, occasionally scribbling meaningless notes on a pad of paper. He glanced at his watch and looked up at the counter. Jastremski was gone, and the woman librarian was stamping cards and slipping them back into books. He waited a few moments until she picked up the books and left the counter. Then he snapped the briefcase shut, stood up and walked casually to the front of the room. He set the thick book on the counter and proceeded through the door at the far end. He descended the stairs to the Lower Level, found Room L3 and stepped inside.

Jastremski sat at a table and motioned for Adam to close the door.

Adam took a seat across the table from Jastremski. "You remember me, don't you?"

Jastremski nodded, his pale complexion now ashen, as though he'd seen a ghost. "The Germans deported you . . . after they arrested . . ." His voice trailed off, and he lowered his eyes.

"It is important that I find my uncle," Adam said, deciding it would be easiest to come right to the point. "I understand you know where he is."

Jastremski didn't respond.

Adam forced himself to be patient. "Will you help me?"

"These are dangerous times," Jastremski said, folding his hands on the table. His fingers were long and thin. They trembled again as they had out in the Reading Room. "One must be cautious."

"I understand."

"Do you? Do you know that the NKVD has been kicking in doors all over the country since the murders near Zyrardow."

"What murders?" Adam asked sharply.

"Three weeks ago two NKVD officers were murdered in some village out by the Bolimowski Forest. Near Zyrardow. One of them was a high-ranking officer. He was making an inspection tour of the rural areas. He was shot through the mouth, I heard. Sounds like an execution, if you ask me."

Adam's spine tingled. Having the NKVD on heightened alert was a problem, but it really had nothing to do with him. *Stay focused. Concentrate on the mission.* He looked Jastremski in the eyes. "Everything you tell me will be kept—"

Jastremski smiled thinly and leaned over the table. He had clearly recovered from the shock of seeing Adam again after all this time. "Save the speech. I've heard it all before. As I said, these are dangerous times. Don't make promises you won't be able to keep if you wind up in the hands of the NKVD."

"OK, no speeches, no promises. But the fact remains that it is vitally important to find Ludwik Banach. Will you help me?"

"As I said, one must be cautious. I'll tell you what I know, then we'll see if it helps you." He paused for a second as though gathering his thoughts, then moved his gaze to the bare walls. "This room was used as a storeroom by Hans Frank's government. They kept all manner of records and documents here, in file boxes, all neatly organized and labeled: concentration camp details, extermination methods, starvation data." He looked down at the table, shaking his head slowly. A moment later he continued. "In the fall of 1941, Banach obtained access to this room. I was never certain how, but I suspected that the German library director, Gustav Kruger, gave him a key."

Adam flinched. *A German gave Uncle Ludwik a key to the room?*

"They weren't *all* monsters, you know."

"I'm afraid I only met the monsters."

There was a look of understanding in Jastremski's eyes. "Once every few weeks, Banach brought documents to me, and I took them to the church."

"And the priest passed them on?" Adam was determined not to mention Natalia.

"I assume so. I never knew who actually received them. I just took them to the church and gave them to the priest. Everything flowed through him. Then in January of this year, immediately after the Germans fled the city, Banach decided to leave Krakow. He said he couldn't be here when the Russians came. But he wasn't well, and I urged him to stay here. We have doctors here. He could get treatment."

"Not well? What do you mean?"

"His time in Sachsenhausen had been hard on him. He had a cough, and his energy was slipping. The Nazis allowed those of us working in the library access to doctors, but Banach refused to go."

"Why?" Adam asked, though he'd already guessed the answer.

"He believed he had tuberculosis, and if he sought medical attention he would be sent to a sanatorium. He was *very* determined to leave Krakow, almost desperate. He kept saying he could not allow himself to be caught by the Russians."

Adam thought it over as the pieces started falling into place. Banach had the copy of Stalin's Katyn Order in his possession, but he knew he would be trapped in Krakow after the Russians arrived, especially if he were confined to a sanatorium. He also knew that Hans Frank's "visitor" would return, searching for the order. "Where did he go?" Adam asked.

"There is an AK contact among the Górale," Jastremski said, "in the Tatra Mountains, beyond Nowy Targ."

Adam remembered the Górale from a student camping trip he'd taken in 1938. They were highlanders—mountain farmers and herdsmen—tough passionate people, the type of people who would protect their friends at all costs. "How will I find him?" he asked.

"Tomorrow, take the evening bus to Nowy Targ but don't get off. A man carrying a wicker basket will get on board."

"Can I go tonight? It's urgent."

Jastremski thought for a moment, then nodded. "I'll arrange it.

Just follow the man with the wicker basket. He'll introduce himself as 'Tytus.' He'll expect a code name in return."

"Tell him it's 'Wolf,'" Adam said as he got up to leave.

Jastremski followed him to the door, checked the hallway then pointed in the opposite direction from which Adam had come. "I suggest you leave by the service entrance in the back. Just follow this corridor and make a left. There's a loading dock, but it's only used on Friday mornings by the janitorial crew. Next to the loading dock is the service entrance."

Forty-Four

15 June

It had been years since the last time Adam was in the eastern section of the Kazimierz District, and the now-decaying neighborhood bore little resemblance to the bustling Jewish market area he remembered. Slowly navigating the mostly deserted, filthy streets, Adam eventually found the address Natalia had written in the newspaper. His first instinct was to share the information he'd received from Jastremski with her. But by the time he arrived at the run-down building, doubts had crept back into his mind.

He stood on the sidewalk, glancing up and down the deserted street, hesitating. He remembered a similar moment back in Warsaw when he had stood outside the breach in the old city wall while Natalia waited for him in the ammunition cellar. He had hesitated then as well, but he'd had to leave when Rabbit suddenly arrived.

Or, had he?

On that night, Natalia wanted to be his friend. A simple thing, a friend: someone to talk to, someone to share his fears, his anger, his hopes for a future. But he didn't have friends; he *couldn't* have friends. It wasn't possible. Friends, relationships of any kind, were a distraction, and distractions led to mistakes.

Assassins could not make mistakes.

He should leave. Get lost for a few hours and take the evening bus to Nowy Targ. That was the sensible thing to do. Focus on the mission. Find Banach and the Katyn Order. Natalia had done her part and there was no reason to put her in any more danger. Back in

Warsaw, she had wanted a friend. But he knew it was far more than that now. If he couldn't be her friend then, he certainly couldn't be her lover now, not ever.

There were no second chances . . . and there would be no *redemption.*

And worst of all, he knew there would be no release from the yearning he felt to touch Natalia, to kiss her, to . . .

He had to leave.

Adam started back up the street, walking briskly, his mind made up. It was the right thing to do.

He approached the end of the block and was about to turn the corner, when he noticed an old man shuffling along the sidewalk on the other side of the street, poking into the gutter with a long stick. Adam slowed his pace. The man looked at him for a moment, then nodded, tipped his grimy, felt cap and shuffled on. Adam stopped and watched as the man proceeded down the street, turned the corner and disappeared . . . alone.

Adam turned and looked back down the street, toward the building where Natalia waited. *What the hell is wrong with me?*

He turned around and walked back to the run-down building, his desire now overpowering. He climbed the stairs to the third floor and found the key behind the radiator. He paused for a moment outside room no. 34 . . . then inserted the key in the lock and pushed open the door.

Natalia sat on the bed wearing only a partially buttoned cotton shirt over her bra and panties. Her knees were drawn up, her arms clasped around them.

Adam glanced around the room, avoiding her eyes. The curtains were drawn, but the window was open at the bottom and a soft breeze fluttered in. "Jastremski was very helpful," he said quickly. "But I've got to go. There's not much time and . . ."

He stopped and looked at her, suddenly struck with a terrible fear that if he took his eyes off of her for just an instant, she'd be gone, like that last night in Warsaw.

Natalia cocked her head and smiled. "You look very hot—and tired." She slid over, making room on the narrow bed, beckoning for him to sit down.

"You know who I am, Natalia. You know what I've done."

"Yes, I do. Now come and sit down. I won't bite."

Adam closed the door and locked it. He set his briefcase on the floor, draped his suit coat over the back of the single chair and sat next to her.

She reached up and stroked the scar on the left side of his face, looking at his damaged ear. "Did that happen at Raczynski Palace?"

He nodded.

"You could have been killed. Why did you—" She stopped and bit her lower lip. "I'm sorry. It doesn't matter." She looked into his eyes. "I was in love with you, Adam."

A knot twisted in his stomach. "And now?" he whispered.

A tear formed in the corner of her eye and trickled down her cheek. "I loved you. I couldn't explain it; we barely knew each other. But I also *hated* you for leaving that night. I hated that you were determined to throw away your life—and *my* life, what we might have had together. And I hated *myself* for not stopping you. And then, the day before yesterday, when you stepped onto that tram . . ."

Adam reached over and brushed away the tear, running his finger slowly down her cheek, feeling as though he had drifted through a passageway, leaving a dark place and entering a brighter one. "That night, at the palace in Warsaw, my last thought was that I had been given a gift. In the midst of all that horror, I had been given a gift—and I threw it away."

"We have another chance, Adam."

He touched her knee, tracing a circle with his finger, looking into her eyes. "I want to believe that."

She placed her hand on top of his and caressed his fingers, reached up and loosened his tie, slowly pulling it off his neck.

With a tremor in his fingers, he undid the rest of the buttons on her thin, cotton shirt and slid it off her shoulders.

She closed her eyes and leaned back, leading his hand slowly up her thigh. Her face was flushed, her hair wet around the edges, sticking to her forehead. Beads of perspiration trickled down her neck and disappeared between her breasts.

Adam leaned forward and kissed her neck.

She snuggled close as his other hand moved around her back, finding the clasp of her bra.

They lay curled together under the sheet as the late afternoon sun filtered through the grimy windowpane. Natalia rested her head on his chest, listening to the soft beating of his heart, feeling a warmth inside she had only dreamt about. If only they could stay right here, curled up in this shabby little room, just the two of them, and ignore everything that was happening in the world, she would be happy.

But that wasn't possible. There were things they had to do. And she had to tell him about the two NKVD agents she had murdered. But not right now. For just a few more moments all she wanted to think about was Adam. She snuggled closer and whispered, "You haven't told me how you managed to get out of Warsaw."

He sighed as he ran his fingers through her hair. "Well, I still had that motorcycle, and the German uniform—"

She abruptly sat up. "My God, you mean that Waffen-SS uniform you wore when you shot Heisenberg? You kept it?"

"Stashed away with the motorcycle. It was almost a month before I could walk—I get these dizzy spells—and I was surprised that the motorcycle and the uniform were still there. But it got me out of the city."

She put her hand on his cheek, leaned over and gently kissed his mangled ear. "Dizzy spells?"

"They come and go, but it's getting better. I don't hear so well out of that ear though."

She furled her brow, gently rubbing his forehead. "The dizzy spells are probably the after-effect of a concussion from the gunshot."

He smiled. "Ah yes, the medical student, whose father was a doctor. So, what about the hearing loss?"

"Hmm, let's see, could be a ruptured eardrum, or possibly a dislocation of the tiny bones in the middle ear. A loud, sharp noise or a blow to the head could cause either one." She slid her forefinger along the thin scar where the bullet had grazed his cheekbone before tearing his ear in half.

"I'm impressed. Apparently you paid attention in class."

"Whichever it is, it appears as though you're damaged goods. Guess I'll have to toss you back."

He slid his hand around her bare back and pulled her on top of him. "Right now?"

"Well, maybe not right now."

Later, they sat on the bed, and Natalia listened intently as he described his meeting at the library. "At least Jastremski doesn't know who *you* are," Adam said. "He told me he never knew who received the documents he got from Banach. He just gave them to the priest."

"When do you have to leave?"

"This evening, by bus to Nowy Targ."

"Is your uncle still there?"

"I don't know. Jastremski's had no contact with him since January. He left him with the Górale at a small chapel somewhere beyond Nowy Targ. I'm to rendezvous with 'Tytus' and use my code name, 'Wolf.' After that, I'm not sure."

Natalia was quiet for a long time, then slowly shook her head. "I can't go with you, Adam. We can't risk getting caught together. You'll be safer on your own."

Adam stared at her, suddenly remembering the other information Jastremski had given him. "Do you know anything about two NKVD agents who were killed near Zyrardow three weeks ago?" he asked.

"Now you know why we can't risk being caught together."

Adam wasn't surprised. Natalia was perfectly capable of shooting two NKVD agents if she had to. And she was right about the risk of being caught together, though at this moment he couldn't bear the thought of leaving her again. "Is there anything else I should know?"

Natalia stood up and stepped across the tiny room, wearing only her white cotton shirt. Adam suddenly felt aroused again at the sight of her small firm buttocks.

She lifted Banach's journal off the top of the bureau and turned around, clutching it to her chest. "Today is Friday. If you're not back by the middle of next week, I'll come up there and find you." She handed him the journal. "Take this with you." Then she picked the rest of her clothes off the chair and began getting dressed.

Adam sighed and set the journal on the bed. He reached for his glasses, then got up and pulled on his trousers. He removed his suit coat from the hook on the wall, withdrew a folded sheet of paper from the breast pocket and handed it to Natalia. "It's a copy of a letter of authorization," he said, "from General Kovalenko of the Red Army. It requires all Russian Army officers to offer their assistance and cooperation. I have the original."

"*You* have a letter of authorization from a Russian general?"

"Whitehall arranged it." Adam explained how Kovalenko was an old friend of Whitehall's—and half Polish.

"And you trust Whitehall?" Natalia asked skeptically.

Adam remembered Whitehall's "deceptions." "I don't know who to trust."

"Has it occurred to you that all of these people could be after the same thing, but for different reasons?"

Adam remained silent, waiting for her to continue.

Natalia paced around the room, running a hand through her short-cropped hair. "We have the journal, so we know a few things for sure. We know that Hans Frank had a visitor in 1942—most likely it was Tarnov—who gave him a copy of Stalin's Katyn Order. We know that the order exists, and we know what it says. As for the rest of your little group of friends—Whitehall, Kovalenko and Andreyev—they *don't* know for sure that Stalin's order actually exists. But they suspect that Tarnov gave Frank *something* that implicates the NKVD in the Katyn murders."

"And they want to find it and make it public to expose the NKVD," Adam said in agreement.

"Or, make sure it never sees the light of day. There are powerful forces at work here, Adam. And the question remains: Who do we trust?"

Adam rubbed the numb side of his face. He felt as if he were riding a runaway train barreling through a long, dark tunnel with no idea what was at the other end. Both Whitehall and Kovalenko had lied to him on more than one occasion. But he had to make a decision. "You have a copy of Kovalenko's letter of authorization. Tarnov is desperate. If I get into trouble and don't return on time you're going to need help. Use that letter to contact Kovalenko or send a message to Whitehall. We don't have any other options."

She turned away and stepped to the window, parting the curtain a bit. The copy of Kovalenko's letter slipped from her hand and fluttered to the floor. "We could leave," she said quietly. "We could forget all this and go up into the mountains, cross over into Slovakia. We escaped Warsaw; we could escape this."

Adam took her shoulders in his hands and kissed the back of her neck. "Is that what you want?"

Natalia was silent for a moment then abruptly turned around, facing him. "Yes, it's what I want. But first, we have to finish this. The Russians burned my village to the ground, and they deported my parents to God-knows-where in Kazakhstan or Siberia." She swallowed hard, her eyes glistening. "And they murdered my brother in the Katyn Forest. They murdered him—shot him in the back of the head—and threw his body in a ditch."

Adam felt her tremble for just an instant, then she stiffened and glared at him. "We have to find that order," Natalia said, her eyes suddenly cold and hard. "We have to *finish* this."

Forty-Five

15 June

The aging bus creaked and groaned, black smoke belching from its exhaust pipe as it toiled along the gravel roadway following the River Raba south from Krakow. The engine labored and the driver jammed the transmission into a lower gear as they climbed the foothills of the Tatra Mountains.

Adam glanced around at the handful of other passengers, then looked out the window and caught a glimpse of the peaks in the distance, remembering how he had hiked through these mountains during the summer of 1938. He had just completed his second term at the Jagiellonian University law school and had taken a break from the legal research he was doing for his uncle. It seemed an eternity ago.

The sun was setting in the western sky, casting long shadows over the grassy meadows nestled between rolling hills and pine forests. The tranquility of the bucolic scene was almost enough to make him forget the danger of the impending mission.

He was close to finding his uncle, but he felt as though he were running toward a door that was about to close. Tarnov and his NKVD thugs were out there somewhere—and they might not be his only problem. As his mind swirled with the uncertainty of who to trust, Adam glanced down at the journal he'd just finished reading. The story of his uncle's incredible journey both haunted and inspired him. He recalled the opening words of his uncle's first entry:

Eight months ago I descended into hell. I have seen the

abyss, the dark chasm of depravity into which man can sink. And I am terrified. I am terrified the world does not know what is happening here. I fear most will not live to tell their story, so I will tell mine and pray that it will emerge from the darkness—that the world may know.

Exhaustion set in and Adam closed his eyes thinking about the afternoon with Natalia, wondering if *he* had finally emerged from the darkness.

When the bus shuddered to a halt at the station in Nowy Targ, most of the passengers collected their battered suitcases, baskets and canvas bags and trudged off the vehicle. Adam remained in his seat. The driver stood outside, smoking a cigarette, chatting with the departing passengers. Eventually a trickle of new passengers boarded the bus, including a stocky man in overalls and a faded plaid shirt, carrying a wicker basket. A few minutes later the driver tossed his cigarette butt on the ground and climbed back into his seat, and the bus lumbered on.

Adam was wide awake now, his senses alive as he sat on the stiff leather seat waiting anxiously for whatever was coming next. Reading his uncle's story and knowing that he was still alive had filled him with a resolve and a sense of purpose that he hadn't felt since Warsaw.

I fear most will not live to tell their story, so I will tell mine and pray that it will emerge from the darkness—that the world may know.

Banach's words drummed in Adam's head, over and over, and he now knew, deep in his soul, that no matter what else happened, the entire story—the bizarre encounters with the madman Hans Frank, the extermination of the Jews and, most important, the discovery of the Katyn Order—had to be preserved and shared with the civilized world. For the first time in as long as he could remember, Adam felt some comfort. If nothing else came of the years of gruesome warfare, the years of mindless death and destruction—finding Natalia and being reunited with his uncle would be enough.

The road grew narrower and the hills steeper as they climbed higher into the Tatra Mountains, the last purple hues of daylight sliding into darkness. The bus bounced along the pockmarked road for another half hour before finally shuddering to a stop. The man with the wicker basket stood up and moved to the door. Adam followed him off the bus.

They appeared to be in the middle of nowhere, and as the sound of the bus' laboring engine receded beyond the hills, the blackness of the mountain night closed in around them though the stars were incredibly bright. The man moved closer, and Adam tensed, clenching his right fist. He wished now he'd accepted the Browning 9mm pistol Natalia had offered. He'd insisted she keep it for her own protection. He hoped he wouldn't regret it.

The man nudged Adam's arm and said, "Follow me and stay close. It's not far, but the road falls off into a ditch."

They trudged along a gravel road in the darkness for perhaps a quarter of an hour. The hair on Adam's neck bristled. He darted his eyes left and right, though he couldn't see a thing in the black night.

Then a shadowy form emerged through the gloom. It turned out to be a modest building with a peaked roof, topped by a cross. Adam waited outside while the man pulled open a creaking wooden door and disappeared into the dark void. A moment later he reappeared in the doorway, illuminated by a kerosene lantern, and beckoned Adam to enter.

It was a mountain chapel, constructed of rough stones and hand-hewn beams, with a stone altar and three wooden pews. The stocky man looked at Adam and tipped his hat. "You may call me Tytus."

"And you may call me Wolf," Adam replied. At the front of the small chapel, an intricately carved crucifix was attached to the stone wall above the altar. The Christ figure had a sorrowful expression. "What do we do now?" he asked.

Tytus pointed to the small octagonal window above the crucifix. "We wait. They'll see the light in the window." He looked at Adam curiously. "You're an American?"

Adam nodded, assuming that Jastremski had told him. "But I was born in Krakow. I came back in '36."

Tytus snorted. "I won't ask why. Jastremski told me a bit about your background, and I don't need to know any more. It's not healthy." He was silent for a moment then said, "You know the Górale?"

"I've read about them and met a few during a camping trip up in this area back in the summer of '38."

Tytus pulled an intricately carved pipe out of his shirt pocket. He took his time filling it with pungent, stringy tobacco, tamping it down and lighting it. He appeared to be in his mid-forties, with thick fingers, jet-black hair and the weathered complexion of a man who made his living working outside. He took a couple of puffs from his pipe, then pointed the stem at Adam. "I've known the Górale all my life. They come down to the lower valleys every year in the spring to work on the farms during the planting season. They come back in the fall for the harvest. In between they pretty much keep to themselves up in these mountains, tending their herds. If you're honest with them, they will do anything for you. They'll open their homes, share their food, give you clothing. But they can be vindictive and cruel as hell if they are deceived. Honor is everything. I don't know what your business is up here, and I don't want to know, but I'll tell you this. Do *not* lie to them."

He puffed on the pipe, then pointed it at Adam again. "They'll be suspicious of you at first. They always are with outsiders; it's in their blood. But be patient and do not lie to them. Not if you want to get out of here."

"I know they fought as partisans during the war," Adam said, "and the Nazis made them pay."

Tytus nodded, exhaling a cloud of sweet-smelling smoke that helped take away the dampness. "Freedom is everything to them. No matter what the Germans did to them—and the Russians later—the Górale fighters kept the routes open all the way to Slovakia. A lot of weapons and contraband passed over these mountains."

"And Polish soldiers," Adam said, remembering rumors of the escape routes back in Warsaw.

Time passed, the heat from the lantern slowly taking away the chill of the night air and the clammy stone walls. Then Adam heard sounds in the distance, the muted clopping of hooves and creaking wagon wheels. The sounds drew closer, until they stopped outside the chapel. Tytus held up his hand, signaling for Adam to remain where he was. A moment later the door creaked open, and a figure filled the doorway.

He was a huge man, with a barrel chest, broad shoulders and long, flowing blond hair. He wore a wide-brimmed felt hat, a black vest over a white linen shirt and coarse, heavy trousers with an embroidered, red strip down the outside of each leg. The big man glared at Adam suspiciously. Then he turned to Tytus and nodded. Without a word, he motioned for them to follow and stepped back into the night.

Forty-Six

16 June

Dmitri Tarnov received a telephone call in his office early Saturday morning. "We've heard from our contact at the library," the voice on the other end said. "Jastremski had a visitor yesterday."

"Yesterday? What the fuck is wrong with you?" Tarnov roared. "Why in the hell didn't someone call me right away?"

Silence.

Then the voice stammered, "I don't . . . Someone should have—"

"*Nichivó!* Forget it, you moron. Who was it? Anyone she knew?"

"*Nyet*. Nobody she'd seen before. She said he was well-dressed and wore eyeglasses, looked like a business man."

Tarnov slammed the phone down.

When Jerzy Jastremski left the library, following his Saturday morning shift, Tarnov was waiting for him, standing on the sidewalk next to a long, black Citroën.

"*Dzień dobry,* Mr. Jastremski," Tarnov said as the slightly built librarian walked past, using the only Polish words he knew, or cared to learn.

Jastremski stopped. *"Dzień dobry."*

"Speak English, Mr. Jastremski?" Tarnov asked.

Jastremski looked wary, but nodded.

"Allow me to give ride home," Tarnov said.

"Thank you, but I prefer to walk," Jastremski said in fluent English. He attempted to step past him, but Tarnov gripped the slender man by the elbow and shoved a pistol into his ribs.

"Get in fuckin' car," Tarnov snapped, "or you die right here." He steered Jastremski to the black Citroën, pulled open the rear door and shoved him inside. Tarnov was dressed in plain clothes—a dark blue business suit and black trench coat—better for this sort of work than the NKVD uniform. He removed the trench coat, folded it carefully and climbed in the auto next to Jastremski.

"What's this all about? Where are you taking me?" Jastremski asked as the Citroën sped through the streets of the Stare Miasto.

"Find out soon enough," Tarnov said. "Now shut up." As they drove on in silence, Tarnov became edgy. Time was running out, and he *had* to find Ludwik Banach. He had no idea whether Banach had what he wanted, or if Jastremski's visitor was anyone worthwhile, but he was damned sure going to find out, and find out fast.

The auto proceeded up Wawel hill and around the castle to the area overlooking the Vistula River. The driver stopped the car and got out. He closed the door and stood nearby, looking out over the river.

"So, Mr. Jastremski, you had visitor yesterday?" Tarnov asked.

"Excuse me, a visitor?"

"At library. You had visitor."

"I'm afraid I don't know what you mean. Several visitors came to the library yesterday, like they do all the time, asking for help finding books."

Tarnov glared at the thin, pale man, laughing internally at Jastremski's feeble attempt at bravado. *We'll find out in a few seconds just how brave you really are, you worthless piece of shit.* Tarnov reached in his pocket and withdrew a key. He dropped it into Jastremski's lap. "Recognize, Mr. Jastremski?"

Jastremski's pale complexion became white as chalk. Beads of sweat trickled down his forehead.

Tarnov smiled. "Yes, of course you do. Key to your apartment. I not return to your wife when we haul her out two hour ago."

"My wife? What've you—?"

Tarnov suddenly smashed his fist into the older man's face, snapping Jastremski's head back against the window. Blood spurted from his nose and mouth. He slumped in the seat, holding his hands over his face.

Tarnov leaned over and grabbed him by the shirt, jerking him forward. "That is what I did to your wife, you AK shithead." He shoved Jastremski hard against the door and screamed at him, "You have one minute to name visitor, what you tell him and where he go!" He leaned closer. "Or I drive you to jail, and you watch while we chop wife into pieces and flush her down fucking toilet!"

Forty-Seven

17 June

Activity at the Kommandatura was at a fever pitch. With the Potsdam conference rapidly approaching, military officers and diplomatic agents from America and Great Britain flooded into Berlin. There were no taxis, and the buses to and from the aerodrome were crowded and stifling hot and usually arrived without most of the luggage. The accommodations assignment desk on the main floor of the Kommandatura was in chaos, and the tempers of those waiting in the endless queue were getting short.

Stanley Whitehall was lucky. His bag had made the trip from the aerodrome, and he pushed his way through the crowd, then slipped into the backseat of a long, black auto with Soviet flags mounted on the hood.

A half hour later, Whitehall was ushered into General Kovalenko's office in the Soviet Military Administration building on Wilhelmstrasse. The general sat at his desk, scowling and thumbing through a thick report. Captain Andreyev, who had been standing near the windows, stepped forward and shook Whitehall's hand. "Good to see you again, Colonel. I trust you made it in without too much difficulty?"

Whitehall set his briefcase on the floor and wiped perspiration from his forehead with a handkerchief. "God, it's a bloody mess at the Kommandatura and even worse at the aerodrome. Gone less than a week and I barely recognize the place."

There was a loud thud as Kovalenko dropped the report on his desk and stood up, stretching and rubbing his eyes. "And this is just the beginning," he growled. "Wait until the entourages of three heads of state start pouring in here, yapping and whining about everything from the bed sheets to the color of the china. It'll be worse than fighting the damn war." The burly general took two large strides around the desk and clapped Whitehall on the back. "Come, my friend, have a drink."

Kovalenko sat across from Whitehall on one of the two leather settees in front of his desk while Captain Andreyev produced a bottle of vodka and three glasses from a cabinet. "So, Adam Nowak is off to Poland?"

"That he is," Whitehall replied. "A bit skeptical perhaps. I can never tell if he trusts me or not."

The general roared with laughter and slapped Whitehall's knee. "You're SOE, Stanley. *No one* should trust you!" He raised his glass and added, "No one except *me,* of course." He downed the vodka in one gulp and turned to Andreyev. "Tell Stanley what we know about Dmitri Tarnov."

Andreyev finished his drink and set the glass on the table. "We've confirmed that Tarnov left Berlin by train several days ago. No one at the NKVD is saying anything. They clam up whenever Tarnov's name is mentioned. But we're certain he went to Krakow."

"He's gone rogue," Kovalenko said. "He's out there on his own on this, probably with a group of thugs he's got something on and knows he can trust. But he's not working within official NKVD channels."

"He can get away with that?" Whitehall asked.

Andreyev nodded. "Regardless of how Beria treated him, Tarnov is still a relative. And that gives him status. He's used it ruthlessly over the years through intimidation, blackmail, performing favors, just enough so he's got his back covered."

Kovalenko stood up and reached over his desk. He picked up the report he'd been studying and held it out to Whitehall. "This is the preliminary agenda for the conference. Buried on about page two hundred is some obscure reference to the Polish borders remaining as they were set at Yalta. That's it."

Whitehall leafed through the report and dropped it on the table, shaking his head. "Stalin's got what he wants. The question of Polish elections is dead, unless Nowak gets his hands on that document—assuming of course there actually *is* a document that implicates the NKVD in Katyn."

Kovalenko shook a cigarette out of the pack of Lucky Strikes that had been lying on the desk. He lit the cigarette and blew a cloud of smoke in the air. "There's a document, Stanley, and it has everything to do with Katyn. Tarnov gave it to Frank, and now he wants it back."

"How can you be so certain?" Whitehall asked, watching the general closely.

Kovalenko's eyes narrowed. "I know *Tarnov*. I know his type and how they operate. There *is* a document, and I'm certain it's a copy of Stalin's Katyn Order."

"Even if Nowak finds it, will it make any difference?" Andreyev asked.

Whitehall continued to watch Kovalenko for a moment, but the general's expression was unreadable. Then he turned to Andreyev. "It depends on what the document actually says. If there is proof the NKVD committed the murders at Katyn and it's made public, it could be just the ammunition Truman and Churchill both need to stand up to Stalin and press the case for Poland."

Andreyev shook his head. "If that happens, Tarnov is finished."

Whitehall turned to Kovalenko who stood looking out the window, rolling the cigarette between his thumb and forefinger. "How much help will your letter of authorization be if Nowak gets stopped in Poland?"

Kovalenko took a long drag on the cigarette. "If he gets stopped by the Red Army or the Polish police he'll be fine. If it's Tarnov, or anyone under his control, he'll be in trouble. That's why I made a copy for him to give to his contact—what's her name?"

"Natalia," Whitehall replied, "and I suspect she's more than just a contact."

Kovalenko shrugged. "Well, if anything happens, and she gets word back to me, I can protest loudly enough to get him out of there. No one—not the NKVD or even Tarnov—can afford a public controversy with this conference coming up."

"What about that message she sent?" Andreyev asked Whitehall. "The bit about, *we are not pathetic pawns on the perilous chessboard*. Do you know what that means?"

Whitehall shook his head. "It's a phrase Banach used in some paper he wrote back in the '30s. A phrase Hans Frank also used in one of his writings. That's what convinced Adam that Banach and Frank knew each other before the war. Damned if I know what it means, though."

Forty-Eight

18 June

Adam stacked the last of the split logs onto the wagon, brushed the dust and woodchips off his shirt, and looked at the tall, husky man holding the double-ended axe. "Is that it?" he asked.

The man brushed his blond hair back and replaced his wide-brimmed hat. He smiled broadly and laid the axe on top of the pile of logs in the wagon. "That's it for now. We should head back; we're late for supper."

The man's name was Piotr and though he spoke Polish, his local Górale dialect was interspersed with enough Slovakian and Hungarian words that Adam had to listen carefully, a task made a bit more challenging with the impaired hearing in his left ear. Since that first suspicious meeting at the chapel, Piotr had slowly warmed up, until now he treated Adam almost as a friend—almost.

They climbed onto the seat of the wagon and waved good-bye to the two other Górale men who'd been helping clear the area of the forest where a stable was to be built. Piotr grabbed the horse's reins with a thick hand, gave them a gentle flick, and the wagon jerked forward, slopping through puddles as they headed toward the cabin.

As the wagon bumped along the muddy road, Adam took in the spectacular scenery. Nestled between two snow-capped peaks, a crystal clear stream trickled down a mountain slope thick with conifers, oaks and birch trees. But he was in no mood to enjoy it. He was restless and getting impatient.

It had been three days since Adam left Krakow. Tytus had departed the morning after they arrived, returning to wherever he came from, leaving Adam with Piotr and his wife, Krystyna, in their three-room log cabin. Adam had learned from Piotr that Banach was indeed among the Górale, though staying with another family in a village higher up in the mountains. It was safer there, Piotr said, farther from Nowy Targ where random patrols of Russian soldiers often made trouble for the locals.

Adam had hoped that by this time he would have already located his uncle and be on his way back to Krakow. But it had rained hard over the weekend, and the route up the mountain was impassable. Perhaps tomorrow, if the weather remained clear, they could make the trip.

The shadows were long by the time they arrived back at the cabin, a sturdy, simple structure, one of three in a small enclave. It was built of logs with small windows and a high-peaked, wood-shingled roof, in the traditional mountain style of the Górale. The aroma of potato pancakes and sauerkraut filled the cabin, and Adam and Piotr washed up while Krystyna set the table with heavy white plates and clay mugs.

"I was getting concerned; he's not usually late for his supper," Krystyna said, gesturing toward her husband. "Was he showing off his wood-splitting skills for you?"

She was younger than Piotr, in her mid-twenties, Adam guessed, quite pretty—and very pregnant. She had thick brown hair put up in a tight bun. Her face was tan, but not weathered, her skin smooth with just a few faint creases at the corners of deep brown, sensuous eyes.

"I probably slowed him down," Adam replied, "but he swings a pretty mean axe."

"That he does. Especially during the contest at Festival Days when all the pretty young girls want to see him flex those big muscles."

Piotr produced a bottle of potato vodka and two glasses, summoning Adam to the table. "Don't pay her any mind," the big man said. "She knows I look at none but her."

Krystyna laughed. "And he knows what I'd do to him if he did." She bent down and gave her husband a peck on the cheek. "He can swing an axe with the best of them, but I can't get him to pick up a broom—even with me in my delicate condition." She added that last with her hands on her hips, nudging Piotr with her backside.

"A man's got his work and a woman hers," Piotr mumbled, pouring the drinks.

"This will be your first child?" Adam said, glancing around the small cabin. There was a fireplace on the opposite side of the single ground-floor room and two sleeping areas in a loft overhead.

Krystyna nodded. "We've only been married a year. Piotr wanted to wait a while, but the good lord had other ideas. Are you married, Adam?"

"No," he said abruptly.

"Well, do you have a girl, a sweetheart?"

Adam felt his face flush, thinking of Natalia and the afternoon they spent in her tiny room in Kazimierz. Is that what they were . . . sweethearts, lovers? His stomach tightened at a sudden foreboding. He'd been bad luck for everyone he ever cared about. Why should this be any different?

"I'm sure you do," Krystyna persisted. "Is she also an American?"

"Krystyna," Piotr interjected, "can't you see you're embarrassing our guest with all your questions? How about our supper?"

She waved a towel at him. "Oh, hush. It won't kill you to wait for a few minutes. If you'd been home on time you wouldn't be so hungry."

After the simple meal Adam helped clear the dishes despite Krystyna's protests, and Piotr's grumbles about setting a bad example. When they were finished they sat around the oak-plank table with mugs of coffee.

"I'd like to see America some day," Krystyna said. "The Statue of Liberty, the Empire State Building. Have you seen the Statue of Liberty?"

Adam smiled. "I sailed right past it the day we came to America. I was eleven years old, and I remember thinking it was very big."

"Did you have a motorcar in America?" Piotr asked.

"My father did. A green Packard with running boards and big chrome headlights."

Piotr's eyes lit up. "Someday I will own a motorcar. A Mercedes-Benz."

Krystyna grimaced. "A German motorcar? After what those bastards did to us? How can you think such a thing?"

"The war's over, and they got what they deserved," Piotr said with a shrug. "It's a fine auto, excellent engineering."

"Hmmmpf," Krystyna snorted and got up from the table. Plucking some knitting from a wicker basket, she sat down in a rocker near the fireplace.

Adam glanced at Piotr, who was smiling at his wife. "Did you serve in the army?"

"Infantry, Fifteenth Division, Krakow Army Group," Piotr said proudly, though Adam detected a sadness in the big man's voice.

"And you made it all the way back here after the capitulation?"

"We were surrounded by the Russians near Grodno. We had nothing left at the end, no food, no ammunition." Piotr folded his arms across his chest. His tone of voice turned cold and hard. "The Russians started rounding us up, herding us into a valley, but they weren't very good at it. They concentrated mostly on the officers. A lot of us just slipped away into the forests. It took me two months to get back here."

Piotr stared into his coffee cup as though remembering the battles, perhaps the friends he had lost.

"How many AK are in this area?" Adam asked. Out of the corner of his eye he could see Krystyna shift in her chair.

Piotr hesitated for a moment, glancing at his wife. "There are others," he said.

Adam waited for more, but Piotr picked up his cup and took a sip of coffee, looking away. "What about the NKVD?" Adam asked. "Have they been in Nowy Targ?"

"They have spies everywhere, the wretched bastards," Krystyna chimed in bitterly. "As bad as the Germans were, the Russians are worse; they're nothing but murderous barbarians."

Adam glanced at her. The fierce glare in her eyes revealed that she, or someone close to her, had suffered at the hands of the Russians. He turned back to Piotr. "Your orders come through Jastremski?"

Piotr didn't respond.

"Jastremski sent me here, Piotr," Adam said, trying not to sound impatient. Tytus had warned him the Górale were suspicious of outsiders, but he was going to need their help. "I'm AK. I was in Warsaw during the Rising. I know Stag and Bor. You can trust me."

Piotr looked at him for what seemed like a long time, his dark eyes searching Adam's. Finally he said, "Jastremski has been here only once . . . with the Instructor."

"The Instructor?"

"Ludwik Banach's code name, the man you're looking for."

Adam smiled. "I'm pleased that you're so thorough. Banach's code name is the Provider."

Krystyna set her knitting back in the basket and stepped over to the table, putting a hand on her husband's shoulder. "We have to be very careful, Adam. The NKVD are ruthless, and very persistent."

Piotr leaned forward with his thick hands folded on the table. For an instant Adam imagined what those hands might have done to him if he'd failed to give Banach's correct code name. "Our leader, Casimir, lives in the village of Prochowa. We'll go there tomorrow if the paths are dry."

"And that's where Banach is?"

"Yes."

"Have you had any news about him?"

"Not since April, when we herded the sheep up to the high pastures. I looked in on him then, at Casimir's home."

"Was he well?"

Piotr hesitated.

"He was very pale and thin," Krystyna said. "He had a bad cough. But he's being well taken care of: good food, a warm bed, and the village has a doctor. It's so much warmer now, maybe he's feeling better."

Adam smiled at her, watching as she rubbed her hands along the sides of her swollen belly. He hoped to hell she and Piotr would survive all this. "Yes, maybe he is," he replied, not allowing himself to think otherwise, not now, when he was so close.

Forty-Nine

19 June

Natalia woke just after dawn and sat by the window in the shabby room thinking about Adam. It was only Tuesday, but she had a sense of apprehension that she couldn't shake. She should have gone with him, but the risk was too great. The NKVD was out there, and if they got caught together that would be the end of everything. There would be no hope of recovering the Katyn Order.

But now, once again, he was gone.

She suddenly felt as though she were suffocating.

An hour later, Natalia jumped off the tram and walked briskly down Sienna Street, heading for the Rynek Glowny. Her stomach growled, and she realized she hadn't eaten anything since noon the previous day. She found the same bakery where she had bought a poppy seed roll the other day, but the only items on the display shelf today were two loaves of black bread. She purchased two slices and devoured them on the way to the Rynek Glowny.

She needed to think, to find a quiet place where she would be safe from prying eyes and could consider what to do if Adam didn't show up by the end of the day. She crossed the square, just coming to life at this early hour, and climbed the stairs of the Mariacki Church.

The first mass of the morning wouldn't begin for another half hour, but there were already several dozen people seated in the pews. Natalia stood just inside the door for a moment gazing around at the intricately painted blue-and-white walls of the immense nave, arcing gracefully upward to the vaulted ceiling. She walked slowly down the ancient stone aisle, made the sign of the cross and slid into a pew. She knelt for several minutes, glancing up occasionally at the altar which for centuries had been adorned with the majestic altarpiece created by the Nuremburg craftsman, Veit Stoss, one of the finest examples of Gothic art in Europe.

Natalia closed her eyes, recalling the magnificent, wooden altarpiece, and its intricately hand-carved central panel, depicting the graceful figure of the Virgin Mary reclining in peaceful sleep in the arms of the Apostles. She felt a warm glow inside, remembering Adam's embrace as they lay in her bed just a few days ago. *Will I ever feel that again?* Suddenly trembling, she opened her eyes and looked at the dark, empty space where the altarpiece had once stood in front of the towering stained glass windows. The Nazis had stolen it, and the altar was now bare and cold, like the soul of Krakow.

She sat back in the pew and, instantly, the hair on the back of her neck bristled as she sensed the presence of someone kneeling in the pew directly behind her. Someone who hadn't been there a moment ago. She sat perfectly still, holding her breath.

A voice whispered, "Conductor, it's me."

Natalia spun around and stared, dumbstruck, at the familiar face.

Rabbit!

Natalia quickly came around the pew and sat next to her teenage friend and comrade-in-arms. "My God, what are you . . . what happened?"

Rabbit was filthy, his face sagging with exhaustion. He looked at her with bloodshot eyes, then abruptly turned away at the sound of footsteps coming down the aisle.

Three elderly women passed by and sat in a pew two rows farther up.

Natalia glanced at her watch. The mass would be starting in fifteen minutes. They either had to leave now, which might seem odd to anyone who noticed, or sit through the mass, which would be unbearable. She nudged Rabbit with her elbow and whispered, "Let's go."

Natalia's mind was bursting with questions, but they both had the discipline to walk in silence for fear of being overheard by NKVD spies. They crossed the Rynek Glowny, then headed north along

Florianska Street, taking some left and right turns into the narrow side streets in case anyone had followed them. Rabbit was emaciated. Natalia knew she had to get him some food and find a place where they could talk.

They passed through St. Florian's Gate, continued north for a few blocks and arrived at the Rynek Kleparski marketplace, where they slipped into the flow of early morning shoppers who trudged through the narrow aisles between the stalls. Most of the stalls were empty. Those that had something to sell offered little beyond wilted vegetables and day-old bread. Luxuries such as meat, eggs and fresh fruit were available only on the black market. With Rabbit at her side, Natalia pushed through several groups of people clutching ration coupons and haggling with vendors. She managed to purchase a small loaf of black bread, a few thin slices of cheese and three apples. Rabbit ate two of the apples before they got out of the marketplace.

There was a smaller neighborhood church around the corner. The early morning mass had just finished. Natalia and Rabbit waited while the parishioners filed out, then slipped into the empty sanctuary. The odor of incense still hung in the air, and sunlight filtered through the stained glass windows as two nuns collected booklets from the pews, then exited through a side door.

They sat for a while eating the bread and cheese until Rabbit slumped back in the pew, wiping his mouth with his shirtsleeve.

"What happened?" Natalia finally asked.

The food seemed to revive him a bit, but there was a look of fear in his eyes that she had never seen before, not even during the most gruesome battles in Warsaw. "NKVD," he said, glancing around. "They broke into the safe house in Lodz. It was a week ago . . . I think . . . just before dawn. I was asleep in the attic. But I woke up when I heard car doors slamming." His eyes darted around the empty sanctuary. He moved closer, lowering his voice. "They knew *everything*."

"Everything? What do you mean?"

"The two NKVD men you shot. They knew all about it. A Polish policeman was with them, and they were looking for a woman and a teen-age boy."

Icy fingers played on the back of Natalia's neck, and she half expected a cadre of NKVD agents to burst into the church with machine guns. "What happened then?"

"They shot someone—the owner of the house, I think. They had Hammer and Zeeka. I climbed out on the roof and got the hell outta there." Rabbit took a deep breath and wiped his mouth with his shirtsleeve again. "I didn't know where else to go, so I came here . . . to find you. You told me about the big church on the market square. I've been goin' there for the last three days. One old nun was startin' to look at me kind of funny, like I was trying to steal somethin'."

Natalia put her hand on Rabbit's shoulder as she tried to absorb the devastating news. Zeeka, Hammer, and how many others, were probably being tortured and murdered because of what she'd done. The NKVD would get the information from them, she was certain of that. One way or the other they'd find out that she had gone to Krakow. *And that was a week ago!*

"You did the right thing," she said, squeezing Rabbit's bony shoulder. "I am *very* glad to see you."

He bit off another chunk of bread. "Now what?"

Natalia thought about it. Since the NKVD was looking for a woman traveling with a teen-age boy, they'd have to split up. And she had to find somewhere for Rabbit to stay. Meanwhile, it was already Tuesday, and Adam hadn't returned. They were going to need help, and there was only one place in Krakow where she had a contact. But she'd been told never to return.

Later that morning, Rabbit walked along the boulevard overlooking the Vistula River, following the directions Natalia had given him to the Kazimierz District. He felt better now than he had for a week. The food and a chance to clean up in the washroom they discovered in the church's lower level had revitalized him, as did the clean shirt that Natalia had managed to buy at one of the stalls in the marketplace. It wasn't new, but it fit and it didn't stink like the one he'd been wearing for as long as he could remember. Natalia had returned to the church's lower level from the marketplace, wearing a gray scarf over her head and carrying a cane and a black felt hat. In her pocket were scissors that she used to cut his long, blond hair. Then she had handed him the hat. He hated hats but wore it anyway, wondering how much good it would do if the NKVD traced him to Krakow.

Rabbit slowed his pace as he entered a narrow walled street leading to the Church of Archangel Michael and Saint Stanislaus. He suddenly felt very conspicuous, certain that he'd hear heavy footsteps behind him at any moment.

Two women stood talking at the entrance of the church courtyard. As Rabbit approached them, he noticed a man on the other side of the street, leaning against the wall, smoking a cigarette. *Is he watching the church?*

At that moment the two women turned and walked across the courtyard toward the church. Rabbit made an instant decision and followed them. He kept a few paces behind as they climbed the steps. At the top landing an elderly caretaker stood with his back to the door, pulling bits of weed from a stone planter. Rabbit hesitated, but one of the women ahead of him held the door open. So he entered the church.

Rabbit let the two women go first, then knelt in the pew and pulled out the rosary Natalia had given him, resisting the urge to glance back at the door. He waited, absently moving his fingers over the beads and trying to ignore the tingling on the back of his neck.

Finally it was his turn. He stepped over to the confessional, knelt at the screen and whispered the greeting Natalia had instructed him to use. "In the name of the Lord I come seeking."

Silence.

Rabbit whispered, "The Conductor sent me."

There was another moment of silence, followed by a rustle of robes, and the priest cleared his throat. "What do you seek?" he said.

Rabbit replied, "Jastremski."

More silence, longer this time. Finally the priest said, "We cannot take any more time here. Three o'clock this afternoon, at the Cloth Hall."

Rabbit exited the church, and hurried down the steps, across the courtyard and through the gate. The man leaning against the wall was still there. Rabbit continued down the narrow street, looking straight ahead. He turned right at the corner, then left at the next street. After five minutes he stopped and knelt down to tie his shoelace. The man was nowhere in sight.

Breathing a bit easier, he walked back along the Vistula, then followed a pathway near the castle that led down to the riverbank. Natalia sat on a bench facing the river.

Rabbit sat down next to her and said, "When I asked about Jastremski, the priest didn't answer."

"Didn't answer? Did he say *anything?*"

"He told me to be at the Cloth Hall at three o'clock this afternoon."

Natalia closed her eyes and pressed her fingers to her temples. Then she looked at her watch. "While we have some time, there are some things you need to know."

At half-past two, Natalia sat at a wrought-iron outdoor table at one of the cafés lining the perimeter of the Rynek Glowny. Most of the cafés were empty, so it was easy to select one that provided a clear view of the massive Cloth Hall on the other side of the vast cobblestone square. Rabbit was two tables away, reading a book about General Pilsudski and the Polish Legions that Natalia had purchased.

Idly stirring a cup of bitter coffee, Natalia thought about the situation. Had something happened to Jastremski? Or had someone gotten to the priest? Was this meeting a setup? She picked up the cup, but her hand trembled and she set it back on the saucer. *Calm down and think.*

As she glanced at her watch, a shadow darkened the table.

She froze.

Slowly, Natalia turned her head and looked up at a man standing over her.

It was the caretaker from the church.

"I'm sorry if I startled you," the elderly man said. "May I join you?"

"Yes, of . . ." She stopped to catch her breath. "Yes, of course. I was expecting the—"

The caretaker shook his head, warning her not to say any more as he slid into the chair opposite. He wore a gray suit with a white shirt and solid blue tie. The suit was clean and neatly pressed but frayed at the ends of the sleeves. He removed his fedora and set it on the table.

It was a warm afternoon, uncomfortably humid as though it might rain at any moment, and the elderly man's high forehead glistened with a film of perspiration as he ran a hand over his thin white hair. "You may call me Leopold," he said quietly. "I saw you sit down and thought I'd save some time." His face was tanned and creased from years of outside work, but his ice-blue eyes revealed the intensity of someone who did a lot more than rake gardens. "And you can tell the boy to join us."

A waiter appeared. Leopold ordered coffee, and the three of them waited in silence until it was delivered. There were only a couple of other people at the café, several tables away, engrossed in their own conversation.

"Jastremski has disappeared," Leopold said abruptly. "So has his wife."

Natalia felt like she'd been kicked in the stomach. "NKVD?" she whispered.

The caretaker nodded and sipped his coffee.

Natalia slumped back in her chair. It had to be Tarnov. She suddenly felt very warm, and sweat trickled down the back of her neck. If Tarnov had gotten to Jastremski, they were sure to find out about Adam. *And they'll know where he went!*

Leopold leaned over the table. "What do you need?"

Natalia drummed her fingers on the table as a dozen thoughts swirled around in her mind. She had to decide exactly what to do, and in what order. She said to Leopold. "It's best if Rabbit and I aren't seen together. Do you have somewhere he can stay for a few days?"

Leopold studied Rabbit, sizing him up. "I have quarters at the church. There's plenty of room. Do you cook?"

Rabbit smiled. "No, but I eat."

"Can you scrape and paint windows?"

"I can if you feed me."

Leopold patted the boy's shoulder. "You paint and I'll feed you. It won't be fancy, but you won't go hungry." He turned back to Natalia. "Anything else?"

Natalia hesitated for a moment, trying to decide how much to say. The more she told this man, the more jeopardy they'd all be in if he were questioned. But if Adam wasn't in trouble already, he would be very soon. She was going to need help. Natalia removed General Kovalenko's letter from the breast pocket of her vest and slid it across the table. It was written in Russian, but she told Leopold what it said.

Leopold slid it back to her, his eyes darting around. Pigeons fluttered about on the cobblestone square among the pedestrians, clopping horses and creaking vendor carts.

"You met a man in the courtyard of the church last week," Natalia said. "You gave him a message to board the tram to Podgorze."

Leopold nodded.

"That man is a friend, and he's on a mission." She spoke slowly, choosing her words carefully. "I'm concerned that he may have been . . . detained. I'm not certain, but I may need help."

"What type of help?" Leopold asked.

"Right now, some advice," she said, tapping Kovalenko's letter on the table before slipping it back into her pocket. "What do I do with this letter, just waltz into a police station and tell them to ring up General Kovalenko in Berlin?"

"As crazy as it seems, that may be an option. A letter like that, signed by a general of the Red Army, should get their attention. On the other hand, the NKVD have planted spies among the police. Do you trust this General Kovalenko?"

Natalia couldn't believe she was even thinking about this. *Trust General Kovalenko? Am I mad?* "Could we send a message to London—to a certain person at SOE?" From what Adam had said about him, Natalia wasn't sure she trusted Whitehall either. But she didn't have any other options, and at least he wasn't Russian.

Leopold appeared thoughtful. "Yes, we could," he said after a moment. "The location of the wireless was compromised recently. It's been moved, and it will take a day for me to arrange it."

In the background a trumpet sounded from high in the Gothic tower of the Mariacki Church.

"Three o'clock," Leopold said. "Rabbit and I should go now. If you want to send a message, meet me here tomorrow at this same time."

Fifty

19 June

On Tuesday the weather was clear. Piotr hitched up the horses to the wagon, and he and Adam left the small cluster of cabins just as the sun crept slowly above the tall mountain peaks. Thin yellow rays filtered through dense conifers. Nuthatches and chickadees flitted about, and an occasional rodent scurried in the underbrush as the horses clopped along the muddy pathway, the wagon creaking along behind. It was a quiet morning, gradually warming as time passed and the sun cleared the treetops.

They had ridden in silence for awhile when Adam said, "You're a lucky man, Piotr. Krystyna is a beautiful woman."

Piotr smiled. "That I am. I don't deserve her."

"Was she in the AK before you married?"

Piotr gave the reins a gentle flick as the horses plodded up an incline. He kept his eyes on the path and nodded. "Her father, Borys, was Casimir's second-in-command. He and Krystyna made regular trips over the mountains into Slovakia back in '39 and '40, guiding our soldiers on their way to France. Since then we've kept the routes open for supplies, weapons, couriers, that sort of thing."

"Is Krystyna's father still—?"

Piotr shook his head.

"What happened?"

"Russians got him, last October. Borys and three others from Prochowa were on their way back from Slovakia. Krystyna wasn't with him, thank the Lord. We were married two months earlier and we were living down here. Borys' group encountered a Russian patrol near the border trying to find their way to Zakopane. They were hunting down some Germans in the area when they got lost."

Adam looked away. He knew from the pain in Krystyna's eyes the night before what was coming next.

"One of the men from Borys' group was wounded, but he escaped and managed to walk back to Prochowa and tell the story. Borys knew the risk, but there wasn't much he could do once they happened to cross paths with the Russians. They were now our *allies,* of course." Piotr spit into the path. "As soon as they got what they needed, the fuckin' Russians just turned on them and started shooting."

Adam thought about Natalia and the story of her village being burned to the ground by the Russians. Her family had disappeared, and her brother had been shot in the back of the head and buried in a ditch in the Katyn Forest. He'd been away from her for three days and it was killing him.

They stopped for lunch in a clearing alongside a stream, and ate heartily—cold chicken with black bread and cider. Piotr asked him again about America, obviously a subject of great interest. It reminded Adam of the night he and Natalia had huddled in the ammunition cellar in Warsaw and he told her about baseball.

"Do you miss it?" Piotr asked.

Did he miss it? It had been so long, and so much had happened that Adam could scarcely remember. In the years since he'd left, the years during which he'd shared the agony of war with the proud and stubborn people of his birth country, his previous life in America had faded to vague recollections. But there was one thing he remembered with complete clarity, one thing he knew he would never forget. "I miss freedom," he said.

Piotr nodded and looked off into the mountains.

The air was crisp, the blue sky crystal clear as Adam watched a hawk gliding in a lazy circle high above the beech and aspen trees. The forest was still thick at this altitude, and he imagined a lynx, or a red deer, or a wild boar keeping a close eye on them from inside the tree line. He remembered Natalia saying she wished they could escape into the mountains. It sounded wonderful . . . if it could ever happen.

Half an hour later they climbed back on the wagon and continued on, climbing higher and higher up the mountain, the path twisting and turning through thinning forests. Eventually the terrain flattened into a plateau, and the path widened into a rutted road, passing through broad grassland meadows populated with long-wooled Podhale sheep. Cabins appeared, nestled between small, neat fields of oats, potatoes and cabbage. A farmer, trudging behind an ox and plow, raised his hand to wave as they passed by.

By mid-afternoon, the village of Prochowa came into view, dozens of cabins clustered close together, all constructed in the Górale style of whole logs, squared and notched at the ends, high-pitched roofs and narrow windows. Men working the fields shouted greetings as they recognized Piotr. Women and children peeked out of cabin windows as the wagon creaked past and drew to a stop in the village center.

It was a grassy square, dominated on one side by a church with a high-peaked roof made of wood shingles. On the other side of the square was a large earthen area ringed with wooden benches and hand-hewn, oak tables. In the middle of the ring, large spits of meat roasted over wood fires, the smoke and tantalizing odor of mutton wafting through the village.

Within minutes the wagon was surrounded by a dozen hardy men dressed in coarse, felt trousers, leather moccasins and wide-brimmed hats. They joked with Piotr and glanced curiously at Adam. Women with long, braided hair partially covered with tasseled scarves or white head-cloths stood nearby, children peeking from behind their ankle-length, embroidered skirts.

Adam anxiously scanned the crowd, but his uncle was not among them. *Should he be?* What had he expected, that Banach would just suddenly appear in the middle of a crowd of mountain highlanders? He realized that he had no idea what to expect.

Piotr stood up in the wagon and held his hands in the air, silencing the crowd. He motioned for Adam to stand and addressed the group in a deep, commanding voice. "Thank you, my friends of Prochowa, for your warm welcome. Allow me to present a friend—an American—who has traveled here by way of Krakow."

That sent a buzz through the crowd. The men glanced at one another and nodded, a ripple of applause, a few cheers. Adam's face flushed. He waved and mumbled a few words of thanks. Then he and Piotr jumped off the wagon, surrounded immediately by well-wishers patting them on the back.

A moment later a thin, regal-looking man pushed through the crowd. He appeared to be in his sixties, with leathery skin and dark piercing eyes. He wore a short black coat over a white linen shirt and gripped an ornate, hand-carved walking stick that Adam recognized as a *ciupaga,* with an axe blade on the top end and steel-tipped spear point on the bottom. The group fell silent.

Piotr removed his hat, bidding good day to Casimir and said, "I bring greetings from Krystyna."

The elderly man smiled broadly. "Ah, Krystyna, I'm told she is with child. Is she well?"

"Getting big as a house. But she can still swat me when I do something wrong."

Casimir laughed. "Women are all the same. She'll settle down a bit when she's chasing after a little one."

Piotr laid his big hand on Adam's shoulder. "Allow me to present a fellow *patriot.*"

The emphasis on the word "patriot" created a flicker in Casimir's eyes, and an unspoken communication passed between the two men. Casimir removed his wide-brimmed hat, revealing a shock of thick white hair. "Welcome to Prochowa," he said, then raised his voice for the rest of the crowd. "We shall have a special meal this evening, in honor of our guest from America."

Adam and Piotr spent the next few hours chopping and stacking firewood near the cooking fires, then touring the village. Adam was bursting with anxiety, barely able to concentrate, expecting that his uncle might appear at any moment, stepping out of one of the simple cottages, or perhaps sitting under a tree with a book. But he tried to be patient and not offend his hosts.

It was a small settlement, no more than thirty or forty dwellings Adam guessed, but incredibly clean and well-organized. Behind the church was a community building where women gathered to weave rugs. A horse stable stood nearby, with harnesses and saddles hung neatly on wooden pegs, the planked floor swept clean with not a trace of straw or manure outside the stalls. There were chicken coops and a turkey roost beyond and downwind from the main village area.

A blacksmith shop was located at the end of a narrow road, along with a millwork shop where several Górale men were hard at work producing shingles, planks and beautifully crafted wooden furniture. A young man in his mid-twenties stepped from behind a turning lathe, wiping his hands on a rag, which he stuffed into the back pocket of his coveralls. "I'm Zygmunt, the shop foreman," the young man said pleasantly. "Would you care for a look around?"

For the next thirty minutes Zygmunt led Adam through his shop, explaining each piece of equipment and every tool, then proudly showed off a set of spindle-back chairs his crew had just completed. Adam shook his head in amazement. Like everything else in the tiny village, the millwork shop was efficiently operated and impeccably maintained, right down to the split-rail fence surrounding the building with not a rail or post askew. He found it hard to fathom that such neatness and order could still exist in this country so ravaged by war.

Later, as the sun was setting and the day's work done, the crowd drifted back to the village center, exchanging good-spirited barbs with Piotr and Adam, moving en masse toward the benches and tables. An all-male crew of cooks hoisted the spits off the fires and set about carving the meat. The village women carried jugs of apple cider and beer to the tables, along with platters of goat cheese and sweet-smelling heavy, dark bread. "It's made from oats," one of the women told Adam, breaking off a chunk and handing it to him. "We call it *chelb*."

Adam took a bite of the chewy bread, suddenly realizing he was ravenous. He glanced around, looking for Banach, but there was no sign of him. There'd also been no acknowledgement from either Piotr or Casimir of the purpose of Adam's visit.

Plates and silverware appeared, followed by enormous platters of roast mutton, potato pancakes and steaming cauldrons of *kwasnica,* a sauerkraut soup that Adam remembered from his childhood days in

Krakow. The noisy crowd quieted for a moment as Casimir offered a prayer, then resumed their chatter as the food was passed.

When the meal was finished, the women cleared the tables, the children disappeared and the men gathered by the fire pits with bottles of potato vodka. Glasses were filled, toasts proclaimed to the visitor from America and the potent drink downed in a single gulp.

After a second round of drinks, this one accompanied by a toast to *Sleboda*—Freedom—three young men moved to the center of the group with two fiddles and a goatskin bagpipe and began to play a lively mountain folk tune. Adam stood at the edge of the group, watching as several of the men joined in the singing.

After a while some of the women drifted back, and the music shifted seamlessly to something a bit slower and more rhythmic. A young woman, perhaps in her twenties, wearing a bright red-and-yellow embroidered skirt, her long blond hair woven into a waist-length braid, stepped up to Adam and took both his hands in hers. "It's called a *góralski,*" she said with a bright smile. "I'm Anastazia, Zygmunt's wife. Come and dance."

Startled, Adam almost tripped over his feet as she quickly drew him into the center of the action. The other couples swirled effortlessly around each other in an eddy of twirling colors, touching only briefly, as the enchanting melody filled the night air. Anastazia was a good teacher, and after a few minutes he was following her lead, taking and releasing her hand, turning and bowing, right up through the grand finale when the entire group joined together in a graceful, serpentine movement Anastazia said was called the *zwyrtanie*.

When the dance ended, Anastazia bowed, smiled again, then hurried off to join a group of other young women, who huddled around her, giggling. Adam had the feeling she'd just won a bet.

Suddenly he felt a large hand on his shoulder and turned to see Piotr standing behind him. The big man motioned for Adam to follow, leading him away from the group of revelers, now all clapping in time to the beat of another song.

It was dark as Piotr and Adam crossed the square except for the warm glow of kerosene lanterns in the cabin windows. Adam's heart pounded as they headed for a cabin just to the right of the church.

Piotr had not said a word, and Adam knew better than to ask where they were going. He'd already figured it out.

Inside the log cabin was a large, high-peaked living area, lit by kerosene sconces on the walls and furnished with handmade wooden chairs and brightly colored, embroidered cushions. A boar's head was mounted above the door. Casimir sat at a round oak table. Another man sat next to him with his hands folded on the table, a serious-looking man, whom Adam had noticed earlier. Casimir introduced him as Doctor Buchinski and motioned for Adam to take a seat.

"You've come looking for Ludwik Banach," Casimir said quietly. Then he turned to the doctor.

Adam could barely breathe. He knew what was coming before the doctor opened his mouth. The words seemed unreal, disjointed, as though they were talking about someone other than his uncle. "He was quite ill . . . we did all we could . . . we kept him comfortable . . . but he grew weaker . . ."

Adam looked at the doctor; his vision blurred. "When . . . ?"

"Just two weeks ago," the doctor said. "He held on longer than I expected." He stood up, placed a hand on Adam's shoulder and left the cabin.

Adam sat in silence alongside Piotr and Casimir, with the same hollow feeling he'd had at Sachsenhausen when he first saw his uncle's name in the Nazi ledger book. He'd always feared his uncle wouldn't survive. *But to get this close? To get within two weeks?*

He looked at Casimir. "Did he leave anything with you . . . any papers . . . documents?" Adam had no idea what these men knew, what Banach might have told them.

Casimir shook his head. "No, there was nothing. Just the few clothes he brought with him." The white-haired man got up and stepped over to a cupboard, returning with a bottle of vodka and three glasses.

Adam was grateful for the drink. He came to a decision as he set his empty glass on the table. "Ludwik Banach—the Provider—was my uncle."

Surprise registered in the faces of the two Górale men, but they remained silent.

Adam continued. "Banach discovered something at the Copernicus Memorial Library before he left Krakow. It was a document. Did he say anything about that?"

"He said only that he had to get out of Krakow," Casimir said, "and that the NKVD would be hunting for him. He stayed with Piotr and Krystyna at first, but we brought him up here as soon as we could, farther away from Nowy Targ. The Russians don't come up here; it's too difficult. They don't know the area, the forests. He was safe here."

"What is this thing he found, this document?" Piotr asked.

Adam studied the two men. The look in their eyes told him they could be trusted. But it was more than that. It was a look that said they were also AK, and they needed to know what he knew. He continued, "Ludwik Banach discovered a document proving that Stalin ordered the NKVD to secretly murder thousands of Polish officers in the Katyn Forest in 1940."

Both men stared at him, their eyes wide with astonishment. After a moment, Casimir asked, "And they know? The NKVD knows about this document?"

"They know the document exists," Adam said. "At least one of them does, an officer named Tarnov. He returned to Krakow from Berlin within the last few days. He tried to locate the same document months ago, back in January when the Russians first came into Krakow. But he couldn't find it. Then, a month ago, I visited the Sachsenhausen concentration camp . . ."

The rest of the story spilled out. Adam talked rapidly, watching the growing concern in the other men's eyes. When he finished, Casimir stood up and paced around the room. Then he placed both hands on the table. "Is it possible that Banach hid the document somewhere in Krakow before he came up here?"

Adam thought about what he'd read in Banach's journal. There were a few days after the Germans left Krakow before the Russians moved in, a few days when his uncle was not under surveillance.

"Did he notify anyone before he left Krakow," Casimir continued, "any type of message that—?"

A message!

Adam pushed his chair from the table and stood up, pacing around the tidy room as a thought formed in his mind. Suddenly it all became so clear, he wondered how he could have missed it. "Of course, that's it!" he blurted out. The answer had been right there all along—in the last line of the journal.

"What is—" Casimir started to say, but Adam held up a hand and stopped him.

"He *did* leave a message," Adam said, "a message I never quite figured out until just now. *Pathetic pawns on the perilous chessboard of the NKVD!*"

Casimir frowned. "I don't understand."

"It's in the library. Stalin's order authorizing the Katyn massacre is in the Copernicus Memorial Library!"

Fifty-One

20 June

Adam left Prochowa just after dawn on horseback. Piotr and Zygmunt followed behind in the wagon. The horse was a bay Carpathian pony, about 14 hands high, broad in the shoulders and sturdy, with an easy gait. Though Adam hadn't ridden in several years, it gradually came back, and after a mile or two he was able to push the horse to a gallop across the meadows, then relax in the saddle as the sure-footed mare made her way down the rugged slopes.

Adam stopped every hour, alongside creeks or small ponds, allowing the horse to rest for a few minutes and graze on the mountain grass. Then he pressed on, his heart aching with grief, his eyes clouded with tears. Ludwik Banach was gone. He had died of tuberculosis in a remote mountain village. For years Adam thought him dead, but he had never really mourned him. And now . . . he had stood in front of the simple wooden cross that morning as the sun came up. And the grief had struck him like a hammer blow. He had recited a silent prayer but it wasn't enough. He would make sure his uncle's death was not in vain. And he would protect the journal. He had given it to Casimir before he left Prochowa, sure the AK leader would safeguard it.

As he pounded down the mountain, hunched forward in the saddle, Adam's anxiety rose to a fever pitch with the stunning realization of where his uncle had hidden the order authorizing the Katyn massacre. And he'd left Natalia alone in Krakow . . . with Tarnov, and God only knew who else, hunting her down.

It was just past noon when Adam spotted the smoke. He slowed the horse to a walk, then guided it up a rocky knoll, a vantage point offering a long view down the mountain. At first there was just a puff, perhaps a kilometer away, darker than the wispy clouds in the background and dissipating quickly. He sat quietly in the saddle and watched, his eyes glued on the horizon. Another puff appeared, then a third, darker than before, lingering longer in the hazy, bluish-white sky. Finally a solid, unbroken plume of dark, black smoke rose above the treetops, drifting off with the breeze.

Adam cursed and jabbed his heels into the mare's ribs. They bolted forward, down the back side of the knoll and back on the trail. He pushed the horse, ducking to avoid tree limbs, ignoring the risk, his mind a blur of fear and rage.

Ten minutes later he arrived at the clearing in the forest where he and Piotr and the two Górale neighbors had been cutting trees a few days earlier. Adam couldn't see the cabins from here, but a plume of thick, black smoke rose above the treetops. He could smell the sharp, pungent odor and hear the crackling of burning wood.

Adam tied the pony to a tree, pulled a rifle out of the saddle holster and checked the five-round magazine. It was a Kar 98k sniper rifle that Casimir had given him. One of the Górale men had taken it from a dead German in '39. He removed the saddlebags and slung them over his shoulder, then hiked into the forest, heading downhill toward the cabins.

It took about a quarter of an hour, moving quickly but quietly through the thick pine forest, before Adam arrived at the crest of a hill where he had a view of the small cluster of cabins. The one belonging to Piotr and Krystyna was on fire. He removed a pair of binoculars from the saddlebags, knelt down and leaned against a tree to scan the area.

He cursed silently as a wave of dizziness blurred his vision, and he suddenly felt nauseous. *Goddamn it, not now!* He waited a moment, closing his eyes and breathing deeply until it passed. He blinked a few times then peered through the binoculars. In the grassy clearing between the remaining two cabins Adam spotted a group of people on their knees, their hands bound in front of them and secured to a low tether strung between two trees. He counted five of them: three women and two men. One of the women was Krystyna. Russian soldiers with rifles slung over their shoulders patrolled the area, some watching the blazing cabin, others watching the surrounding hills and forest. He counted at least a dozen.

Piotr had told him that Russian soldiers were prowling around Nowy Targ, terrorizing the locals. But these weren't Red Army soldiers. They were NKVD riflemen. And this was no random act of terrorism. Adam slowly scanned the area, looking for Tarnov between the wisps of black smoke. He didn't see him, but he knew he had to be there.

He scanned back to the group tied between the trees just as one of the riflemen shouted something at the man tied next to Krystyna and jabbed the barrel of his carbine into the man's forehead. Adam couldn't hear everything from this distance, but it was obvious the rifleman was angry, probably demanding information. The man being questioned spit at the Russian. An instant later, the top of his head exploded.

Adam's fingers clamped down hard on the binoculars as the sound of the gunshot reached his ears, followed by muted screams from the others tied to the rope. He dropped the binoculars, picked up the rifle and raised it to his shoulder. He peered through the scope, twisting the adjusting knob to bring it into focus. The rifleman had moved a step to his left and leveled the gun at Krystyna. Adam sighted in on the side of his head and squeezed the trigger.

The man's body went rigid as the bullet blew away the right side of his head. Adam moved his arms to the left and smoothly chambered another round, searching for a second target. He found it and fired. He swung farther to the left, found a third target and fired. He swung the gun to the right and found a fourth target. This one turned toward him, raising his rifle. Adam squeezed the trigger and shot him in the chest.

He looked up from the scope and quickly surveyed the grassy clearing between the cabins, while removing a fresh five-round magazine from the saddlebags. Three Russians were on the ground, lying still, apparently dead, and one was still thrashing about, blood oozing from his chest.

But Adam spotted two others sprinting across the clearing, coming directly toward him. He snapped the fresh magazine into place, sighted in and located the one on his left. He squeezed off a round and moved the gun slightly to the right. He spotted the other rifleman diving to the turf and fired a shot into his back. He looked up and scanned the area again. Now six riflemen were down, but the others had disappeared. The people tied to the rope were all on their knees, their backs rigid as though frozen in shock.

Adam stuffed the binoculars into the saddlebag and crept slowly back down the hill. He moved to his right, staying below the crest of the hill. Above the crackle of the blazing fire, he heard muted shouts in Russian coming from his left, the direction of the trail. He stopped and turned his head to hear more clearly through his good ear, knowing that would be the route the Russians would take as soon as they recovered from their surprise.

He continued moving, circling to his right for another five minutes, then climbed carefully back up the hill. He looked around and assessed his position. He had a clear view of all three cabins and the people in the clearing tied between the trees. Fortunately they were upwind, out of danger from the fire, and from this position he'd be able to pick off anyone who approached them. To his left, between his position and the trail, the terrain was thick with pine trees, obscuring his view. And with the impaired hearing in his left ear, he doubted he'd be aware of footsteps or snapping twigs over the roar of the blazing fire. He turned to his right and spotted a rocky outcrop that jutted from the slope a few meters away. He grabbed the saddlebags, dashed over and crouched behind the rock wall.

With his back covered, Adam removed two fresh magazines from the saddlebags and set them on the ground in front of him. Then he scanned the area again with the binoculars. The four remaining people tied to the rope had settled down a bit, though the blond woman next to Krystyna was sobbing. He scanned slowly, trying to detect any movement, but the riflemen had hunkered down, no doubt searching the hillside through their own binoculars, trying to locate him.

Adam leaned back against the rocks and thought about his predicament. Piotr and Zygmunt were behind him with the wagon, but they wouldn't arrive for at least another hour, perhaps two. The Russians would certainly have learned that Krystyna's husband had left earlier with the wagon, and when they found Adam's horse they would assume Piotr was following behind. But Adam was cut off from the trail, with no way to warn Piotr. Their only chance was if Piotr and Zygmunt spotted the smoke and snuck into the forest before the riflemen ambushed them. It was a slim chance. And Adam knew that Krystyna and her neighbors were the bait. Tarnov was down there—waiting for him.

A half hour passed. Nothing happened, no movement in the clearing except the people tied to the rope, who sagged from fatigue. Adam stretched, rocked his head back and forth, then raised the rifle to his shoulder and peered through the scope. The Kar 98k rifle felt good in his hands. It was about the same weight as the Springfield he'd used in Warsaw, and the muzzle velocity was similar. But the Kar's bolt action was smoother, and its specially mounted Zeiss scope far superior. It had twice the resolution of the Springfield's scope and didn't fog up.

Adam adjusted the focus. Two riflemen came into sharp view, moving cautiously along the side of a cabin. He weighed the options. If he took the shots, he'd expose his new position. On the other hand, it was an opportunity to lower the odds.

He fired twice, striking the second rifleman in the neck before the first one hit the ground. Then he grabbed the saddlebags and darted off, sprinting from tree to tree as a volley of return fire ripped through the forest.

After a couple of minutes he slowed and dropped to his knees, overcome with another wave of dizziness. His stomach heaved and he sat down, leaning back against a tree, praying he wouldn't pass out.

Adam waited, wiping sweat from his brow, breathing deeply. Gradually his vision began to clear, and his stomach settled down. Holding onto the tree, he slowly got to his feet. He waited another minute, then continued circling to the right. He stopped and knelt behind another outcrop of rocks. He still had a view of the people in the clearing, so he crouched low and waited.

Time passed. The fire was dying out, the cabin reduced to a charred heap of rubble. He shifted and switched knees. His right foot tingled and his back hurt, but he stayed low, certain he'd be seen if he tried to stand.

Then, a gunshot!

A shout in Russian.

Another gunshot, from the direction of the trail.

"Over there!" someone shouted in Polish. It sounded like Piotr. Then a heavy blast from a shotgun, two more rifle shots and a loud, deep voice bellowing in agony.

Adam peered into the trees, cupping his hand behind his good right ear, and listened. Then he turned back to the clearing, brought the rifle up to his shoulder and searched for movement.

Nothing.

Several minutes passed before two men staggered into the clearing: Piotr, his shirt soaked with blood, and Zygmunt, his arm around Piotr.

Adam scanned the periphery of the clearing, searching for riflemen, but they were concealed from his lines of vision. Piotr and Zygmunt reached the people tied to the rope and slumped to the ground. Piotr crawled over to Krystyna and embraced her.

Then a loud voice echoed through a bullhorn in fractured English. "Attention, Mr. Nowak! We know you here. I order you come out and show yourself."

Adam recognized Tarnov's voice but didn't respond.

Tarnov bellowed again. "Come out now, or we shoot another these people."

Adam raised the rifle and peered anxiously through the scope, scanning the corners of the remaining two cabins where he thought the sound came from. Sweat dripped from his forehead. He gritted his teeth. *Just a glimpse, that's all I need. Just a—*

Adam blinked at the crack of the gunshot and looked up. The man tied at the end of the rope was splayed out, face down in the grass, the top of his head gone.

Piotr struggled to his feet, shouting obscenities. A gunshot blew bark off the tree beside him. The big man stood his ground for a moment, then dropped to his knees.

Tarnov's voice echoed through the forest again. "Last chance,

Nowak. Come out, or we shoot one by one."

Adam weighed the possibilities. Tarnov had followed him up here. He must have gotten the information from Jastremski. Jastremski didn't know about Natalia . . . but who else had Tarnov gotten to?

Adam realized that holding his ground here wasn't going to accomplish anything except getting Piotr, Krystyna and their unborn child killed, along with the rest of their neighbors. Tarnov was a monster, and he was desperate. There was no limit to what he might do. And time was running out. Cursing silently, Adam stood up and threw down his rifle. He wasn't completely out of options—but the only one that remained would be tough to pull off.

Adam stepped out from behind the rocks with his hands up and slowly descended the hill. When he reached the edge of the clearing, three riflemen burst from the cover of the trees and were on top of him in an instant, shouting and cursing in Russian. A rifle butt thumped him in the chest, and Adam fell backward, gasping. Then a heavy boot kicked him in the back. A jolt of pain shot all the way up to his neck. One of the riflemen, a giant with hands the size of dinner plates, grabbed him under the arm and jerked him to his feet. The Giant shouted at him, spraying Adam's face with spit.

Adam tried to pull away, but his legs were like rubber and he stumbled. The Giant held him up, while another rifleman jammed a gun barrel into his stomach. Adam sagged, gasping for breath. A third rifleman, a short, beefy man with a pockmarked face and a broken nose, groped Adam's waist and trouser legs, searching for weapons.

Finally, Tarnov appeared and shouted a terse command in Russian at the Giant, who jerked Adam upright and pinned his arms behind his back. The broken-nosed rifleman stepped aside and pointed a carbine at Adam's chest.

Tarnov wore a black trench coat and strolled slowly across the clearing, with only a casual glance at his dead riflemen. He stepped up to Adam and abruptly spit in his face. "Filthy American dog," he snarled. "No Airborne troopers save you this time."

Adam stared at him silently, remembering Tarnov's livid glare that night at the Kommandatura. It was the same now.

Tarnov took a step closer, unclipped a bayonet from Broken Nose's carbine and held it under Adam's chin. "Where is Ludwik Banach?"

Adam remained silent.

Tarnov flicked the bayonet.

Adam jerked his head back as a sharp, burning sensation shot through his chin. Blood dripped onto the front of his shirt. He took a breath through his teeth and exhaled slowly before speaking, trying to ignore the pain. "In my shirt pocket . . . a letter from General Kovalenko. You should read it."

Tarnov blinked. Then he handed the bayonet back to Broken Nose with another command in Russian. The Giant held both of Adam's wrists in a vise-like grip while Broken Nose reached into his shirt pocket, withdrew the letter and handed it to Tarnov.

Adam watched closely as Tarnov read Kovalenko's letter. For just an instant the NKVD major's eyes widened, then he abruptly crumpled the letter in his fist and dropped it on the ground. "General Kovalenko long way from here." Tarnov's voice was firm, but Adam saw a flicker of uncertainty in the Russian's eyes.

"There's a second copy of that letter," Adam said, "with a friend in Krakow. If I don't return by tomorrow, my friend will contact the general."

Tarnov's face reddened. The veins in his neck bulged. He slapped Adam hard across the face, knocking his glasses off. "Tell me where is Banach, or you not *live* until tomorrow."

"He passed away," Adam said.

Tarnov frowned, and his eyes narrowed. "Passed which way?"

"He *died*. Two weeks ago."

Tarnov punched him in the side of the head. "Lie! It is lie!" He drew a pistol from his holster and stomped over to the people tied to the rope. He held the gun to Krystyna's head.

Piotr roared another obscenity and swung his leg at Tarnov, catching him behind the knee. Tarnov stumbled and dropped the pistol. Instantly, Broken Nose charged Piotr and rammed the stock of his carbine into the big man's forehead. Piotr collapsed backward. Tarnov retrieved his pistol and got to his feet. He pointed the weapon at Piotr, who was shaking off the blow and struggling to sit up.

"Leave them alone!" Adam yelled. Blood dripped from his nose, and his ears rang. "They've done nothing!"

Tarnov glared at him. "Where is Banach?"

"He died, Goddamn it! I told you that!" The effort of shouting intensified the throbbing in Adam's head. A wave of dizziness washed over him.

Tarnov's face turned crimson. He aimed the pistol at Piotr's leg and pulled the trigger, blowing away the Górale man's kneecap.

Piotr bellowed in pain, thrashing about and clutching his leg. Krystyna shrieked, over and over in a long, forlorn howl.

Tarnov grabbed Krystyna by the hair, yanked her head to one side and shoved the barrel of the pistol against her temple. He looked at Adam with wild eyes. "Tell truth, fucking dog! Or she—"

"Stop!" Adam shouted, louder this time. His head pounded, and his stomach churned with nausea. "Goddamn it, stop! I'm telling you . . . the truth! Ludwik Banach died of tuberculosis, two weeks ago. He was an old man . . . a sick man!" He paused to catch his breath. The pain was growing, smothering him, and he feared he would pass out. "I just found out yesterday. I'm telling you . . . the truth. Now . . . leave these people alone!"

Tarnov released Krystyna's hair and shouted a string of commands at another group of riflemen who had stepped into the clearing. One of them carried a coil of rope. He sprinted over to Zygmunt and secured his wrists to the main rope with the other captives. A second rifleman hustled over to the smoldering cabin, picked up a scrap of wood and handed it to Broken Nose. One end of the wooden shaft was still in flames.

Then Tarnov shouted at the Giant. The huge man gripped both of Adam's wrists in one of his massive hands. With the other hand, he picked up Adam's glasses and put them back on his face. "I want you see clear," Tarnov snarled at Adam. He pointed at the stout, blond woman crouching on the other side of Krystyna.

Broken Nose stepped over Piotr, who was covered in blood and only barely conscious, and approached the other woman. She struggled against the ropes, her eyes wild with fear. "No! Oh God, no! Please!"

Broken Nose kicked her onto her back, stomped his boot on her forehead and thrust the flaming shaft of wood against her chest.

The woman shrieked wildly, legs thrashing.

"Jesus Christ!" Krystyna screamed at Broken Nose, "You bastard! Stop!"

Zygmunt lashed out with his feet, trying to kick Broken Nose, but he couldn't reach him.

"Stop it! Goddamn it! Stop!" Adam shouted, desperately trying to break loose from the Giant's iron grip.

Broken Nose kept his boot on the woman's forehead, pinning her down as her white cotton blouse caught fire. She shrieked long, agonizing wails, over and over again, until Broken Nose turned pale and backed off. He dropped the flaming stick on the ground and looked the other way. Finally the woman shuddered, wheezed one last time and passed out.

Tarnov snapped a command to Broken Nose, then put his boot on Krystyna's shoulder and shoved her onto her back. Krystyna grunted, her simple, cotton dress stretched tight over her swollen belly.

Broken Nose picked up the burning scrap of wood and dutifully stepped forward. Tarnov shouted at Adam, "Where is document? You care about this woman. I know. I save her for worst. You lie, she burn next!"

Krystyna spat at Tarnov. "Go to hell, you son of a bitch!"

Tarnov kicked her in the stomach. Krystyna grunted in pain, drawing up her knees.

Adam's eyes clouded with tears as he struggled to stay on his feet and focus his vision on Tarnov. *Stay calm. Stay calm, Goddamn it . . . and think!* He took a deep breath, forcing himself to concentrate. He could tell by Tarnov's reaction earlier that Kovalenko's letter gave him pause. Tarnov was NKVD, but Kovalenko was a Russian general, and there'd be trouble—not what anyone wanted with the Potsdam conference coming up.

"Last chance, Nowak!" Tarnov bellowed. "Where is document?"

Krystyna lifted her head. Her forehead glistened with sweat as the rifleman held the burning wood close to her face. "No, Adam!" she cried. "No! Don't tell him!"

Adam hesitated a moment too long, and Tarnov flicked his head toward Broken Nose. The rifleman jabbed the burning stick against Krystyna's neck.

Krystyna howled and jerked her head, kicking her feet wildly, squirming away. Broken Nose stepped toward her and pressed the red-hot stick against her neck a second time as Krystyna writhed helplessly. Her long, agonizing screams sliced through Adam's soul like a hunting knife.

"Stop!" Adam screamed. "Stop! I'll tell you what I know! Just get that son of a bitch away from her!"

Tarnov waved a hand at Broken Nose who again tossed the burning stick to the side. "If you lie, I burn off ears. Then I work on baby."

Adam swallowed hard, choking back the bile in his throat as Krystyna rolled on her side, moaning, curling her legs into a fetal position. He glared at Tarnov, quickly running through all the possibilities in his mind as the NKVD officer approached him. "The document you're looking for is in Nowy Targ."

Tarnov spit in his face again. "Fucking lie! Why you go up mountain if document in Nowy Targ?" He shouted a command to Broken Nose, who stepped over to Krystyna and jerked her head back, exposing the charred and blistering skin on the side of her neck.

Krystyna shrieked again, then convulsed violently, gagging on her own vomit.

Seething with rage, Adam jerked his arms with every ounce of strength he had left. He broke free of the Giant's grip, lunged at Tarnov and grabbed him around the neck. He squeezed and dug in his fingernails as Tarnov ripped at his hands. An instant later, the Giant brought a massive fist down on Adam's shoulder.

Adam's arm lost all feeling, and he dropped to one knee. His grip fell away from Tarnov's neck as a double image of the Russian oscillated back and forth in his field of vision.

Tarnov punched him in the face. "Lies! Fucking lies!"

"I didn't know . . . the document was in . . . Nowy Targ . . ." Adam gasped as the Giant grabbed his wrists again. "I didn't know . . . until the Górale people told me. Banach hid it there . . . when he passed through." Adam struggled to breathe. Sweat ran down his face. Would Tarnov take him along to Nowy Targ? Maybe not. The city was so close Tarnov could leave him under guard for a short time. *All I need is one more day and Natalia will contact Kovalenko.*

Tarnov glared at him. "Where in Nowy Targ?"

Adam's foggy mind was just barely a step ahead. "In a locker at the bus station . . . number 39."

"Key! Where is key?"

Adam shook his head. "No key . . . they didn't have—" Tarnov punched him again. Adam's head jerked back and a bolt of pain shot through his forehead.

"Burn pregnant woman's face off!" Tarnov roared. He shouted the command a second time in Russian.

Broken Nose hesitated.

Adam screamed at Tarnov, "It's true! Banach was an old man . . . he lost the key . . . but he remembered the number—39—it's the year he was arrested!"

Adam kept his attention riveted on Broken Nose, who still had not moved toward Krystyna. Out of the corner of his eye he saw a flash of movement. A crunching blow slammed the back of his head. Everything went black.

Fifty-Two

20 June

The new location of the wireless was a dilapidated garage on Filipa Street, north of the Stare Miasto District on the other side of the Rynek Kleparski market. Leopold had been waiting for Natalia outside the café on the Rynek Glowny. As soon as he spotted her, he turned and walked away. Natalia followed him, walking hunched over with the cane. She wore the gray scarf over her head, a gray sweater and a black-and-red, flower-print skirt she'd obtained from a secondhand store. It was the first time she'd worn a skirt in years.

She remained at a discreet distance behind Leopold until the elderly man disappeared inside the garage, leaving the door ajar. As soon as Natalia stepped into the dank, dirt-floored building, Leopold pulled the creaking door closed behind her. A young, bearded man with a cigarette hanging from the corner of his mouth sat in front of a wireless set. Rabbit stood next to him, peering over his shoulder, obviously engrossed in the equipment.

Seemingly oblivious to Natalia's presence, the bearded man tightened the connections to a twelve-volt battery, donned a headset and slowly adjusted the dials of the Canadian-built wireless set, one of the few still in the hands of the AK. He listened intently, then adjusted the dials again.

Natalia removed her scarf, leaned the cane against the wall and handed Leopold a slip of paper with the message she wanted to send. After lying awake most of last night tossing and turning, she had finally decided that it was Whitehall she would contact.

Leopold sat down on the other side of the wireless and wrote out the code. Then he handed it to the bearded man, who began tapping on the key. When he finished, the man disconnected the battery, lifted the wireless set off the workbench and placed it inside a wooden crate. He covered the crate with a canvas tarp, set three worn-out tires on top of the tarp and left the garage without a word.

"So, now what?" Rabbit said, with that same eagerness that Natalia recalled from their street battles in Warsaw.

"Now we wait," Natalia replied, though the delays were driving her crazy. It was all she could do not to get on the bus to Nowy Targ. *And do what, take on Tarnov alone?*

Leopold nodded. "We'll meet back here tomorrow at noon and see if we get a reply."

Natalia put a hand on Rabbit's shoulder. "You're OK?"

"Yeah, sure," the boy said. "Mr. Leopold kept me busy painting windows today."

Natalia smiled. "That's fine. Tomorrow then."

Natalia left first so Leopold could lock up the garage. He and Rabbit would return to the Church of Archangel Michael and Saint Stanislaus by a different route so they wouldn't be seen with her. She crossed the tram tracks that ran along the busy Avenue Basztowa, and passed through St. Florian's Gate back into the Stare Miasto, heading for her dingy room on the east side of the Kazimierz District. She had no idea who else lived in the building, if anyone, though she was certain she'd heard someone in the hallway when she woke that first morning. Like the other places she'd gone to find smuggled packages when she was part of the channel, the room was secure, carefully selected and away from prying eyes. She figured she'd be safe there for another day. At least it had a bed, running water and a toilet.

It was almost five o'clock, and the Rynek Glowny was busy with pedestrians returning home from their jobs and queuing up at the few shops with something to sell. A scattering of people sat in the cafés around the perimeter of the market square, sipping watered-down beer and cheap wine.

Natalia smiled at the driver of a horse-and-carriage that passed by.

The horse snorted, its hooves clopping loudly on the cobblestones. The driver tipped his hat. She grinned to herself and glanced toward the Mariacki Church, then stopped dead in her tracks.

In front of the church, two khaki-uniformed NKVD troopers were questioning a petite young woman with short black hair, who had been riding a bicycle. Natalia kept her eyes focused straight ahead and quickened her step as she passed by. It could be anything, she told herself. The NKVD was always questioning somebody about something. But Rabbit's words flashed back like a thunderbolt. *Those two NKVD agents you shot! They knew all about it!*

As she continued across the Rynek Glowny, Natalia felt completely exposed, as though she was the only person on the immense square, and someone would shout her name from the top of City Hall Tower and freeze her in her tracks. Then a car would roar up and a half-dozen agents would leap out and—

She shook her head as she reached the south end of the square, turning quickly onto Avenue Grodzka where another horse-and-carriage passed her going in the opposite direction. She thought it was going to be a long time until noon tomorrow.

Fifty-Three

21 June

Adam's head hurt like hell. The throbbing sensation along both temples woke him, and he struggled to sit up. It was dark. He blinked, then reached up and felt for his glasses. Remarkably they were still there. He blinked again and saw a thin shaft of light above his head.

"Adam?" It was a man's voice, a whisper, close by.

"Zygmunt?"

"Yes. Thank God you're alive."

"Are Piotr and Krystyna here?" Adam began to make out forms as his eyes cleared. Zygmunt was sitting up. Next to him, two shadowy humps lay on the floor.

"Piotr's still unconscious," Zygmunt said. "He was bleeding badly. I tried to stop it, made a tourniquet with my belt."

"What about Krystyna?"

"Over here." Zygmunt motioned with his hand, and Adam crawled closer.

Krystyna lay curled up, breathing shallowly, her arms wrapped around her protruding belly. There was something white around her neck.

"I did the best I could. Tore strips from my shirt," Zygmunt said. "There was some holy water in the bowl near the door. I think the moisture helped ease the pain a bit." He touched her shoulder gently. "Adam is awake," he whispered.

"Adam?" Krystyna tried to lift her head but cried out and stopped. "Are you hurt?"

Adam struggled to hold back the tears. He touched her shoulder. "I'm fine. Don't try to move."

"How is . . . Piotr?"

"He's still unconscious," Zygmunt said, "but the bleeding has stopped."

"That's good . . . isn't it?" she whispered in a raspy voice. "Can you . . . move me closer?"

Slowly, with Zygmunt holding her shoulders and Adam her legs, they slid her a meter or two across the wooden floor, now sticky with congealed blood. Adam could feel her body jerk as she struggled to hold back her screams. She rested her head on Piotr's chest, then took his right hand and placed it on her stomach. "It's moving. Can you feel it?" she whispered to her husband in a barely audible voice before drifting off.

Adam felt Piotr's forehead. It was cold and clammy. The big man's breathing was erratic.

"I loosened the tourniquet every fifteen minutes or so, judging by the angle of the moonlight," Zygmunt said quietly. "After a few hours, the bleeding had slowed enough to take it off. He was also shot in the side, just above the hip, when they attacked us in the wagon. He's lost a lot of blood."

Adam nodded and caught Zygmunt's eye in the gloom of the chapel, silently acknowledging his efforts. The Górale were incredibly self-sufficient, they had to be, but in this case it probably wouldn't be enough. "What about Krystyna?"

Zygmunt glanced at her, but Krystyna's eyes were closed. "She was badly burned," he whispered. "I'm afraid she's going into shock. Infection will kill her if we don't get help."

"Where are we?" Adam asked, but he thought he knew the answer as his senses started to kick back in—the hard wooden floor, a shaft of moonlight through an octagonal window. "The chapel?"

"Yes. There's just the four of us. They took Maria away."

Adam hadn't known the third woman's name, but he could imagine what Tarnov's men did to her. He tried to stand, but a jolt of pain shot through his head. He felt nauseous again and leaned back against the stone wall. "How long have we been here?"

"I'm not sure. Nine or ten hours at least."

"I'm sorry . . . it's my fault, I shouldn't have come."

Zygmunt shook his head. "They'd have killed us anyway. That's the way they are."

Krystyna stirred and managed to turn her head toward the two men. "What document . . . is Tarnov . . . looking for?" she asked.

The pain in her voice cut Adam to the quick. He touched her shoulder gently. "It has to do with . . ." He swallowed hard and continued. "It has to do with the murders of Polish officers back in 1940."

"Katyn?"

"Yes."

"Tarnov was involved in that?"

"Yes, he was."

She was quiet for a few minutes. Adam thought she might have drifted off again and leaned closer. In the moonlight he saw a tear trickling down her cheek. She blinked and their eyes met. "You're not just a diplomat . . . are you?"

Adam didn't respond.

"I saw how you . . . shot . . . those soldiers." Krystyna reached up and brushed her fingers along his cheek. "I'm glad . . . you're here now." Then she closed her eyes again.

Adam slumped back against the stone wall, sick to his stomach. He had the sudden urge to strangle someone. He'd never felt this helpless in his life. Krystyna was carrying Piotr's child. Three days ago they were a young, happy couple who'd risked their lives for their country. They had been looking forward to peace and quiet, to raising a family in their simple mountain existence. *Then I came along! This is my fault!* Adam closed his eyes, clenching his fists, wishing with all of his soul for just three seconds alone with Tarnov.

Several minutes passed as Adam leaned against the stone wall, forcing the rage to subside. It was Wednesday night, or more likely early Thursday morning. Natalia had said she'd wait until the middle of the week before coming to find him. But she wouldn't come alone. They had discussed that. He had told her to use Kovalenko's letter, or contact Whitehall, and he was certain that's what she'd do.

She was too smart, too well trained, to try anything foolish. She'd get help. Would she use her copy of Kovalenko's letter and go to the Krakow police? Or would she contact Whitehall? Either way, Kovalenko would know that something had happened, and he'd take action.

Unless they lied to me again.

Adam pushed the doubts from his mind. It was too late to worry about that now. When he gave Natalia the copy of Kovalenko's letter he'd made the decision to trust the Russian general. He sat quietly and listened for noises from outside. He couldn't hear anything, but he was certain they were being guarded. Pressing both hands against his temples to ease the pain, he forced himself to keep thinking. The fact that Tarnov had locked them in the chapel instead of continuing to torture and kill the Górale villagers proved he was concerned about Kovalenko's letter. Tarnov had to do something about that.

Would he be able to track down Natalia?

Another wave of nausea struck him, and Adam swallowed hard, wondering what else Jastremski might have told Tarnov under torture.

The priest?

Jastremski had said that everything flowed through the priest, so if Tarnov got to the priest . . .

Adam massaged his temples again, trying to stay calm. Even if Tarnov learned about Natalia, it didn't mean that he knew where she was. But Tarnov was desperate. He was going to do *something,* and Adam knew they had to get out of here before he returned.

He glanced around in the shadowy darkness of the chapel. He remembered the structure from the night with Tytus when there'd been a lantern, and he realized an escape was wishful thinking. The building was about ten meters on a side and stoutly built, with a thick, wooden floor, no cellar, and solid stone walls. The single octagonal window was high in the peak of the roof and, at any rate, too small to crawl through. And there were NKVD rifleman outside.

After a moment Zygmunt said, "They'll be expecting me back in Prochowa."

Adam turned toward him.

"My horse was tied behind the wagon," Zygmunt continued. "I told Casimir that I would head back at first light today. If I don't return by noon he'll know something's happened. They'll come looking for us."

Fifty-Four

21 June

On Thursday morning Rabbit sat at the small table in the caretaker's quarters and carefully spread marmalade on his third slice of black bread. He hadn't eaten this well in months, and he couldn't even remember the last time he'd had marmalade. The living quarters, which adjoined the caretaker's workshop in the lower level of the Church of Archangel Michael and Saint Stanislaus, consisted of the kitchen, a small sitting room, bedroom and a bathroom. Rabbit had spent the last two nights on the sofa in the sitting room, which was the most comfortable place he'd slept since the NKVD raided the safe house in Lodz.

He'd had nightmares about that terrifying incident almost every night since it happened, and it was something he wondered about now as he finished the thick, chewy piece of bread. During the entire two months of the Rising in Warsaw, he'd never had nightmares, not even after his friend Bobcat had been killed by the flamethrower in the sewer. That had been the most horrendous thing he'd ever experienced, and certainly he was a lot closer to Bobcat than he was to Zeeka or Hammer or the other AK operatives in Lodz. But there was something so evil about the Russian NKVD that even now he shivered as he thought about it.

Leopold had been busy in the workshop, and at precisely eight o'clock he stepped into the kitchen and poured a cup of coffee. Just as he had done the day before, he spread marmalade on a slice of bread, put the coffee and the bread plate on a tray and left to deliver them to the priest, saying he'd be back in a few moments.

Rabbit finished his breakfast, cleared off the table and went into the workshop where Leopold had set up several wood-framed window screens that needed scraping and painting. They had to meet Natalia at the wireless site at noon so there was no time to lose. Rabbit got right to work.

Scraping the dried-out, flaking paint from the first screen, Rabbit thought about Natalia and her friend, who she said was off on "a mission." She'd been vague about both the friend and the mission, and he wondered what could have been important enough to make her leave the safe house in Lodz. But he was glad she did. If she hadn't, she'd be dead. Like Hammer. And Zeeka . . . He wouldn't think about that.

It was almost nine thirty when Rabbit finished scraping all the screens and was ready to start painting. He wondered where Leopold was. He needed the old man to show him which paint to use. The caretaker had said he'd be right back when he left to deliver the breakfast to the priest. That had been more than an hour ago.

Rabbit stepped outside and walked around to the courtyard to check the gardens that surrounded the fountain, but Leopold wasn't there. He climbed the winding stone steps that led to the main entrance of the church, but the doors were locked. *Can he be doing some chore for the priest?*

Out of curiosity, Rabbit walked around to the other side of the church and the adjoining monastery. He stood off at a distance. It would be very out-of-place for him to enter the monastery, he thought. He had not met the priest—other than the few minutes he'd spent whispering into the confessional screen—and he certainly couldn't just knock on the door and ask for Leopold.

He decided to go back to the workshop and wait when something caught his eye. The arched wooden door of the monastery was ajar. And there was a black object on the ground next to the door. Rabbit took a few steps closer. It looked like a shoe.

He took a few more steps, coming still closer.

It was a man's shoe: black leather and freshly polished. It certainly wasn't Leopold's. The caretaker had been wearing his work boots that morning. Rabbit picked up the shoe. The laces were still tied, and there were scuff marks on the heel and along one side.

Rabbit suddenly dropped the shoe and spun around. He backed up against the wall of the monastery, his eyes scanning the courtyard.

Nothing.

He glanced down at the shoe again, then put his hand on the thick wooden door of the monastery and gave it a gentle push. The heavy door creaked on its hinges and swung inward, revealing an alcove.

An image flashed through Rabbit's mind of the knife he'd used to slice the bread that morning, and he wished it were in his hand right then. He stuck his head into the alcove. "Hel—" His voice caught. He coughed and tried again. "Hello?"

He stepped into the alcove and knocked on the door to the priest's private quarters.

No response.

He knocked again, but this door was also ajar and it swung inward a bit.

Rabbit put a hand on the door and pushed it open. He took a step, stopped and listened. He took another step and found himself in a tidy, simply furnished parlor with two chairs on either side of a fireplace. On the other side of the room was an archway that led to what appeared to be a dining area. He grabbed the iron poker from the hearth and stepped across the wood-plank floor to the archway.

He stopped and listened, but the only sound was his own breathing. He exhaled slowly and peeked around the archway.

Two of the chairs were overturned, and Leopold lay in a pool of blood in the center of the room. His throat had been slit.

Rabbit tightened his grip on the poker, his eyes darting around the room. Holding the poker in both hands, he stepped carefully around Leopold's body and pushed open the swinging door to the kitchen.

Nothing.

He crossed the dining room, checked the bedroom and the toilet.

There was no sign of the priest.

Still gripping the poker, Rabbit slowly backed out of the priest's quarters and through the alcove. He stood with his back against the thick, wooden door, looking around the courtyard, trying to comprehend what had happened.

While he was scraping screens in the workshop on the other side of the church, someone killed Leopold. But why? And where was the priest? It was almost certainly the priest's shoe Rabbit had found. *Kicked off during a struggle?* Did whoever killed Leopold, abduct the priest?

Rabbit checked the courtyard one last time, then sprinted to the gate. He glanced down the long, walled street, then dropped the poker and walked away from the church without looking back.

Twenty minutes later Rabbit found himself at the same pathway leading down to the Vistula River where he'd met Natalia after going to "confession" at the church on Tuesday. There was no one around, so he followed the path to the bench and sat down, staring out at the slow-moving water. Was it the NKVD? They'd been hunting for him ever since Natalia shot two of their agents three weeks ago. Did they follow him to Krakow and to the church?

Did they get Natalia?

Rabbit stood up and paced around. Something didn't make sense. Why would they arrest the priest? And why didn't they come into the caretaker's quarters and get him? They killed Leopold, why not him?

Then it dawned on him. They weren't after *him*. Whoever it was came to arrest the *priest*. This had nothing to do with the NKVD agents Natalia shot. This was something else, and Leopold had gotten in the way.

He walked down to the riverbank and tossed a stone in the water, watching the ripples drift outward in ever-widening concentric circles. When he met Natalia after going to confession at the church on Tuesday, she had told him about her friend who was on some type of mission. She had instructed him to ask the priest about Jastremski. But it was obvious there was more to it than that. And whatever was going on, it was also obvious by what just happened that the whole thing was starting to fall apart.

Rabbit walked back up the hill to the pathway and looked in both directions. A man on a bicycle rode past, and he could see other people strolling toward him from the direction of the castle. He couldn't stay here. He wouldn't be meeting Natalia at the wireless site until noon, and he had no idea where she was now. He needed to get lost for a couple of hours.

Natalia paced around the tiny third-floor room, checking her watch every five minutes. She tried to sit and read the newspaper she'd picked up earlier that morning, but she found herself reading the same sentence over and over, with no idea what it said. The walls seemed to be closing in on her. She was frustrated and angry. She should have gone up to Nowy Targ yesterday, though she had no idea what she would have done once she got there.

But something had gone terribly wrong; she was certain of it. And here she was, still in Krakow, waiting for a reply to her wireless message while Adam might be . . . She checked her watch again. Still two hours before she was to meet Leopold and Rabbit at the wireless site, but she had to get out of the room or she'd suffocate.

Hunched over with her cane and wearing the gray scarf and flower-print skirt, Natalia took a different route from Kazimierz to the Stare Miasto, then wandered about aimlessly, blending in with the crowd. An hour later she stopped on Avenue Mickiewicza. Across the street was the Copernicus Memorial Library.

Where Ludwik Banach had worked.

And Jerzy Jastremski.

Natalia stood and stared at the stately, modern structure that occupied an entire block. A heavy weight of helplessness pressed down on her. Adam was somewhere up in the mountains looking for Banach, and Jastremski was the only one who knew exactly where.

And now *he* was gone.

Time crawled past and still she watched people going into and coming out of the library. She had to move on. She was going to draw attention to herself. She consulted her watch again and was relieved to see that it was time to meet Rabbit and Leopold. She headed for the rendezvous.

As she approached the ramshackle garage, Natalia spotted Rabbit waiting outside. He walked up to her and took her elbow, turning her away from the garage door. "I've got to talk to you," he said. They moved around to the back of the garage. Rabbit's eyes darted around.

He leaned close and whispered in her ear, "They killed Leopold."

Natalia took a step back and stared at Rabbit. "Leopold . . . when?"

"Early this morning. I found him in the priest's dining room. He was . . ." The boy made a slitting gesture with his forefinger across his throat.

"What about the priest?" she demanded.

Rabbit shook his head. "He was gone. Someone took him away."

"Tarnov," Natalia said. It slipped out before she could stop herself.

"Who?" Rabbit asked.

"I haven't told you the whole story. I will, but not now. First we have to find out if there's a reply to our message."

They walked around to the front of the garage again, and Rabbit pulled open the door. The same bearded wireless operator sat hunched before the radio. He looked at them with a frown. "Where's Leopold?"

"Murdered," Natalia said, removing the scarf and running a hand through her hair. "At the church this morning."

The young man dropped his cigarette on the earthen floor and ground it out with his boot. "Who did it?"

"NKVD," Natalia said.

"Shit! I've got to get this unit packed up and moved out of here. We can't risk any further transmissions."

"What about my message?" Natalia asked. "Did you get a reply?"

He nodded. "Just before you arrived." He handed her a slip of paper with scribbles on it.

"It's not decoded?"

The man started disconnecting wires. "Leopold does that."

Natalia clenched her teeth, forcing herself to stay calm. "Can you do it?"

He stopped and stared at her. "You want *me* to decode it? You don't even know me. What if it's something you don't want me to know? Or something *I* don't want to know. That's Leopold's job."

"What the hell is wrong with you?" Rabbit blurted out. "Didn't you hear the lady? Leopold is dead!"

The young man leaped to his feet. "Hey, you little shit, I don't take—"

Natalia stepped in front of him and poked a finger into the man's chest. He was taller than she was but skinny and, despite the scrawny beard, didn't appear to be more than about twenty years old. "Listen to me, and listen carefully. I'm on a mission authorized by the British SOE. Several people have already been killed, and if you don't decode this message *right now* other people will die." She slipped her right hand under her sweater, feeling for the handle of the Browning 9mm pistol tucked in the waistband of her skirt.

"That's not my concern, lady."

Natalia took a step back, pulled out the pistol and aimed it at the skinny young man's head. "You'd better *make* it your concern, mister. And you'd better do it *right now!*"

His eyes widened, and he held up his hands, backing away. "Hey, take it easy. I don't want—"

"Just shut up and decode the damned message!"

Beads of sweat appeared on the young man's forehead. His eyes darted back and forth between Natalia and Rabbit. Then he snatched the paper from Natalia's hand and sat down at the stool. "You're fuckin' crazy," he sputtered. "Just put away the gun. I'll decode the Goddamn message, then I'm packing up and getting out of here."

It took only a few minutes, and he handed Natalia the decoded message.

PIRATE ARRIVING 22 JUNE
KRAKOW CENTRAL STATION
1500 HOURS

"June 22nd? That's not until tomorrow! What the hell are they—"

"It's a part of the new code," he said, packing the wireless set into a wooden crate. "They set the date one day ahead, an extra precaution in case the message is intercepted."

"Then he's coming today?"

"That's what it says: three o'clock this afternoon. And now, unless you're going to shoot me, I've got to get this stuff out of here."

Rabbit helped the young man hoist the crate into a wheelbarrow. The man threw a tarp and two tires over it and pushed it out of the garage, giving Natalia a wide berth, muttering under his breath.

"Who's *Pirate?*" Rabbit asked after the wireless operator was out of sight.

Natalia had no idea, and she also wondered how they would recognize each other. She shrugged. "We'll find out soon enough. It's probably best if we stay here until it's time to meet him."

Rabbit nodded. "And now you can tell me what the hell is going on."

Fifty-Five

21 June

Natalia spotted him from across the street. He was tall and thin, wearing a gray pin-striped suit, a fedora and a black patch over his left eye. Some pirate, she thought. At least he didn't have a parrot on his shoulder. After a moment the "pirate" looked in her direction. With a slight nod of her head, Natalia communicated she was the one he was to meet. Then she turned away and, hunched over with her cane, headed back toward the garage.

She didn't look back, but Natalia knew he was behind her, following at a safe distance as they crossed the Rynek Kleparski market, busy at this hour with people picking over the half-rotten potatoes and the few loaves of stale bread that remained in the stalls. When she arrived at the garage, Natalia slid the door open and stepped into the dimly lit interior. Rabbit was waiting for her, standing next to the workbench where the wireless unit had been. She pulled the Browning from the waistband of her skirt.

The thin man with the eye patch appeared a few minutes later. At this closer distance Natalia noticed heavy scars across the left side of his face. She raised the pistol and pointed it at him.

The man carefully set his briefcase on the dirt floor, then slowly removed his hat. "I am Captain Andreyev, an associate of Adam Nowak's and chief aide to the late General Andrei Kovalenko."

Andreyev. Natalia remembered the name from what Adam had told her. His Polish was very good, with a slight Russian accent, but she was so startled by the rest of what he'd said that she barely registered his fluency. "Did you say, the *late* General . . . ?"

Andreyev held his hat in both hands and nodded. "The general was killed in an automobile accident."

A chill crawled up Natalia's back. "When did it happen?"

"Yesterday."

Natalia stared at the Russian who stood calmly in the center of the gloomy, dilapidated building. Kovalenko was dead? It couldn't be a coincidence. Someone must have murdered him. Who . . . and why? Because of the letter he gave Adam? *The letter I have a copy of!* She pushed a ladderback chair toward Andreyev and took a stool facing him, still pointing the gun.

There was an awkward silence until Andreyev leaned forward intently and addressed her. "I apologize for being so blunt, but General Kovalenko's accident has been a shock for all of us. Perhaps I should explain—"

"Yes, perhaps you should," Natalia cut in abruptly.

"I assume that Adam Nowak told you about General Kovalenko's relationship with Colonel Whitehall of the SOE, and the general's sympathetic position toward Poland."

"We don't need his Goddamn sympathy."

"Nevertheless, I was General Kovalenko's chief aide. I've been involved in all of his dealings with Colonel Whitehall on the issue of Poland. It was Colonel Whitehall who asked me to come here." Andreyev's eyes moved to Rabbit, then back to Natalia. He seemed to ignore the pistol pointed at his chest. "In the first message you sent to Whitehall, you indicated that you'd found something of importance."

Natalia didn't respond.

"May I ask what it was?"

Natalia hesitated, suddenly feeling very exposed. Was this really Andreyev? What if Tarnov had sent someone to impersonate him? But they'd received a coded wireless message from Whitehall, and Andreyev showed up at the right time and place. *But even if he is Andreyev . . . can I trust him?*

"Natalia?"

"Don't rush me, Goddamn it! This is all happening pretty fast."

"Yes, of course, I understand."

"Do you?"

"I understand how hard—"

Natalia leaped to her feet, pointing the pistol at Andreyev's forehead. "My family lived in a village near Lwow, *Captain Andreyev!* Until September of 1939. Now I don't know *where* they are—except somewhere in *Russia,* if they're still alive!"

Andreyev didn't flinch, but beads of sweat trickled down the sides of his face. He looked directly into her eyes. "General Kovalenko's mother was Polish, Natalia. He is . . . was . . . a supporter of Poland's independence and its quest for freedom. He was—"

"Were you in Warsaw, Captain?" Natalia demanded.

"Yes, I was."

Rabbit spoke up. "And you watched from the other side of the river while the Nazis destroyed our city?"

Andreyev's eyes moved toward the boy, but he did not respond.

Natalia gritted her teeth in frustration. Adam was in trouble, probably captured by Tarnov. What the hell was she doing here in an abandoned garage talking to a *Russian*? "Why are you here, Captain?"

"I'm here to help you. That's what you asked for."

"Who killed General Kovalenko?"

"Major Tarnov was responsible for that. *He's* the enemy, Natalia."

Natalia kept the Browning trained on Andreyev's forehead. Was it really that simple? Tarnov was the enemy and everyone else—Whitehall, Kovalenko, Andreyev—were allies, trying to help the down-trodden Poles? Was it possible that Kovalenko, a Russian general, cared enough about Poland that even after his death his chief aide was willing to defy the NKVD and risk his own life to help in the quest for freedom?

"What was it you found, Natalia?" Andreyev asked.

She glanced at Rabbit.

The boy stood perfectly still and met her eyes. He nodded.

Natalia hesitated. "A journal," she said quietly. "I found Ludwik Banach's journal."

Andreyev waited.

She realized there was no other choice. Adam had told her to contact Whitehall and that's what she had done. Andreyev showed up exactly as the coded reply to her message said he would. She had to trust him. "Banach's journal made reference to a document, an official order signed by Stalin. It was given to Hans Frank by a visitor from Russia in November of 1942." She described the contents of the order while Andreyev listened without expression.

"Do you have it?" he asked when she was finished.

"The journal?"

"The *order,* Natalia." The Russian captain's voice took on a hard edge. "Do you have the order?"

"No."

When Andreyev spoke again his patient tone of voice had returned. "Do you know where it is?"

Natalia lowered the pistol but kept her eyes locked on him. She had to trust him . . . but he was still a *Russian.* "No, I don't," she said. "And neither does Adam. That's why he was searching for Banach."

Rabbit spoke up again. "Are you here to help us find Adam, or to get your hands on the copy of Stalin's order?"

A flash of irritation crossed Andreyev's face. "I'm here to do both. But, I'll be honest: Finding the order, and making it public, was vitally important to General Kovalenko. It's vitally important to Colonel Whitehall, and it should be to *you.* It could make a difference in what gets decided about Poland at the Potsdam conference. The fate of your own country—"

"And that matters to *you,* Captain Andreyev?" The pistol was at her side, and she tightened her grip on it. "The fate of Poland matters to *you?*"

Andreyev got to his feet, but Natalia stood her ground. "It mattered to Kovalenko," Andreyev snapped. "And *he* mattered to me. I'm sorry about your family. I'm sorry about what happened in Warsaw and in the Katyn Forest. I'm sorry about the whole damn war, but that doesn't change what's important now. What's important now is to find that copy of the order and—"

"What's important to *me,*" Natalia retorted, "is to find Adam Nowak."

Andreyev nodded. "Very well, then. I suggest we get started. Do you know where he went?"

Natalia turned to Rabbit again, thankful that her friend was there. She had decided to trust Andreyev because she had no other choice. But she felt a great comfort having someone beside her that she knew she could rely on, someone she trusted without question.

Rabbit was silent but his eyes communicated agreement. Natalia continued. "Adam made contact with someone who told him that Banach is with the Górale in the Tatra Mountains, somewhere beyond Nowy Targ. Adam went up there to find him, but he should have come back by now. His contact has also disappeared."

Andreyev's expression hardened. "His contact is probably dead by now. But Tarnov would have beaten the information out of him before he killed him."

Natalia glanced at her watch. It was quarter to four. "We should go to Nowy Targ this afternoon and try to make contact with the Górale."

"Tarnov will have men watching the bus station," Andreyev said.

"Can you get an auto?"

Andreyev thought for a moment then nodded. "I'm here unofficially, but I have a few resources I can access. I'll meet you back here in one hour."

Fifty-Six

21 JUNE

THE DRIVE UP TO NOWY TARG took longer than they expected, and Natalia grew more apprehensive with each agonizingly slow kilometer. Andreyev did the best he could, maneuvering the Russian GAZ-11 through the narrow, winding roads, at one point darting past a battered, rusted truck laden with sacks of grain and coming so close to the edge of the road that Natalia thought it would all end right there. Rabbit, of course, thought it was great sport.

The city appeared quiet as they crossed a bridge over the Bialy River, and proceeded along twisting cobblestone streets lined with three-story, stucco buildings. Natalia guessed most of the locals were home having their supper. They parked the auto behind the bus station—a drab, brown building, with peeling paint and boarded up windows—and set out on foot. As they passed the front of the station, the dozen or so people standing in line at a bus stop eyed them curiously. In a small, remote city like this outsiders easily attracted attention, and Natalia felt more than a little conspicuous, especially walking down the street with a Russian officer. At least Andreyev wasn't in uniform, though the GAZ-11 they drove into town was a dead giveaway.

Farther down the street they spotted a pub. It was a chalet-style structure of stone and white stucco, with a steep, wood-shingled roof. The door was open, and Natalia heard voices from inside. "As good a place to start as any," she said.

Inside, the room was long and narrow, with a copper-topped bar on the left and a half-dozen round, wooden tables along the right. A scattering of pictures, mostly faded prints of mountain landscapes, hung haphazardly above the tables. A ceiling fan creaked overhead, and a stuffed boar's head glared at them from the wall behind the bar, yellow teeth clenched around a limp rabbit.

"I hope I don't end up like that," Rabbit whispered to Natalia, jerking his thumb toward the boar's head.

The only other patrons were two young men wearing dark trousers and matching green shirts, like uniforms of some sort, who sat at the far end of the bar with mugs of beer, conversing with the bartender. They both shot quick glances at the trio entering the bar, then turned back to their beers. Andreyev motioned toward one of the tables, and the three of them sat down. The table was low, with barely enough room to slide their legs under it. Andreyev sat facing the door.

After a bit more conversation with the two men, the bartender wiped his hands on a cloth, then walked around the bar to their table. He was in his sixties, Natalia guessed, slightly built and practically bald with wisps of gray hair around his ears and the back of his head. He smiled politely when Natalia ordered three cups of coffee and returned to the bar. They'd had some discussion ahead of time about who should do most of the talking. It could appear odd for a woman to be the one asking questions when a man was present, but with Andreyev's Russian accent, it seemed the better risk.

The bartender returned and set the coffee cups on the table. "Anything else?" he asked. "We have vegetable soup tonight."

Natalia spoke up, reciting the question they had also discussed ahead of time. "We were expecting to meet someone here, but we were delayed along the way. His name is Tytus; do you know him?"

The bartender's eyes were blank, his expression unreadable. "No, sorry, no one by that name." He walked back to the bar with a slightly quicker step and rejoined his friends.

Natalia sipped the coffee slowly, trying hard not to choke. It was even worse than the bitter, ersatz concoctions served in Krakow and smelled earthy, as though brewed from tree roots. "I'm sorry, did you want some soup?" she asked Rabbit. The boy was always hungry.

"Nah, not from here," he replied. "I don't trust that guy."

"An intelligent observation," Andreyev said quietly.

"Especially considering the auto we drove into town," Natalia said.

The three of them continued in trivial bits of conversation to pass the time, having decided to wait for twenty minutes before moving on to another place.

They didn't have to wait that long. One of the men wearing the green uniform shirt polished off his beer, got up and left through a rear door.

"He'll be back," Andreyev said.

"Should I follow him?" Rabbit asked eagerly. "He'd never spot me. I'm good at that."

Andreyev shook his head. "We all stay together. Let's see how this plays out."

Andreyev had changed clothes back in Krakow when he'd gone to get the auto. Instead of the pin-striped suit, he now wore gray slacks, a black turtleneck sweater and a short, lightweight leather jacket. He carried a pistol in an ankle holster under his right trouser pant.

Natalia sat facing the rear of the bar, and the hair on the back of her neck bristled when the same man returned ten minutes later. Instead of taking his seat at the bar, however, he stood in front of the rear door with his arms folded over his chest. He now wore a black denim jacket over the green shirt. She assumed he was armed.

A moment later, Andreyev tensed and slowly slid his hands off the table. His right foot scraped softly along the wooden floor.

Two other men stepped through the front door. They both wore the same green shirts under black denim jackets.

One of the men pulled the door closed and stood in front of it. The second man approached their table. He was young, in his mid-twenties Natalia thought, tall and broad-shouldered with short blond hair. He had hard, blue eyes, and he fixed them directly on Andreyev. "Why are you looking for Tytus?" he asked.

"Are you Tytus?" Natalia asked.

He ignored her and pointed at Andreyev. "I want *you* to answer the question."

Andreyev sat with his back ramrod straight, his hands still under the table. "We need his help."

The men standing in front of the two doors both took a step forward, and the man sitting at the bar slowly turned around facing the table. "We don't help Russians up here," the blond man said. "Now, what the fuck are you doing here?"

Andreyev appeared unfazed. "There are two things you should know," he said calmly. "The first is that I may be a Russian, but I am here unofficially and I mean no harm to you or anyone else."

The blond man spat on Andreyev's shoe. "And what's the second thing?"

"The second thing is that I'm holding a Tokarev T30 in my lap, pointed directly at your crotch. If one of those three goons so much as twitches, I'll blow your balls off."

Natalia noticed the man sitting at the bar move slightly, as if to slide off the stool. He stopped abruptly when Andreyev, who hadn't taken his eyes off the blond man, barked, "Don't even think about it! Keep your ass on that stool or your friend is dead before your feet hit the ground!"

The blond man glared at Andreyev for a long tense moment. Finally he turned to Natalia. "Are you Russian too?"

"Polish."

"All right, then. Before we all kill each other maybe you should tell me what you want."

"We're looking for Tytus."

The man didn't respond.

"Do you know Tytus?" Natalia pressed.

"What if I do?"

"If you do then you'll know that he met a man named Wolf last Friday."

Again, he didn't answer.

Natalia leaned forward. "This is important. The man called Wolf is an American who fought with the AK in Warsaw. He needed to make contact with the Górale. We think he may have run into trouble, and we need to find him."

The blond man grunted. "You're AK, and you're running around with a fucking Russian. How stupid do you think I am?"

Andreyev broke in, his tone of voice sharp and authoritarian. "Have you seen any other Russians around here in the past few days?"

The man hesitated.

"If you did, they were probably NKVD. If they find Wolf before we do, they'll not only kill *him,* but they'll also kill every one of the Górale that Tytus took him to meet." Andreyev paused and then added, "And after that, they'll come for you."

"They're going to come for all of us sooner or later," the man said. He was silent for another moment, his eyes flicking back and forth between Andreyev and Natalia. "Yes, I know Tytus met a man called Wolf," he said finally. "He took him to a chapel farther up the mountain where they made contact with the Górale. Tytus left him there and came back the next day."

"Have you seen any Russians around here?" Andreyev repeated impatiently.

"Hell, all the time. Red Army hooligans, usually drunk and looking for trouble. We're with the local militia, and they like to push us around."

"What about NKVD?"

The blond man tilted his head toward the bar. "Tell him, Jacek."

The man named Jacek spoke up, but stayed firmly planted on the bar stool. "It was early yesterday morning, before dawn, a group of NKVD riflemen and a man in a black trench coat. They headed farther up the mountain."

"How did they know where to go?" Andreyev asked.

A sudden emotion passed over the blond man's face. He grimaced. "They took Tytus with them—after they murdered his wife."

Natalia slapped her hand on the table. "Jesus Christ! It's Tarnov! We've got to get up there. Now!"

Andreyev pushed his chair back slightly, and put both hands on the table. They were empty. "Is there anything else we should know?" he asked the blond man.

The man looked down at Andreyev's hands and smiled. "The one in the black trench coat drove back into town yesterday evening," he said, "along with two of the riflemen. They went to the bus station and forced the manager to open all the lockers. Then they headed back toward Krakow."

Natalia's stomach lurched. "Shit!"

On Thursday evening Tarnov had dinner alone at a restaurant just off the Rynek Glowny in Krakow's Stare Miasto District. It was located on the ground floor of a small hotel whose name he couldn't pronounce, a small, simply decorated establishment that he'd frequented with Hans Frank back in the days when the Russians and Germans were allies. Frank had always enjoyed Krakow, Tarnov recalled, thought it was a magnificent city, filled with glorious Medieval treasures and rich history. *The man was a fool.*

Tarnov tossed back his glass of vodka and poured another from the bottle the waiter had left on the table. How could he have trusted a lunatic like Frank with the only copy of Stalin's Katyn Order? He thought back to the previous evening. Of course, the order wasn't in a locker at the Nowy Targ bus station. He wasn't surprised. He had suspected Nowak was lying, but he couldn't waste any more time. He'd had to take care of the Kovalenko business. But Nowak and those Górale sheepherders would pay dearly for their sins, and Tarnov knew he'd get what he wanted, one way or the other.

His dinner arrived, the house specialty, a fried pork cutlet in thick sauce with a potato pancake. Tarnov sighed, forcing himself to relax. It was too late to drive all the way back tonight. Nowak was secure for the moment, locked in the mountain chapel under heavy guard. And now, with Kovalenko out of the way, he'd be able to operate without interference. But first, there was one last issue to deal with.

When Tarnov finished, he lit a cigar and sipped cognac, occasionally glancing at the hand-carved clock on the fireplace mantel. A bit later his aide, a young and eager NKVD lieutenant named Resnikov entered the restaurant. Resnikov had committed more than a few "indiscretions" over the years, particularly with young boys. Tarnov had protected him from the do-gooders within the NKVD, and Resnikov was grateful. He could be trusted.

Resnikov removed his hat and stood at the table until Tarnov acknowledged him and gestured for him to sit.

"Well?" Tarnov asked, setting his cognac snifter on the table.

Lieutenant Resnikov hesitated. "I haven't found anyone, sir."

"Damn it!" Tarnov snapped. "I *know* there's someone out there, Lieutenant. Someone who has the other copy of Kovalenko's letter."

Resnikov was silent, his eyes dropping to the table. After a moment he cleared his throat. "*Prastítye,* but with the general's death . . . does it matter?"

Tarnov glared at the young officer. "We can't take any chances. Whoever it is could still cause a problem."

Resnikov sat up straight. "Give me an order, sir."

Tarnov tapped his fingers on the cognac snifter. "Let's go over this again. When that librarian, Jastremski, revealed where Ludwik Banach went, he gave up Adam Nowak's name . . . his 'visitor' at the library."

The lieutenant nodded. "He couldn't stand to see his wife tortured."

"And when you interrogated him a second time, he gave you the name of the priest, his contact in the smuggling operation."

"Da."

"But when you interrogated the priest earlier today, he didn't provide any new names?"

"Nyet."

Tarnov continued to tap his fingers on the glass. The priest didn't have the copy of the Katyn Order. They'd already torn apart his quarters at the monastery and found nothing. *There has to be someone else, someone the priest was working with.*

"The priest is still alive," Resnikov offered, "though he's in pretty tough shape."

Tarnov finished off his cognac and pushed his chair back. "Then go at him again, right now, until he gives you a name."

Fifty-Seven

21 JUNE

THEY SLIPPED QUIETLY through the forest, their moccasin-covered feet making barely any sound at all. It was approaching dusk on Thursday evening, and there were eight of them, the best of the Górale hunters in Prochowa. Three were armed with shotguns, the others carried their own hand-fashioned *ciupagas*. They moved quickly with an unspoken communication born of years in the wilds of the Tatra Mountains.

Casimir held up a hand, and the band of hunters stopped, melting silently into the trees. He caught the acrid odor of charred wood on the breeze and instantly knew what had happened. He made eye contact with Mikolai, his second-in-command. It was all that was necessary, and Mikolai disappeared, continuing on down the mountain in silent reconnaissance.

In less than a half hour Mikolai returned from the other direction, knelt next to Casimir and whispered, "Piotr's house is destroyed. The other two are intact."

Casimir held his breath as Mikolai gave him the rest of the report. Piotr's neighbors had been shot, their bodies still lying in the grassy area between the cabins. Both of their wives were dead, one badly burned and shot through the head, the other one raped and stabbed. Mikolai had found her body inside one of the cabins. Piotr, Krystyna and Zygmunt were missing. "I also counted the bodies of eight NKVD riflemen, most of them shot in the head," he said.

Casimir closed his eyes and breathed slowly, visualizing what must have happened. Then he looked at Mikolai. "The American?"

"Since he was on horseback, he must've arrived first and seen the fire. He probably shot the riflemen."

"Then he must be with Piotr and the others," Casimir said. "They're being held somewhere until this NKVD agent, Tarnov, gets what he's after."

Mikolai's eyes narrowed. "The chapel."

The blond man's name was Karol, and he and his militia comrade, Jacek, agreed to guide Natalia, Andreyev and Rabbit up the mountain, as far as the chapel. "The chapel's been there as long as anyone can remember," Karol said as they bumped along the gravel road, all jammed into the GAZ-11. "It's used as a safe house, a way to send signals to the AK contact among the Górale."

"You're AK?" Natalia asked.

"No. Tytus is the only one left. Russians took care of the rest." He shot a quick glance at Andreyev. The Russian captain sat in the front passenger seat with his eye on Jacek, who was driving. Andreyev ignored the comment. "But I know where the chapel is," Karol went on, "and Tytus told me what the signal was some time ago. Just in case. We can only drive partway. Then we have to walk."

It was after dark when they arrived at a point where the gravel road turned to the left and headed back down the mountain. Jacek pulled the GAZ to the side of the road and shut off the engine.

Karol took the lead, and the group set off up the mountain, following a narrow pathway that dropped off sharply into a ditch. Rabbit followed behind Karol with a bounce in his step, clearly enjoying the adventure. Jacek was third, then Natalia. Andreyev brought up the rear.

The path wound through thick stands of conifers. Though it was dark, the moon was rising, and Natalia could make out Jacek's shadow in front of her. The underbrush tickled her fingers, and it was deathly quiet save for the muted thump of their footsteps on the dirt path.

They had trudged along for about ten minutes when Natalia heard an owl hoot off to her right. A moment later there was a second hoot, from her left.

A sudden flash of movement.

Jacek's shadow disappeared.

Natalia stopped, but before she could turn her head, a hand clamped tightly across her mouth. Another hand grabbed her elbow, and in an instant she was on the ground being dragged off the path and through the underbrush. She struggled, kicking her legs, but it did no good. Her assailant was too strong.

Then he stopped. Terrified and barely able to breathe, Natalia looked up. The moonlight was brighter, and she could tell they were in a clearing. A shadowy figure crouched in front of her. It was a man with long hair flowing from beneath a wide-brimmed hat. He held something in his hand that looked like a long pole with an axe head on the end. Natalia remembered reading about the strange weapons in school. She was amazed they still used them. Slowly the man lowered his hand from her mouth but maintained his grip on her elbow. He raised his forefinger to his lips.

A moment later the underbrush rustled, and another man with long hair and a wide-brimmed hat suddenly appeared, dragging Rabbit. The boy kicked furiously and shook his head back and forth. The man stopped and put a knee on the boy's chest. Still struggling, Rabbit turned his head and caught Natalia's eye. Even in the moonlight she could see the fury in his eyes.

The man gripping Natalia's arm leaned over and whispered in her ear. "Tell the boy to settle down." He spoke Polish, but his accent was strange.

She turned to Rabbit and whispered. "It's OK. Just . . . do as they say."

Rabbit glared at her defiantly. But a moment later he gave in.

Another man stepped into the clearing and knelt down in front of Natalia. This one also carried a *ciupaga,* but he was older, with leathery skin and white hair. "If I let you sit up, you must promise not to make a sound," he said.

Natalia nodded.

The older man motioned to Natalia's assailant who released her elbow. Natalia sat up.

"Who are you? And what are you doing here?" The older man asked.

"Who are *you?*" Natalia shot back. "Where's the rest of our group?"

For an instant he looked amused, but his expression changed quickly, becoming serious. His eyes were dark, black pits. "My name is Casimir. And the rest of your group is unharmed . . . for the moment. Now answer my question."

These were obviously Górale, and Natalia felt a glimmer of hope. "I'm looking for Wolf," she said.

He frowned.

Goddamn it, is he using his real name? "Adam Nowak," she said quickly. "I'm Adam's friend, Natalia. He came up here last week, searching for his uncle, Ludwik Banach. Have you seen him?"

Casimir studied her, his expression now curious. "And you and your friends just barged in here, stumbling in the dark, hoping to find him?"

Natalia felt her face flush, and she struggled to control her impatience. *I'm so close, so damned close!* "Yes, that's exactly what we're doing. Now, please tell me. Have you seen him?"

Casimir stood, held out his hand and helped her to her feet. The Górale hunter holding onto Rabbit did the same. "I've met your friend, Adam Nowak," Casimir said. "He was ambushed by the NKVD yesterday. We believe your friend and a few of our people are locked in the chapel—which at the moment is heavily guarded by riflemen."

He paused at a rustling in the underbrush. A moment later Karol, Jacek and a very disgusted looking Andreyev were pushed into the clearing by three Górale hunters carrying shotguns.

One of the hunters shoved Andreyev a step forward. "This one's Russian," he said to Casimir. "The other two are friends of Tytus."

Casimir stepped up to Andreyev. "Are you NKVD?"

"No," Andreyev replied curtly.

"Who sent you here?"

"He's a friend," Natalia said. "He's helping us."

Casimir kept his eyes on Andreyev. "We found Tytus' body in the forest on the other side of the chapel."

"We had nothing to do with that," Andreyev said.

Casimir abruptly took a step backward and thumped his *ciupaga* on the ground. Instantly, two Górale hunters charged from the trees and knocked Andreyev to the ground. One of them produced a rope and grabbed Andreyev's wrist, but the Russian lashed out with his other hand, smashing his fist into the hunter's face. Andreyev tried to stand, but a Górale with a shotgun stomped hard on his chest and shoved the double-barreled weapon into his face.

"What the hell are you doing?" Natalia shouted at Casimir. "I said he was a friend!"

Casimir ignored her, and within seconds Andreyev was subdued, his wrists bound behind him. The Górale hunters forced Karol and Jacek to the ground, tied their hands behind them, then bound all three men's feet together.

"I hope you know what the fuck you're doing," Andreyev snarled. "Those NKVD riflemen won't be carrying spears."

Casimir turned to Natalia. "One of my men will stay here and keep an eye on these three. You and the boy are coming with me."

In the moonlight, Natalia could see that the chapel was heavily guarded. She and Rabbit followed closely behind Casimir, who led the way as the silent Górale hunters proceeded in a wide circle through the forest, gradually surrounding the sturdy, stone building. Six NKVD riflemen with carbines slung over their shoulders stood near a fire about ten meters from the front of the chapel. They smoked cigarettes and joked while meat roasted on a spit over the flames.

Casimir stopped and gestured to one of the hunters, who carried a shotgun and appeared to be the second-in-command. Without a sound, he and five others broke away and slipped deeper into the forest, heading toward the front of the chapel. Two of the five also carried shotguns.

Casimir motioned for Natalia and Rabbit to follow and continued on through the trees toward the rear of the building. A young Górale hunter wearing a black scarf around his neck, trailed closely behind. Casimir led them past the chapel and up an incline into a thick stand of conifers. The ground was spongy with fallen needles. The night air smelled of pine.

Casimir stopped and dropped to one knee, motioning for Natalia and Rabbit to come closer. "You will remain here until we take the building," he whispered. He gestured toward the young hunter with the black scarf. "Tajik will come for you. If you ever want to see Adam Nowak alive, do not make a sound."

With Rabbit at her side, Natalia knelt on the soft ground watching Casimir and Tajik slip silently into the forest, armed only with their *ciupagas*. Rabbit took her hand. "These guys know what they're doing," the boy whispered. "I wish I could see them whack the fuckin' Russians with those axes."

Natalia wished she felt that confident. It was obvious the Górale were fierce and stealthy hunters. But they were up against heavily armed NKVD troopers. *Adam's life depends on mountain men with spears?*

Pine needles pricked her back, and she adjusted her position, peering into the moonlit forest. She could just barely make out the rear of the chapel—a black, square silhouette against the flickering yellow light of the fire. She watched, and listened.

A shadow slipped through the trees.

Another shadow.

Natalia squeezed Rabbit's hand, listening, straining to hear, every nerve in her body tingling.

Tree limbs creaked in the breeze.

Then a grunt and a muted thud.

Rabbit nudged her elbow and pointed toward the chapel. A flash of movement, a sweeping arc through the firelight.

Another grunt, and a thud.

Quiet.

Then an owl hooted.

A second owl answered.

Without warning, a deafening shotgun blast echoed through the forest.

A second blast, followed by a concussion of rapid gunfire, hammered Natalia's eardrums.

Then it was quiet.

Natalia knelt on both knees, riveted to the spot, barely able to breathe.

A shadow, very close.

It was Tajik, at the base of the hill, motioning for them to follow.

Fifty-Eight

22 JUNE

THE NKVD'S MAIN INTERROGATION ROOM was buried deep in the Dragon's Den, a cave below Wawel Castle, which Medieval legend held was once inhabited by a man-eating monster. It was sufficiently isolated so that none of the clerks and administrative officials who worked in the castle would be bothered by screams and crunching bones.

Early Friday morning Lieutenant Resnikov stood outside the interrogation room, waiting for the thugs inside to finish their work and haul what was left of the priest back to his cell. The young lieutenant was annoyed. When they'd broken the priest's nose, blood had spurted everywhere, and his freshly pressed uniform shirt was ruined. The priest had been tougher than he thought, and breaking him down had taken a while, but Resnikov finally got what he needed. He stuck his head inside the interrogation room, grimacing from the stench of blood and body odor, and gave a few last instructions to keep the priest alive. Then he walked away, cursing to himself about the shirt.

When Resnikov reached Tarnov's office, he was not surprised to see that the door was open and the lights on at this early hour. He was about to enter when he heard the telephone receiver bang down and Tarnov bellow, "Goddamn idiots!"

Lieutenant Resnikov backed away, but Tarnov suddenly appeared in the doorway, face flushed, eyes blazing. "You! Get in here! *Bystrýey!*"

Resnikov cautiously stepped into the office.

Tarnov slammed the door behind him and barked, "Adam Nowak escaped!"

Resnikov's stomach twisted in a knot. "*Góspadi!* How could that happen?"

"The fucking incompetent riflemen you assigned to guard Nowak and his friends were attacked. Malinovsky went up there early this morning, found them all dead. All twelve! Most of them were killed with fucking axes and spears—" Tarnov stopped and waved his hand dismissively. "The details don't matter. We've got to find that son of a bitch, understand?"

The young lieutenant nodded quickly.

"Now, tell me what you got from the priest."

Resnikov took a deep breath, trying to ignore the beads of sweat trickling down the side of his face. "Tough old bastard. Held out for a long time. But he finally admitted that Ludwik Banach was smuggling Nazi documents from a secret storage room located in the Copernicus Memorial Library. It confirms what we got from Jastremski. Banach gave the documents to Jastremski, who passed them to the priest."

"Did he say what kind of documents?"

"He said they were from Hans Frank's secret files but claims he never read them, just passed them along."

"Passed them to whom?"

"A woman. He claims he only met her a few times. He described her as young, plain-looking, with brown hair. He referred to her as the Conductor."

Tarnov scoffed. "It's a fucking code name, completely useless. Does he know where she is?"

Resnikov smiled. His thugs had to practically kill the priest, and they made a hell of a mess, but it was worth it. "He gave me an address," he said proudly.

"An address? Good work! Where is it?"

"In the eastern section of the Kazimierz District."

"Get my car."

Adam woke with a start when he felt a hand brush across his cheek. Natalia smiled at him, then leaned over and kissed his cheek. He looked around, but the room was a blur without his glasses. "Where are we?"

She smiled again. "You were *really* sound asleep. We're in Nowy Targ, in an upstairs bedroom in Karol's house."

"Karol?"

"A friend of Tytus. He's with the local militia."

Adam thought for a moment. It started to come back: the gunfire outside the chapel, Casimir bursting through the door, Górale hunters . . . then Natalia. There were others. This Karol must have been one of them. "What about Piotr and Krystyna?" he asked.

The smile disappeared from Natalia's face. "Piotr died on the way down here. You were unconscious in the backseat of the car. Krystyna's holding her own. She's in the hospital. Karol snuck her in late last night under a different name."

Adam's eyes clouded. "Her baby?"

"The doctor says the baby should be fine, as long as Krystyna can fight the infection. They're doing what they can."

Adam wiped his eyes, then sat up slowly, wincing as a bolt of pain shot through his ribs. He wondered how many were broken. Natalia handed him his glasses, and he spotted a familiar face on the other side of the tiny, wallpapered room. "Rabbit?"

The boy beamed. "It's me, Captain Wolf."

Adam turned to Natalia. "I don't understand . . . how . . . ?"

"Don't you remember? He was there last night, at the chapel. So was Andreyev."

"Andreyev?" The room began to spin. *Christ, what's wrong with me?*

"You should lie down again," Natalia said, placing her hand on his shoulder. "You were in pretty tough shape when we found you last night."

"No, just give me a minute. What time is it?"

"Six o'clock. And that would be in the *morning*. Friday morning."

"Yeah, yeah, don't get smart. So, Andreyev is here, in Nowy Targ?"

"Yes, we'll get to that in a minute. First, tell me about your uncle."

Adam rubbed the left side of his face. It seemed like his visit to

Prochowa had happened a long time ago. "He died . . . two weeks before I got to the village . . ."

When he finished the story, Natalia took his hand, squeezing it gently as their eyes met. After a moment she said, "There's something we have to tell you."

"What is it? You look like—"

"General Kovalenko is dead."

Adam flinched and another jolt of pain shot through his ribcage. "What the hell . . . what happened?"

"Andreyev says Tarnov arranged for Kovalenko's death in an auto accident."

"Jesus Christ, I can't believe—"

"You can't believe that Russians would murder their own generals? They've been doing it for—" Natalia stopped and bit her lower lip.

"I can't believe this happened *now,* that Tarnov could act that fast." Adam stood up. The dizziness had subsided. He stepped over to a bureau on the opposite wall and looked in the mirror. There was a black-and-blue lump on his forehead, and the left side of his face was red and swollen.

"Tarnov certainly did a number on you," Natalia said. "I'm surprised you're able to stand up."

"Casimir said you took out eight riflemen," Rabbit said, grinning.

Adam smiled at the boy. "Thanks for looking after Natalia."

"Yeah sure, we make a good team."

Adam's head pounded and he felt like hell, but his injuries were nothing compared to what Tarnov had done to Piotr and Krystyna. *If it's the last thing I do, I'm going to get that fucker.* "I want to talk to Andreyev," he said to Natalia.

"Rabbit will get him." She glanced at the boy, and he hurried from the room.

"What have you told Andreyev?"

"Everything. I'm still not sure we can trust him, but we had no other choice."

"You did the right thing. If we want to get out of here alive, we'll need his help."

• • •

It wasn't long before Rabbit returned with Andreyev. Adam leaned against the bureau. He was afraid if he let go he might fall down. He held out his hand. "Good to see you again, Captain."

Andreyev shook his hand, peering into his face. "You look like hell."

"Thanks for the compliment. Natalia told me about General Kovalenko. Tarnov could make that happen?"

"Tarnov's operating on his own. But he's got friends, dangerous friends. He can get to anyone."

"To you?"

Andreyev shrugged. "He could. But I don't think he'd try. Not right now, anyway. Given what's at stake for him, Tarnov probably felt he had to take the chance and get Kovalenko out of the way. If the general had seen Natalia's message he would've raised hell. I can't do that. No one would pay any attention." He paused for a moment. "Do you have the Katyn Order?"

Adam shook his head.

"But you know where it is."

"It's in the Copernicus Memorial Library."

Andreyev blinked. "Stalin's order about Katyn is in a *library?*"

"I'm certain of it."

Andreyev looked around at all three of them. "When does the library open?"

Natalia answered, "Ten o'clock." She took Adam's hand and stood back to study his torn, bloodstained shirt and filthy trousers. "We can't do much about your face, but Karol will give you some clean clothes, after you've had a bath. Then I'll bandage those ribs."

Tarnov was livid. He paced his office. It was 9:30 in the morning, and more than three hours had passed since the futile raid on the shabby room in Kazimierz, but he was still beside himself. *We missed her! She was there! I know it . . . I can feel it!* He picked up the phone and screamed at the operator: "Get Lieutenant Resnikov in here!"

When Resnikov stepped into his office, Tarnov jabbed his finger into the young officer's chest. "Can you get any more from that fucking priest? Would he know where the woman went?"

The lieutenant shook his head. "We could try, but I doubt we'd get anything. He's almost dead. I gave them instructions to keep him alive, but it's been several hours." The young lieutenant shifted his weight from one foot to another as silence hung in the room.

Tarnov took a deep breath to settle down. He sat at his desk and stared out the window, then abruptly swiveled around and snatched up a pencil as something occurred to him. "You said Banach was smuggling documents out of the Copernicus Library."

Resnikov nodded.

Tarnov tapped the pencil on the desk. "Everything seems to focus on that library. Hans Frank stored secret files there. Banach and Jastremski worked there and smuggled out the files. Nowak went there to make contact with Jastremski." The pencil snapped in half, and Tarnov tossed it at the wastebasket, missing. He stood abruptly, hands on his hips and glared at Resnikov. "So what the hell does it all mean?"

The lieutenant cleared his throat. "Uh, I'm not—"

"What do we know for *certain?*"

"For certain? I don't think—"

Tarnov ignored him. "What we *know* is that Banach left Krakow abruptly last January and traveled up to the Tatra Mountains. Then Adam Nowak came along and followed him up there. But, when we caught up to Nowak, he was headed back *here*. And he didn't have the document . . ." Tarnov's voice trailed off.

"Document, sir? What document are you—?"

"*Nichivó!* It doesn't matter! Don't worry about the fucking document. It's *Nowak* we're after. He was on his way back here, to Krakow. *Why,* lieutenant? Where do you suppose he was going?"

"The library?"

"Exactly! The Copernicus Memorial Library."

Fifty-Nine

23 June
10:00 AM

Adam still felt uncomfortable sitting next to Captain Andreyev in the front seat of the GAZ-11. He knew that he had no choice. He had to trust Andreyev, but the shock of General Kovalenko's murder still bothered him.

"Are you sure you're up to this?" Andreyev asked. "Even with clean clothes, you still look terrible."

"I'll be fine as long as I don't run into Tarnov again." *That's a lie. I want that bastard!*

"I guess that depends on whether or not Tarnov makes a connection between you and the library," Andreyev said. "He got to your friend Jastremski, and the priest. He'll probably figure it out before long."

Adam's ribs felt better now that they were bandaged, but he still winced as the black motorcar bumped over a pothole. "It didn't take Tarnov very long to get to General Kovalenko, did it?" he replied, but regretted the comment when he saw the flash of pain on Andreyev's face. Perhaps this Russian could be trusted after all.

Andreyev turned onto Avenue Mickiewicza and drove past the imposing structure of the Copernicus Memorial Library. At the end of the block he turned left, circled around the building and pulled into a narrow, cobblestone lane behind the library.

Adam breathed a sigh of relief when he saw a truck with the insignia of a janitorial company parked in front of the open dock door.

He'd remembered correctly Jastremski's comment about the dock door only being used on Friday mornings. He turned to Andreyev. "You know what to do?"

The Russian nodded. "I'll be on Avenue Mickiewicza at the south end of the library in thirty minutes. If you're not there, I'll come back here to the loading dock. I'll repeat the process every fifteen minutes unless . . ."

Adam nodded. "Yes, I know—unless the NKVD or the police show up."

"If that happens, I won't be able to—"

"It won't happen. Tarnov hasn't figured it out yet." Adam got out of the car and watched Andreyev drive off. He reached into the pocket of his suit coat and felt the Browning 9mm pistol Natalia had given him. A part of him hoped Tarnov *would* show up.

The janitorial truck was empty, and there was no one around at the moment. Adam checked his watch. It was five minutes past ten. With a groan, he climbed onto the loading dock and stepped into the building.

Natalia entered the library at precisely 10:15, noticing only a scattering of people at the tables in the ground floor gallery. She wasn't surprised. It was Saturday, and it was summer, with the start of the university's first fall term after the war still a month away. Following Adam's instructions, she walked past the information desk and headed for the curved, marble stairway leading up to the Reading Room. As she passed the bust of Copernicus in the center of the circular gallery, Natalia glanced to her left. At a table on the far side of the room, Adam sat with his head down, reading a magazine—right where he had said he'd be.

The Reading Room was vacant except for a middle-aged, paunchy man wearing a gray felt cap, who sat at a table near the rear, leaning over an open book as though he was having trouble making out the print. The librarian on duty—a bald, tired-looking man of about fifty—sat behind the counter at the front of the room sorting index cards.

As Natalia approached the counter she silently rehearsed what

Adam had instructed her to ask for—the *Proceedings of the Academy of German Law, 1935,* the conference where Banach first met Hans Frank. It would be a large leather-bound volume, which Adam remembered from his uncle's personal collection. He was convinced that Banach had hidden the copy of Stalin's order in the book before leaving Krakow.

Natalia's mouth was dry, and she felt very exposed, but so far things were proceeding as planned. They had decided she would be the one to ask for the book because, if he were questioned later, the librarian would be less likely to remember her than Adam, who looked like he'd just stepped out of a boxing ring.

When the librarian finally looked up from his index cards, Natalia smiled. "I wonder if you could help me. I'm looking for the proceedings of a legal conference."

The man set aside the stack of cards. "Well, I will certainly try. What is the name of the organization?"

"The Academy of German Law," she replied. "The conference was in 1935."

The man scratched his chin, then walked over to an immense card catalog and pulled open a drawer. He slowly thumbed through some index cards, then slid the drawer closed and opened another. Natalia fidgeted while he repeated the process a third time before finally turning back to the counter, looking pleased with himself and holding up an index card. "I believe I've found it," he announced. "I'll return in a moment."

When he disappeared into the stacks, Natalia's neck began to tingle, and she glanced around the room again. No one was there except the paunchy man hunched over the book. She took a deep breath to calm down and thought about the phrase that Banach wrote in the last page of his journal—*pathetic pawns on the perilous chessboard of the NKVD*. As a code, it was ingenious. It was a memorable phrase, but Banach knew that Adam was the only person who would connect it to the event where Banach had met Hans Frank before the war—the conference of the Academy of German Law in 1935.

After an excruciatingly long time, the librarian returned and set the book on the counter. It was indeed a thick, leather-bound volume with gold printing on the spine that read:

THE ACADEMY OF GERMAN LAW
PROCEEDINGS OF THE ANNUAL CONFERENCE
14 – 19 JULY, 1935

"It's a reference book and not to be checked out," he said, "but you're welcome to take a seat and spend as much time as you need."

Natalia thanked him, gathered up the book and moved to a table near the windows. She sat down with her back to the open room, shielding the book from view. Her palms were sweaty and she wiped them on her trousers, then opened the book and carefully thumbed through the pages.

There! Two sheets of paper folded in thirds and inserted into the middle of the volume. Natalia examined the first one. It was a carbon copy of a document, typewritten in Russian and dated 5 March, 1940. She could make out only a few words, mostly names—*J. Stalin, L. Beria,* and others she didn't recognize. A number of signatures were scrawled across the document. She looked around the room a third time, then unfolded the second sheet. It was a translation into Polish in the same precise handwriting she recognized from Ludwik Banach's journal.

As Natalia read the translation her eyes clouded with tears. It was all there, exactly as Banach had described in his journal—an order, signed by Joseph Stalin and every member of the Soviet Politburo on 5 March, 1940, authorizing the execution of twenty-seven thousand Polish "nationalists and counterrevolutionaries," including more than four thousand officers of the Polish Army in the Katyn Forest.

She sat for another moment, immobilized, staring at the despicable document with tears trickling down her face. She thought about her brother, Michal, shot in the back of the head, his body lying in a ditch in that Russian forest. The document could not bring him back, and it could never heal the wounds . . . but at least now there was proof. At least now, after all the pain and the sorrow, after everything that had been taken away, the dark, silent secret would be exposed.

Natalia carefully refolded the two sheets of paper, slipped them into the pocket of the vest she wore under her sweater and returned the book to the counter. As she left the Reading Room, she had the feeling that tomorrow would be a better day.

A quarter of an hour earlier, just after Natalia entered the Copernicus Memorial Library, Rabbit crossed Avenue Mickiewicza and stood on the corner opposite the massive building. He slipped his right hand into his pocket and felt the smooth walnut handle of the knife Karol had given him before they left Nowy Targ. It was a risk, of course. If he were stopped and searched, being armed was an immediate death sentence. But he didn't intend to be searched.

He pulled out the pack of cigarettes Adam had also given him, leaned against the side of the building and lit one. Adam had said it would make him appear more casual. Rabbit was feeling a lot of things right now, but casual wasn't one of them.

He thought about Natalia and Adam—*the Conductor and Wolf*—in the library risking their lives for a piece of paper. They had real names, the first people he'd known in a long time who did. Natalia had asked his name the other morning as they sat by the river, the morning she told him what was really going on. But he didn't have another name to give her, at least not one he wanted to remember. He was Rabbit. He'd been Rabbit since he was eight years old and woke up in the middle of the night surrounded by smoke and flames, his parents lying dead under a heap of rubble in their parlor. He and his brother had run out of the house and into the streets crowded with people shrieking and crying. Since then he'd stayed alive for six years by running fast . . . and he didn't need another name.

He wondered about the piece of paper they were all so eager to get their hands on. Natalia had told him what it was about and that it might help Poland gain its freedom. Rabbit doubted that was true. He doubted that a piece of paper, no matter what it said, would make any difference to the tens of thousands of Russian soldiers and NKVD agents who were now crawling over the country. As far as Rabbit was concerned, they were no different than the Germans, and the only thing that would ever make a difference was another army, with more soldiers and more guns. As far as he could tell, that was all that ever mattered.

Rabbit stiffened and took a quick drag on the cigarette as a long, black Citroën drove past him on the other side of the avenue and stopped in front of the main entrance of the library. An NKVD trooper got out of the auto, followed by an NKVD officer and a short, stocky man wearing a black trench coat. The three of them hurried into the building while another trooper emerged from the driver's side of the auto and stood guard on the sidewalk.

Goddamn it!

Rabbit wasn't expecting this. Adam had stationed him outside the library just as a precaution. They weren't even sure that Tarnov knew Adam had escaped, much less that he would show up at the library, right here, right now.

Rabbit hesitated for a moment, then crossed the wide street and walked toward the auto. Generally very little traffic moved on Avenue Mickiewicza given how few people in Krakow owned automobiles, but suddenly there were no pedestrians around either. No doubt the sight of a long, black auto roaring up and the NKVD piling out was enough to cause passersby to take a detour. So, with no one else on the street, Rabbit gained the trooper's undivided attention as he drew closer.

The trooper stepped into the middle of the sidewalk and shouted something in Russian. Rabbit didn't understand. But he knew what the trooper intended by the way he pointed for Rabbit to go back the way he had come.

Rabbit continued on, quickening his pace, talking loudly and rapidly: "I forgot my books, I'll just be a minute, no problem, it will just take a minute."

As Rabbit came closer he could see that the trooper was no more than seventeen or eighteen years old, and it was obvious he didn't understand a word of Polish. But Rabbit's torrent of words was just enough to cause the Russian a moment of distraction.

Rabbit continued jabbering and walking faster, his right hand in his trouser pocket, clutching the knife. The trooper shouted again, louder this time, and pulled a pistol from the holster on his belt.

Rabbit pretended to stumble and dropped to his knees.

The trooper stepped forward and raised the gun. But he hesitated for an instant.

It was enough.

Rabbit sprang up, thrust his hand underneath the stunned trooper's outstretched arm and shoved the knife into his chest.

The young Russian uttered a loud grunt, doubled over and dropped his weapon on the ground. Rabbit paid no attention to him as he withdrew the knife and slashed two of the auto's tires. Then he grabbed the pistol and sprinted toward the library.

Sixty

23 JUNE
10:30 AM

ADAM GLANCED OVER THE TOP of his magazine just as Natalia emerged from the Reading Room. Even at this distance, and even though she walked hunched over with the cane, he could tell by the way she held her head that she'd been successful. He set the magazine on the table and was about to push his chair back when Natalia stopped. She was halfway down the stairway, staring at the library entrance.

Adam turned toward the entrance and saw a uniformed NKVD trooper emerge from the atrium and approach the information desk. Behind him was another NKVD soldier, this one with the distinctive blue hat of an officer. A third man stood behind the officer, short and stocky, wearing a black trench coat.

Tarnov.

The trooper snapped at the receptionist in Russian. The young lady looked flustered and stood up, wiping her hands on the sides of her skirt. The officer stepped forward and said something that Adam couldn't quite hear, and made a gesture as if reading a book. The receptionist frowned, shook her head, then pointed toward the stairway.

Adam picked up the magazine and lowered his head, peering over the top as Tarnov and the officer marched across the circular gallery. The trooper remained at the information desk, resting his right hand on the butt of the pistol strapped to his waist.

Adam slipped his hand into the pocket of the suit coat he'd

borrowed from Karol and gripped the handle of the Browning. *Sit still . . . just for a moment.*

It was almost more than he could bear, but he knew he had to give it a moment to play out. Natalia wore a gray head scarf and walked with a cane. Even if Tarnov had beaten her description out of the priest, he'd be looking for a young woman. Perhaps she'd slip past him. It was a slim chance, he knew, but it was better than a three-on-one firefight.

As Tarnov and the officer reached the Copernicus bust halfway across the room, Tarnov barked some instructions, and the officer continued on toward the stairway. Tarnov stood in the center of the cavernous room, looking around at the dozen or so persons sitting at tables, all of them now scrunched down in their chairs, heads buried in books. He stepped over to the table closest to him and knocked the book away from a terrified woman.

Adam slid the Browning out of his pocket and held it under the table. It was heavier than the Walther P-38 he'd used in Warsaw. The barrel was shorter, and it didn't have the same comfortable feel in his hand. But it was all he had. He glanced toward the stairway.

Natalia hobbled down the steps. She passed the NKVD officer at the bottom of the stairway. A few steps farther, and he turned suddenly toward her and snapped, "*Prikrashchát!*"

Natalia hobbled on.

The officer shouted again and took a long stride toward her, reaching for her arm.

Natalia spun around and whacked him on the side of the head with the cane.

The blow knocked the stunned officer to the floor.

Natalia dove on the ground and rolled under a table.

Tarnov jerked his head toward the commotion, pulled a pistol from a shoulder holster inside his coat and started toward Natalia.

Adam jumped to his feet, brought the Browning up with both hands and aimed at Tarnov. Just as he pulled the trigger a wave of dizziness swept over him, and the bullet ricocheted off the bronze Copernicus bust. It toppled off the pillar and bounced on the marble floor with a deafening *clang!*

Chaos erupted. People screamed and crawled under tables. The receptionist at the information desk bolted out through the atrium.

Tarnov dropped to one knee, turned and fired at Adam, blowing away a bookshelf directly behind him.

Adam toppled the table on its side, crouched behind it and concentrated on the stairway. The NKVD officer was on his knees, reaching for the pistol on his belt. Adam exhaled slowly, took careful aim and fired. The officer collapsed backward, clutching his stomach.

Adam flinched as a gunshot from the direction of the information desk slammed into the table. Splinters flew in every direction. A chunk of wood struck his head and blood ran into his eyes. His ears ringing, blinking his eyes against the blood, Adam crawled under the next table.

Sirens wailed in the distance.

Tarnov's coarse voice echoed through the room. "Throw out weapon, Nowak! In two minutes, more NKVD come!"

Adam searched the room for him. *Where was the son of a bitch?* He finally spotted him, crouching behind the pillar.

Before Adam could figure out how to reach Tarnov, the trooper at the information desk ran to the closest table and abruptly shot the man cowering there in the back of the head. The trooper tipped over the table, dropped to one knee and fired in Natalia's direction.

Adam stuck his head above the table, aimed the Browning at the trooper and squeezed the trigger. He missed, knocking a painting off the wall on the far side of the room.

A woman leaped from her chair and ran screaming toward the entrance. She made it only a few meters before the trooper gunned her down. He moved to aim at Natalia again, but a gunshot from the direction of the atrium hit him in the back, exploding through his chest in a burst of red.

Adam turned toward the entrance and saw Rabbit sprinting from the atrium to the information desk, a pistol in his right hand. The boy ducked behind the desk just as Tarnov fired at him from behind the pillar. Then Tarnov darted from the pillar and rolled under a table.

The sirens grew louder.

Adam stood and fired at Tarnov.

Tarnov swore loudly.

Adam dropped to his knees. He looked under the tables and saw the Russian crawling toward the far side of the room, trailing blood. Cursing his dizziness, Adam lay prone on the floor and propped his right arm against a table leg for support. He sighted in on Tarnov's back and squeezed the trigger.

Tarnov shuddered. He groaned, then lay still.

Adam stood up slowly. He leaned on the table for support as the suddenly quiet room spun around in his field of vision. Then he staggered toward Tarnov, holding the pistol out in front of himself.

Tires screeched outside the building.

"Adam!" Natalia shouted.

Adam continued on toward Tarnov, desperately wanting to make sure the bastard was dead.

"Adam! There's no time!"

Adam stopped, his stomach churning, his temples throbbing. "Up the stairs! Now!" he shouted.

Natalia screamed, and pointed toward the front of the room. "Rabbit! Jesus Christ!"

Rabbit stood halfway between the information desk and the stairway, swaying from side-to-side, the front of his shirt covered in blood. He slid slowly to the floor.

Natalia rushed past Adam and dropped to her knees next to the boy. He lay curled in a ball, clutching his stomach, blood oozing between his fingers. Adam followed her and knelt down on the other side. "How bad?"

Natalia shook her head.

Rabbit thrashed his legs. His face contorted in pain as Natalia carefully rolled him onto his back. Blood had soaked through his shirt and the front of his pants. She ripped the scarf off her head, folded it and pressed it against the boy's abdomen. He cried out and clawed wildly at her arm.

Heavy boots stomped into the atrium.

"Shit! They're coming," Natalia said.

Adam scooped up Rabbit, struggled to his feet and bolted for the stairway. Natalia trotted alongside him, pressing down on the bloody scarf as they hobbled up the stairs and down the hallway.

They burst into the Reading Room, slipping on the blood dripping from Rabbit's wound. The startled librarian backed up against the card catalog. The man with the felt hat huddled under the table. Natalia held the scarf against Rabbit's stomach.

"Fuckin' . . . Ahhh . . . no . . ." Rabbit moaned. He twisted and jerked in Adam's arms.

"Hurry, through that door!" Adam shouted. He motioned with his head toward the far end of the counter and prayed that Andreyev would be at the loading dock.

Natalia kicked open the door, and they ran down the steps to the lower level. At the bottom of the stairs, she grabbed Adam's arm and jerked him to a halt. She peeled away the blood-soaked scarf and dropped it on the floor, then quickly pulled off her sweater, folded it in half and pressed it hard against the flow of blood from Rabbit's abdomen.

The boy grunted and clawed again at her fingers. Then his head rolled back, and his arms went limp.

"Stay with me, Rabbit," Natalia shouted. "Stay with me!"

Trailing blood, they ran past Room L-3 and down the hallway to the service door next to the loading dock. Natalia pushed open the door, and they burst through to the cobblestone lane.

Andreyev stood next to the GAZ-11. He jerked open the rear door.

"Lay him on his back!" Natalia commanded as she crawled into the vehicle and crouched on the floor of the backseat.

Adam eased the boy onto the seat, then crawled in next to her. Andreyev slammed the door shut, jumped in the driver's seat and they sped away from the library.

Natalia lifted the sweater and opened Rabbit's shirt, exposing the bullet wound in his abdomen. It was no larger than the size of a ten-groszy coin, but blood pulsated out, running onto the seat and the floor of the auto in a dark, sticky mass. She reached around underneath him feeling for an exit wound, but there was none.

"Give me your coat," she said to Adam. "Quick!"

Adam pulled off his coat, and Natalia folded it up, pressing it against Rabbit's stomach. She grabbed Adam's right hand and placed it on the folded coat. Blood was already seeping through. "Press down firmly, right here, use both hands," she said, grabbing his left hand and bumping against him as the auto careened around a corner, tires screeching. "Keep pressure directly on the wound. We've got to stop the bleeding. It's the only chance he has!"

Andreyev shouted from the driver's seat, "Can he hang on until we get out of the city?"

Natalia placed her fingers against Rabbit's neck, directly under his chin, and knew instantly the boy was in deep trouble. His pulse was racing as his heart struggled to keep up with the loss of blood and rapidly falling pressure. "His heart rate's going wild; he's losing too much blood! He could go into shock!" She leaned over and put a hand on Rabbit's forehead. "Rabbit, can you hear me? Stay with me!"

The boy's eyes rolled from side-to-side. "I hear . . ."

Natalia slid her hand under his head. "That's it, that's it, stay with me, Rabbit." She turned to Adam. "Keep pressing down, hard!"

"We can't stop," Andreyev said. "The NKVD will have every hospital within five kilometers surrounded in the next few minutes."

"I know that," Natalia snapped. "Just get us the hell out of here!" She looked up, straining to see out the back window of the speeding auto and get her bearings.

"Where are we going?" she yelled to Andreyev.

"Through Kazimierz and over the river to Podgorze, then farther south from there."

"There's a village I know about a few kilometers south of Podgorze," Adam said. "They had a doctor, a friend of my uncle. Do you think he can make it?"

Natalia looked at the boy. Rabbit's eyes had closed. She leaned close to Adam and whispered, "I don't know. This is bad." She held up her hand. It was covered in dark, sticky blood. "I think the bullet hit his liver." She turned back to Rabbit. "Can you hear me, Rabbit? Are you with me?"

The boy's eyelids fluttered. "Conductor . . . I . . . can . . ."

The auto raced on, swerving around corners, barreling down avenues at top speed. Natalia couldn't see much from her position on the floor of the sedan, but after what seemed like an eternity Andreyev yelled back to them again. "We're crossing the river into Podgorze," he shouted over the roar of the engine and squealing tires. "I don't see any tail, but we have to keep going."

"Just let us know when we're south of Podgorze!" Adam shouted back.

Natalia leaned over the boy. "Rabbit, are you still with me?"

He didn't respond.

"Rabbit! Stay with me!" She turned her head to the side, her ear just above his mouth. She could barely feel his breath. She put her fingers to his neck again and checked his pulse. It was getting weaker. His face was the color of chalk. She slapped his cheek. "Rabbit! Please, stay with me!"

The auto bumped hard over a pothole, then swerved around a corner. Natalia was thrown against Adam again, knocking his hands off the bloody coat. She gently lifted the coat and examined the wound. The bleeding had slowed to a dark oozing. She slid her fingers under the boy's chin and checked his pulse.

Nothing.

She swallowed hard and switched to the other side of his neck and checked again. Nothing.

She slapped his cheek, harder this time. "Please, stay with me, Rabbit! Open your eyes!"

The boy lay still. His chest stopped moving.

Goddamn it, no!

Tears clouded her eyes as Natalia stared at the boy's still face. She ran her hand through his matted, blond hair. He looked peaceful, almost serene. She remembered the first time she had met him, at the massacre in the hospital square in Warsaw, a battle-hardened veteran at the tender age of thirteen. She remembered his cool, quick action with the NKVD agents at the village near the Bolimowski Forest. But most of all, she remembered how he'd laid his head on her lap after his friend Bobcat had been killed in the sewer. He'd asked her why God would let these things happen. She hadn't been able to give him a good answer then. And she certainly couldn't now. She studied his face for another moment, then leaned over and kissed him on the forehead. "Oh Rabbit, I'm so sorry."

Adam put his hand on her shoulder.

She slumped against him, shaking her head, letting the tears flow.

They rode in silence as the auto sped through Podgorze and the southern suburbs of Krakow. A quarter of an hour later, Andreyev pulled over to the side of the road and stopped near a flat, open field surrounded by deserted factory buildings. Parked in front of them was an old farm truck, faded and rusty, a load of hay in the back. There was no driver.

Andreyev got out of the car, opened the rear door and motioned for them to get out. Then he turned away and walked a few paces into the field.

With Rabbit's body lying in the backseat of the car, the three of them stood in silence for a long tense moment. "You can't go back," Andreyev said. "None of us can. The NKVD will be tearing Krakow apart within the hour." He motioned with his head toward the farm truck. "The key is in the ignition. It doesn't look like much, but I'm told it runs well. You can be in Nowy Targ by this afternoon, and from there you can make your way to Prochowa. Your Górale friends should be able to get you safely over the mountains into Slovakia."

Natalia turned to Adam. Her eyes were red from crying. She clenched her jaw firmly in that look of defiance he remembered from Warsaw.

"We can't stay in Poland," he said quietly to her.

"And I certainly can't take you back to Berlin with me," Andreyev said. "Tarnov's murder will put every Russian officer in Europe on alert, looking for you."

Natalia reached in her vest pocket and withdrew the copy of Stalin's order. "What about this?"

Andreyev held out his hand. "I'll make sure it gets to Colonel Whitehall."

She stared at the Russian for a moment, clutching the precious document with both hands. Then she turned to Adam and handed it to him. "Here, it's your decision." She turned away and walked a few steps farther into the field.

Adam followed her. Gently, he placed his hands on her shoulders. "Captain Andreyev is right. It's the only way."

She turned around and looked into his eyes. "Can we trust him? After all this . . . Rabbit . . . your uncle . . . can we trust him?"

Adam was quiet, his eyes searching hers. Finally he nodded. "Andreyev is taking an enormous risk. We just murdered three NKVD, and he's arranging for our escape. If he wasn't sincere he could just as easily have turned us over to them." He gazed up at the blue sky. A flock of swallows flew overhead. "We'll go up into the mountains and into Slovakia. Just like you said you wanted to do. From there we can go anywhere."

"What about Rabbit?"

"We'll take him with us," Adam said, swallowing hard, his eyes clouding up. "We'll bury him in Prochowa next to my uncle . . . and some of the other patriots who sacrificed their lives for this."

Natalia reached up and touched his face. "Is it finished?"

"Yes. For now . . . it's finished."

Epilogue

Potsdam, Germany
2 August 1945

Colonel Stanley Whitehall sat in the back row of delegates who had gathered in the courtyard of the Cecilienhof Palace in Potsdam on the last day of the conference. The leaders of the "Big Three" sat side-by-side in wicker chairs on the veranda, while lower-level ministers circulated among the delegates, passing out thick packets of the declarations, decrees and proclamations that would govern postwar Europe.

Whitehall got up to leave. He already knew the outcome. Poland was lost. The Soviet-controlled communists from Lublin were recognized as the legitimate government, the free elections touted at Yalta submerged and forgotten. His shoulders sagged a bit more than usual as he lumbered across the immaculately manicured lawn.

Then, as he reached the walkway at the edge of the courtyard, Whitehall turned back and took one last look at Joseph Stalin, dressed in his white uniform tunic, smiling broadly at a horde of photographers. Would it have made any difference if Roosevelt hadn't died, or if Churchill hadn't been ousted in the British elections?

Perhaps.

But he knew what it really came down to. The Russian dictator wouldn't be sitting quite so smugly if the copy of the Katyn Order had ever surfaced.

• • •

Later that afternoon, in the drawing room of the mansion in Grunewald, Whitehall poured a drink at the sideboard and handed it to Tom Donavan. He motioned for him to take a seat. "So, what have you learned?" Whitehall asked, as he settled into the other chair.

Donavan set his glass on the coffee table and plucked an envelope out of his briefcase. "We finally received a dispatch from the AK chaps up in Nowy Targ."

Whitehall opened the envelope and read the message.

A AND N OFF TO THE HILLS
PIRATE HAS THE PRIZE

He had never met Natalia, but Whitehall breathed a heavy sigh of relief, surprising himself over how worried he'd been about Adam. Then he downed his glass of whiskey in a single gulp and leaned forward, frowning. "So, what the hell happened to Captain Andreyev?"

Donavan took a quick sip of his drink. "I first checked with the Soviet delegation at the Kommandatura. They went through their files but didn't come up with anything. Then I visited the Soviet Military Administration Headquarters."

Whitehall grunted. "Wouldn't guess those chaps were very cooperative."

"Not at first," Donavan said. "But I showed them Kovalenko's letter, and that got some attention. Apparently, even after his death, the general still has some influence. Had to sign my life away, of course, but then a Red Army major took me in tow and I spent an hour sitting across the table while he rifled through personnel files."

Whitehall got up and poured another drink. He looked out the leaded-glass windows at the sunlit terrace. "And what did he find?"

"They have no record of a Red Army captain named Andreyev."

Whitehall spun around. His drink splashed onto his fingers. "No record? That's preposterous! The man was General Kovalenko's chief aide. I met him myself—several times, for God's sake, in this very room!"

"I said the same thing to the Red Army major, a bit more diplomatically, of course."

"Well?"

"According to *their* records, General Kovalenko didn't have an aide. Never liked the concept, or some such thing."

Whitehall shook his head in disgust and tossed back what remained of his drink. He glared at Donavan. "So, that's it? There's no Captain Andreyev?"

"He never existed."

The Journal of Ludwik Banach

My name is Ludwik Banach.

Eight months ago I descended into hell. I have seen the abyss, the dark chasm of depravity into which man can sink. And I am terrified. I am terrified the world does not know what is happening here. I fear most will not live to tell their story, so I will tell mine and pray that it will emerge from the darkness—that the world may know.

In November of 1939 I was arrested in Krakow, along with two hundred other professors, lawyers and doctors who had been invited to a seminar at the university. German soldiers, storm troopers of the SS, marched into the assembly and forced us out at gunpoint. We were loaded into trucks, then into foul-smelling railcars. For five days we had no food, almost no water. We had no room to lie down. I was sure this was hell. And then we arrived in Oranienburg, Germany, and entered Sachsenhausen—a large camp, enclosed with brick walls and barbed wire fences.

Then I knew what hell truly was.

Perhaps someday I will have the courage to write about life in that dark abyss. Thousands of us labored at back-breaking jobs with little food or water in a camp so filthy and infested with rats and lice that most died of typhus within six months. Perhaps someday, when the memory is not so fresh and raw, I will be able to write about it . . . but not today.

Today is the tenth of August, 1940, and I will begin to record the incredible events that have transpired since my unexpected and abrupt release from Sachsenhausen one month ago. The story begins on the morning of my last day in that living hell.

10 July 1940

During the morning roll-call I was pulled from the ranks and marched to the commandant's office. I was confused and frightened. No one had ever been pulled from the roll-call and taken to the commandant before. If anyone committed an offense they were just shot on the spot and dragged away, their body thrown onto a cart with the other dead.

The commandant's deputy, Ludwig Rehm, and our block leader, Hans Fricker, were waiting for me in the office. Rehm glared at me for a long time, his coal black eyes and red, twitching face a mask of hate. Abruptly he spit in my face. Then he turned away and nodded at Fricker, who told me I was being released into the custody of the Governor General of Poland and would be transported back to Krakow.

I was so astonished, I was certain I hadn't heard him correctly. Fricker pointed to a suit of clothing hanging on a hook. When I took the clothing, he gave me a shove. He took me to the guard's quarters and ordered me to shower and change clothes. He handed me a small vial of kerosene to kill the lice in my hair. Though in a state of shock from the incredible news, I lingered as long as I dared, reveling in the luxury of soap and water. It was the first shower I'd had in eight months.

I arrived back in Krakow after two days traveling. This time I had a seat in a normal railcar, guarded by a pair of drunken Wehrmacht soldiers. Apparently I was no longer of interest to the SS.

I was taken by auto to Wawel Castle and locked in a small, but clean, room in the lower level. I had no idea why this was happening or what fate awaited me but, strangely, I was not afraid. Perhaps it was because I could not conceive of anything worse than the hell of Sachsenhausen where I would certainly have died. My heart grieves for my friends, those whom I have left behind. There is little chance any of them will survive.

I had a dark sense of foreboding at what I would find here in Krakow. But I was also intrigued at the prospect of seeing the Governor General of Poland. I had learned he was the German legal scholar Hans Frank, with whom I became acquainted while attending European legal conferences in the '30s. My memory of Frank was of a highly intelligent, if somewhat conflicted, man caught up in an impossible situation during the rise of Nazism.

We had last met in 1935, in Germany, at a conference of the Academy of German Law, which Frank founded, and we corresponded on a regular basis for several years afterward. Frank was, at that time, a zealous proponent of human rights and an independent judiciary. But over the years, as fascism tightened its grip on German society, the tone of his letters changed, and I sensed he knew he was fighting a losing battle. Our correspondence had ceased, of course, with the German invasion of Poland. I had already been arrested and deported to Sachsenhausen by the time Frank came to Krakow as Governor General.

26 July 1940

On this day I met the Governor General of Poland. Since arriving in the city on 12 July, I had been confined to my room. I had seen no one except the guards who brought me two meals and tea each day. I had been allowed to bathe and given clean clothing. I put on weight and regained much of my strength. But all the time I couldn't help thinking about my new captor, Hans Frank. Why was I here? What did he want from me?

Following the morning meal, I was led up to the third floor of the castle, shown into a large, well appointed office and left alone.

A moment later the door opened, and a German officer stepped in. Though I hadn't seen him in five years, I instantly recognized Hans Frank.

He bowed slightly, clicked his heels and addressed me by name. He offered me a chair and a cup of coffee, and we talked for more than an hour. It was perhaps the most bizarre hour of my life. Here was a man I had known as an intelligent, widely respected legal scholar, one of the best in Germany if not all of Europe—a man with whom I had discussed ideas, debated legal positions and corresponded with for years. And on this day, cast on opposite sides of a brutal war, we sat in a room adorned with the swastika flag and the Nazi eagle, in the royal castle of Poland, and chatted about old times. I could barely sit still, so great was my anguish over the atrocities I had witnessed at Sachsenhausen: the beatings and murders, the inhuman brutality—atrocities that Frank certainly knows about, has perhaps even ordered.

The meeting ended abruptly when an aide knocked on the door, explaining that Frank had a telephone call.

That afternoon I was transferred to a larger room at the other end of the castle. The room had a desk and chair and a box of German language books. As I sat at the desk, I could not imagine what was in store for me. But that was insignificant next to the question burning a hole in my heart. Was it possible that I would be reunited with my dear wife, Beata? Could God be that generous?

2 August 1940

After days of waiting I was finally led from my room to an automobile outside the castle. A moment later, Hans Frank joined me in the backseat. As we drove through the streets of Krakow, my beloved city that I hadn't seen in almost a year, it was all I could do to control my emotions. Red-and-black swastika banners flew from every flagpole. Placards with the German word ACHTUNG in bold, black letters across the top, followed by lists of rules and regulations, were posted on buildings. People stood in long queues at bakeries, their faces gray and drawn, their heads bowed. The streets were practically deserted, the only other vehicles being German military trucks and the long, black autos of the Gestapo.

Frank leaned over suddenly and said that he would explain how things are to be in Poland. There will be no education for Poles beyond the fourth grade. The universities and libraries will remain closed. All Polish press, theatre and cabarets will be censored. References to Polish history, culture and literature will not be tolerated. Possession of radios by Poles is prohibited and will be replaced with loudspeakers in public areas.

This was a different Hans Frank from the other day. This Frank was stiff, unsmiling and authoritarian. I listened silently, my heart sinking with the realization that the Germans intend to destroy the very fabric of Polish life, to reduce us to a nation of slaves. My despair turned to anger. I struggled to maintain control, forcing myself to remember that the man sitting next to me was no longer the scholarly, affable gentleman I had known, but the Nazi governor overseeing the occupation of my country. My skin crawled.

A few minutes later, the auto stopped in the area west of the university. We got out of the car, and I looked up at the magnificent edifice of the new Copernicus Memorial Library. Years ago I was involved in its conception. My dream, this world-class facility, had been completed just days before the outbreak of the war.

Frank nodded at me, and we entered the building. Inside, dozens of people were at work, methodically unloading crates of books, stocking shelves and typing labels. Frank led me on a tour of the new facility. We passed Feldgendarmes standing guard in every room as Polish workers moved about with armfuls of books and documents.

I recognized several of the Poles as librarians from the university.

After a while, Frank stopped at the top of a sweeping marble stairway overlooking the main floor of the library. We were alone. He said that what he told me in the auto has been commanded by the Fuhrer—the Fuhrer who has been influenced by Heinrich Himmler and the SS. He said this with contempt in his tone of voice. He said that it shall be the law of Poland, and, as the Governor General of Poland, he is obligated to enforce the law.

Abruptly, his demeanor changed; his eyes brightened and he smiled, waving his hand toward the vast space below. He said he had ordered the transfer of the entire collection of the old libraries of the university into this new building for safe-keeping. This is being done, he said, to keep them out of the hands of Himmler and the rest of the SS barbarians who can barely read, let alone appreciate science, literature and art. He told me this is why he has spared me. He knew I had been instrumental in the planning of this new library, and the transfer of thousands of books and documents would require the assistance of former Polish librarians, working under the supervision of trusted professionals. He looked me in the eye emphasizing the word *trusted*.

I stared at him, dumbfounded, not knowing how to respond. It had been nine months since my arrest, since I was last in Poland. But at Sachsenhausen we heard stories whispered in the bread lines and latrines, told by the most recent arrivals from Poland, stories of murder and brutality, the stripping away of Polish culture, of Polish life, all on the orders of Hans Frank. And now, Hans Frank had brought me back to Krakow—as a "trusted professional"—to supervise librarians? I could only stare at him and nod. It was as if I'd slipped into a bizarre dream.

Frank led me down a hallway and into an elegant office. A short, thin man with gray hair stepped around from behind a massive mahogany desk. He was impeccably dressed in a gray, silk suit. Frank introduced him as Gustav Kruger, the director general of the new Staatsbibliothek Krakau, as this library will now be known. Frank said that he will check on me from time to time, but I shall report directly to Herr Kruger. Then he turned and left the office.

Kruger offered me a chair, then handed me a small, greenish-grey, four-page booklet emblazoned with the eagle and swastika above the word *Kennkarte*. I opened it. Inside I found my passport picture, my name and date of birth, and my address, which was an apartment unfamiliar to me but located just a few streets away. It also listed my occupation as "librarian." The Kennkarte, which identified me as *nichtdeutschen*, a non-German with no Jewish ancestry, also specified curfew hours and the number of food coupons to which I was entitled.

Kruger told me I am free to come and go within the city limits of Krakow. His tone was bland and bureaucratic; his eyes avoided mine. He went on to advise me that I am required to be present in the library from seven o'clock in the morning until six o'clock in the evening, Monday through Saturday. Then he leaned across the desk, looked directly at me and told me I will be watched. That it is the Governor's explicit order. I am not to make any telephone calls, nor contact family or friends, and all of my correspondence will be read.

I hesitated for a moment, then took a chance and asked Herr Kruger if he knew what has become of my family. He shook his head.

11 August 1940

It is Sunday, my first day off from work. Yesterday, while helping to sort boxes of books at the library, I discovered this leather-bound notebook. Its pages were blank, and it was small enough to slip into the breast pocket of my suit coat. Removing books from the library is strictly prohibited. They enforce the rule by having

Feldgendarmes stand guard at the main door of the library. But they are usually preoccupied with their cigarettes and jokes, and no one is ever searched. Thus it was a simple matter to bring this notebook to my apartment where I spent yesterday evening recording the events of the last month.

This morning I sat in my apartment for a long time, working up the courage to visit my home. I waited for this day for nine months, thinking every hour in the hellhole of Sachsenhausen about my Beata, and my nephew, Adam—praying for the day when we would be reunited. But this morning, when the day arrived and I had at last an opportunity, I remembered Herr Kruger's warning, and I was paralyzed with fear.

As I walked down the street toward my home, I sensed someone following me. I slowed my pace, hoping he would pass me by. When he didn't, I glanced back at him and he approached me. He was a tall man in a dark blue suit. I knew instantly he was Gestapo. He stood very close to me, and I pressed my hands to the sides of my trousers to hide the trembling. I will never forget what he said: "Your wife is no longer here. She has been sent to a work camp."

I suddenly felt dizzy and backed up against a tree. I tried to ask where she had been sent, or what he knew about Adam, but nothing came out. The Gestapo man stepped even closer and said, "Do not make any further inquiries, Dr. Banach. No inquiries, about anyone."

After he left, I sat on the grass under the tree and cried . . . like a baby. Then I wandered about aimlessly until it was dark. My sorrow turned to rage, rage to despair. Beata and Adam are gone. Where? Sachsenhausen? At the work camp I watched every day, praying I wouldn't see them among the new arrivals. Could I have missed them?

The thought is too terrible to contemplate.

19 August 1940

This past week has been the most painful of my life. Every moment of every day I think about Beata and Adam. During all the dreadful months at Sachsenhausen my only solace was the belief that they were safe. Beata is an intelligent, beautiful person, and she has not been involved in any anti-German activities. Adam is an American citizen, and America is not at war with Germany. Time and time again, as I lay awake on the sleeping rack at Sachsenhausen, I was able to relieve my anxiety by imagining them going about their business in Krakow: walking along the river, shopping on the Rynek Glowny, sitting down to Sunday dinner.

But now, even that has been stripped away. At times my despair has been so great that I have contemplated the unthinkable. But I must continue on. Beata and Adam could survive; wherever they have been sent, there is a chance they could survive. And as long as there is that chance, I will survive as well.

Here in Krakow, the heel of the conqueror has crushed the life out of the city.

The university is locked up, as are all the schools, bookstores and museums, along with the White Eagle Pub where I debated the future of Poland with my colleagues and students. None of us got it right. They are all gone now. I have learned from the Polish workers at the new Staatsbibliothek Krakau that those who were not arrested with me in '39 were rounded-up this past spring in an action personally ordered by Frank. More than thirty thousand Polish leaders, politicians, teachers and artists in all the major cities—the last of Poland's intelligentsia—were arrested and thrown into prisons. It was called the *AB Aktion,* a shortened version of a typically cumbersome German term meaning "peace-bringing action."

When I arrived at the library this morning a truck was parked at the dock, and workers were unloading another shipment of books. Who will be left in Poland able to read them?

3 September 1940

I have been employed at the new library for a month. The word "employed" is hardly applicable since all of the Poles, including me, work eleven hours a day for starvation wages. The money is actually irrelevant, since there is little in the shops to buy, and even if there were more, our ration cards limit us to the bare amount necessary to sustain life. My official responsibility is to assist in "Germanizing" Jagiellonian University's magnificent collection. It is to be reorganized emphasizing German works and purging Polish works. The university is to re-open one day as the German University of Krakow.

My unofficial task, as Herr Kruger has informed me, is to keep the Polish staff in line as we complete this task. Purging the Polish works is heartbreaking for all of us, especially the Polish librarians who have dedicated their lives to the preservation of our literature, science and arts. I have begun to suspect that it is equally distasteful to Herr Kruger. A few days ago, he said that Governor Frank is depending on us to complete this task. There was a certain look in his eye, a look I have seen before whenever he has met with Frank, a look of sorrow which I'm not sure I can explain.

16 October 1940

Frank stopped in today, presumably to check on the progress of the library. Instead, he and I sat alone in the Reading Room while he expounded at great length about the Jewish ghetto being created in

Warsaw. All of the city's Jews, as well as thousands from surrounding towns, are to be relocated to a separate area within the city. Soon this will happen in Krakow, Frank said, since it is his desire that Krakow shall be the "cleanest" city in the General Government of Poland. When this "malignancy" has been eliminated, he said, conditions will improve for the Poles.

Then he leaned across the table and whispered, "When your wife returns, Dr. Banach, she will be proud of what we've accomplished."

I was so stunned I could barely breathe. It felt like an eternity before I recovered. Then, embarrassed with how timid my voice sounded, I asked where Beata is. Frank stared at me without responding, then casually changed the subject and began asking questions about the various collections in the library: the legal journals, and the works of art, history and geography. It went on for another twenty minutes before he finally dismissed me.

The man is a monster.

I returned to my small shabby apartment, seized with fear for Beata's safety, as well as Adam's. As I write this, it is hard to keep my hand from trembling, knowing that my fate, my family's fate—perhaps all of Poland's—lies in the hands of Hans Frank. Before retiring for the night, I will find a better hiding place for this journal.

25 December 1940

It is my second Christmas without Beata and Adam. I miss them so much it is impossible to describe. I attended mass at the Mariacki Church but had to leave halfway through. The memories overwhelmed me. Frank sent over a small ham and a slice of chocolate cake. (What goes on in this man's mind?)

I shared the ham with Jerzy Jastremski and his wife, Helena. He is one of the Poles working on the project whom I knew from our former life. He is a quiet, gentle man, a former librarian at the law school, and we have become friends. They invited me to their apartment for Christmas dinner and were delighted to see the ham. But I must admit, I saved the slice of cake for myself and ate it when I returned to my own apartment. I took my time. It was the first chocolate I've tasted since the invasion in '39.

Toward evening, I was shocked when Herr Kruger appeared at my door with a bottle of schnapps. "For a Christmas drink," he said, which I found remarkable. Though always respectful and polite, he rarely engages any of us during the workday except to give instructions or ask questions about books and documents. Tonight, he was at first ebullient and talkative, chattering about his wife and three daughters back in Hamburg, joking about what they must have spent on Christmas presents. He went on about how they may join him here in Krakow one day, if the situation improves. After a while, though, his mood changed: he became sullen and spoke very little. I think he was quite drunk.

12 March 1941

This winter has been a long, cruel one. We hear that people in the villages are starving. There has been no further mention about Beata from Frank or anyone else. I am ashamed at my own helplessness, and at times I become so infuriated I want to kill someone. It is all I can do to keep myself under control. Frank is so unpredictable that I fear for my life whenever he's around, even though he treats me with respect. I never know what's going on behind his dark, penetrating eyes.

The Krakow ghetto is a reality. Over the last several months, I have watched its construction from a distance. Brick walls now seal off more than twenty thousand Jewish souls in a section of the city where only a few thousand people previously lived. We hear reports of four and five families crammed into every apartment with hundreds of others living on the streets. In each building around the periphery of the ghetto, the windows and doors have been bricked over, preventing those trapped inside from even a glimpse of the rest of the city. Eventually I stopped watching. It is more than I can bear.

Having experienced Sachsenhausen, and now witnessing the treatment of Krakow's Jews, I realize with great sorrow that the Nazis have dragged Germany into a chasm of depravity I never believed possible of the civilized and culturally advanced country I knew. That the country which gave us Bach and Brahms, Goethe, Nietzsche and Albert Einstein also gave us Adolf Hitler tears away the very fabric of my belief in mankind.

Frank visited the library today for a meeting with Herr Kruger. As he was leaving, he stopped at the table where I was working. He has done this frequently during his visits, stopping by to chat, as though we were still professional colleagues discussing legal principles. Today he expounded on how he has tried to guarantee a "right of reprieve" for all those arrested during the *AB Aktion*—arrested on his orders—but how his efforts have been in vain because of Himmler and the SS. Then he rambled on for more than ten minutes about how the Jews of Krakow would be kept safe in the ghetto from the ravages of the SS. I listened silently, my stomach churning. Why does he tell me these things? Does he think I actually believe this nonsense, that this barbarism is not his doing, that it is all Himmler's? What can I say in response to this madness?

As Frank was leaving I noticed Herr Kruger standing nearby, watching. There was that hint of sadness I've seen before in his expression.

22 June 1941

Now it is summer, but that brings no relief to us. We work long hours at the library as we did all winter. But then yesterday work came to a halt. Germany attacked Russia! Everyone whispered about this incredible event. What it means for Poland is impossible to predict, except that we will have many more months of war on our soil.

Will Russia now become allied with Britain and America? Has Hitler gone completely mad? Certainly he cannot expect to defeat Russia while fighting Britain and America at the same time. The Americans have yet to enter the war, but it is only a matter of time. With America's industrial might combined with the horde of millions that Stalin will throw into the breach, how can there be any outcome other than the defeat of Germany? But then the Russians will stomp into Poland. And who will be left to drive them out?

8 July 1941

Books are being smuggled out of the library. I have struggled with the potential danger of recording this activity in this journal, but then it is probably no more damning than most everything else I have written. And if this journal ever reaches the civilized world, it is important to record for history that some of us are attempting to preserve what we can of Polish culture.

The schools in Poland have been closed for almost two years, but teaching continues. It continues in the cellars and attics of people's homes, in the backrooms of shops and warehouses, wherever people can gather with their children out of sight of the Gestapo. Months ago, those of us working in the library learned of these activities and focused our efforts on smuggling out Polish books, passing them on to operatives in the Resistance to aid in the continuing education of our young people. The candle of learning must not be extinguished, no matter the danger.

The task is complicated because of the extreme danger if we should be caught. It would be a death sentence for all of us, of that I am certain. It is complicated and hazardous, and today it almost ended in disaster, but for a very strange occurrence which I cannot fully explain.

Herr Kruger approached me late in the afternoon holding a sheet of paper that he said was a message from a local Gestapo agent. The agent reported that a box of Polish books had been discovered hidden in the back of a grocer's cart not far from the library. The Gestapo agent interrogated the grocer about the source of the books, but the man insisted they were from his family's private collection and that he was delivering them to his daughter. The books were confiscated and the grocer shot for subversion.

I held my breath as Kruger said this, swallowing hard for fear I would get sick. The Gestapo agent wondered if the books had been smuggled out of the library, Kruger said, but he had assured him they had not come from the Staatsbibliothek Krakau. Then he turned away without further comment.

18 October 1941

Autumn has come, and we face another brutal winter under German occupation. Reports trickling out from the Krakow ghetto describe deteriorating conditions beyond anything we could have imagined. Within the last month, another six thousand Jews from surrounding villages have been herded behind the brick walls. Desperate people are chopping up furniture for fuel and bartering what few possessions they have left for bread and potatoes. Every day horse-drawn carts laden with corpses exit the ghetto through the heavily guarded entrances.

Frank spoke to the workers in the library today, telling us how pleased he was at our progress and how the Staatsbibliothek Krakau will soon become the most renowned institution in the Third Reich. He praised Herr Kruger for his leadership, then dismissed us to resume our work.

Later, on his way out of the building, Frank asked me to walk with him to the door. He said that he was pleased to hear from Herr Kruger about my excellent work at the library. Then he added that he was certain Beata will be pleased when she returns to see what has been accomplished. The comment drove a stake of fear into my heart. I was so stricken that I stood mute as he turned away and walked to his waiting automobile.

At six o'clock, just as the workers were about to leave, Herr Kruger summoned me to his office. We spoke for a few moments about the progress of the library, then he asked me what Frank and I had talked about. I repeated what Frank had told me about my work in the library. He asked if Frank had mentioned his future plans for the ghetto. I said that he had not, and as I said this I noticed that Kruger's face was pale and his hand trembled. He stared at me for several moments, then stood up and bid me good night.

19 October 1941

As I was about to leave my apartment this morning, I noticed an envelope which had apparently been slid under the door sometime during the night. Inside was a key with the marking "L-3" embossed on the head. I was dumbfounded. Who could have left it? What could it possibly mean? L-3 is a designation for a room on the lower level of the library. I hesitated for a long time, wondering what to do, my mind conjuring up all manner of possibilities, none of which made any sense. Finally, I removed one of my shoes, slipped the key inside and left for work.

Just as he had last night, Herr Kruger summoned me to his office at six o'clock, as everyone was leaving. He said that he had advised the night shift guards that I would be working a few hours later this evening. He looked at me for a moment as though trying to decide what to say next. Then he told me that the guards take a forty-five minute dinner break at seven o'clock, up on the third floor.

A few minutes after seven, I sat at my table in the Reading Room thinking about the inexplicable conversation with Kruger. I hesitated for several more minutes, then got up, walked across the large room to the door at the far end of the counter and descended the service stairs to the lower level. I located room L-3, unlocked it and stepped inside.

The room was filled with shelves containing dozens of cardboard file boxes. In the center of the room, a small table held one box marked with the word "Podgorze," which is the section of the city where the ghetto has been constructed.

I opened the box. As I went through the documents inside I was astounded. They included detailed plans for the construction of the ghetto, calculations of the number of people that could be crammed into various types of houses and apartments, and predictions of death rates due to starvation and disease. My hands were shaking as I removed document after document, each filled with gruesome details of the carefully planned imprisonment and extermination of Krakow's Jews. And everywhere I found the signature of Hans Frank.

I glanced at my watch. It was seven thirty. I went through the documents a second time, removing several I judged to be most important and replaced the lid on the box. Scarcely able to breathe, I left the room, locked it and went home. In my apartment, I hid the documents beneath the floorboards of the closet where I keep this journal.

12 January 1942

I have been assigned "night duty" every other week since last October. There is always a single cardboard file box on the table in room L-3. The boxes include drawings, specifications and detailed work plans for concentration camps all over Poland. There are memos from Frank to various officials in Berlin, with attached reports written by Frank's subordinates, describing in academic detail the gradual starvation of the Polish population. There are reports itemizing the thousands of tons of agricultural production diverted to Germany each month and others documenting the tens of thousands of Jews arriving in Poland, transported from Western Europe in trucks and railroad box cars. It is so incomprehensible that I sometimes wonder if this is really happening or if we are all caught in some cruel, demented dream.

Shortly after my "night duties" began I realized what had to be done with documents I'd smuggled out of the library. The channel has been resumed. Many are taking risks to preserve what little is left of our humanity. May God grant that our efforts are not in vain.

18 January 1942

Frank summoned me to his office in Wawel Castle today. This was the first time I have been there since I was assigned to work in the library seventeen months ago. I was terrified. Had he found out about the documents I'd been smuggling? Had he discovered the channel?

When I was shown into the office, Frank ordered me to sit and stood over me waving a sheaf of papers. "This is proof of their madness!" he shouted, dropping the papers on a table in front of me. I did not reach for them. I have learned not to anticipate anything where Frank is concerned.

He paced around the office, clearly agitated, explaining that a conference had been held at a suburb of Berlin called Wannsee. General Heydrich had presided. Finally realizing this had nothing to do with me, my fear subsided a bit and I was able to concentrate on what he was saying.

Frank's voice dropped to a whisper as he leaned close to me. He said they had discussed a "final solution" at the conference and intended to gas all of the Jews. He asked if I could imagine it—gassing all of them. He wondered out loud how it could be possible, how it would be organized. His eyes were wide, and he stared at me for a long time, as though he were trying to envision the event. Then he abruptly snatched up the papers and waved his hand, indicating that I was dismissed.

As I stood to leave he said a remarkable thing: "I did not attend. I sent Colonel Buhler instead. Remember that, Dr. Banach."

1 June 1942

The last five months at the library have been uneventful. Our work has progressed steadily, and Herr Kruger seems pleased. I had not seen Frank since January, then today I was summoned to his office. After inquiring about the state of the library, he informed me that he will soon be leaving for a visit to Germany to deliver a message directly to the people. He will be giving a series of public lectures, he said, emphasizing the importance of an independent judiciary within a totalitarian system and promoting the idea that a "police state" can never be tolerated. He leaned across the desk, looked me directly in the eye, and said, "This is what you and I have always believed, Dr. Banach," as though we were still colleagues.

I was frightened by the intensity of his gaze, and all I could do was nod in agreement. He waited, as though expecting me to say something that would validate his intentions. Over the many months since my return to Krakow I have realized that Frank seems to be concerned about what I think of him. It is as though he needs someone to talk to, someone who reminds him of his former life before the madness consumed him. His comments about fighting for the "right of reprieve" for those he had arrested in the *AB Aktion,* about protecting the Jews from Himmler, about not attending the Wannsee conference, all of it is some attempt to make me think he is above all the brutality and murder. Yet, the hundreds of documents in room L-3 tell a very different story.

As he continued to stare at me, I finally mustered the courage to ask if he thought it wise to lecture on that subject at this time in Germany.

On his desk, Frank keeps a framed photograph of himself standing next to Adolf Hitler. He picked up the photo and looked at it closely, as though trying to make out some small detail. Then he set it down and, with a wave of his hand, dismissed me.

21 August 1942

Late this evening Frank called me to his office unexpectedly. He was sitting at his desk in his shirtsleeves, his tie undone. There was a bottle of schnapps on the desk. He poured himself a drink, swallowed it in one gulp and leaned forward. His eyes wandered about the room. He mumbled about the Fuhrer stripping him of his party offices as he rolled the empty glass between his thumb and forefinger.

"The lectures in Germany . . ." he started to say; then his voice trailed off. He slumped in the chair and was silent for a long time.

Then he abruptly shoved the chair back and stood up, ramrod straight. He jabbed a finger in the air and screamed, "That fucking Himmler!" He paced around the room, whispering something to himself, then stopped next to my chair, looked down at me and said that he was to remain as Governor of Poland. He asked what I thought of that but continued on without waiting for an answer. He said that he will have no power in the party but will remain as governor of Germany's largest occupied territory. "Who has ever heard of such madness?" he said.

I believe Frank is losing his mind.

28 November 1942

It has been three months since my last entry. On most days I am too tired to write. Life has dragged on, one dreary day after another. "Night duty" continues, and the channel remains intact. I have been assured that the documents I am risking my life (such as it is) to smuggle from the library are being passed on, but the brutal oppression of the citizens of Poland continues. Deportations from the Krakow ghetto have begun, and I have heard rumors that as many as fifteen thousand Jews have already been sent "to the east." No one knows where they are really going, but my heart sinks when I remember Frank telling me about the "final solution." How can this madness continue? Is it possible that the rest of the world doesn't know? Or don't they care?

Frank came into the library early this morning. I had not seen him since that day in August when he had been stripped of his party offices. But today he was in a jovial and expansive mood, talking rapidly about how well the war effort is going, how the Russians will soon be defeated. We sat at a table in the Reading Room, and he pulled his chair close. He whispered that he had a visitor recently, a Russian visitor.

I didn't know what to say so I remained silent, knowing this was generally the best course of action when Frank was in a talkative mood. He continued whispering even though there was no one else nearby. He said that his Russian visitor had brought him a gift as a token of his friendship. The Russian had asked for his protection when the Bolshevik empire collapses under the might of the Wehrmacht.

14 April 1943

Another five months have passed since my last writing. I fear that this journal has lapsed into tedium, but such is my life. I continue to work in the library six days a week, with "night duty" as usual. The rest of the time, I sleep. My friend Jerzy Jastremski and his wife continue to invite me to supper at their apartment, but I usually decline. I am too tired to be a good conversationalist. And I have developed a hacking cough. Jerzy wants me to see a doctor (it is allowed for workers in the library), but I fear being sent to the hospital. I remember the "hospital" at Sachsenhausen, from which no one ever returned.

Frank visited the library this evening. I was gathering up my things to leave when he motioned for me to accompany him as he walked down one of the corridors. I followed him, waiting as always for him to initiate the conversation. After several minutes he stopped and said that the German Wehrmacht made a discovery in Russia a few days ago. It was a mass grave in the Katyn Forest near Smolensk. He said the Russians had murdered more than four thousand Polish army officers back in 1940. They were shot in the head and dumped in a ditch. Frank said that Stalin is blaming Germany, but it was the Russians who committed the murders.

The news was like a blow to the stomach. I could barely breathe as I thought of the many Polish officers I knew, some of them sons of my closest friends, fine young men in the prime of their lives and professional careers. Is this what happened to them? Were they put down like dogs and left to rot in a ditch? I looked away and blinked several times, trying to clear the tears from my eyes.

Frank, of course, was oblivious to my discomfort. He said that he had known about the murders for some time. He asked if I recalled his visitor last November. Thanks to this visitor and the gift he brought, Frank said, he has proof that it was the *Russians* who committed this despicable act. He said that proof—solid evidence—was always useful.

15 January 1945

I return to the journal now after almost two years because something happened today that may actually provide meaning for my continued existence. For the last two years I have slogged through life, merely staying alive on the slim hope that Beata and Adam have managed to survive. And so I have kept on, one day after another.

Today I discovered the "solid evidence" Hans Frank boasted about back in April of 1943. It is a carbon copy of a single document authorizing the massacre in the Katyn Forest! I found it neatly folded in a non-descript envelope intermixed with dozens of other envelopes and file folders in the final box of documents left on the table in room L-3.

I was just in time. The Nazi occupiers are cleaning out everything: their headquarters at Wawel Castle, their personal homes and apartments, even the storage rooms at the library. The streets of Krakow are clogged with all manner of German vehicles piled high with furniture, silverware, paintings and rolls of carpets—rats hoarding their booty before jumping ship as the Red Army closes in. But what is to become of *us?*

16 January 1945

The Nazis are gone—just like that, Hans Frank among them—in a frenzied exodus from the city. After more than five years, the streets of Krakow are now devoid of the black uniforms of the SS and the green uniforms of the Feldgendarmes. It will be several days, I'm told, before the khaki uniforms of the Red Army and NKVD fill these same streets. I will not be here to see it.

When I removed that document from that final box in room L-3, I instantly knew that this was what Frank had alluded to—the proof he had received from his Russian visitor.

And I knew why I had survived. I *must* make sure this piece of evidence is shown to the people of the world, that they may see the true nature of Stalin and his henchmen—barbarians every bit as evil as the Nazis they have just defeated. Perhaps this damning evidence, exposed in the court of world opinion, will convince the Americans and British to stand up to Stalin and deny his ruthless ambitions for Poland.

I have translated the document. It took more than two hours, and when I finished I was shaking so badly I dropped the thin piece of paper on the floor. I picked it up and read it a second time, scarcely able to believe that such a thing would ever be put on paper.

The translation of the entire document is too long to include in this journal, but this is the essence of its contents:

On 5 March, 1940, at the request of NKVD Commissar Lavrenty Beria, an order was signed by Joseph Stalin and every other member of the Soviet Politburo, authorizing the execution of twenty-seven thousand Polish "nationalists and counterrevolutionaries." The various groups of Poles and their places of execution were itemized—including the four thousand officers of the Polish army whose graves were discovered by the Germans in the Katyn Forest.

17 January 1945

I need worry no longer about the safety of my beloved Beata. Before departing yesterday, Herr Kruger did me one last service and told me the truth. Beata died more than two years ago at the concentration camp at Dachau. Though hearing of her death ripped my soul apart, I was not surprised. I realize that all of Frank's comments about Beata returning were designed to keep me in a state of perpetual fear and to prevent me from communicating with anyone. I only thank the Lord that she is at peace. I asked Herr Kruger about the whereabouts of my nephew, Adam, but he was not able to furnish any information.

Now, I have but one last thing for which to live. This will be my final entry of the journal. I have been up all night, and I know what I must do. The copy of Stalin's order authorizing the massacre in the Katyn Forest must not fall into Russian hands.

To whoever reads this journal: find Adam Nowak and tell him that we shall never be pathetic pawns on the perilous chessboard of the NKVD.

Ludwik Banach

Professor of Law, Jagiellonian University
Member, Polish Bar Association

Author's Note

The incident that has become known as the Katyn Massacre was, without a doubt, one of the most heinous war crimes ever committed. More than twenty thousand Polish Army officers and civilians were secretly murdered by the Soviet NKVD during April and May of 1940. The murders were actually carried out at several different sites in Russia.

In addition to the Katyn Forest near Smolensk, where the graves of more than four thousand Polish officers were discovered, at least three thousand persons were murdered at a secret camp near Starobelsk, six thousand at a camp near Ostashkov, and as many as fourteen thousand at other places of detention. In addition to army officers, the victims included chaplains, university professors, physicians, lawyers, engineers, teachers, writers and journalists.

This unprecedented crime was initially discovered by the German Wehrmacht as they advanced through Russia in April 1943. The Soviet Government denied any knowledge of the incident and claimed that the murders had been committed by the Germans.

The Polish Government-in-Exile, and in particular Prime Minister Wladyslaw Sikorski, had been pressing the Soviet Government for years about the apparent disappearance of Poland's army officers. The discovery of the graves in 1943 heightened the controversy and eventually led to Joseph Stalin's decision to break off diplomatic relations with Poland. On 4 July 1943, Prime Minister Sikorski was killed in an airplane crash seconds after takeoff from an airfield in Gibraltar. The incident has never been completely explained.

The controversy over the Katyn Massacre continued until 13 April 1990, when Soviet President Mikhail Gorbachev publicly acknowledged the Soviet Union's responsibility for the murders. On 14 October 1992, fifty-two years after the secret murders were committed, the Soviet Government finally produced the order of 5 March 1940, which authorized the execution of more than twenty-seven thousand Polish "nationalists and counterrevolutionaries," including the Polish officers in the Katyn Forest. The order was drafted by the Commissar of the NKVD, Lavrenty Beria, and was signed by Joseph Stalin, along with every member of the Soviet Politburo.

The horror of Katyn continues to this day. In April 2010, the president of Poland, Lech Kaczynski, along with his wife and more than ninety other Polish dignitaries, died in an airplane crash in Russia. They were en route to a ceremony commemorating the seventieth anniversary of the Katyn massacre. On 26 November 2010, the Russian parliament officially condemned Joseph Stalin by name for the mass execution of Poles at Katyn. The parliament declared that the Soviet dictator and other Soviet officials had ordered the "Katyn crime" in 1940.

In writing *The Katyn Order,* I chose to begin the story with another great tragedy of World War Two, the Warsaw Rising of 1944. Like the Katyn massacre, the facts of the Warsaw Rising were suppressed for decades after the war by the communist authorities governing Poland. Consequently, the story of the Rising is not well known in the West, and is often confused with the Warsaw ghetto uprising of 1943. They were, in fact, two completely different events.

By the summer of 1944, it was clear that Germany would be defeated by the Allies. American and British forces were liberating France, Belgium and the Netherlands, while Soviet forces were pushing into Poland. The German Army was in retreat. Having no illusions about what "liberation" by the Soviets would mean for their future, Poland's home army, the AK, acting on instructions from their Government-in-Exile in London, attempted to seize the opportunity to take control of their capital. What ensued was the Warsaw Rising, a catastrophe of epic proportions, that resulted in the loss of tens of thousands of lives, and the destruction of one of the world's great cities. Winston Churchill, who agonized over the struggle for Poland's capital as it unfolded day-after-tragic-day, described it this way in his memoirs:

> The struggle in Warsaw had lasted more than sixty days. Of the 40,000 men and women of the Polish Underground Army, 15,000 fell . . . The suppression of the revolt cost the German Army 10,000 killed, 7,000 missing and 9,000 wounded. The proportions attest to the hand-to-hand nature of the fighting. When the Russians entered the city three months later, they found nothing but the shattered streets and the unburied dead. Such was their liberation of Poland, where they now rule. But this cannot be the end of the story.

For more information on the Warsaw Rising, consult the website, www.warsawuprising.com.

The Katyn Order is a work of fiction. The order signed by Joseph Stalin and the Soviet Politburo is an historical fact. Whether a copy of the order ever existed, however, is a matter of the author's speculation. The characters in this story are fictitious, but all of the events are true and the majority of places described are real, as far as my research could confirm. There are a few notable exceptions: the Copernicus Memorial Library in Krakow and the Tatra Mountain village of Prochowa are products of my imagination, as are the Church of the Sacred Mother, the Polonia Bank, and the Bomb Shelter Pub in Warsaw. I also elected to have the dining room of the Adlon Hotel survive the fire.

Ludwik Banach is also a fictitious character, as is his relationship with the real historical person Hans Frank. Banach's journal is fictitious, but it incorporates many historical facts, including the arrest of more than two hundred Polish intellectuals by the Nazis, and the existence of the Sachsenhausen prison camp and the Academy of German Law.

McBooks Press is committed to preserving ancient forests and natural resources. We elected to print this title on 30% post consumer recycled paper, processed chlorine free. As a result, for this printing, we have saved:

19 Trees (40' tall and 6-8" diameter)
8,629 Gallons of Wastewater
6 Million BTU's of Total Energy
524 Pounds of Solid Waste
1,792 Pounds of Greenhouse Gases

McBooks Press made this paper choice because our printer, Thomson-Shore, Inc., is a member of Green Press Initiative, a nonprofit program dedicated to supporting authors, publishers, and suppliers in their efforts to reduce their use of fiber obtained from endangered forests.

For more information, visit www.greenpressinitiative.org

Environmental impact estimates were made using the Environmental Defense Paper Calculator. For more information visit: www.papercalculator.org.